THE LIES
WE TELL

'*Reading* Buried Lies *is painful. I mean, I remember it all so damn well. Lucy kept trying out different sun-creams in the office and I went on secret dates. But all that frivolous stuff stopped after Texas. So be warned. The story I'm about to tell is much weightier. Much darker. It's no longer about* Buried Lies. *Now I want to talk about Mio.*'

MB

PRELUDE

'Who are you?'

TRANSCRIPT OF INTERVIEW WITH
MARTIN BENNER (MB).

INTERVIEWER: KAREN VIKING (KV),
freelance journalist, Stockholm.

MB: Who are you?

KV: My name is Karen Viking. I was a close
friend of Fredrik Ohlander, whom you
worked with before.

MB: Really? A close friend?

KV: Yes. But I can understand you being
suspicious, so I'm going to share all
the information I've got with you. After
Fredrik died . . . you know he's dead,
don't you?

MB: Yes, I know. I'm very sorry about
that.

KV: Me too. He was one of my very closest
friends, almost a brother to me. I . . .
Well, anyway, a few days ago Verner, his
partner, called me. He'd found a thick
sealed envelope with my name on it in
Fredrik's safe-deposit box at the bank.

Apparently it said that no one but me was allowed to open it.

MB: Okay.

KV: I went and got the envelope from Verner that same evening. It contained a large bundle of papers and a short letter from Fredrik explaining that if he disappeared or died, I was to contact you. He wrote that the two of you had met after you got into trouble and that it was vital that the story you had told him was preserved.

MB: Did he ever mention to you the fact that we were working together?

KV: No. But a few of us suspected he was working on something very sensitive.

(Silence)

KV: If I understand correctly, you and Fredrik hadn't actually finished. Because the story was still going on. Or have I got that wrong?

MB: No, and presumably that's why Fredrik thought it was so important for the two of us to meet. Because he knew we'd only reached the interval, and that I would have wanted the second act to be as well documented as the first.

KV: So what's the current state of affairs? Is the second act over?

MB: Yes. Everything's over now.

(Silence)

KV: Okay, so how do you want to do this? Do
you want to tell me what's happened?

MB: I'd be happy to. The fact that Fredrik
entrusted you with this task means
I can trust you. So I will. But you
do need to understand and accept
the ground-rules. Everything I tell
you has to stay between us. You can
only publish the story if I die or
disappear. Is that understood?

KV: Absolutely. As you can see for yourself,
Fredrik said as much in his letter.

MB: How much do you know, then? How much
did Fredrik manage to write down before
he died? All of it?

KV: I think so. But perhaps it would make
sense for you to read it for yourself?
He wrote one long version, as well as
a shorter summary. It looks like he
was thinking about turning the longer
version into a book. Fredrik gave it a
great title.

MB: Really?

KV: *Buried Lies*.

BURIED LIES

Summary

M y name is Martin Benner, and I'm a lawyer. Until recently I had it all: women, a career, a seriously rich life and a wonderful daughter. My life has changed. And I'm no longer safe. Possibly because I've got weaknesses. I'm constantly on the hunt for the ultimate high, both professionally and in my private life. And that's taken its toll, sadly. On my relationship with Lucy, with whom I work and occasionally sleep, for instance.

A man came to my office. He said his name was Bobby, and he wanted my help. His sister had got herself into a hell of a lot of trouble. She had been put on trial for five murders she didn't commit. The papers called her Sara Texas. Her real name was Sara Tell.

Bobby asked me to represent his sister. And find her missing son, Mio. His sister's first lawyer had done a lousy job. Bobby thought I could do better. There was just one problem. Sara was already dead. She killed herself after absconding from a supervised excursion from prison. That was the day before the verdict was due to be announced in court. All the legal experts agreed that she would have been found guilty of all the murders. There was plenty of evidence. And there was also the fact that she'd confessed.

Despite all that, I said yes, but only to the first part of the job: clearing Sara's name. I wasn't bothered about Mio, her missing son. He disappeared from his preschool the same afternoon his mum escaped from her guards. The police were assuming she'd killed him as well as herself. I had no reason to think otherwise.

Fairly soon I realised that there were holes in the police investigation. It looked like they'd been sloppy; there were several loose ends to follow up. Sara had worked as an au pair in the USA, in Texas, and that's where she was supposed to have committed her first two murders. But her best friend Jenny, who had also been an au pair in Texas, had her doubts. Serious doubts. So Jenny came to see me, to tell me she could give Sara an alibi for the time of the first murder.

Then everything happened very quickly. Jenny was murdered. And so was Bobby. Only the Bobby who died wasn't the man who had come to my office. The police said there was a witness who claimed to have seen Jenny get run down and killed by a car that resembled mine. A Porsche. That witness statement, combined with the fact that I had been in contact with both victims, was enough to make me a suspect. The investigation was led by an acquaintance of mine, Didrik Stihl. A man whose company I enjoyed, and who had proved useful in the past (and who also happened to have led the investigation against Sara), but now he suddenly became a person I wanted to stay as far away from as possible.

Lucy and I went to Texas. I thought that if I could manage

to prove that Sara was innocent of one of the murders, I'd be able to get her cleared of the rest as well. And I thought that if I managed to clear Sara's name, then my own problems would sort themselves out. I wouldn't end up being prosecuted for the murders of Jenny and Bobby, and my life would go back to normal. To a great extent I was driven by my love for Belle, my four-year-old niece, whom I'd looked after since she was nine months old and her parents died in a plane crash. I do my best to be a good father, and I love Belle more than anything and anyone. Something which, I might add, turned out to be a serious weakness.

In Texas we found out more than we could ever have imagined. It became clear that Sara had in fact committed the first murder of which she was accused. But it had been self-defence. We also found out that Sara had worked as a prostitute and belonged to a network run by a mafia boss. A network built around the trade in drugs and women's bodies. The mafia boss's name was Lucifer.

Sara had had a very particular relationship with Lucifer. She had been his secret lover, and fled home to Sweden when she realised she was expecting his child. But she couldn't get away that easily. Lucifer was a man with plenty of contacts, and an extensive network of informants. It wasn't long before he knew both where she was, and why she had left.

Lucifer flew to Stockholm and asked Sara to go back to Texas with him. She refused. As punishment, and as a way of putting pressure on her, he told her that each time she said no he would have someone murdered, someone who in the future she risked being accused of having murdered. She said no three times, and Lucifer killed three people in Stockholm. Before long, Sara was in police custody, accused of no fewer than five murders. Two in Texas, three in Stockholm. Her son, Mio, was placed with foster parents.

Sara escaped when she was on a supervised excursion from prison. I assumed it was so she could get herself and her son to safety, but exactly how that was supposed to happen we didn't actually know. Either way, her son had vanished. He wasn't at his preschool, nor with his foster parents. In her despair, Sara jumped from Västerbron. Mio was never found.

He wasn't the only child to disappear. My own beloved Belle was abducted. I had left her in Sweden when Lucy and I went off to the States. To make her as safe as possible I'd taken her to stay with her grandparents out in the archipelago. She was also under the protection of a man named Boris, an old client of mine. A client – and also a mafia boss. But not even that helped. She disappeared while I was in Texas, and wasn't returned until two days later. Lucifer wasn't a child-killer, he just wanted to stop me. An anonymous man called my mobile to tell me that I could have her back on loan. He had already taken her once, and he could do so again. Unless I helped him find Lucifer's missing son, Mio. As long as I agreed to help, I would be allowed to keep Belle.

Which is where I am now. My daughter has already been kidnapped once, and if I don't get my act together I could lose her forever. I have to do everything I can to find the missing boy, Mio. And I also have to try to find out who's trying to frame me for two murders. Because Lucifer claims not to be behind that particular aspect of the story.

Lucifer. I would dearly love to know who he is. To give the

evil a face, and to help me rid myself of the bastard. There's some evidence to suggest that Lucifer is a sheriff I met in Houston, Esteban Stiller. But I daren't poke about in that. Because then Belle would die.

There's nothing more important in my life than Belle. I know that now. So for her sake I'm trying to stick to the rules of the game and not seek out too much information. But the hunger's there in my blood, and I can't do anything about that. It's like walking a tightrope. I have to keep my eyes focused firmly ahead of me and not look down.

Because if I do, I know I'd fall.

PART 1

'When Mio vanished.'

KV: So what did you think of *Buried Lies*?

MB: Bloody good. So, let's get started. I
talk, you write. Just like I did with
Fredrik.

KV: Where are you going to begin? With
what happened right after you got Belle
back?

MB: Of course. The first few days can be
summed up pretty easily. First we went
to hospital to get Belle checked over.
Then we went home to my flat and stayed
there. I only went out to see Fredrik
and the police, nothing else. And then
I set to work with the tasks I'd been
given.

KV: And what were they, exactly? Just so we
know we're on the same page.

MB: I had to find out what happened to Sara

Texas's son, Mio. That was the task
Lucifer had given me. And then find out
who was trying to frame me for two
murders, and why. Because Lucifer wasn't
involved in that; he'd made that very
clear.

KV: There was no reason to think he might
be lying?

MB: We'll get to that. But first there's
something else I need to make clear.

KV: Okay?

MB: Reading *Buried Lies* is painful. I mean,
I remember it all so damn well. Lucy
kept trying out different sun-creams in
the office and I went on secret dates.
But all that frivolous stuff stopped
after Texas. So be warned. The story
I'm about to tell is much weightier.
Much darker. It's no longer about *Buried
Lies*. Now I want to talk about Mio.

KV: Okay, let's try something, then: if you
were going to write this story yourself,
what would the first sentence be?

(Silence)

MB: This: 'In my nightmares, I was buried
alive.'

1

SUNDAY

In my nightmares, I was buried alive. It was the same scenario every time. At first I never understood what was about to happen. Tight-lipped people held my arms fast and forced me to walk forwards. Not slowly, not quickly. It was night, and the sky was black. The air was warm and close. We were moving through what looked like an abandoned industrial estate. The outlines of huge, dark machines rose up around us, like shadows cast in iron. I wanted to ask where we were, where we were going. But the gag wouldn't let me speak. It chafed in my mouth, tugging at the corners of my lips. The fabric was rough against my tongue. And there was something going on with my legs. They were tied together with rope, meaning I could only take short steps. I was forced to take many more steps than my guards. And that terrified me.

How many times do you feel afraid as an adult? Not many. Mainly because there aren't all that many things that scare us. We know that most things sort themselves out, that it's silly to get hung up on little things. It's one of the blessings of growing older: escaping the constant paranoia and fears of youth and getting some perspective on things. The only drawback is that this liberation from fear makes us so painfully aware of what is really worth being frightened of.

The loss of our nearest and dearest.

The loss of our own health or life.

And, in rare instances, fear of pain or anxiety.

As I half-walked and was half-dragged through the abandoned industrial landscape, I knew I was going to die. That's one of the most interesting things about nightmares in general. We often know how they're going to end. Because on a subconscious level we already have an idea of why we dream the things we do. We know which real events and experiences have triggered different reactions inside us, and it's partly from these events that fear takes its nourishment. Memory has almost unlimited power over our thoughts.

The nightmares started to torment me as soon as I got Belle back. After I'd been to Texas. In my sleep I tried both to resist and wake up at the same time. I never once succeeded. The nightmare continued without me being able to influence it at all. The silent, black-clad men moved as relentlessly as the tide. I chewed and chewed on the gag, trying to make some sort of sound. It was impossible. No one wanted to explain where we were going. No one wanted to tell me what I'd done.

Eventually I realised anyway. I started to recognise where I was. Understood what the machines surrounding us were, and what they had once done to the earth. I had been there before. I had never planned to go back. I started to howl and tried to resist. But the men just carried on. I was left dangling from their arms and my feet and lower legs scraped along the ground. The jeans I was wearing were ruined, and soon it started to hurt.

I never stopped trying to make myself heard. Not even when we were standing beside the hole that had already been prepared. I wanted to ask for forgiveness, explain that it had all been a terrible accident. But I couldn't get a single intelligible sound out. That was when the sobbing would start. Hoarse, hot, corrosive. My whole body would shake as I pleaded for my life. No one listened. Instead I was shoved headfirst into the pit. It was deep, at least two metres. I landed hard on my stomach and felt something break. A rib? Two? Something caused a sudden flash of pain in my left lung and I tried to roll over.

By this point they had already grabbed their shovels and started to rain soil and sand down on top of me. They worked silently and systematically, burying me alive. They never slowed up. Not when I got to my knees, nor when I stood up. My hands were tied behind my back and I knew I wouldn't be able to climb out. So I stood there and screamed silent screams while mortal dread galloped off with the last of my reason. I met death standing up. When the earth reached my chin my vision was already starting to fade.

I never woke up until the top of my head was covered.

'What do you dream about, Martin?'

Lucy tried to catch my eye across the breakfast table. She had seen me sweat between the sheets far too many nights in a row. When I didn't reply she went on: 'It seems like the same dream recurring over and over again. Is that what it is?'

'I don't remember. Is it really so surprising that I'm

dreaming a load of fucked-up nonsense after everything we've been through?'

After everything we've been through. A lie, but there was no way Lucy could know that. The dreams had a single source: Texas. I kept quiet about that.

I took a mouthful of coffee and burned myself.

'Damn.'

Lucy was still looking at me.

'You keep tossing about,' she said. 'Screaming.'

I put the mug of coffee down.

'Really?' I said. 'So what do I scream, then?'

I asked mainly because she expected me to.

'"I know where he is." You scream, "I know where he is." But you don't, do you?'

For a moment time stood still.

'Martin, you don't, do you? Where Mio is?'

I came to my senses and shook my head.

'Of course I don't.'

We ate the rest of our breakfast in silence. I thought about how secrets are like every other sort of shit. You can bury them as deep as you like, but sooner or later they find their way up to the surface anyway. Especially if you return to the scene of the crime of your own accord.

Lucy thought I was screaming that I knew where Mio was. Only I knew what I was really going on about. *Who* I was talking about.

'*I know where he is.*'

Oh yes, I knew, alright. But the person I was talking about didn't have a damn thing to do with Mio.

Or did he?

2

The living and the dead. The boundary between the two is brutally sharp. So painful and frightening. By the time the nightmares got the better of me I was already in a terrible state. You tend to be after you've been accused of two murders, been on a crazy roadtrip through Texas and then lost and regained your daughter. I had no real appreciation of how urgent my mission to find Mio was. To be honest, I didn't really care either. Not at first. According to the Bible, the earth was created in six days. And on the seventh day God rested. We turned that upside down. Lucy and I rested for six days. Then we got to work. On a Sunday.

'What are you going to do first?' Lucy said.

Not such a stupid question.

'Try to put a face to him. And pay a visit to the place where he disappeared, the preschool.'

I had no idea what Mio had looked like. Had he been short or tall for his age? Fat or thin? With long or short hair? It bothered me that so much time had passed without me reacting to the absence of pictures. I hadn't stumbled across a single photograph of the kid, in any context. Not in the records from the police's preliminary investigation, and not in the media either. I used to be on good terms with the police; I could simply have asked where all the pictures of Mio had gone (assuming there had ever been any). But I no longer had any contacts of that sort. And I didn't want to arouse the police's curiosity about why I might want a picture of Mio.

So who, if not the police, might potentially have a photograph of Mio? There was a maternal grandmother. And an aunt. Jeanette and Marion. I decided to contact both of them. Neither of them called me back. Hours passed. Never mind, I had plenty more important things to be getting on with. Such as visiting the last place anyone saw Mio.

The car started with a roar. My fucking gorgeous Porsche 911. It smelled of leather, as if it were new. But apart from that it didn't feel particularly new. Nice cars and young children aren't a good combination. Belle did her best, but there were still traces of her everywhere. But Belle was hardly the biggest problem. After everything that had happened, it just didn't feel anywhere near as much fun to drive. I had asked Boris – the old mafia boss – to get his guys to check the car after I got home from Texas, and they had removed a bug, a tracking device installed by the police so they could keep an eye on me. To make life harder for my adversaries, Boris's men had attached the bug to a delivery van instead. My new pattern of movement would probably cause a fair amount of confusion among the police.

It was already afternoon when I picked Belle up then

drove south. She had spent the day with her grandmother, my mum, Marianne. Belle looked happy when she realised we weren't going straight home. Her eyes shone with enthusiasm. The shortness of her memory almost frightened the life out of me. How could she look so happy? It was only just over a week since her father's parents had died in a fire and she herself had been kidnapped. Shouldn't she be beside herself with – I don't know – grief, fear, anxiety? Perhaps it was odd, but I wasn't actually too concerned about the kidnapping. She had been gone less than forty-eight hours, and had probably spent most of that time asleep, stuffed full of tranquillisers. For perfectly understandable reasons she remembered nothing of all that. But she remembered her grandparents, and sometimes asked about them. So she ought to be grieving for them. Missing them. Or so I thought, as an adult.

Belle had a different perspective. I had explained that Grandma and Granddad were gone, and would never be coming back. But Belle's only four years old. She doesn't understand a word like never. She doesn't understand that some things, some states are infinite.

'They died,' I said. 'Just like your mum and dad did.'

And Belle nodded so wisely, without any sentimentality. She knows her parents died in a plane crash when she was a baby. She knows I'm not her real dad, but her uncle, her mother's brother. But that doesn't mean she understands the significance of what I tell her. She doesn't understand that she could have had a completely different life if my sister and brother-in-law hadn't died. A life with two engaged and devoted parents who loved barbecues and renting summer cottages on Öland, going skiing in the winter and watching movies at weekends. Normal people with normal lives and worries, who would have other families round for meals and who would doubtless have seen to it that she had other siblings.

I parked the car a couple of blocks from our destination.

'We're getting out here,' I said, helping Belle out of the car.

I squeezed her hand as we walked along the pavement. She was a lot like her mother. I hadn't really given it much thought before, but she was. And still is. In terms of appearance, Belle is very much her mother's daughter.

'Where are we going?' she said.

'We're going to walk past a preschool,' I said.

Mio's preschool. The Enchanted Garden. But I didn't say that.

I could actually have gone past the preschool before I picked Belle up rather than after. But I wanted to have her with me. It looked better. A lot of people mistrust men they see creeping around a preschool late in the afternoon. Particularly if they look like me. Tall and black. Skin colour trumps everything else in Sweden. The fact that I'm wearing a ludicrously expensive shirt and hand-stitched shoes from Milan doesn't make any difference. The first thing that strikes other Swedes when they see me isn't uncomplicated success.

There were a few children playing outside the preschool. Maybe there weren't any other playgrounds nearby, so the preschool's would have to do, even though it was Sunday. The sun was still relatively high in the sky. There was still a chance to make the most of the summer. For anyone who had the time. I didn't.

Belle looked at the children with interest.

'Are we going to play with them?' she asked, taking a step in their direction.

My grip on her hand tightened automatically.

'No,' I said. 'We're just going to walk past.'

If Belle was incapable of understanding the significance of her parents' death, she certainly couldn't comprehend the value of walking past an interesting-looking playground without going near it. Without joining in.

'Why?' she said.

I heard the change in her voice. From happy to sullen and disappointed. Like an abrupt shift from sun to snow in April.

'Because we don't know the children in this playground.'

I was happy with my answer. Perhaps Belle was too, because she fell silent.

When we reached the gate to the playground I slowed my pace slightly. Not to the point where we were standing still, but enough to heighten my powers of observation. Taking photographs was out of the question. If I wanted pictures, I'd have to come back later.

This was where he disappeared, I thought.

But how the hell did it happen?

Children don't just disappear. They get mislaid by adults who neglect their duty of care. I had read the file relating to the investigation the police had carried out into Mio's disappearance. The preschool teachers had said it was a perfectly ordinary day. Mio had been dropped off by his foster parents that morning. He had been tired, and had a bit of a cold, but perked up after lunch. At two o'clock the staff put the children's coats on and took them outside. An hour later they served the afternoon snack outside, even though it was autumn and already cold. But it was sunny and dry, and the children were having such a nice time. It was, as one of the teachers said, all very peaceful.

Perhaps that was the problem. That it had been so peaceful. Perhaps that made the staff drop their guard. So much so that they didn't notice when one of the children suddenly wasn't there. Not until his foster mother showed up to collect him. By then the sun had gone and no one knew what had happened.

I let my eyes sweep across the playground. It was surrounded by a metal fence that had to be seventy centimetres high. There were bushes growing in a bed on the inside, but they didn't cover the whole boundary. A grown-up who felt like swinging a leg over the fence could easily do so without getting caught up in the vegetation. But a four-year-old child? Hardly.

I looked for weaknesses. A hole in the fence, perhaps, or a point where there was no fence at all. There was nothing like that. Mio must have walked out through the gate the last time he left his preschool. Or been lifted over the fence by an adult.

Belle was dragging her feet. Her sandals scraped the tarmac as she failed to pick her feet up properly. In a matter of minutes she would lose it completely. That was something she definitely hadn't got from her mother. My sister was hopeless at raising objections, at making her presence felt. I used to hate seeing her back down in the face of the people around her. Her boss, her husband, her colleagues. Me.

'I want to go home,' Belle said.

'Soon,' I said.

One of the children in the playground caught sight of me. He frowned as he looked at me and Belle warily.

I didn't like the feeling of being watched – not even by a small child – so I squeezed Belle's hand and said, 'Let's go home and make spaghetti bolognese.'

We turned and walked back to the car. I helped Belle with her seatbelt and got in behind the wheel. I did a U-turn and drove past the preschool one last time. Belle looked at the children playing on the swings but said nothing. She doesn't make a lot of fuss, Belle. She knows it isn't worth it, that that isn't the way to get what she wants.

The Enchanted Garden was out in Flemingsberg. I pulled out onto Huddingevägen and drove north towards the city centre.

'I'm hungry,' Belle said as we headed into the Söderleden tunnel.

I glanced at the time. No, she wasn't. She was bored.

'We'll soon be home,' I said.

It was summer, a Sunday. Barely any traffic at all. The pulse of the nation's capital had slowed dramatically.

But the fun and games weren't over yet. It happened at the pedestrian crossing outside the Gallerian shopping mall on Hamngatan. A truck was coming in the opposite direction. An old lady was waiting at the crossing. I put my foot on the brake-pedal.

Nothing happened.

I put my foot down again, more out of surprise than panic. The brake-pedal wasn't responding at all. The woman was stepping out onto the road.

'Fucking bloody hell.'

I blew my horn repeatedly. Pressed the bastard brake-pedal. And thought: is she going to be the second person I've killed?

3

It didn't happen. Terrified, the old lady threw herself backwards and watched me fly past. And the unbelievably unsettling thought that my desperate brain had just formulated vanished. As if it had worked out for itself exactly how unwelcome it was.

Instinctively I stamped as hard as I could on the brake-pedal. So hard that I practically stood up from the seat. Then it was as if something beneath the pedal burst, and the car stopped so abruptly that the airbags went off.

Belle started screaming. Behind me I heard other cars' tyres shriek on the tarmac. I held my breath (you tend to do that when you're being crushed by an airbag) and waited for someone to smash into us. Nobody did.

Utterly confused, I threw the door open and managed to get out. I ran round the car and pulled Belle out as well.

'There, there,' I said, brushing the hair from her cheeks. 'It turned out ... okay.'

Plenty of people had stopped to stare at all the cars that

were standing motionless. The old woman was sitting on the pavement, shocked but unharmed.

'Come on,' I said, taking Belle by the hand.

I went back round to the driver's seat of the Porsche. I crouched down and peered at the floor of the car. What the hell was that smell? I leaned closer. At first I didn't understand a thing. But that smell – I recognised it. Belle clung to me as I stuck my head inside the car. And realised what was wrong.

An orange. An orange that Belle had been planning to take to her grandmother's but had dropped in the car. The fact that it could have rolled in under the brake-pedal was beyond her imagination, and mine too. But it was nothing malicious. Not this time.

Lucy laughed so hard she was actually crying (it was wonderful to see that beautiful smile again) when we got home and I told her what had happened. As for me, I didn't have any difficulty keeping a straight face.

'I think I'm going to hate that Porsche by the time this is over,' I said.

'The Porsche?'

'I was so damn sure someone had messed with the brakes, Lucy. So fucking sure.'

Lucy stroked my cheek.

'I've already started to get dinner,' she said.

'Smells good,' I said.

And thought to myself: what the hell are we doing? We're not playing happy families, are we?

Lucy had spent every night with me since I got Belle back. I hadn't had any reason to question it. Belle and I needed her, there was no more to it than that. But now quite a few days had passed. Enough for me to start feeling panicky. Belle is the only person I've ever lived with as an adult. I think that's been good for me. I'm not really made to have other people too close to me. Lucy and I never lived together, even when we were a proper couple. That was mostly my fault, or thanks to me, anyway. I'm scared of everyday life, the same way other people are scared of war and environmental disasters. I have to be able to withdraw, recharge my batteries. Alone, or in the company of another woman. Whatever it takes to keep everyday life at bay.

Most people I knew said I was stupid when I refused to move in with Lucy. I was told plenty of times that I was immature. No passion lasted forever. All infatuation eventually turns into love. Everyday routine couldn't be avoided forever. It was just something you had to get used to. And start loving.

I stirred Lucy's bolognese sauce listlessly. I was, and am, made differently. I do not love the everyday.

'How did you get on?' Lucy said. 'Did you see anything?'

Memories peppered me like bullets from an automatic rifle. Children. Tarmac. Buildings. A playground. A boy who couldn't take his eyes off me.

I described everything.

'The children were outside when Mio disappeared,' I said. 'Which makes me wonder how on earth it could have happened at all. A child of Mio's age couldn't have climbed over a fence like that. And he couldn't have opened the gate on his own.'

'We'd already worked that out, though, hadn't we?' Lucy said. 'That he didn't go off on his own, I mean. We just don't know who took him.'

'True,' I said. 'We're talking about a big open area here. The playground's not some leafy space with plenty of corners to hide in. Whoever took Mio must have done it right in front of the teachers' eyes. Or on the other side of the building. But then someone ought to have reacted when Mio started heading in that direction. There's nowhere to play round there.'

I walked away from the stove and started to lay the table. Lucy tipped fresh pasta into boiling water. I wasn't only playing happy families. I'd also become a private detective. The sort who sneaked round empty preschools measuring the length of the fence surrounding them.

'It was dark when Mio went missing,' I said. 'It was November, almost four o'clock in the afternoon.'

'The playground must have been lit up, then,' Lucy said. 'And the streetlamps must have been on at that time.'

'Of course,' I said. 'But that doesn't mean there are no shadows or dark corners.'

Lucy drizzled some oil over the pasta.

'None of the teachers remembers seeing him go,' I said. 'Or being picked up by either of his foster parents. You don't just walk in and take a child. You say hello to the staff and ask how the day has been.'

I could hardly believe those words were coming out of my mouth. I was never going to have children. Now I was standing in my own kitchen telling Lucy what it's like, picking up a child from preschool. As if she didn't know that just as well as I did.

Lucy called out that dinner was ready. Belle came trotting in with a doll under each arm.

'No more than one doll at the table,' I said.

Instantly she dropped the short-haired one on the floor. She sat the other in the high-chair next to her own place at the table.

'What about the car?' Lucy said.

I pulled a face and looked at the time.

'I suppose I'll have to take it round to the garage when we've finished eating,' I said. 'Oranges smell like shit when they dry out.'

So that was the last thing I did on my first day back at work. I took my Porsche to a garage that was open on Sundays and left it there. I drove home in a hire-car. Completely unaware of what a brilliant move that was.

4

MONDAY

The phone rang just after midnight. The first thing I thought when I opened my eyes was that I hadn't had time to start dreaming yet. Lucy woke up a moment after me. Because I was still in purely formal terms suspected of a double murder, we assumed that my mobile was being bugged. So I had several different ones. The one that was ringing now was the oldest of them. The only one I possessed when this whole bizarre sequence of events began. The one I thought the police were monitoring.

'Answer it, then,' Lucy said.

She'd become so impatient. But so had I.

I pressed the wrong button several times before I finally managed to shut the phone up.

'Martin.'

My voice sounded rough and sleepy.

'I know what you're looking for.'

I fell silent. It was a woman's voice. I didn't recognise it, didn't know who she was.

'Sorry?'

'I ... I have to see you. There's something I want to tell you. About Mio.'

My pulse quickened, abruptly, rapidly.

'Who are you?' I said.

I wanted to make the conversation as short as possible. The police had to be kept out of this. At all costs. I'd promised that to Lucifer.

'I can't tell you. Can we meet?'

'What, now?'

'Would that work?'

At least a dozen alarm bells went off inside my tired head. How did she know who I was? There hadn't been anything about me – so far – in the papers. Now that I came to think about it, there'd been surprisingly little about any of it in the papers. I'd seen a few small articles about two hit-and-run incidents in the centre of Stockholm, but no one seemed to be linking them. And I hadn't seen anything about a suspect being questioned by the police. *Why not?* Since when had the police stopped leaking like a sieve? How the hell could two murders with a connection to the heavily reported case of Sara Texas *not* get greater coverage in the press?

The voice on my mobile spoke again.

'So can we meet up now?' she said.

I got annoyed.

'Not unless you tell me who you are and why you think I'd want to meet you in the middle of the night,' I said.

Lucy looked at me, wide-eyed. I ran my finger over her bare shoulder. It would take a fairly compelling argument to get me out of bed.

Then the woman said: 'Bobby told me about you.'

I froze.

'I don't believe you,' I said.

'Before he died. I met him. He said you'd come and see me and the others at preschool. To find out what happened to Mio. He gave me your number.'

My mouth felt bone-dry. It didn't matter if the police heard this.

'So you work at Mio's preschool, then?'

'Yes.'

'You have to give me something more,' I said. 'Tell me why it's so important that we meet.'

'Because I know things,' the woman said. 'Things I don't want to say over the phone. But I'm prepared to say that I saw something that afternoon. When Mio disappeared.'

She whispered the last sentence.

'You saw something?' I repeated slowly.

'Yes,' she said. 'Are you going to come?'

Every sensible part of my brain protested. No, I wasn't going to head out into the night alone. No, I wasn't going to trust an anonymous woman who called me out of the blue. But curiosity got the better of me. In that respect I hadn't changed. Once a thrill-seeker, always a thrill-seeker.

'You have to tell me your name,' I said.

She hesitated.

'Susanne,' she eventually said. 'My name's Susanne. Are you coming?'

I swallowed and avoided looking at Lucy.

'I'll come,' I said. 'Now I want your phone number so I can call you from a different mobile.'

Perhaps Susanne had her own reasons to be scared of the police, because she refused to give me her number. In the end

I gave her another number for her to call me on. One that I had thought was secure up to that moment, but which would be useless within a day or so if the police really were listening in and had found out about it. When the police decide to listen to someone's telephone conversations, the surveillance is always limited to specific numbers. If it later turns out that the person they're bugging is using other phones and numbers, the police have to go back to the prosecutor and request permission to monitor those as well. And that process can take a number of hours, days even.

It would be dishonest to suggest that Lucy gave me her blessing when I told her what I was about to do.

'You're mad,' she said loudly as I got dressed.

'Shhh, you'll wake Belle,' I said.

'You can't be serious,' she said. 'You've got to have someone with you. Surely you understand that?'

Oh yes, I understood. But the only person I could think of whose hand it might have been worth holding was Boris the mafia boss. And I didn't want to bother him for no reason. Not after everything that had happened when he was watching over Belle. The less contact we had, the less likelihood there was of the police realising that he and I knew each other.

Which in itself was also pretty laughable – my anxiety about the police: I'd never been scared of them before, but now regarded them as irrational adversaries with the potential to wreck my whole life.

'I'll be at this address,' I said, giving Lucy a note on which I'd scrawled all the details. 'If you don't hear from me within an hour, call the police. We'll just have to hope they do something sensible if it comes to that.'

Lucy shook her head. She was sitting in bed with her knees pulled up under her chin. Her red hair was dancing over her shoulders. She was wearing nothing but pants and a thin vest. The more erotically inclined part of my brain – previously the larger part, to be honest – came to life. What wouldn't I give just to be able to stay at home and have sex with Lucy instead?

'Back soon,' I said, and left the bedroom.

I put the car-keys in my pocket. I was going to meet the woman who'd said her name was Susanne outside the Blå Soldat bar at Gullmarsplan: an obscure place with peculiar opening hours. The car awoke with a rumble as I turned the key in the ignition. That was when the adrenalin really started to pump. Bobby had been thorough, I had to give him that. He had tugged at far more threads than I had realised. It bothered me that he wasn't alive to enjoy the fruits of his hard work. Instead I was now working for a different client, and was busy trying to make Bobby's sister's absolute worst nightmare come true. I was trying to reunite Mio with his biological father. But it was also possible to see things in a different light. I was trying to save my daughter's life. And my own. That had to act as some sort of justification. Even for Bobby.

The car rolled through a Stockholm that was full of life. I like cities that never sleep. Stockholm's a little bit like that. There are always people on the move. As least as long as you're in the city centre. As soon as you get beyond the old toll-gates the excitement stops. The streets become darker, the people sparse.

But nowhere I passed on the way was as deserted as the place where I was to meet the secretive Susanne. The Blå

Soldat was closed and shuttered up. A large note on the door informed me that the bar had gone bust two weeks earlier. There were no plans for it to re-open.

I stood on the pavement for a while, waiting. Apart from the distant sound of cars on the motorway, there was no noise at all. A short way to the south the Globe arena rose up, huge and white. I looked at the time. I'd give Susanne another five minutes, then head back home again.

The second-hand moved like a projectile over the clock-face. Ten minutes later I was still standing there, now full of an anxiety I hadn't felt earlier. I was missing something. Something very important. I shivered and set off reluctantly back towards the car.

Get out of here, for fuck's sake, a ghostly voice whispered in my head.

Then a different voice said: *It's already too late.*

I began to move faster. Almost as if I'd just found out that the Blå Soldat was going to explode within three seconds. I revved the engine and drove away. Holding the wheel with one hand, I fumbled with the seatbelt with the other. Then I called Lucy.

'Everything okay?' I said.

'Fine. How about you?'

Her voice sounded worried.

'I'm on my way home,' I said, and ended the call.

Because Susanne had withheld her number I had no way of contacting her. But she could have called me if she was running late and couldn't get to our meeting in time. But she hadn't. That could only mean one of two things.

She'd been prevented from coming by something that also meant she was unable to let me know.

Or she had never intended to show up.

It didn't really matter which it was, because either way, the feeling that I had walked into a new trap was just as strong.

5

After the incident with the orange I had hoped that the nature of my nightmares might change, but sadly that wasn't the case. Once again I was buried alive, standing in a deep pit. Once again I woke up drenched in sweat and tangled in the bedclothes. If only the bastard sun would rise so a new day could start.

'You're not getting any sleep,' Lucy said anxiously.

'Oh, it's fine,' I said.

But my brain was starting to get sluggish and my eyes itched. Those nightmares were an omen, nothing else. I knew exactly where they came from; I knew exactly why they had started to torment me after I'd been to Texas. But despite that, I couldn't break free of them. All I really wanted to do was curl up in a foetal position and beg to be left alone. But that sort of thing only works if there's someone you can direct your pleas at, rather than the sins in your past.

Lack of sleep does something very destructive to people. It tends to affect me by making me far too sensitive and slow-witted. And that's a terrible combination for someone living under the threat of death. My nocturnal excursion was still troubling me as well. My firm conviction that I'd walked into a trap and landed myself in even more trouble was seriously stressing me out.

'It doesn't necessarily mean someone was fucking you about,' Lucy said as we were preparing breakfast.

Porridge for Belle, yoghurt with fresh berries for Lucy, and coffee and a sandwich for me. To hell with diets, I say. Moderation is rarely best, but when it comes to food it undoubtedly is. Don't eat too many sweets, don't drink too many fizzy drinks, don't eat too little fibre and protein. And don't worry so much. Life's fragile enough as it is. Who knows, maybe next time you'll be the one the mafia are after.

'No, of course not,' I said. 'It's just a coincidence that someone called me in the middle of the night and said she had something to tell me about Mio's disappearance. Just a harmless prank call.'

Lucy raised her eyebrows.

'That's not what I meant. I was thinking that there could be a perfectly logical reason why she didn't show up.'

'And didn't call?'

Lucy shrugged her shoulders.

'Give her a bit of time. She'll probably get in touch again.'

Belle came into the kitchen in her pyjamas. The doll was propped up in the high-chair and then we were ready to start a new day. Lucy and I had stuck to a clear strategy since this whole inferno began: we would do our best to carry on with ordinary life. For Belle's sake, but also so it wouldn't be so obvious to anyone looking on from the outside that our life was collapsing. I was a murder-suspect, after all. The police needed some sort of proof that I wasn't just waiting to be locked up. I was an innocent man, and I had to behave like one. Go to work, do the preschool run, do my two hundred spins on the hamster-wheel of everyday life.

'What are you going to do today?' Lucy said.

'I've got the names of the people who were working in Mio's preschool when he went missing,' I said. 'I thought I'd check them out.'

Lucy didn't seem convinced.

'It's not as if no one's done that before,' she said. 'The police talked to every member of staff, and . . .'

'Thank you, I've read the file containing the interviews. When I said I was going to check them out, I didn't mean I was going to talk to them.'

Lucy frowned.

'No?'

'No. I'm going to see what they're doing now. See if they're still working at the same preschool. If they're even still alive. If any of them is called Susanne.'

Belle was slapping her porridge with her spoon. Milk and jam splashed out onto the table. She hadn't done that since she was two.

'Don't do that,' I said sharply.

She stopped, but didn't eat anything. This was something she'd started with since the fire and kidnapping. She wasn't eating well at all. That was why I was so quick to get cross. Because I was worried she'd starve to death and leave me alone that way instead.

Lucy stroked my arm.

'Belle, can't you try eating some?' she said.

Her voice was much gentler than mine.

Belle shook her head.

'It's not nice,' she said.

I looked down into her bowl.

'Is it the wrong jam?' I said.

She didn't answer.

'How about if you sit with me?' Lucy said. 'If you come and sit on my lap and we help each other out? Would that feel better?'

Belle slid off her chair and slipped round the table. She climbed up into Lucy's arms and buried her face against her chest. Anxiety was pricking at my soul like needles. I really had no idea what she'd been through during the hours she was at the mercy of the kidnappers. At the hospital they hadn't been able to detect any signs of abuse or other mal-treatment. But they did find traces of sleep-inducing drugs in her blood. She didn't seem to have a single memory of when she was snatched from her grandparents' cottage out in the archipelago.

The police and doctors all guessed that she'd been sedated in her sleep and carried out of the house before it was set alight. When I asked Belle what she could remember, she said she'd fallen asleep while her grandmother was reading her a story, then woke up when I lay down beside her. But by then she was no longer in her grandparents' summerhouse, but in my room at the Grand Hôtel. None of us knew how she'd got there.

'No preschool today,' Belle said.

Baby talk, with no subject or verb. When had we last heard that? My instinct had been to get her back into her usual routine as quickly as possible, and spending her days at preschool was an important part of that. But perhaps not, if she was so tired and wasn't eating anything either.

'I'll call Signe,' I said.

Signe, the au pair, was one of the rapidly shrinking group of people I still trusted. Largely because I was so dependent on her.

'And I'll call the preschool,' Lucy said.

She went on feeding Belle like she was a baby while she made the call. One spoon, two spoons, three spoons. Then Belle twisted her head away. Lucy tempted her with some orange juice instead. And then another spoonful of porridge.

One spoon for Mummy, and one for Daddy, a voice chanted inside my head.

Signe arrived half an hour later. Lucy and I went off to work shortly after that: Lucy to get on with work, me to search for someone else's child. It was half past eight when we got in the car. Twenty minutes later we were at our office on Kungsholmen. Lucy shut herself away in her room. I sat down at my desk and took out the police investigation file into Mio's disappearance. I had been confused and tired when I received the phone call during the night. She had said her name was Susanne. But had there been anyone of that name working at the Enchanted Garden at the time?

I had my answer after a brief read-through. No. There was no Susanne at the Enchanted Garden. Naturally. She had lied about her name. I tried to tell myself it was perfectly understandable. But I still wanted to find her. Because the woman who called had claimed to work there.

And said she'd been given my phone number by Bobby before he died.

Why trick me into leaving the flat in the middle of the night?

I hated having so many questions and so few answers. Over and over again I kept reliving the feeling of not being able to stop the Porsche at the pedestrian crossing. It could have been for real. I could have killed another human being.

Again.

I rubbed my forehead with clenched fists. Hard, hard. Inside my skull a single thought was throbbing: I'm not a killer. *I'm not a killer.*

Lucy knocked and walked in.

'I'm going out to a meeting. Lunch later?'

Lucy and me. Me and Lucy. It was starting to feel claustrophobic. I used to have a large social network that I was careful to maintain. There was no way that could just have withered away. Unless this was just what happened in the summer? People escaped from the city and those who were left were the loneliest of the lonely.

'Sure,' I said. 'Let's go for lunch when you get back.'

She nodded and turned to go. It struck me that she must be feeling just as isolated as me.

'By the way,' I said.

'Yes?'

I gulped. There ought to be limits to what I felt I could ask of Lucy. Even so, the words came out of their own accord.

'If the police want to know where I was last night, for whatever reason ...' I began.

'I'll say you didn't leave the flat,' Lucy said. 'Anything else?'

I shook my head. A false alibi, just like that. As if it was the easiest thing in the world for a lawyer.

Lucy left the office. I sat there wondering what had become of us. And decided it was time to deal with something else altogether.

6

There are always witnesses. Always. Even if someone is murdered, mugged or raped in complete seclusion, then at least the perpetrator (and the victim, if they survive) is a witness. Those are the sort of people you need to get hold of if you want to know what happened. People who saw something, heard something.

I was looking for two witnesses. Firstly, one who saw Mio being taken from the Enchanted Garden. The police claimed there was no one who'd noticed anything suspicious. The boy was there, and then he wasn't. How this actually happened, no one seemed to have the slightest idea. I don't believe in stories like that. Mio disappeared from a playground full of children. Belle can see whatever I'm doing or not doing from what feels like a distance of a thousand metres. And she comments on everything: if I cough, sneeze, or – on very rare occasions – happen to break wind in her vicinity. In other words, there was no chance whatsoever that Mio could have disappeared from an admittedly fairly dark but still well-populated playground without one of his friends seeing something. Or one of the teachers.

But I was also looking for another witness. A witness who could solve a mystery. The mystery of who was trying to frame me for murders I hadn't committed. Finding Mio wouldn't make any difference if I was still facing a life sentence. Someone had said they'd seen a Porsche that looked like mine run down and kill a young woman a few weeks earlier. Jenny had died just a few blocks from her hotel. Bobby had been run down and killed shortly after that. There were no witnesses that time. According to the police this wasn't a problem. Because the police were quickly able to link Bobby to me, and that was the end of it: it *was* my Porsche that had killed two people the same night. And I was the person who had been sitting behind the wheel.

When it came to the witness who saw a Porsche hit Jenny Woods, everything was much simpler than with Mio's disappearance. Because at least there was a name. The only problem was that the preliminary investigation was still confidential, which in turn meant that the witness's name was difficult to get hold of for an outsider like me. The fact that something is difficult rarely means that it's impossible. But I was going to need help.

I'm the sort of man who understands the value of building a network of contacts at an early age. I rarely turn down an invitation to a party, and there's not much I don't get asked to attend. I've become the sort of person other people are happy to know, and that's an important factor for success. That's why mafia bosses like Boris contact me, and that's why I know people like Madeleine Rossander.

Madeleine Rossander was at university the same time

as me. An incredibly clever woman. And she has enough energy to fire up an entire army if she wanted to. Be that as it may, Madeleine and I have something in common (besides the fact that we're both extremely focused on our careers and are the sort of people other people want to know): we both used to be in the police. Me, because I thought it was a way of getting closer to my father. I don't know why Madeleine did it. But I know that she, just like me, concluded that it was a big mistake. She didn't fit in on the thin blue line. She wanted too much, thought too much, criticised too much. All in less than two years. Then she told the force to go to hell and she became a lawyer instead.

The trick when you tell so many people to go to hell at the same time is to make sure that the exceptions understand that they really are exceptions. People love feeling that they're special. Madeleine was well aware of this and played her hand perfectly. As a result, she still has a handful of friends within the force, and they'll do anything for her when called upon.

She picked up on the second ring.

'This is Martin Benner,' I said. 'Have you got time to talk?'

'Sure. How are you? It's been ages.'

I detected a trace of anxiety in her voice, and that bothered me. No matter how hard I tried, it was difficult to put a brave face on things and behave normally. Were other people starting to wonder what had happened to me?

'There's been a lot going on recently,' I said curtly.

'Nothing serious, I hope?' Madeleine said.

'No, just far too much of the same old thing.'

Or not.

I've been trying to get justice for a suspected serial killer.

I've been accused of committing two murders myself.

My daughter was kidnapped by a mafia boss known as Lucifer.

Her grandparents have been murdered.

And now I'm trying to find a missing child.

Up until then I hadn't confided in anyone but Lucy, Boris and Fredrik. That was unsustainable. If I wanted Madeleine to help me, I'd have to tell her something about what I needed help with.

I let out a cough as the words collided in my throat.

'To be honest, things aren't great right now,' I said. 'Could we meet for lunch?'

'Sure,' Madeleine said. Her voice changed. 'How about the end of the next week? I can do . . .'

'Today, Madeleine,' I said. 'Today.'

I'm a man of simple needs and relatively few friends. Or rather – extremely few friends. My circle of acquaintances is magnificent and prodigious, but it's constantly changing and not united by any particularly strong bonds. Everyone is replaceable and, to be perfectly honest, I spend a lot of time with people I don't particularly like. But Madeleine is an exception. In all respects she is to be counted as a real friend. My only problem is that I haven't really given her much proof of that.

I informed Lucy by text that lunch was cancelled. Then I got in the car and drove to KB, 'the artists' bar', where I'd arranged to meet Madeleine. She was already sitting at one

of the more secluded tables, and her face lit up when she
caught sight of me.

'Okay, I'm really bloody curious now,' she said.

I gave her a quick peck on the cheek. The smell of her
perfume hit me. I didn't recognise it.

'You smell nice,' I said.

She burst out laughing.

'Chanel,' she said. 'Some new sort, apparently.'

'Apparently?' I said, raising one eyebrow. 'You didn't buy
it for yourself?'

'No, as a matter of fact.'

She smiled, but her face soon settled into a more serious
expression.

'What's happened, Martin?' she said.

More than anything, I would have liked to have been in
a position to give her the uncensored version of what had
become of my life, but that was impossible. I had to carry
on being careful and not make any silly mistakes. So I said
no more than was strictly necessary.

'I have reason to believe that someone's trying to frame
me for something I didn't do. Two murders. And the police
aren't exactly handling the investigation brilliantly. Quite
the opposite, in fact.'

Madeleine raised a glass of water to her lips. She put it
down again without drinking any.

'You're suspected of two murders?' she said.

'Yes.'

But a bit less now, after Lucifer burned my daughter's
grandparents alive, I thought silently to myself.

'What can I do for you?'

'There's a witness,' I said. 'One of the murder victims is

supposed to have been run down by a car that looks like mine. There's someone who saw what happened. I'd like you to use your contacts in the police and get hold of a name for me.'

We maintained eye-contact while I spoke. What I was asking was no small favour. For the first time in my life I saw Madeleine left speechless. Under other circumstances that would have been very amusing. Now it was terrible.

'I don't know what to say,' she said.

'Yes, ideally?' I said, feeling my cheeks burn.

'Of course,' she said, and nodded. 'Of course. But ... You said two people had been run down by your car.'

'No. By a car that looked like mine.'

Madeleine put one hand to her cheek and brushed a lock of hair aside.

'But you did know the victims?'

'Yes.'

She fell silent. She was like me – she didn't believe in coincidences.

'I've got an alibi for the night of the murders. I was at the hospital with Belle.'

'Well, then,' Madeleine said, relieved. Then she became serious again. 'Is she okay?'

'She's great,' I said. 'She fell and broke her arm, but she's fine again now.'

Maybe not fine. She still had her arm in plaster. And a scar on her forehead. I tried to avoid looking at it.

A waitress came over to take our order. I hadn't even looked at the menu, but Madeleine ordered two salads of the day for us.

'What I don't quite understand,' she said, 'is why you're having trouble with the police if you've got an alibi?'

That's the disadvantage of hanging out with smart people: they pick up on things that don't stand up in daylight.

'Oh,' I said. 'You know how retarded detectives can be. Getting hung up on pointless details.'

Madeleine looked at me sternly.

'What sort of pointless details?'

I held my arms out.

'I went outside the hospital to get some fresh air. At three o'clock in the morning. A security guard found me and told the police that I most definitely hadn't spent the whole night inside the hospital.'

I grimaced and waited for Madeleine's response. To my surprise she looked like she was about to burst into laughter.

'I don't know anyone else who could have something like this happen to them,' she said. 'No one at all. But go on. How did all this start? Are you in trouble with a client who's now trying to frame you for murder, or what?'

They were reasonable questions. Extremely reasonable, in fact. But I had no answers that I felt like sharing with her. Which is more or less what I said.

'It's probably best if I don't know too much,' she said.

I could have kissed her. I didn't.

'Thank you,' I said. 'Thank you.'

She drank some water. I watched her long, slender fingers as they held the glass. No new ring. The man who bought perfume for her understood the value of proceeding slowly.

'How are the kids?' I said.

'Fine, thanks. At long last they've accepted that their father and I are divorced. I think they're happy with life.'

'And your ex?'

'Less happy, evidently.'

'Sore loser,' I said.

'Exactly,' she said.

We sat in silent camaraderie until our food arrived. Madeleine wielded her cutlery with such force it looked like she was planning to kill whatever was on the plate. She'd got divorced several years ago. It was the only way to get her husband to pull his weight at home.

'You just want the name?' she said.

I cut tentatively at a piece of chicken.

'It would be great to get hold of a photograph as well,' I said. 'I've scoured the preliminary investigation file I got hold of from the police like an idiot, looking for one, but I can't find anything.'

Madeleine didn't understand.

'A photograph of the witness?'

'Of a missing boy you might have heard of. By the name of Mio.'

7

Without the name of the witness who claimed Jenny had been run down by a Porsche, I had nothing to go on. So I was left with the hunt for Mio. Madeleine and I parted with a promise to be in touch again soon. We smiled and hugged each other warmly. But when she turned and walked away I knew that something had changed. Madeleine was (and is) a loyal friend, and would do whatever she could to help me. But seriously – how relaxing is it to spend time with someone suspected of having committed two murders?

Madeleine didn't think she'd have any trouble getting hold of both the name of the witness and a photograph of Mio. But I was more doubtful.

'There must be a picture of the boy,' she said. 'How else would the police have been able to look for him?'

I'd been wondering that too. All I knew for certain was that there wasn't a single photograph of him in the material I'd been able to check for myself. The boy was like a ghost. I could sense his presence somewhere close to me, but I couldn't reach him. And that bothered me. Or rather, it frustrated me. Because I'm not the sort of man who believes in fairy tales, nor ghosts either, for that matter. The fact that I still didn't know what he looked like was starting to annoy me more and more.

Jeanette Roos, Mio's maternal grandmother, didn't want anything to do with me. His aunt, Marion, did eventually reply to the message I'd left on her phone. She didn't have any photographs of her nephew, she said in a text message. Of course not. She hadn't cared a damn about her sister, so why would she have any pictures of her child?

I only have two personal photographs on my desk. They're both of Belle. But that certainly wasn't the case when my sister and brother-in-law were still alive. I blushed when I realised that if Belle had gone missing while my sister had been alive and someone had asked if I had a picture of her, the answer would have been no. Belle had been a baby when my sister died. She was of no interest to me. My sister and I used to meet up occasionally, for dinner or a drink. There was nothing wrong with my sister, but her husband was a different matter. If it hadn't been for him, we'd have seen far more of each other. But I wouldn't have had any photographs of Belle. In that regard I wasn't the slightest bit better than Marion.

I thought about Sara's brother, Bobby. He had genuinely loved her, and wanted to clear her name. He ought to have had some pictures of his nephew. On his phone, if nowhere else. But I had no idea how I was supposed to get hold of that. I have to admit that I was starting to feel disheartened. Bobby had been based in Switzerland when he died. That was where he lived and worked, and that was where he had a girlfriend. Maybe I could get hold of her, ask her to dig out some old family photographs from whatever he had left behind? But in order to do that, I needed to know what her name was, and how to get hold of her. And I didn't.

I snatched up my phone and called Marion Tell again. This time she answered at once.

'I thought I made it clear that I don't have any photographs,' she said.

'You don't, but Bobby's girlfriend might,' I said. 'How do I find her?'

'Goodness, I've got no idea. But perhaps she'll be moving back home now that Bobby's dead.'

'Home? So she's not from Switzerland?'

'No, certainly not. They moved down there together. He went to work as a lorry driver, she as a hairdresser.'

It was difficult to imagine a more unlikely move. Statistically speaking, they had to be pretty much unique. No one moves to Switzerland to drive lorries or cut hair. No one. Yet that was precisely what they had done.

'Why?' I said. 'Why in God's name did they move?'

'Bobby claimed he'd earn more money there. And there was all the fuss about Sara. I don't think he was feeling that great.'

I toyed with a pen on my desk. Sara's family didn't know I was suspected of having murdered Bobby (even if Bobby's mother already held me responsible). So in that respect there was nothing odd about Marion being so unguarded when she spoke to me. But Marion was also a woman who had lost both her brother and her sister in the space a year. Her only siblings. Regardless of whether she'd been close to them or not, their deaths ought to have left some sort of mark on her.

'How do you mean, "all the fuss about Sara"?' I said. 'I thought she got her act together when she became a mother?'

Marion sighed.

'I suppose she held it together, more or less. But there was still something chaotic about her life. If you ask Mum, she'd say Bobby moved after Sara died, but that's just her getting mixed up. He moved some time before that. I kept out of the way, didn't want to get involved in all that nonsense. I assume it had something to do with her old friends. Those violent thugs.'

Something chaotic about her life. Yes, that was certainly one way of putting it. I bit my lip to stop myself blurting out what I knew. That Sara had managed to have a child with Satan himself, and that he hadn't given her a moment's peace after she fled with his unborn child in her womb.

'I want to get in touch with Bobby's girlfriend,' I said. 'What's her name, and how do I reach her?'

'Her name's Malin,' Marion said. 'I don't know how you could contact her. I have absolutely no interest in helping you.'

I ignored her comment.

'You never met her?'

A stupid question, but one that was worth asking.

'No. But I assume we're likely to meet tomorrow.'

I was surprised.

'So soon? Could you tell her from me that—?'

'No, no, and no. I'm not going to pass on any messages from you. Tomorrow is Bobby's funeral. And you know what? I think you should come.'

'Er . . .' I began.

'Yes, come along,' Marion said. 'You seem to have been

much closer to Bobby than I was. Come along to the funeral and feel like a member of the family.'

Her voice was dripping with sarcasm and made me squirm.

There was no way I could go to Bobby's funeral, was there?

My grandmother once said that before you turn sixty you attend less than five funerals, and then a countless number of them after that. She wasn't a nice person, my grandmother. So I didn't go to her funeral. Nor did my mum, Marianne, or my sister. What would we have been doing there? Celebrating the fact that the old bag was dead?

Before I decided to go to Bobby's funeral, I'd been to three in the past. A friend's, my brother-in-law's, and my sister's. The last one was the toughest. Someone had heard my sister say that if she died, she wanted everyone to wear bright clothes at her funeral. So I showed up in my best summer suit and a pale blue shirt. There was a big photograph of my sister on top of the coffin. The contrast between us couldn't have been more pronounced. In the picture she was so blonde that her hair looked almost white. She had a fetching suntan. On her lap sat little Belle, just as fair as her mother. And there I sat, in the front pew. Her black half-brother. A man hardly anyone recognised because my sister and I preferred to meet up alone or not at all.

It was a fantastic, beautiful summer's day, and the singing of the children's choir had almost raised the roof. My brother-in-law had a separate funeral. It rained then. My mother couldn't stop crying as she buried her only daughter. Lucy was the same. But I just sat there staring at the white coffin and trying to understand how such a young person could just cease to be from one day to the next. I still haven't got to grips with that. Or else I simply haven't accepted it. I hate the fact that life is finite.

'Are you crazy?' Lucy said when I told her of my plan later that evening. 'Surely even you can see that there's no way you can attend the funeral?'

'You mean because the police think I was the person who ran him down and killed him?'

'Duh, yes.'

'Lucy, no one knows about that stupid theory. Thank God.'

'What if the police are there?'

'The police? Why the hell would they be at Bobby's funeral?'

She shrugged.

'Maybe to see if the murderer shows up?'

'But Lucy . . .'

I couldn't help laughing. I ought to have been screaming, though. Yet another night at home with Lucy. We had now reached a – to my mind – dizzyingly large number of them.

I became serious.

'They only do that in films,' I said.

We ate in relative silence. Relative, because Belle was playing at being a one-man band on her side of the table. She ate a surprising amount, and Lucy and I had to restrain ourselves from bursting out in celebration in front of her.

'How did you get on with the preschool staff today?' Lucy said as we were clearing the table. 'You said you were going to check them out?'

I admitted that I hadn't got very far. And then I told her about Madeleine Rossander. Lucy listened attentively.

'Good move,' she said. 'She's trustworthy as well as very useful.'

Madeleine and Lucy are very different. Something to do with maturity. I always think of Madeleine as being older than me and Lucy, even though she isn't. We were actually born in the same year. But she has a depth, a solidity that neither Lucy nor I possess.

I checked the mobile in my left pocket. No missed calls from Madeleine. Nor from the mysterious Susanne. In the other pocket was my other mobile. My normal one. The one I used to use before my life turned into an adult version of musical chairs.

I put the plates in the dishwasher. Lucy rinsed the saucepans. Belle was feeding her doll with water. Then my old phone rang. Lucy and I both started. I took it out from my pocket. I recognised the start of the number on the screen instantly.

'Hello, Martin, how are you?'

Didrik Stihl's voice exuded hearty common-sense. Even so, hearing it made me feel nervous. Any contact with Superintendent Stihl could only mean problems, or more bad news.

'Fine, thanks.'

'That's good to hear. Listen, can you come in tomorrow?'

I felt my heart lurch. Up to that point my visits to Police Headquarters hadn't exactly contributed anything of great value to my life. And I had other plans for tomorrow. Because I was going to a funeral.

'What am I suspected of doing now?'

'Another murder.'

I practically stood to attention.

'Sorry?'

But Didrik ignored me.

'So we'll see you tomorrow? Ten o'clock?'

'Not a fucking chance,' I said. 'What the hell are you playing at? You can't behave like this. Calling here and ...'

And what? Unsettling me. Getting me off balance. Making me panic. I forced myself to think sensibly. Didrik would never have called and said what he had if they had anything solid to go on. He wanted to scare me, trick me into saying or doing something stupid. He wasn't going to win that easily.

'Who's dead?' I said.

'We can take that tomorrow,' he said.

'Wrong. We can take that now.'

'Ten o'clock tomorrow morning,' Didrik said. 'Try not to be late.'

I tried – as quickly as I could – to work out whose turn it was. Who else knew too much? Who else had to die?

A name popped into my head: Elias Krom. The guy who had come to my office pretending to be Bobby. The guy who dragged me into this whole mess.

'It's Elias Krom, isn't it?'

I said it so fast that I just managed to get it out before he ended the call. I heard Didrik breathing down the line. He wasn't going to get away with what he'd just done. Making nuisance calls to someone suspected of murder.

'See you tomorrow,' he said.

And hung up.

8

TUESDAY

Just after one o'clock my phone rang again. Just like the previous night. The difference was that this time I wasn't asleep when it rang. Instead, I was lying awake on my back, staring up at the ceiling. I was starting to become terrified of the nightmares that were plaguing me. Terrified because I was finding it more and more difficult to hold their origin at bay. The very grubbiest of secrets. So grubby that not even Lucy knew about it. If only we hadn't gone to Texas. Then things wouldn't have got stirred up the way they had been.

And then there was the problem of the fresh impetus the police had found. I couldn't deny that it was making me feel stressed. Lucy was lying asleep by my side. She kept stirring anxiously. When the phone started to vibrate on the bedside table she sat bolt upright in bed. Like a soldier who had lain down to rest in the middle of a battle and had been woken up suddenly.

I have to admit that I gave my mobile a couple of hard stares before I finally reached out and answered it.

'Yes?'

There was silence at the other end. But only in the sense that no one was saying anything. I could clearly hear someone breathing. Even though she hadn't said anything, I knew it was the same woman who had called the previous night: Susanne.

'Tell me what the fuck you want or I'm hanging up.'

I didn't recognise my own voice. I had become a man without any slack. There was no longer any space for a pleasant tone. Nor for patience.

'I'm sorry I didn't come yesterday.'

So was I. But I also felt relieved. I had been worrying about what might have happened to her. In case I got blamed for it.

'What happened?'

'I couldn't make it.'

'Yes, I'd worked that much out for myself, that wasn't what I asked.'

'I didn't dare. Okay? I chickened out. I didn't dare meet you. Sorry.'

It sounded like she was crying. Good. Because I have no respect for people who cry when they apologise.

'Who are you so afraid of?' I said.

I didn't really want to continue this conversation on the phone. Even though she had called the new number I had given her, there was a significant risk that it was already compromised.

She was thinking the same thing.

'Can I risk telling you over the phone?' she said.

It was a damn good question. The only thing I knew for certain was that I had no inclination whatsoever to set out on any more nocturnal excursions.

There was a clattering sound, as if she'd dropped her phone.

'All I know is what I saw,' she went on. 'Nothing else.'

'When Mio disappeared?'

'That's right.'

I wondered what the best way to proceed was. I was relatively sure that I wasn't being watched. At least not to the extent that there were officers sitting in a car outside my home at nights eating takeaway food. But if they were listening to my calls, the problem was the same as it had been the previous night. It wouldn't take them long to get to any place that Susanne and I arranged to meet. After a short pause for thought, I decided to sacrifice another phone but to refuse any invitation to meet.

'I'll give you another number to call,' I said.

When I put my mobile down and picked up a different one, Lucy touched my arm.

'What's going on, Martin?'

'I think she's got something to tell me.'

Lucy looked at me thoughtfully.

'Okay,' she said.

She got out of bed.

'I'm thirsty. Can I get you a glass of water as well?'

'Yes, please.'

She walked out of the bedroom. I hated watching her go. I was seized by an unreasonable and pathetic terror that it might be the last I saw of her. It occurred to me that that was a significant factor behind the fact that we were now living together. That I couldn't bear not knowing if she was still alive.

The third mobile rang. We were regularly buying more

and more. If I had to stop working as a lawyer I could probably get a job as a switchboard operator.

'This time I want you to tell me everything over the phone,' I said abruptly when I answered. 'No more meetings until I know what you've got to say.'

'I appreciate that you don't trust me, but ...'

'I don't trust anyone right now. Don't take it personally, that's just the way it is.'

She fell silent. Or was browbeaten into silence, maybe. Either way, she didn't say anything.

'I don't know where to start,' she said eventually.

I did.

'Start with Bobby,' I said. 'How did you come into contact with him?'

'He came to the Enchanted Garden. Angry and upset. The police had already been several times, and then he turned up some time later. He frightened a lot of the staff. They said they'd call the police if he didn't leave.'

Her words were coming more easily now.

'Did he threaten the staff?'

'Not directly. At least that's how I saw it. I was a temp at the preschool at the time, they used to call if they needed me. I had a few weeks' work there when Mio was placed with his foster parents, and then again when he went missing. I wasn't working the day Bobby came to the school, I was only there to pick up a reference. That might be why I saw things differently.'

'How do you mean, differently?'

Lucy came back carrying a glass of water. She'd spilled some on her vest, making it partly transparent. That would have made me crazy with lust before, but now it didn't bother me. Maybe that was what being a grown-up meant?

'Like I said, all the others seemed frightened. But I just thought he seemed so sad. The look in his eyes was so unhappy, not at all wild or angry. When he had been driven out from the Enchanted Garden he sat in the car and wept. I saw him when I went out a little while afterwards. I . . . I couldn't keep quiet any longer. I gave him my phone number. He called an hour or so later.'

I rubbed my eyes in an attempt to clear my thoughts.

'Why did Bobby come to the preschool? And when?'

'He came late last spring. It was like he couldn't stop thinking about his dead sister and had figured out that he wasn't going to be able to put what happened to her behind him. He said someone must have seen something. That he didn't believe a child could just vanish the way Mio had done. He wanted to know why the staff were lying to the police.'

Bobby had been thinking along the same lines as me. There's always someone who saw something. Always.

'Was that what they were doing, then? Lying to the police?'

'No,' she said quietly. 'But the police didn't talk to everyone.'

I straightened up.

'Sorry?'

'It's true. They didn't talk to me, for instance. According to the rota, I'd already gone home by the time Mio disappeared, but they asked me to stay on in a different class when my shift was over. Those hours were accounted for separately. I assume the police didn't notice that.'

'So you were in the playground when Mio went missing?'

I heard the woman who called herself Susanne clear her throat over the phone.

'No. I was inside with one of the children. He had a cold and was running a temperature, and I had to wait until his mum came to pick him up. He was sitting on the floor playing with the Lego. And I was standing at the window, itching to go home.'

I felt my pulse rate increase.

'You were standing by the window? What did you see?'

'The back of the preschool. There's no playground there, just a car park and the loading area. The children can't get round there because of the fence that keeps them out at the front.'

My heart was beating even harder.

'What did you see?' I repeated.

My voice sounded hoarse.

'They came out of nowhere. I could only see them from behind, but I know it was Mio. I recognised his hat and coat. But most of all, his yellow wellington boots. He was walking beside a tall woman who was holding him by the hand.'

'He was walking? She wasn't carrying him?'

'No, it didn't look like she needed to. He knew her.'

I couldn't stay on the bed any longer and had to stand up.

'Who was she?'

'A girl, Rakel. She did some part-time work at the pre-school up until the autumn Mio disappeared.'

I tried to take in what she'd said.

'And you've never told anyone this?' I said, feeling myself getting angry.

'No one ever asked.'

Her defence was unexpectedly shrill. I changed tack.

'What time was it when he went missing?'

'Half past three. The police arrived at four. By then I'd just left.'

I took a deep breath.

'Why in God's name didn't you sound the alarm when he was abducted?'

'I didn't know he was being kidnapped! Back then, everything to do with Mio was a bit odd. And Rakel had worked with us for a while. I was sure there was some logical explanation for why she was picking him up.'

Conviction does funny things to people. They seem to become irrational, for instance.

'Okay, but you must have heard the news on the television and radio?' I said. 'There was a national alert for Mio.'

When Susanne replied it was in such a quiet voice that I could barely hear what she said.

'I didn't dare tell anyone what I'd seen.'

'Why not?'

'For the same reason I hardly dared call you. I'm scared something will happen to me.'

'Have you been threatened?'

'No. But ... it's complicated.'

'That's not good enough,' I said.

And that was when Susanne snapped. That was when the wretched tears started.

'She saw me do something silly,' she whispered.

'Who did?'

'Rakel.'

'Something so silly you were scared she'd say what she'd seen if you said you saw her with Mio?'

'Yes.'

I sighed.

'Okay, now I really am curious,' I said. 'What did you do that's so terrible that you didn't dare say you'd seen a child being kidnapped?'

'I stole some things. One of the teachers was moving house and had been given permission to store some boxes in an empty office. I happened to see her digging about in one of the crates. She had some really nice jewellery in a little wooden box. I can't explain why I did what I did. But I went back that evening and stole the box. And that's when Rakel saw me.'

A bird moved outside the window, far too close. I've hated birds ever since I was a child. The window was open and I gestured to Lucy to close it.

'What was Rakel doing at work at that time of day?' I said.

'I don't know. All I know is that she saw what I did. She confronted me the next day. "I saw you stealing. Bear that in mind."'

'Hang on – she said that?'

'Yes.'

I was thinking out loud.

'She didn't say she'd tell the others that you were the thief? Because I can imagine there was a hell of a fuss once the theft was discovered.'

'There was. I hardly dared accept any more work there.'

Why hadn't Rakel told either the police or her colleagues that she had witnessed the theft? That struck me as important, the fact that for some reason she didn't want to reveal that she'd been at the preschool at the same time. Or she simply didn't want to draw attention to herself.

'I didn't know what to do,' Susanne said. 'But ... I really needed the money. So I sold all the jewellery. I actually got quite a good price for it. It solved all my problems.'

Solved her problems and created a load of new ones, I thought. Her actions also prompted a lot more questions. Far more than I felt I had time to ask.

'I'm afraid I'm still having trouble understanding your behaviour,' I said. 'Did Rakel do anything else to scare you into keeping quiet?'

Susanne hesitated for a while before answering.

'It was just as she was about to go out through the gate of the car park with Mio,' she said. 'She stopped under one of the streetlamps. Then she turned round, almost as if she knew I was watching her. She looked straight at me. And then she raised her hand and put one finger to her lips. I swear – if looks could kill, I wouldn't be here today. I was so frightened I darted away from the window. And I didn't say a word to anyone. Because I knew something terrible would happen to me if I did.'

I thought for a while. There were gaps in the logic of her story; we would have to talk again, several times.

'Even though you were so terrified, you evidently carried on working there,' I said. 'And despite the fact that you were the thief. Didn't you feel any shame?'

'The preschool had been told to make big cutbacks. I was pretty sure they wouldn't want me any more, that they'd have to get rid of all the temps. But then they offered me a longer contract. I couldn't afford to turn it down.'

The words came so easily to her. She couldn't afford to turn it down. Couldn't say no. Things ended up the way they did. I couldn't remember the last time I'd spoken to someone who took so little responsibility for things.

'You said nothing to anyone,' I said. 'Until Bobby turned up at the school. Then, all of a sudden, you decided to talk to him.'

'It wasn't until I saw him that I realised what I'd done. I couldn't live with that. It didn't matter how frightened I was – I had to tell someone. So I told him. After that we stayed in touch. He told me he'd gone to the police, but that they hadn't believed him, and said I'd have to go myself. Then I got scared again. The next time Bobby called he mentioned your name. He told me you'd be getting in touch with me. But you never did. In the end I called Bobby. A man answered, said he was a police officer. He told me Bobby was dead. Then I hung up.'

I sighed.

'Have the police been to see you yet? They could have traced your call if they wanted to.'

'Hardly. I made the call from an unregistered pay-as-you-go mobile. Like I'm doing now.'

It was my turn to fall silent.

'Susanne, what do you want me to do with this story of yours?' I said after a while. 'You won't tell me what your real name is. And you don't want to involve the police.'

'There must be some way you can use what I've told you anyway!'

'Come on, tell me your name, for God's sake. I know it isn't Susanne.'

'No.'

'Rakel, then? You must be able to give me her surname.'

'Minnhagen,' Susanne said. 'Her name is Rakel Minnhagen.'

I wrote it down.

'I'm going to have to call you again,' I said. 'Give me your number.'

She refused.

'Don't think you can tell me what to do,' she said. 'I make the decisions.'

9

'So who am I supposed to have killed now?'
My meeting with Didrik Stihl and his colleague really wasn't the place for humour, but I didn't have the energy to think tactically. I was pleased to see that Didrik's colleague was clearly surprised. He hadn't expected me to be aware of the reason I had been summoned to Police Headquarters again.

As usual, Lucy was in complete control of her facial expression and didn't move a muscle. Didrik ignored my remark.

'What were you doing the night before last?' he said.

'Why?'

'Just answer the question.'

'I was at home.'

'All night?'

No, I was out trying to find a mysterious woman who says her name is Susanne.

'Yes.'

'Who can vouch for that?'

'Lucy.'

Didrik leaned back with a sigh.

'You realise you're going to have to reallocate the roles in this little performance, don't you? Lucy can't be both your legal representative and the person giving you an alibi, Martin.'

'No?'

Didrik gestured in a way that reminded me of how I usually reacted when Belle was being particularly difficult. But he didn't scare me. It was good to get confirmation of the fact that they didn't have me under twenty-four-hour surveillance. If they had, he wouldn't have had to ask where I was that night.

'Perhaps you'd like to get to the point?' Lucy said. 'If not, we've got plenty of things to be getting on with instead of just sitting here.'

'I can imagine,' Didrik's colleague said.

His name was Staffan. If he had told me his surname was Stalledräng, like the old Christmas carol, I wouldn't have been surprised. I thought it was a shame that police officers who try to make insinuations usually fail. Partly because they don't understand what the word 'insinuation' means.

'Let's get going,' Didrik said sharply, making me wonder if he was talking to me or to his colleague. 'Martin, we're going to have to impound your car again. Is it parked outside?'

Was he joking?

'You can't be serious. Who's been run down this time?'

Didrik didn't answer my question.

'Is the Porsche parked outside?' he repeated.

'No. We walked here.'

One of our more spontaneous decisions. Walking from the office instead of taking the car.

'Do you have any firm suspicions you want to share with us, or can we go?' Lucy said.

I liked the fact that she was pushing them to move faster, even if I was terrified of ending up in a situation where I left Police Headquarters without knowing what had happened. Or who had died.

'There's been another death,' Didrik said. 'And a witness who says the victim was run down by a man driving a Porsche 911. It's fairly obvious that Martin would spring to mind in circumstances like that.'

The fact that we had once been friends seemed completely incomprehensible. I started to feel sick and wanted nothing more than to get out of there.

'Elias Krom,' he said.

I did my best not to react. And succeeded reasonably well.

'Anyone you know?' Staffan asked me.

This time he tried to look sly. And failed.

'No,' I said.

'No?' Didrik said. 'Are you quite sure?'

'Yes,' I said. 'I don't know Elias. But I have met him. He was the man who came to my office, pretending to be Bobby.'

Didrik looked at me seriously.

'So Elias Krom was the one who first got you involved in Sara Texas's case?' he said.

'Yes.'

'I thought you said it was Bobby.'

I sighed. Very deeply.

'I thought it was. Then I realised that it couldn't have been. But I've already told you that.'

'Of course,' Didrik said. 'It's just that you neglected to mention Elias. Why?'

The correct answer was because Lucifer had told me to stop talking to the police. But of course I didn't say that.

I shrugged instead.

'You never seem particularly interested in what I've got to say.'

'You never have much to offer,' Staffan retorted.

I didn't respond.

First Jenny. Then Bobby. And now Elias. Everyone who had provided me with information was dying, one after the other. How was that possible? Who was keeping such a close eye on me that he or she could find someone like Elias? Someone who had been a total stranger to me until Boris gave me his contact details. I'd never even called Elias; I just went round to his home. And I was fairly confident I hadn't been followed there. But only fairly confident. Lucifer's associates had known I was staying at the Grand Hôtel that night. How they knew that was beyond me. The thought was unavoidable: had Lucifer ordered Elias's death?

I didn't think so. It was far too clumsy.

'Martin?'

Lucy put her hand on my arm.

'We're done here,' I said, and stood up.

'You seem very calm, considering what you've just been told,' Didrik said, getting to his feet.

It was a statement of fact.

'Exactly what have I been told? That a man I met on a few occasions has been murdered. That a witness saw him get run down by a car that resembles mine. All very unpleasant. But this time the whole thing seems pretty straightforward.'

'How so?'

I couldn't tell if Didrik was amused or disconcerted.

'Because this time, Didrik, you're asking the wrong questions.'

He folded his arms over his chest and waited for me to go on.

'You asked where I was the night before last. But you forgot to ask where the Porsche was.'

Talk about someone's jaw dropping. The question is, why had Didrik been so convinced of my guilt? Why hadn't they arrested me?

'Tell me,' he said curtly.

'My car is in for repair,' I said. 'Belle dropped an orange on the floor. The orange rolled under the brake-pedal. Things got very messy when I had to stop the car suddenly. I dropped it in to be cleaned up two days ago, and I don't yet know when I'll be getting it back. To be honest, there's no real rush. At night it's locked up – indoors – at the garage. Call and check. There was no way I could have picked it up on the night of the murder. Nor could anyone else, for that matter.'

I couldn't help enjoying my moment of triumph. Finally something had gone my way.

'Give us a call when you want to have a serious conversation about Martin's Porsche and its involvement in these murders,' Lucy said. 'Because by now it must be obvious that what we said was right all along – that someone is trying to frame Martin for these crimes.'

Didrik lowered his eyes and looked at his notebook.

'It's possible that we'll come to the conclusion that Martin's car wasn't involved in the latest murder,' he said.

'Just like it wasn't involved in the others,' Lucy said.

Didrik swallowed hard and didn't respond. He was under as much pressure as I was. I liked that.

'Your perpetrator is getting careless,' I said. 'The first killings, the double murder, was scrupulously carried out. That evidently wasn't the case the night before last. Presumably he or she reasoned that it would be enough to use any old Porsche.'

I sounded very confident, but I was actually terrified. Because there was a microscopic possibility that the latest murder had been committed using my Porsche. That the killer had somehow managed to get it out of the garage. The question was: how would that affect what the police thought about my involvement?

'Like I said, call us,' Lucy said.

We left the room. Didrik walked to the main entrance with us.

'One last thing,' he said as we were standing by the revolving doors.

I nodded.

'Do you know someone called Boris Micanovic?'

I don't know where my self-control came from, but to my immense surprise I managed to appear unconcerned. I didn't have time to notice how Lucy reacted.

'No,' I said. 'Why?'

Didrik shook his head.

'Forget it, it was just a thought.'

I had two choices. I could drop the discussion and walk out. Or stand there arguing. I chose the latter. Because I wanted to know why Didrik was asking about the mafia boss I had been very close to in the recent past.

'Okay, that's more than enough of you throwing out questions at random,' I said. 'Who is this Boris, and why do you mention him?'

Didrik seemed to hesitate, but not for very long.

'His name cropped up in the investigation into the murder of Belle's grandparents,' he said.

Ah. I thought I was going to have a heart attack. My fingers and hands went numb, and the pressure on my chest was like an elephant standing on it.

'Who is he?' Lucy asked.

Good, she was on board as well. Rather cooler than me.

'A mafia boss,' Didrik said. 'One of the big ones.'

'And you think I know him?' I said. 'You don't have a very high opinion of me these days, do you?'

Didrik tilted his head to one side.

'I'm not sure you deserve a high opinion, Martin,' he said.

That was more than I could bear.

'Well, thanks very much for today,' I said, and headed for the revolving door.

'No, thank you,' Didrik said.

'Say hi to Rebecca.'

I don't know why I said that. Maybe to remind him that we had once known each other. I hadn't seen Didrik's wife for several years. Didrik wasn't the sort of man who ever said much about his family. Apart from the time he and Rebecca adopted their only child. He talked so much then that he almost sent me to sleep with all the details.

When Didrik didn't answer I glanced over my shoulder. Didrik was standing frozen to the spot.

I stopped and searched my memory. Had they got divorced? Or – even worse – had she died?

'What is it?' I said. 'I didn't mean to put my foot in it.'

Didrik came back to life again.

'Don't worry,' he said. 'I'll tell her.'

He turned to go. Then he seemed to remember something he'd forgotten to ask or say.

'By the way,' he said. 'Elias Krom.'

'Yes?'

'He's not dead.'

Lucy and I looked first at each other, then at Didrik.

'But you said ...'

'No, I didn't. You did. I didn't ask about Elias because he'd been run down, but because you mentioned his name on the phone yesterday.'

Thoughts were flying through my head like missiles.

'So who's dead, then?' Lucy said.

Didrik pulled a face that was hard to read.

'Fredrik Ohlander,' he said. 'A journalist. Apparently he was working on something seriously top secret.'

I swear, it was like falling from a great height. Fredrik Ohlander was dead. The only person to whom I had entrusted the whole of my story, with the exception of Lucy and Boris.

'You're looking a bit pale,' Didrik said. 'How did you know him?'

I didn't have to lie about that, at least.

'We were students together, back in the day.'

'I didn't know you studied journalism?'

'I didn't. He studied law. But only for a couple of terms.'

Didrik nodded.

'You don't happen to know what this secret project was that he was working on?'

'No.'

My reply was blunt and pointed.

'Oh, well,' Didrik said. 'We'll just have to find out for ourselves.'

Then he turned on his heels and walked away. This time he didn't come back.

PART 2

'I killed a man.'

KV: Bloody hell. So you had no idea Fredrik
was dead until then?

MB: No. We'd agreed not to be in constant
contact. Largely out of consideration
for his safety. But clearly that wasn't
enough. He died just over a week after
we last met.

KV: You must have been extremely scared.

MB: Scared, but mostly sad. I felt horribly
guilty.

KV: You couldn't have known what was going
to happen.

MB: No, but after everything else that
had happened I should have had some
idea. Or at least done a decent risk
assessment.

KV: Those nightmares . . .

MB: We're getting to that.

KV: And . . . what you said about . . . you killing someone.

MB: I never said that.

KV: You said that if you'd killed the woman on the pedestrian crossing, you'd have killed another person.

MB: We'll get to that as well.

(Silence)

KV: So Elias Krom was alive and well. That's something.

MB: Yes, although to be brutally crass, he was less important to me than Fredrik. Or rather - the two can't be compared. Fredrik knew every last fucking detail of my story. No one else did. Apart from Lucy and Boris, of course. But neither of them knew I'd been talking to Fredrik.

KV: Seriously? That's what I don't understand. How could the murderer have known you'd told Fredrik everything?

MB: I had my own theories about that, and eventually got confirmation that they were correct. But we haven't got to that part of the story yet.

KV: Seems like you had a hell of a lot to do. Find Mio. Find out who was framing you for murder. Find out who killed Fredrik.

MB: It was clear to me that the last two had to be connected. There was a pattern. Jenny and Bobby died because they provided me with information. I could only assume that Fredrik died for the same reason. He was a man who knew too much, and who had the potential to start talking. Especially if anything happened to me.

KV: And something did happen . . .

MB: A lot of things happened. And pretty quickly.

KV: Unpleasantly quickly, I'd have said. But let's do as you say. Take one thing at a time. What was the first thing that happened after you left Police Headquarters?

MB: I had a drink. Then I went to a funeral.

10

I was starting to think of myself as a dangerous man. The sort of man you shouldn't come anywhere near. Lucy and I left Police Headquarters hand in hand. Metaphors are useless, but just then it was fair to say that problems were gathering above our heads like storm-clouds. Fredrik Ohlander was dead. That was something I really hadn't expected.

'I need a drink,' I said.

'Now? It's only just gone eleven o'clock.'

'Then we'll have an early lunch today. Lunch and something to drink.'

We jumped in a taxi and drove to Riche. I prefer hanging out in Östermalm, even if I end up in other parts of the city like Kungsholmen or Vasastan surprisingly often. When we were picking the location for our office, Lucy was adamant that we should establish ourselves in Östermalm. I wasn't convinced. I didn't want it just round the corner. Kungsholmen felt like a smart choice. Close to Police Headquarters, and also on an island. Islands are good.

You're in no doubt about when you leave them. All you have to do is cross a bridge and you've left all the mess behind.

The taxi taking us to Riche crossed Kungsbron. Lucy looked out over the water.

'Who was he?' she said.

'Who?'

'The man who died. The man you said you were at university with.'

The man you said ... I could hear the doubt in her voice, and it bothered me.

'I was at university with him. But he switched subjects and became a journalist.'

'Why haven't I ever heard of him?'

'Because I've never socialised with him.'

'But you must have had some sort of contact with him, seeing as he was run down in a car that was apparently very similar to yours?'

I saw the taxi-driver twitch in the rear-view mirror.

'Let's talk about it later,' I said.

Lucy didn't reply.

We arrived and I paid the driver. Lucy went into the restaurant ahead of me. A waitress showed us to a table in the window.

'Something to drink?'

'A glass of white wine,' Lucy said.

'G&T,' I said.

The waitress disappeared.

Lucy focused her gaze on me. It wasn't warm, but jet-black. Furious.

'After everything we've been through,' she said. 'And you're still – *still* – keeping things secret from me.'

If only you knew, I thought.

The nightmares floated up to the surface again. I did what I usually did and pushed them back down again. They weren't relevant; they'd only come to life because of our trip to Texas. While we were there they hadn't been a problem at all. I'd had to focus on my own survival, on the mystery of Sara Texas. I'd managed to keep the past at bay, with one exception: my memories of my dad. His betrayal, our farewell, his death. But now I could feel the whole mess slipping out of my grasp. The past, and the lies, were breathing down my neck. It was only a matter of time before I'd have to get to grips with things.

I took a deep breath and wished my drink had arrived.

'There's a perfectly natural explanation for why you didn't know about Fredrik Ohlander,' I said.

And I told her what there was to tell. That after everything that had happened, I wanted to leave some sort of record behind if I died or disappeared. That I wanted to make sure my story was documented in the event that I was unable to tell it myself.

Lucy listened impassively.

'Too many people had died,' I said gruffly. 'Don't ask me what I think now that Fredrik's gone too. This really is unbelievably fucking unpleasant.'

Our drinks arrived. Lucy sipped her wine, I my G&T.

'Do you regret not having something stronger?' I said.

'Regrets are pointless,' Lucy said.

Her remark could have been directed at me, it was hard to tell. The alcohol made its way into my bloodstream and offered temporary respite.

'Who knew?' Lucy said.

'No one.'

'Rubbish, he's dead.'

'That's what's so terrible. I didn't even tell *you* about Fredrik.'

Lucy drank more wine.

'He could have talked.'

That thought had also occurred to me. Particularly after what Didrik had said about him working on something 'seriously top secret'. Had Fredrik felt the need to get the details of my fucked-up story confirmed?

'Who else could he have talked to?' Lucy said.

'Anyone,' I said. 'I gave him all the names.'

Lucy crossed her legs.

'Anyone,' she said. 'Any one of all the people you yourself have talked to. You know what that means, don't you?'

I did. It meant that whoever killed him was one of the many people I'd met in the past few weeks. In Sweden, and in Texas. It was a nightmare scenario.

'We need to find out what he did after he and I met,' I said.

A hopeless statement.

'There's a lot we need to find out,' Lucy said.

Another hopeless statement.

Little more than a week ago she had been absolutely exhausted. Now her batteries were recharged, but there was a flatness far too close to the surface.

My mobile rang. It was Madeleine.

'I've got the name you wanted,' she said.

'Great!'

My outburst made the other guests turn round. I calmed down.

'But I haven't managed to get hold of a picture of Mio.'

I couldn't help feeling disappointed. But disappointment wasn't the dominant emotion. Once again I was left wondering how it was possible. How could not even the police have a photograph of a child who had been the subject of a nationwide search?

'Can we meet up?' Madeleine said.

I glanced at the time.

'I'm having lunch at the moment. Then I'm going to a funeral.'

'A funeral?' Madeleine said. 'Who's died?'

'Far too many people,' I said. 'Would five o'clock work?'

Fear came out of nowhere. I started looking round automatically. Lucy noticed my fluttering gaze and frowned. I ignored her. Was I being watched? Could I trust that the phone was secure? Or was I sentencing Madeleine to death as well?

From one death to another. In American films funerals are always incredibly well-attended. The reality is often very different. We aren't as popular as we like to imagine. And really – how many people do you want to attend your funeral? All your old shags? The forgotten and forsaken? People you've trampled on and shoved in the shit? Or all the old relatives whose names you don't even know and therefore don't give a damn about? The moment I got out of the car a short distance from the church where the service was going to be held, I made up my mind to write a guest-list. If I was going to die in the near future, I wanted to make sure the right crowd gathered at the funeral.

I had no desire whatsoever to attract any unnecessary

attention. So I had already decided in advance that if there weren't many people there, I wasn't going to go in. Either there'd be enough of a crowd to hide in, or there wouldn't. There wasn't. I recognised Jeanette Roos from a distance of a hundred metres. She hated me, and would kick up a hell of a fuss if she caught sight of me.

I slipped behind a large tree. They'd chosen a church out in Nacka. I had no idea what their connection to the place was, but I was grateful for all the greenery surrounding the church, the churchyard and the car park. I didn't particularly want to show myself, and I needed easy hiding-places.

Marion, Bobby's sister, was approaching the church from another direction. She nodded to her mother and walked right past her. I tried to remind myself what sort of childhood she'd had. How tough it must have been. But I couldn't do it. I don't know how many times I end up rejecting my own mother's outstretched hand each month. She keeps begging for a full-blown mother-son relationship, and I keep saying no. But only to a full-blown relationship. A half-arsed one is fine.

Jeanette was in pieces. I could see that easily enough from my ridiculous hiding-place. She was standing next to a younger woman who stroked her back from time to time. There was no sign of the priest. And hardly anyone else either, come to that. There was a group of young men, four or five of them, maybe, a short distance away. One of the men glanced in my direction. It was Elias Krom.

My heart did an extra beat and I pulled back. The whole hiding-behind-a-tree thing wasn't really right for me. The next time I looked out, they had all gone inside the church. Everyone except Elias. He was still standing outside smoking. His hand was shaking. Then he stubbed his cigarette out and started walking in my direction.

Really good players know when to capitulate. I'm one of them. I knew I'd messed up. So I stepped out from behind the tree and waited for Elias.

'What are you doing here?' he said.

Hunted people easily run out of energy. Elias looked like he'd spent years running for his life.

'I was thinking of attending the service, but that probably isn't a good idea.'

'There's hardly anyone here,' Elias said. 'Best you don't come in.'

I couldn't disagree.

'Who was the woman standing next to Jeanette?' I said.

'Malin. Bobby's girlfriend.'

'I need to talk to her. Can you arrange it?'

He stared at me, wide-eyed.

'I've done you enough favours,' he said.

'Me?' I said. 'You're not getting me mixed up with Bobby now? He was the one who told you to pretend to be him and sneak into my office, not me.'

'I didn't sneak in.'

'So what? I need to talk to Bobby's girlfriend. If I give you a phone number, can you see that she gets it?'

He shook his head and started to back away. His whole body was trembling.

I stepped forward and grabbed hold of his arm.

'What's happened?' I said. 'Why are you so nervous?'

He gulped several times before answering. His eyes were flitting about the churchyard so erratically that it was hard to follow them.

'Someone's following me. Not all the time, but nearly. Just when I start to breathe out, the bastard comes back. I don't know what he wants, and I don't know who he is. But I think it's going to end badly. Like it did for Bobby and Jenny.'

I chose my words with care.

'I get that you don't trust me,' I said slowly. 'But I'm still going to ask you to do this. Because otherwise this will never end. I can guarantee that.'

'Did you get your kid back?'

His words hit me like a punch, even though that wasn't his intention.

'Yes, she's okay. But ... I've only got her back on loan. You understand? There are things I need to sort out. Like finding out who killed Bobby, for instance.'

Elias ran his fingers through his hair. It was greasy. There was dirt under his fingernails.

'I don't want to get involved. Sorry, but that's how it is. I wouldn't be here today if I didn't care about Bobby, but now I have to think of myself.'

'That's exactly what I'm telling you to do!' I said, in a voice that was louder than I intended. 'You won't be able to sort this out on your own.'

'What do you mean, "this"? What the fuck is "this"? I don't understand a thing. I just want my fucking life back!'

If he spoke any louder he'd wake the dead from their eternal slumber. Now it was my turn to look round at the churchyard and beyond. There was no one in sight. But that was hardly proof that neither of us was being followed.

'Just fix it for me to talk to Bobby's girlfriend,' I said. 'Do that, and I won't bother you again. Okay?'

He rubbed his face hard and blinked.

'Okay,' he said. 'Okay.'

He put his hands in his trouser pockets.

'You should go into the church now,' I said. 'Before they come looking for you.'

'I will,' he said. 'Why is it so important for you to talk to Bobby's girlfriend?'

I had no desire to elaborate on that, so merely said: 'I think Bobby did a lot of looking for his nephew on his own. He may have left a load of stuff behind. Such as a picture of Mio, for instance.'

Elias blinked again. His eyes seemed to be irritating him.

'A picture of Mio? Haven't you already got one?'

'No.'

Elias's hand flew up from his pocket. He scratched the corner of one eye.

'He looked a lot like you.'

'*Me?*'

My eyebrows shot up in surprise.

Elias nodded thoughtfully.

'A lot like you,' he said. 'Same colouring.'

A gust of wind made the trees tremble. I stood there in silence and watched as Elias went inside the church. I had unexpectedly found out something I hadn't known a thing about before.

11

Evil's name was Lucifer, and he lived in Texas. I had made a solemn vow to Lucifer's associate that under no circumstances would I try to find out any more information about the big mafia boss. If I did, Belle was dead, and possibly also Lucy. The fact that I had now found out the colour of his skin was hardly the result of any conscious snooping. His skin was the same colour as mine. Dark. Or black, depending on your choice of words. The question was, what could I do with that particular nugget of information?

Lucy looked surprised when I told her what I'd found out.

'I don't know why it matters,' she said, 'but I've got a feeling that it does.'

I agreed with her. Not knowing who Lucifer was bothered me more than I could put into words. He was the man who had kidnapped my daughter. He had murdered her grandparents. He had threatened to kill me and was using me as a coerced agent in Stockholm. Sooner or later I would give in to the temptation to find out who he was, and see to it that he disappeared from my life permanently.

Lucy was studying me carefully.

'Don't even think of it, Martin,' she said. 'Just let it go.'

She was asking the impossible, and she knew it. But she was also asking the only sensible thing.

She changed the subject.

'How was the service?'

'Not a fucking clue, I didn't even set foot inside the church.'

'Wise.'

We were sitting in Lucy's office. She was behind her desk, I was slumped like a teenager in one of the visitors' chairs. At the start of the summer our office had resembled a youth club. We had been planning a trip to Nice, and Lucy was busy trying out different sun-creams. That all seemed such a long time ago now. Lucy was leafing through some papers she had in front of her. She seemed older, somehow, or more taut, than she had done just a few weeks earlier. I probably did too. We had stopped laughing. It couldn't really get much worse than that.

'We ought to do something fun,' I heard myself say.

Lucy shifted her focus from her papers to me.

'We ought to get our lives back first,' she said.

And what if we can't? I wanted to ask. What the fuck do we do then?

'I'm going to go and see Madeleine now,' I said.

Another change. I never used to tell Lucy who I was going to see and when.

'Anything I can be doing in the meantime?' Lucy said.

I stopped and considered.

'The woman who's called me two nights in a row now calls herself Susanne, and she says someone called Rakel Minnhagen abducted Mio from his preschool. That's worth digging into. Check the preschool's staff properly; I haven't had time. I don't know exactly what we're looking for, so keep your eyes open.'

Lucy jotted down some notes and nodded. I looked on, feeling anguished. We were chasing lots of different threads at the same time, and whatever I did left me feeling inadequate. It was a horrible feeling. If I'd been obeying a senior officer, he would have yelled in my face: 'One thing at a time, Benner! Hold this damn investigation together!'

But I had no commanding officer, and there was no way I could hold my investigation together.

'Do they know us at the preschool?' Lucy said.

'No,' I said. 'Why would they?'

'You tell me, I was just checking. Anything else?'

'Passport photographs,' I said. 'Don't forget to dig out passport photographs of the people working at the school when Mio disappeared. We need to know what they look like.'

I'd barely finished speaking before Lucy and I were struck by the same thought.

'Bloody hell,' Lucy said.

We'd been stupid. Ridiculously stupid.

'Mio,' I said. 'Check to see if he had a passport.'

There were at least ten smokers standing outside the bar where I was meeting Madeleine. She had chosen the location, not me. A backstreet I'd never heard of, near Gullmarsplan. Not far from the Blå Soldat bar where Susanne had wanted to meet. The taxi-driver had to use satnav to find it.

'I appreciate the need for caution, but isn't this taking things a bit far?' I said once we were seated.

We were sitting at a small corner table. I avoided touching the walls. They were so filthy I'd have got stains on my clothes if I leaned against them.

'Sometimes you have to think outside the box,' Madeleine said.

She put a brown envelope on the table. A waiter took our order. I carried on where I'd left off at lunch. Another G&T. Madeleine ordered a beer. The waiter disappeared.

'How did you get on?' I said.

She'd already told me, admittedly, but I didn't have time for small-talk. I was treading water in the Mariana Trench. It was exhausting, and very hard work.

'Good and bad.'

She ran her hand over the envelope. With a mixture of fascination and horror, I realised that she was nervous. It was unusual to see Madeleine nervous.

'You know I'm happy to help you, Martin. But not with absolutely anything. And not at any cost. I've got children. I can't risk their safety for your sake.'

'I haven't asked you to,' I said.

It was impossible to keep my voice steady. I lowered it as I went on: 'What the hell's happened?'

Madeleine shook her head briefly.

'Nothing,' she said. 'It's just a feeling I got. There's something that doesn't make sense about this whole thing.'

Our drinks arrived. Madeleine took several deep mouthfuls of her beer. My G&T tasted terrible.

'I don't usually have any trouble getting information out of the police,' Madeleine said. 'This time it was different. It's as if the preliminary investigation has been flagged with big red warning signs. I had to come up with all sorts of peculiar excuses that would normally have been completely unnecessary.'

'But you did manage to get the information?'

'Only half of it, like I said on the phone. I've got the name of the witness who saw Jenny Woods get run over. But no picture of Mio.'

A woman walked past our table. I got the impression that she slowed down as she went past. Madeleine and I sat in silence until she'd gone.

'Isn't that a bit bloody weird?' I said in a low voice. 'That there aren't any pictures of the kid?'

'I'm not saying that there aren't any pictures,' Madeleine said. 'I'm saying that the person I spoke to couldn't find any, not a single one.'

'What, you think someone's hidden them? Someone inside the police?'

She shrugged.

'I don't know what I think,' she said. 'All I know is that it's just like you said: extremely unlikely that the police don't have any pictures of the child. That's one of the very first things they ask for whenever anyone disappears.'

I considered what I already knew. That Mio looked like me. That told me everything and nothing.

'Who's the witness?' I said.

I don't know why I thought it was so important.

'A woman by the name of Diana Simonsson. Do you recognise the name?'

'No. Should I?'

Madeleine pushed the brown envelope towards me.

'Open it,' she said.

I did as she said and pulled out a sheaf of papers. At the

top was a black-and-white photograph of a young blonde woman.

'What about now? Do you recognise her?'

I shook my head. She was a complete stranger to me.

I started to look through the documents. It was a district court judgement. I read the first page with bemusement. It was a rape case. What did this have to do with anything? Rape is the most heinous of all heinous crimes. For that reason I very rarely agree to defend anyone suspected of it. Because I have immense difficulty sympathising with what they've done. And because I never feel completely sure of what they *haven't* done. But there are exceptions. And I had one of them in front of me.

My own name shone out as if it was written in burning letters. I had defended the suspect. And Diana Simonsson had been the plaintiff, or the victim, to put it more plainly.

All of a sudden I remembered her as clearly as if it was yesterday. She'd been completely hysterical when the verdict was announced. Later that day she turned up at my office and gave me a bollocking, screaming that I was the devil's lackey, that she'd never forgive me for what I'd done. I told her that if she didn't leave my office at once, I'd call the police. I also said I understood that she was disappointed, but that she couldn't take that disappointment out on me. It was the court that convicted or cleared people. And every-one had the right to a defence. Even people suspected of sex-crimes. She left my office in a state of near meltdown. I waited until I heard the door close behind her. Then I called the police and filed a report against her. Something for which I was now very grateful.

'Are you kidding?' I said. 'The police's star witness, who

swears she saw a Porsche 911 run down and kill Jenny Woods, is a woman who hates me because I managed to get the man she accused of raping her cleared at his trial?'

'Pretty much,' Madeleine said. 'I was wondering why you weren't being held in custody. I think we know why now.'

I didn't believe that.

'What are the chances that she of all people would be standing there at that particular moment?'

'Big enough, apparently,' Madeleine said.

'No way,' I said, pushing the file away from me. 'The same sick mind that planned Bobby and Jenny's deaths made sure there was a so-called witness to one of the murders.'

'You don't think she was there?'

'Not a chance.'

'Someone told her to make a false statement?'

'Yes. Why else would she make do with only identifying the car? She ought to have recognised me as well.'

'A false witness. Martin, how often does that actually happen in real life?'

'That doesn't matter. What matters is that it's happening this time.'

Madeleine drank some more beer. The noise-level in the bar was steadily increasing. Someone started playing darts. Sharp projectiles pierced a board on the wall. A smell of sweaty armpits drifted past, making me screw up my face.

'Why did they need a witness?' she said. 'Wasn't there any forensic evidence?'

'No,' I said. 'Nothing to tie me and my car to the crime scenes. Well, there was something. The Porsche had – still has – a dent on the bonnet that I can't explain. But I don't know what that proves.'

'So you think whoever was driving stopped the car and got out to examine his victims?' Madeleine said. 'And called in a witness to strengthen the evidence?'

'Maybe. But it's more likely that the witness was part of the plan all along. If there was some credible way of linking my car to the first victim, there wouldn't be any problem tying it to the second one.'

More darts hit the board. Madeleine looked at the man as he took aim and threw them.

'Who else has access to your car apart from Lucy?' she said.

I opened my mouth, then closed it again.

'Lucy?' I said. 'Sorry, you think Lucy is mixed up in this?'

My heart stood still even at the thought of it.

'Anyway,' I said, 'I wouldn't say that she "has access" to my car. No one does, except me. Lucy hasn't got her own key to the Porsche, and never will have.'

Madeleine wouldn't look me in the eye.

'It must have been someone who could get hold of your car, Martin. No one had better access than you. And Lucy, simply because she's so close to you. She could have got the keys from you easily enough that evening at the hospital.'

I shook my head.

'You're talking as if it's definite that it was my Porsche that was used that night. But, as I've already said, there's no evidence to support that. Nothing.'

'That depends how you look at it,' Madeleine said. 'You're dismissing the witness. I'm less convinced. I checked the database of vehicle registrations. Guess how many Porsches of that model there are in Greater Stockholm? Three. The police have spoke to the other owners and written off both them and their cars. I've seen parts of the preliminary investigation. I took the opportunity to get hold of excerpts while I was sorting the other stuff out. There was no sign of a break-in on your garage door. Same thing with the car. You know as well as I do that you can't break into or hotwire a car without there being some sort of evidence afterwards. And if it was your car, Martin, you're going to have to accept that the crimes were committed by someone close to you.'

I went on protesting.

'If it was even a Porsche that ran down and killed Bobby and Jenny. God knows how much that witness was paid to come up with her story.'

I could see the doubt in Madeleine's face. How could I describe the extent of the madness with which I'd been confronted in recent weeks, which had left me believing that the impossible was actually possible? Normally I'd have agreed with Madeleine and said that obviously it was a Porsche that had hit Jenny and Bobby. And no, you certainly couldn't get into a locked Porsche and start it without leaving some sort of evidence. But this was so far beyond normal that it was impossible to explain to the uninitiated. Nothing was the way it seemed.

'I can't thank you enough for your help,' I said.

My conscience was making my blood run slowly. There was a name that I'd been trying my utmost not to think about since we left Police Headquarters. Fredrik Ohlander. The journalist who had died. Was that my fault as well? Quite possibly.

'I hope I won't regret it,' Madeleine said.

She might as well have slapped me in the face. If anything happened to Madeleine, if she met the same fate as Fredrik, I'd be destroyed.

'Me too,' I said. 'Me too.'

And I realised, when our eyes finally met, that we meant very different things.

'Madeleine, I didn't do the things they're saying. I didn't hit those people.'

I couldn't believe I was having to say that. It was hardly surprising she was accusing Lucy of everything that had happened. The alternative was evidently accusing me.

Madeleine swallowed hard.

'You were the one who taught me that the truth is rarely anything but the most obvious solution,' she said quietly.

'I know. But that basic rule doesn't apply this time. I swear, you have to believe me.'

She nodded her head slowly.

'I'm trying,' she said. 'I'm trying.'

12

Restlessness is often the cause of poor judgement. That applied to me too. I didn't want to go back to the office after Madeleine and I parted. It was too late; I'd soon be going home anyway. But I realised I didn't want to be there either.

'Take care,' Madeleine said as she gave me a hug.

And then she was gone.

I wanted to call after her, say I might need her help again. But I knew that wouldn't be fair. It was clearly dangerous for other people to be anywhere near me. Madeleine was one of the few people I respected and liked. I didn't want to drag her into this mess if I could help it.

So what was I going to do if I wasn't going to go home or back to the office? Belle and Lucy were waiting for me. Following my new custom, I fished my mobile from my pocket and sent Lucy a text.

'Going to be late. Need to sort something. M.'

Then I dug out another phone number: Veronica's, the woman I'd met at the Press Club. Our encounters felt so distant now, as if they belonged to a different century. We'd met only twice. Since then I hadn't had time to see her, seeing as all hell had broken loose. What was rather more surprising was the fact that Veronica hadn't contacted me either. I'd guessed she was the sort of woman who had problems with relationships in which sex didn't mean love. But her not phoning seemed to indicate otherwise.

Since Lucy and I got on that plane to Texas I hadn't spared other women so much as a thought. But that had changed now. Impatience was running through my body like an itch. I've always found fresh energy from having sex. With as many women as possible. That's why I prefer to define myself as single, and it's why I don't want to have a partner or get married. Whenever the stress or boredom get too much, I need the opportunity to relieve the pressure.

Veronica was a good option. We'd already met and I knew she was good at sex. It wouldn't require any tedious preliminary work to get her into bed. The only thing holding me back was the memory of how we had met. I'd first encountered her when I was out having a drink with Didrik Stihl. My intention had been to pump him for information, but that hadn't gone particularly well. Whereas, in contrast, my pick-up techniques worked rather well. Veronica had been stuck with a boring date and was more than happy to let herself be led astray.

I stifled a sigh and put the phone to my ear. It started to ring. The fact that I had bumped into Veronica while I was having my last friendly meeting with Didrik was irrelevant. She was a completely separate chapter from an entirely different book. And I was horny and restless. I needed sex (with someone other than Lucy), and I needed it right away.

A voice answered after just two rings. A very mechanical voice, belonging to one of the phone companies' automated systems.

'This number is not in use,' the voice said. 'Please check that you have dialled correctly.'

I stared dumbly at my phone. There was no question that I had misdialled – the number was already in my list of contacts. Puzzled, I called again. And got the same message.

Under normal circumstances I would merely have shrugged and moved on to the next name on the list, because I'm rarely if ever short of someone to fuck. But just then the circumstances were very far from normal. I had stopped believing in fate and coincidence. Maybe there was a perfectly natural reason why Veronica had changed her number. Natural and harmless. Unless the truth was rather different. Natural, but potentially life-threatening.

I'd become paranoid, I had to admit. But I couldn't afford any more mistakes or misjudgements. I needed to know who I could trust and who I should write off. So I hailed a taxi and went round to Veronica's. At least there was nothing wrong with my memory. I'd been to her flat on Södermalm twice. I very rarely take women back to mine. If Belle were to wake up in the middle of the night she mustn't find me in the bedroom with a – to her – unknown, naked woman. Or on the kitchen table. Or standing up against the wall.

One of my mobiles buzzed. I'd soon have to get myself a handbag. My trousers were stuffed full of mobiles to a degree that could only be described as unattractive.

To my surprise I found a text message from Elias. He'd spoken to Bobby's girlfriend. She was prepared to meet me.

'Can she come to your office tomorrow?' he wrote.

I confirmed that that would be fine, and thanked him for his help. He didn't reply.

The taxi pulled up outside Veronica's door. It struck me that I didn't know her surname. Berntsson? Bertilsson? No matter, I knew I had to ring the third bell from the top on the entry-phone. I pressed it again and again. No answer.

My heart-rate speeded up and I took several deep breaths to stay calm. There was no reason to panic. Obviously Veronica was at work. But my anxiety refused to accept rational arguments. It was squirming through me like a worm. Did I even know what her job was? Was there anywhere else I could get hold of her?

Just to put my mind at rest. Just to help me calm down.

I didn't give a damn about whether or not I got to have sex. Lucy was still the best I knew; I didn't need to look for someone else to practise relaxation techniques.

I tried ringing one of Veronica's neighbours. No answer. I tried again and heard an elderly woman's voice through the speaker.

'Yes?'

I never need to lie in order to sound important or authoritative. Telling people what my job is always does the trick. There was no reason to do anything different this time. But I did try to say as little as possible about myself.

'I'm sorry to bother you,' I said. 'My name is Martin, I'm a lawyer. I'm trying to get hold of your neighbour, Veronica. It's urgent.'

Silence.

'Veronica?' the woman said.

'Yes?'

'There's no Veronica here.'

Shit. Pissing fucking shit.

I hesitated, but only for a moment.

'Could I possibly come in?' I said.

'By all means,' the voice said. 'Come up and ring the bell. The name on the door is Svensson.'

There was a buzz and the door opened.

There was a lift, but I chose to take the stairs. It was Lucy who got me started on that. You should never miss any opportunity to exercise your buttocks and thighs. Sure enough, one of the doors on the third floor was marked Svensson, whereas the door Veronica and I had gone through was unmarked. Had that been the case when I was last there? I couldn't remember.

I hardly had time to ring the bell before the door marked Svensson opened. An elderly woman welcomed me in with a twinkling smile. I liked her instinctively. She was old – she had to be over eighty – but extremely spry. It's important to make a distinction between people's physical and mental age. There are thirty-year-olds who behave as if they were seventy, and ninety-year-olds who never seem a day over forty-five.

'Harriet,' the woman said, shaking my hand.

'Martin,' I said. 'I'm sorry to impose like this. Like I said, I'm trying to contact Veronica next door.'

I pointed towards the door to the neighbouring flat.

Harriet stepped out onto the landing and followed my finger with a look of surprise.

'There's no one called Veronica living there,' she said.

'There was a few weeks ago,' I said.

She shook her head firmly.

'No,' she said. 'That's not right.'

I did my best not to lose my grip. Panicking wouldn't help.

'Okay,' I said. 'Okay. Let me put it like this: a few weeks ago I paid a visit to that flat. I was there in the company of a woman who called herself Veronica. Tall and blonde, very attractive. She had keys to the flat and there was nothing to suggest that she hadn't been there before. Does she sound like anyone you've seen coming and going?'

I tried to remember what the flat had looked like. Small, just two rooms, bedroom and living room. White walls, fully tiled bathroom. Kitchen cabinets from Ikea. Neutral, timeless furniture. Green plants and soft sheets. Pictures on the walls, but not many photographs. I ransacked my memory. The more I thought about it, the more certain I became: I hadn't seen a single photograph. The only things in the flat that could be described as personal were a few items of clothing tossed on the sofa and bed. I should have opened the fridge. To see if it was empty.

'Yes,' she said. 'I think I've seen the woman you're talking about. She seemed very nice. But I only saw her here a couple of times. Like all the others who use that flat.'

'All the others?' I said dumbly.

Harriet nodded.

'This building is owned by a housing cooperative, and I'm on the committee,' she said. 'All the flats belong to members of the cooperative. Apart from that one, which is used as shared accommodation for guests. So your young lady must know someone who lives here in the building, who let her borrow it while she was visiting. We don't have a member called Veronica.'

I nodded as my pulse quickened. It would be such a relief

to find that everything had a logical explanation. I had lied to Veronica, telling her my house was suffering from damp and that we'd have to meet at hers. The fact that she may have lied to me in turn didn't necessarily have to mean anything funny. Maybe she hadn't even been lying: the flat could well have been her home on the days when she and I met. She was under no obligation to tell me where she really lived.

'Perhaps you should go round knocking on my neighbours' doors,' Harriet said with a wry smile. 'To find out which one of them she knows.'

Naturally I didn't do that. But I did go up and down the stairs, looking at the names on all the doors. I didn't recognise any of them. When I eventually left the building I still had the distinct feeling that I had been tricked.

13

The flat smelled of garlic when I got home. Belle came rushing out and threw her arms round me. The plaster on her arm hit my neck hard. The spring in her little legs would probably carry her all the way to gymnastics gold at the Olympics if I could only get my act together to sign her up for classes.

'Daddy, we did sculpture today. Come and look!'

She let go of my neck and promptly fell on the floor. She leapt to her feet again and pulled at my hand.

Before the kidnapping she never called me anything but Martin. Now she only said Daddy. A tiny part of me thought that was wrong. For the same reason it had always been wrong: she already had a daddy. A dead one, admittedly, but one who was still more authentic than I was.

Lucy was standing in the kitchen peeling prawns. Her face lit up when she saw me, then darkened again when she saw my worried expression.

'What's happened?'

'We'll talk about it later,' I said.

It wasn't altogether obvious that I was going to tell Lucy what had happened. But, on the other hand, there was no one else I could share my anxieties with.

Belle's creations were lined up on the kitchen table. Three little brown clay figures that looked a bit like Gollum.

'They're great,' I said.

To start with, all the crap Belle dragged home from pre-school with her used to drive me mad, but over the years I've learned to appreciate it. All the drawings, stone trolls and bits of plastic tat were at least proof that she was doing something each day. I liked that.

My shirt was sticking to my back. The air was humid and oppressive. Grey clouds were gathering in the sky.

'There's going to be a storm,' Lucy said.

'Rain,' Belle said.

'And probably some thunder and lightning,' I said.

Belle turned pale so quickly that I didn't register it at first.

'No lightning,' she whispered. 'No lightning.'

Tears as big as blueberries were rolling down her cheeks. She's terrified of storms. I tell myself that it must be something to do with the plane crash that snuffed out her parents' lives. There was a ferocious storm that night. But Belle could hardly know that. And she wasn't on that plane.

'Okay,' I said. 'No lightning.'

As if I had the slightest control over the weather.

Gently I lifted Belle up in my arms. Once again she wrapped her arms round my neck, holding so tight that I almost couldn't breathe.

'There was loads of lightning,' she said. 'Loads.'

I stroked her back.

'When, sweetheart?'

She was breathing very close to my ear.

'When I was sleeping at Grandma and Granddad's. They said it was nothing to worry about. But I was ever so scared.'

I froze mid-movement. Up until that moment Belle hadn't said a word about what had happened before or during her kidnapping. We had assumed she couldn't remember anything because she was sedated. Now, out of the blue, she was talking about thunder and lightning. What else could she remember?

From the corner of my eye I could see Lucy staring at us. I prayed silently that Belle wouldn't notice how agitated we were that she was talking. If she did, there was a risk that she would simply clam up again.

'Do you remember talking to anyone else apart from Grandma and Granddad?' I said.

Belle didn't answer. We sat down to eat, but it was impossible to get anything into her. Her eyes kept roaming over the large windows facing the terrace and the dark, stormy sky beyond. When thunder rumbled in the distance and the first raindrops started to hit the glass, I got up quickly from my chair.

'Come on, Belle,' I said. 'Let's go and read a story.'

We went and sat on her bed. I closed the window and pulled the blind down. The room became dark and I took out a torch. Belle was delighted, and held it perfectly still while I read. Two books later she was fast asleep, safe from the storm, resting limply against my chest.

I stroked her hair and tried to make some sort of sense of what she had said. There had been thunder. Grandma and Granddad had said it was nothing to worry about. There was no more to it than that. No matter how much I wished there was.

'A flat for guests?'

Lucy looked as confused as I had been when I told her what I'd found out on my visit to my former shag's flat.

I nodded solemnly. After mulling things over for a few hours I was now sure: there was something funny about Veronica.

We were sitting under the roof out on the terrace, watching the flashes of lightning chase each other across the sky.

'Why . . . I mean, how did you find that out? Why did you go round to see her?'

I have certain rules that govern my life. One is that I never lie when asked a direct question. Especially not when it's Lucy asking it, and all the more so if what she wants to know about is my sex-life. But this time I wasn't sure if I should stick to the truth. I didn't think I should. It was better to lie.

'I can't explain,' I said. 'It was a . . . an impulse. I wanted to check out everyone I've met over the past few weeks.'

'Everyone?'

'Oh, you know what I mean.'

Lucy looked away.

'Can't it just have been a coincidence?' she said after a while. 'Maybe she allowed herself to be picked up for the simple reason that she thought you were hot. Maybe she was in the city for a course, or was visiting a friend and had just borrowed the flat. Who knows, maybe she lives in a completely different part of Sweden.'

'That thought occurred to me too,' I said. 'But that doesn't explain why her mobile number no longer works.'

'Did she say what her surname was?'

'Don't remember. I might not have been told.'

'Martin, for God's sake.'

'What? Do you know the surnames of all your fucks?'

Lucy became serious.

'Yes.'

'Seriously?'

'Yes. And to be perfectly honest, I think that would apply to most normal people. You know who you sleep with. Or else you don't sleep with them.'

I didn't know what to say, so I kept quiet. I didn't agree with her in principle, but that discussion could wait.

'Did she say what she did for a living?' Lucy said.

Another question I couldn't answer with any confidence.

'She said she was an accountant.'

'How dull.'

I laughed, loud and unforced.

'I know,' I said. 'That's what I thought.'

Lucy sighed.

'So what's to say she was lying, really? Maybe she *is* an accountant. Maybe she did borrow the flat from a friend who lives in the building. There are hundreds of reasons why someone might need temporary accommodation. Getting a new bathroom put in, something like that.'

'How do you explain the phone number, then?'

Lucy said nothing.

The wind turned and the rain started to push us back towards the wall, almost scornfully. In the end we were pressed up against the window.

'By the way, how did you get on investigating the staff at the preschool? Did you get hold of any passport photos?'

'I've got their names and details in my handbag. I'll be getting their passport photographs tomorrow. I'm not sure I'd call it investigating, though. I doubt we'll be able to do much with what I managed to find out.'

I didn't feel up to looking at Lucy's findings. That would have to wait until the following day, when I could see the passport photos as well. I had other things to think about.

'Her phone number,' I said. 'If I can get an explanation of why that's changed, I'm prepared to buy the rest of it.'

Lucy pulled her feet up onto her chair.

'Who knew you were going to the Press Club that evening? That was where you met her, wasn't it?'

I nodded quickly. She was asking an extremely pertinent question. If I didn't meet Veronica by chance, she must have known I was going to be there at that time.

'Only you and Didrik,' I said.

Lucy said nothing at first.

'Only me and Didrik,' she repeated after a while.

A flash of anxiety made my stomach clench. Madeleine's question from lunchtime echoed in my head.

Who else has access to your car apart from Lucy?

I shivered involuntarily. Of course my car wasn't involved. And of course Lucy wasn't caught up in everything that had happened.

'What is it?' she said.

'Nothing,' I said.

New thoughts appeared. They set off quickly towards fresh targets, a long way away from Lucy.

'Didrik,' I said quietly.

Lucy started.

'Surely he can't be involved in whatever it is we think is going on?'

I shook my head.

'No,' I said. 'I really don't think so. If that was the case, Didrik and his colleagues would have been keeping an eye on me before Bobby and Jenny died. Anyway, it just doesn't make any sense. The police simply don't work that way. Honey-traps only happen in films.'

'Honey-traps?'

'Pretty women enticing men and sleeping with them to get information.'

Lucy pulled a cardigan over her shoulders.

'Right,' she said.

'Come on, Lucy. We've always . . .'

'I know,' she said. 'I know.'

Of course she knew. Lucy wasn't stupid; she knew why I'd tried to contact Veronica again. There was a rumble of thunder and flashes of lightning went on striking randomly selected patches of ground.

'He teased me,' I said quietly.

'Who did?'

'Didrik.'

'When?'

'When I was flirting with her. Well, maybe not teased. Pulled my leg. He mostly just sounded jealous.'

Didrik has a lot of talents, but was he a good actor? I wasn't sure. The idea that he could have set up a honey-trap at the Press Club was laughable. But on the other hand – if that was the case – he was hardly the only person to have surprised me in recent weeks. That is the downside of knowing an awful lot of people very superficially: you can soon end up feeling alone and uncertain.

'What was she like to talk to?' Lucy said. 'Did she ask a lot of questions?'

I shook my head. Lucy would have hit me if she knew the images that popped into my head when I thought of Veronica. Warm bodies, sweat and breasts that were far too large. Hers, not mine.

'Not that I remember.'

'So what would be the point of meeting you?' Lucy said. 'What did you have that she wanted, if not information?'

I closed my eyes. What did I have with me that evening at the Press Club that she might have wanted, and couldn't get hold of any other way?

I opened my eyes again.

'I don't know,' I said. 'Not yet. But trust me – it won't be long before we get to the bottom of this.'

14

WEDNESDAY

I was wrong. It took an inordinate amount of time for me to realise what Veronica wanted from me. And by the time I did so, it was too late.

But I had no idea about that when I made my way to the office the following morning. Another bad night with too little sleep. Another morning of anxious glances from Lucy and irritating comments about how I looked. Irritating because I had so little to say about why I was sleeping badly. I thought I was comfortable with my lie. I was wrong about that too. Big revelations were on their way, and I didn't have the faintest clue.

The weather gods were very good at setting portentous background music to the drama that was unfolding. First, before it all began, we'd had an unusually warm summer. Then Bobby came to my office and the rain started. I'm not saying that there's a perfect causal connection between these events, but I'm confident that it's more than mere coincidence. Day after day the bad weather hung on. Until the day when Bobby's girlfriend Malin came to see me. Then the sun returned.

She rang the doorbell at ten o'clock. Lucy was in her room having a telephone conference call with a client. I was sitting drinking coffee. It had been a long, sleepless night. Thoughts I wasn't prepared to share with any living person were going round inside my head. The nightmares that had been tormenting me at night up till then had found fresh impetus and were now tormenting me during the day as well.

I hated the feeling of being doubly exposed. The problems I had in real time were bad enough – the past had to be held at bay. I no longer believed it was remotely possible that I had met Veronica by chance. Which meant that someone had made sure she was at the Press Club on that particular evening. And the only people who had known I was going to be there were Lucy and Didrik.

Assuming Didrik hadn't mentioned to anyone that we were going to meet up. Someone like that Staffan. It bothered me that I kept finding myself in situations where I needed Didrik's help but couldn't get it. That was no use to either of us. Particularly not if the mess I found myself in was somehow linked to the police. But how could that be the case? Could there really be people inside the law and order machinery of the state who were mixed up in everything that was afflicting me and my family?

So, Bobby's Malin showed up at ten o'clock. She wasn't at all what I was expecting. Which happens fairly often. I was, and remain, a person with certain prejudices. We all are. That's how we remember and sort the people we meet in different situations. Prejudices also mirror our expectations. In Malin's case this was particularly unfortunate. Because my expectations were formed on the basis of the encounters I had had with a man calling himself Bobby, but whose real name was Elias. I'd never met Bobby, so I couldn't possibly know what he had been like, or what sort of person his girlfriend might be.

Malin was very straightforward. I respected her automatically, almost like the way I did when I first met my friend Madeleine Rossander. Certain people simply demand that of you. If you don't comply, you don't get anywhere near them.

'I'm pleased you got in touch,' Malin said once we'd introduced ourselves.

She spoke with a Norrland accent, making her voice sound calm and measured.

'And I'm very pleased you've come to see me,' I said.

I had to stop myself. There was so much I wanted to say, so much I wanted to ask. At the same time I was weighed down by a guilty conscience. But that was irrational. It was Bobby who had sought me out. It was he who had turned my life upside down, not the other way round. Even so, I had the perturbed sense that I had caused him great harm.

I let my confused reasoning boil down to: 'I'm so sorry that Bobby died. If there's anything I can do, let me know.'

Malin tilted her head to one side. Her eyes were too bright; it was obvious she'd done a lot of crying recently. I felt unexpectedly envious. There were so many times in my life when I should have cried but didn't.

'Bobby had such high hopes of you,' she said.

She couldn't have inserted the knife with greater precision. I didn't know how to respond.

'He talked about you long before he came to see you.'

I had to interject: 'He never came to see me, Malin. He sent Elias.'

'Bobby was so used to not being taken seriously. That's why it happened that way.'

'I know that. But why Elias? He's hardly the sort of person who wins other people's confidence.'

'He probably was in Bobby's world. Besides, Elias was very sympathetic towards Sara, whatever one might think. And Ed, who was the obvious choice, didn't want to do it.'

I nodded dumbly. Ed, Sara's unpleasant ex-boyfriend, hadn't been prepared to help Bobby contact me. But he had passed the task on to Elias. Very noble.

'I understand that Bobby made a number of inquiries of his own into what happened to Sara and her son,' I said. 'Far more than Elias told me about.'

Malin blinked several times.

'When Sara came home from the USA, pregnant, she was a complete wreck. We thought things would get better once the child was born, but she just got more and more paranoid. It was painful to witness.'

'So you and Bobby were already together then?' I said, unable to conceal the surprise in my voice.

Another prejudice – that Bobby wouldn't have been capable of maintaining a long-term relationship.

'We got together when we were seventeen,' Malin said. 'It was him and me against the world. He didn't have anyone but me, and I didn't have anyone but him. Sounds pathetic, doesn't it?'

Her question took me by surprise.

'No,' I said. 'Not at all.'

'Not at all? How many other teenagers only have each other?'

I didn't know. I just knew that I had been one of the

lonely ones. That my dad was absent and my mum an addict, and therefore incapable of looking after me and my sister properly.

'Did Sara ever tell you and Bobby what she had been through in the USA?' I said.

Malin looked me straight in the eye.

'I don't know what you mean by "what she had been through", but we understood that she had had serious problems with her boyfriend there. The man who was the father of her child.'

I nodded stiffly.

'She had a tattoo at the back of her neck,' I said. 'The word Lotus. Did she tell you how she got that?'

Malin shrugged.

'She said it was a drunken prank, and that she regretted it.'

A drunken prank. That was one way of describing the tramp-stamp that was meant to tell a certain sort of person who you belonged to. Lotus was the nickname Sara had been given by Lucifer. It had been branded into the back of her neck as a permanent reminder that she would never be free.

'I see,' I said.

'You mean she was lying? That the tattoo actually meant something more?'

I held my hands out, not altogether unlike really bad doctors when they want to suggest that their patient might be right after all.

'No, not at all,' I said.

Malin fiddled with the strap of her wristwatch. I noticed that the hands were standing still and showing the wrong time.

'I know that Bobby, via Elias, asked you to get justice for Sara,' she said. 'How far did you get?'

All the way. I got all the way to the miserable, shitty truth that Sara wasn't a serial killer, just an exploited prostitute.

'Not as far as I would have liked.'

'But you stopped working on the case when Bobby died?'

I folded my hands on my desk and leaned forward.

'Yes,' I said. 'I did.'

'They're saying Bobby was murdered. You must have been scared.'

'Very scared.'

'So was Bobby. That's why he didn't tell anyone he'd come back to Stockholm.'

There it was again. The alarm bell telling me that I was missing something vital.

'Someone must have known,' I said. 'Otherwise he wouldn't have died.'

'He told Elias, obviously. But not his mother. Nor any of his other friends.'

'Apart from Ed?'

'No, not even him. Ed put Bobby in touch with Elias. But he had no part in what happened after that. He keeps to himself, always has so many things going on.'

Once again I saw Elias before me. Trembling and shaking with nerves. The memory conjured up such angst that it created a sinkhole beneath me. I almost had to cling onto the desk to stop myself tumbling into it.

'Is Elias the sort of man who can keep quiet?' I said.

'Yes, absolutely. He comes across as a bit rough but Bobby and I trusted him.'

Even though he'd been in prison, I felt like adding. Even

though in his youth – which wasn't actually all that long ago – his hobby had been beating people up on the street, which got him a conviction for assault. Calling him a bit rough was an understatement.

'Malin, someone must have known,' I said. 'It's as simple as that. Think about it. What happened once Bobby got to Stockholm? Did he just sit holed up in a flat somewhere, or did he meet anyone? Did he say anything about that?'

My mobile rang. Loudly.

'Sorry,' I said, and rejected the call.

I opened the top drawer of my desk and dropped the phone inside.

'No, he didn't tell me anything about what he was doing after Sara died,' Malin said quietly. 'But I realised he wasn't done with his inquiries. He must have used up all his holiday, he travelled to Stockholm so many times. I thought he should hand it all over to you, especially what he found out at Mio's preschool.'

I felt the hairs on the back of my neck stand up.

'What did he find out at Mio's preschool?'

'He'd got in touch with one of the teachers there. She was sure she'd seen Mio being abducted.'

The hairs on the back of my neck settled back down again. I already knew about that. Why hadn't Bobby shared what he'd already found out with me, either via Elias or by abandoning the deception and getting in touch with me himself? It was incomprehensible.

'You said you didn't care about Mio,' Malin said quietly, as if she could read my thoughts. 'Bobby was so worried that you wouldn't understand how important he was in this whole thing.'

'So why didn't he tell me all he knew?' I said.

'He wanted to see how you worked first,' Malin said. 'What if you'd blown him out? Then he'd have given you far too much information, and all for nothing.'

That was an explanation I wasn't prepared to accept, but I didn't say so.

'So he met Susanne,' I said. 'Who else?'

'Susanne?'

'If it's the same woman I've been in contact with at Mio's preschool, that's what she says her name is.'

Malin shook her head.

'I don't know what her name was.'

That reminded me that I still hadn't looked through Lucy's list of the school's employees.

'Either way, he met one of the teachers,' Malin said. 'She claimed she knew who abducted Mio. Rakel, I think her name was.'

Malin's voice cracked and I realised that I was holding my breath.

'Did he find her?' I said. 'Did they meet?'

Malin swallowed several times.

'No. He died before he figured out how to find her.'

It was hard not to feel sorry for Bobby. He had meant so well yet not managed to finish the job. Someone ran him down. Using my car. Or a Porsche that looked like mine. Malin still knew nothing about that, and that was the way it was going to stay.

'You wanted to see me?' she said. 'That's why I'm here today.'

I pulled myself together for the conclusion to our meeting.

'I'd like a photograph of Mio, if you've got one.'

'Elias was right, then. That's what he said, that you wanted a photograph. What for? I mean, you're not working on Sara's case any more.'

'True. It's too dangerous. But Bobby was desperate to know what happened to Mio. I've been thinking that it doesn't cost anything to do a bit of cautious digging.'

It was stupid lie. It burned my tongue. Bobby was dead. Why would I care what he did or didn't want?

Malin opened her handbag and took out a small picture.

'This was taken at preschool a few weeks before he went missing,' she said, putting it down in front of me.

Even though I already knew what I was going to see, I was surprised. Mio hadn't inherited any of his mother's colouring.

'You'd think he was adopted, wouldn't you?' Malin said.

She didn't mean any harm by that: it was a simple statement. I couldn't take my eyes from the picture. Mio the ghost-boy finally had a face. He was much smaller than I had imagined. With serious, wide eyes that stared straight into the camera. He looked smart. A checked shirt and a knitted tanktop that was slightly too big for him.

'He looks a fine lad,' I said. 'Can I keep this picture?'

'Sure. I've got others.'

Malin closed her handbag and got to her feet. I stood up as well.

'You know,' she said, 'Bobby thought it was terrible when Mio ended up with foster parents. Social Services didn't think Bobby was mature enough to look after a child, and they evidently didn't care enough about me to even spare me a thought. Bobby's no longer here, but I am. If Mio is still out there somewhere . . . I'd like the chance to offer him a home.'

I could have burst into tears at that moment, but I didn't.

'I'm not a magician,' I said. 'But I'll see what I can do.'

Malin held out her hand and I took it.

'Sara had high hopes of you, too,' she said. 'Almost as if she really did think you were a magician.'

'Sara?'

Malin let go of my hand.

'Yes.'

'You mean Bobby? He – or rather Elias – was the one who came here and asked me to help. After hearing an interview with me on the radio.'

Malin laughed. It was a warm laugh.

'He may have said that, but if he did it was a lie. It was Sara who gave Bobby your name.'

The sun reached in through the window; beams of light danced across the desk.

'When?' I said. 'Sara had been dead six months by the time Elias came to see me.'

I searched my memory frantically. Had I ever met Sara? I didn't think so.

Malin smiled gently.

'You asked what Sara told us about her time in the US. There was someone else apart from that boyfriend, unless it was the same person. Sara called him Satan. But we didn't hear about him until the police started causing trouble for her.'

I held my breath, waiting for her to go on.

'Bobby was so desperate to help Sara, but she kept brushing him off,' Malin said. 'She got her lawyer to tell him there was no point. Bobby kept trying, but she refused to have anything to do with him. Because she was being held in isolation there was no way for us to see her, and her lawyer was useless. All Bobby had to go on once she was gone was what she had said before she was arrested. She was aware that she was in danger, and tried to do something about it. But she asked the wrong person for help. One time she told Bobby that she regretted not turning to you instead. That you were someone who could get at Satan.'

Someone who could get at Satan.

'Why did she think I could do that?' I said in a voice that was more tense than I would have liked. The hairs on the back of my neck were standing up again.

'Because you know each other.'

'Sorry?'

'Look, Sara sometimes said crazy things. I mean, Satan. He doesn't even exist. Her lawyer said we should forget what she'd said, that it was just nonsense. According to him, the important thing was that she'd confessed to all the murders. But Bobby didn't agree. Not at all. About any of it. Bobby thought it was worth taking a chance and turning to you. Sara was already dead by then, so what harm could it do if he contacted you?'

All hell could break loose. Because Satan did exist, but Malin couldn't have known that.

Once again the ground opened up beneath my feet. The abyss, so infinitely deep. Sara had been surrounded by so many bad people, but none worse than the man who shared Satan's name.

Satan was very definitely a specific person. Satan was Lucifer.

And now I could hear Sara's voice echoing from beyond the grave:

You know each other.

Not a fucking chance. That couldn't be true.

'I don't understand,' I said. 'In what context did this person called Satan say he knew me? How are we supposed to have met?'

'I don't know. Why, are you taking this seriously?'

More than anything else I'd heard in the past few weeks.

'In what way did Sara think I could have made a difference for her?' I said in a voice that didn't sound like mine.

Malin looked uncertain.

'She said that someone Satan hated so much must be capable of getting the better of him,' she said in a thin voice.

It was like a storm had started to rage inside my office. I expected all the papers to fly up from my desk and land in a heap on the floor.

He knew me and he hated me.

I didn't understand what Malin was talking about.

A misunderstanding, I thought. The whole thing was a misunderstanding.

Even if on some level I knew that couldn't be true.

'So why didn't she come to see me, then?' I said. 'Why didn't she ask me to be her lawyer? I'd have been happy to help her.'

Malin lowered her eyes.

'I don't think it was in your capacity as a lawyer that you could have helped her. It sounded more like she was thinking of ... well, something else. Either way – because of all that other stuff she didn't dare contact you. She simply didn't dare trust you; she wasn't sure you'd be on her side.'

Distinctly uncertain as to whether I wanted to know the answer to my question, I said: 'What other stuff, Malin? Why didn't Sara think she could trust me?'

Malin said nothing. She fiddled with the catch on her handbag, unsure if she should answer my question.

'She said you'd killed someone,' she eventually said in a whisper. 'The man she called Satan had said that you were the only lawyer in Stockholm who'd been able to get away with murder.'

15

That was the thought which I couldn't allow to exist – that it wasn't a coincidence that I'd been dragged into the story of Sara Texas and her son. That I had my own role to play, whether I was aware of it or not. A role that was somehow connected with my very dirtiest little secret. Those bloody nightmares. In which I was always buried alive, standing upright. They collided with what I'd just heard from Malin. Well, perhaps they didn't collide – they created a potential bridge between past and present. A bridge that frightened the life out of me.

Once Malin had gone I felt so drained I could have fallen asleep. But I didn't. Instead I just sat at my desk for a long time. Memories from the time when I had extinguished another human being's life had set fire to my brain. There had been three of us. It had been hot. And dark. So terribly fucking dark.

I tried to organise my thoughts and made a decision.

Then I stood up and went to see Lucy.

'There's something we need to talk about,' I said.

Lucy sat perfectly still on her desk-chair while I recounted what I'd been told. I held the finale back. I knew it would change everything, forever.

'Baby, he knew who I was way before I got dragged into this mess.'

It had been a long time since I'd called her baby. Life had become so serious that only our proper first names worked.

Lucy ran her fingers through her hair.

'We mustn't lose our grip now, Martin,' she said.

'What do you mean by that?'

'I think I almost agree with Sara's lawyer. We can't suddenly start thinking that everything Sara ever said was true. If – and I mean *if* – it turns out that she really was referring to Lucifer, and *if* you really do know him, we still have no reason to start saying incomprehensible things are suddenly comprehensible. You used to be a police officer. You worked in Texas. Almost twenty years ago, maybe, but you could have come across him in some situation that seemed inconsequential to you but was crucially important to him. *If it's actually true at all.*'

I undid the top buttons of my shirt and felt the sweat on my chest and back. Our trip to Texas had opened the gates to a madness I had done everything I could to forget. Now the past had caught up with me. The way in which it was blurring with what was happening now was close to magnificent.

Lucy saw the change in me.

'Martin, what's happened?'

I twisted my head so I could see out of the window. Stockholm was bathed in sunlight. The city never looks more beautiful than it does then. Blue water, blue sky, blue blood in the royal palace.

'Blue is for other people,' my mum used to say when I was growing up.

And dressed me in a green sweater with patches on the sleeves.

I took a deep breath. I had to find the words to say something I had never spoken about. And I had no idea what the consequences might be.

'Something happened when I lived in Texas. I've never talked about it. To anyone. Yet Malin mentioned it a little while ago.'

A different sort of surprise appeared in Lucy's face. There was still a limit to my ability to confide in her.

I killed another person.

There's no other way to describe it.

I, Martin Benner, killed another man. By mistake.

'Benner, we're going to bury this problem,' my boss told me that evening.

And that's what we did.

I hated remembering the minutes after the shot went off. When I was standing in the rain, shaking with shock as I called my boss. He said: 'Stay where you are.'

Two hours later we were standing far from Houston in an abandoned oilfield. I can still feel my boss's heavy hand on my shoulder.

Benner, we're going to bury this problem.

It was so easy at the time. Rendering what had been done undone. Very few people knew what had happened, and they all kept the secret. The camaraderie of the police force is unique; it doesn't exist within any other group of people.

'I killed a man. By mistake.'

I said.

To Lucy.

And saw her image of me change irrevocably.

Because there are things we think we will never hear. Lucy had definitely never expected me to tell her I had killed another human being. Her face was completely white as she listened to the story I thought I had buried forever in the sand.

'It was dark,' I said. 'The middle of the night. I was a police officer, had been for a little less than a year. My partner and I were sitting in our patrol car, talking. A call came over the radio. A wanted drug-dealer had been seen a few blocks from where we were. We were eager for some action. I responded to the call as fast as I could. 'We've got it,' I said. And off we went. Foot to the floor, flashing lights, the whole circus. Ridiculously amateurish. We saw the guy from a distance of a hundred metres or so. He was running along the pavement, terrified. It was raining and he lost his footing. We caught up with him in three seconds and leapt out of the car. By then he was back on his feet and running like a lunatic, straight into a dead-end lined by long-abandoned workshops. There wasn't a single light in any of the windows. Neither my partner nor I had a torch on us. We ran, and we shouted. 'Stop! For fuck's sake, stop!' In the end he did. When he turned round he had one hand inside his jacket.'

Lucy ran the tip of her tongue over her lips.

'So you shot him?'

'My partner fired a warning shot, straight up in the air. We yelled at him to show his hands, and stick them up. At once. But he didn't. Instead he grinned and went on feeling inside his jacket. When he eventually pulled his hand out ... It was raining, hitting me right in the face. I couldn't see properly, but I was as good as certain he was holding something in his hand. That and the grin were all it took. I fired one shot. I was aiming for his leg but hit him in the torso. He died within minutes.'

Lucy didn't say a thing. She looked like she was about to ask if I was mad, but thought better of it. In the meantime I carried on talking. I told her what my boss had said, and what we did with the body. And how I left Texas, and how my partner had later died.

'I don't know what to say,' she said. 'I really don't.'

I took several deep breaths.

'It wasn't murder,' I said.

'Okay.'

'What do you mean, okay? It wasn't.'

'Okay.'

'Lucy . . .'

'I need to get some fresh air. Sorry, but this . . . I don't know what to say.'

Lucy stood up.

'No, so you said. Several times.'

'*Have you any idea how you sound?* Do you realise what you just told me?'

Probably not. Because I had just put into words something I had never spoken about. There had actually been long periods of my life when I had managed to forget what had happened. At least in the sense that I stopped thinking about it. Stopped thinking about the fact that I had once stood with a shovel in my hand digging a grave for a man I had shot. Even when we were in Texas I'd managed not to think about it. But I'd had Sara Texas to concentrate on. My own future. And my dad.

'How the hell did your boss come up with the idea that you should conceal what had happened to the guy? Why not go the usual route and claim self-defence? You thought he was armed. People get away with that all the time. Especially in Texas.'

'He was unarmed,' I said. 'We searched him and found nothing. Nothing at all. No gun, no drugs, nothing. But I did find his wallet and ID. I'd shot the wrong guy. We looked him up in our records, and the police didn't have a thing on him. Or at least nothing big, I should say. He belonged to a gang of young troublemakers the police had been keeping an eye on.'

Lucy picked her handbag up from the floor and put it over her shoulder. She really was going to leave.

'So he was just a bit of a nuisance?'

'Yes.'

'How old?'

'Seventeen.'

Lucy reacted as if I'd hit her in the face.

'Bloody hell,' she whispered.

I jumped up.

'Lucy, don't get this out of proportion. I—'

'Out of proportion? *Out of proportion?* Martin, you shot a child! And buried him in an oilfield!'

She started to cry as she strode towards the door. I caught her and tried to hold on to her. She pulled free.

'Don't touch me, I need to be alone.'

'I wasn't that old either!'

That was my only defence. The only thing that helped me sleep at night. That I had been so young, and should never have been allowed to end up in that situation.

Lucy stopped a short distance away from me.

'I understand that,' she said. 'But why haven't you told me about this before now? Given everything that's happened in the past few weeks?'

'Even in my wildest fucking imagination I had no idea that it had anything whatsoever to do with Sara Texas.'

I had raised my voice, and it felt good. Because nothing I had told Lucy had been a lie. I had simply chosen not to tell her the whole truth about why I stopped being a police officer in Texas. And – hand on heart – I hadn't had the slightest idea that that terrible night had anything to do with Sara's tragic fate.

I shook my head, my whole body trembling.

'I don't understand,' I said. 'I don't understand what conclusion I'm supposed to come to now. Lucifer knows me, hates me, even. Because of what happened in Texas? Or something else?'

Lucy quietly brushed the tears from her cheeks.

I was clutching at straws. They snapped the moment I touched them. But I went on trying.

'Maybe it's a misunderstanding,' I said. 'Sara can't have meant Lucifer when she talked about Satan.'

Lucy shook her head and walked out of the room. I followed her to the door.

'When will you be back?'

The level of self-control it took not to physically hold her in the room was new to me.

'When I've finished thinking,' she said. 'You're just going to have to wait, Martin.'

PART 3

'They're dying now.'

TRANSCRIPT OF INTERVIEW WITH
MARTIN BENNER (MB).

INTERVIEWER: KAREN VIKING (KV),
freelance journalist, Stockholm.

KV: You shot a seventeen-year-old boy?

MB: Yes. My only defence is that I
was very young. I should never have
been put in that situation. That
defence works for me. But I can't
answer for how other people feel
about it.

(Silence)

KV: I don't think I quite understand. You
called your boss and told him you'd shot
a guy. What exactly did he say after
that?

MB: That we should stay at the scene until
he arrived.

KV: You weren't to call for an ambulance?

MB: The guy was already dead.

KV: But you just went and buried him. His family . . .

MB: I know. I know. It had been a turbulent time for the police district I was working in. Several of my colleagues had been accused of using excessive force in a number of different situations. The gorillas in Internal Investigations were starting to get seriously pissed off with all the incidents. My boss was terrified that my fatal shooting would be the straw that broke the camel's back. He probably envisaged his career coming to an abrupt end that night. If I was convicted of manslaughter or anything like that, some of the guilt would rub off on him. He'd have been fired and would have lost his pension. The whole lot. The Americans are ruthless when it comes to questions of personal responsibility.

KV: You never questioned the extreme immorality of what you did?

MB: Of course I bloody did. Many, many times.

KV: Did you talk about it? You and your partner?

MB: We never worked together again after that night. He requested a transfer to another district, and we lost contact. Some time later he got shot on duty.

KV: And by then you'd already moved back to
Sweden?

MB: Yes. I left what happened behind.
The circumstances surrounding my
life at that time really were pretty
exceptional. It was like waking up
from a nightmare. I left all the crap
in the States – the shooting, my
disappointment in my dad – and returned
home a different person. Something like
that.

KV: Your dad, yes. You had no contact with
him after that?

MB: I did actually return to the States
some years later and looked him up
again. But he still didn't want anything
to do with me.

KV: I don't really remember, although I know
I read something about it in Fredrik's
notes. Your parents met in the USA?

MB: They met in Sweden, but moved to the
USA so that I would be born there and
have American citizenship. They planned
to move back to Sweden a year or so
later. Marianne, my mum, moved first
with me and all our stuff. My dad never
followed. He abandoned us.

KV: Abandoned is a strong word.

MB: Think of a better one if you can.

KV: Sorry, I didn't mean it like that.

(Silence)

KV: Actually, about the fatal shooting in
        Texas . . .

MB: Yes?

KV: There's no mention of it in what Fredrik
        wrote.

MB: I know. There was no reason to tell
        Fredrik about it. I couldn't see how it
        was relevant, on any conceivable level.
        And besides . . .

KV: What?

MB: I barely thought about it when I was
        in Texas with Lucy. I was completely
        absorbed in other things. My dad, for
        instance. So I never mentioned it to
        Fredrik. Which is why there's nothing
        about it in *Buried Lies*.

(Silence)

KV: So what was the next step? What did you
        do after that?

MB: I looked at the pictures of the
        preschool staff that Lucy had got hold
        of. And went on waiting, just like
        before.

KV: Waiting?

MB: For even more people to die.

KV: And did they?

MB: Yes. God, yes.

16

Serious plays always stretch to several acts. There are intervals between the acts, giving members of the audience a chance to stretch their legs and buy refreshments. So that they can handle another bout of misery. But I never got that sort of break. Life just rushed on, carrying me with it. I kept thinking that it was ridiculous, that I needed to catch my breath. But fate, or whatever the hell it was, had other ideas.

The pictures were in a brown envelope on Lucy's desk. I took it back to my own room and put it down next to the other material she had dug out, but didn't open it. I couldn't bear to. I needed a chance to recover before I got slapped in the face by any more surprises. God only knew what I had ahead of me.

Not to mention what was already behind me: decades of skilful avoidance, all to create some degree of distance from the worst thing I had ever done and experienced. Was Lucifer, of all people, going to come along and rip open that old wound?

That can't be how I know him.
There can't be any other reason.

Then one of my mobiles rang. There was only one person who had the number of that particular phone: Boris. The mafia boss who had promised to protect Belle, and then lost her.

'Yes,' I said when I answered.

'It's me. Can you talk?'

Boris's voice sounded hoarse and anxious.

'Of course. I was thinking of getting in touch anyway,' I said.

Boris was outside somewhere. It sounded like he was walking into a headwind. Just like I was, only more literally.

'Not over the phone,' Boris said. 'We need to meet.'

'When?'

'How about now?'

I ran my finger across the envelope I had taken from Lucy's office. More surprises, more bad news, heading my way. I felt that very clearly.

'Sure. Where?'

'Same place as last time.'

For a moment I wasn't sure. What did he mean? Then I realised he must mean the time we met out on the island of Skeppsholmen. The same night I was called by one of Lucifer's associates and entered into a pact with the mafia boss. The same night I got Belle back.

'I'll be there in thirty minutes,' I said.

'Good.'

Lucy and I had decided on a sudden whim to cycle to the office. It's an excellent way of getting around Stockholm. I would be able to get to Boris relatively quickly.

It was while I was trying to remove the bicycle lock that she walked past. I didn't recognise her at first, half hidden as she was behind a pair of enormous sunglasses. Then my memory cleared and came into focus. It was Didrik Stihl's wife. Our eyes met as she pushed her sunglasses slowly up into her hair.

'Hello, Rebecca,' I said.

I had time to ask myself if Didrik had told her about the suspicions against me before she reacted. She stiffened at first, then turned white as a sheet. Finally her cheeks blushed vividly. Oh yes, she knew. Otherwise she wouldn't have been so embarrassed.

'Oh, hello, Martin.'

It looked like she was trying to smile, but it didn't quite work. The smile got caught halfway and ended up as a brittle grimace. And it also looked like she didn't know if she should stop and talk, or carry on walking. She decided to stop. But not for long.

Her behaviour irritated me. The lock came loose and I freed the bicycle.

'Everything okay with you?' she said.

The same grimace again. And her voice cracked as she spoke.

'Fine, thanks,' I said. 'Excellent, even.'

I smiled my widest smile and felt my cheeks strain.

'That's great,' she said. 'Really great.'

She lowered her sunglasses again, like a curtain. The performance was already coming to an end. She was about to move on.

I remembered how uncomfortable Didrik had been at our last meeting when I told him to say hi to Rebecca. I looked at her carefully. Something wasn't right. Something beyond the fact that she was agitated at having bumped into her husband's former friend (or whatever we had been) who was now suspected of several murders.

'How about you?' I said.

'Oh, I'm fine too,' she said.

'Are you on holiday or just out for a morning walk?'

I don't know what made me ask such a ridiculous question. It was a transparent attempt to pry into what she was doing. She had no reason to tell me anything about her life.

'I'm not sure you could call it a holiday,' she said. 'I've got a few days off and took the chance to come up here.'

'Come up here? How so?'

'To Stockholm. I live in Denmark these days. In ... out in the countryside.'

So she and Didrik were separated. Since when? I wondered. When we had met at the Press Club he had been married to Rebecca. But why should he have been telling the truth? Didrik and I weren't particularly close friends. Until our meeting at the Press Club we hadn't seen each other in over a year. Why would he have told me he'd left his wife? Or vice versa, whichever way round it was.

Rebecca nodded quickly.

'I need to get going,' she said. 'Look after yourself.'

'You too,' I said. 'Sorry to hear about you and Didrik.'

For a moment she looked confused, then she smiled briefly and walked on. The confusion that had flashed across her face spread to me. Had I misunderstood something? Had they not split up after all? But they must have done, because Didrik could hardly be living in Denmark.

I cycled off along Sankt Eriksgatan, still mulling things

over. Perhaps the fact that Didrik and his wife had split up wasn't merely an irrelevant detail. Perhaps I had actually just been supplied with a very important snippet of information. I had no way of knowing. That bothered me. Hugely.

I didn't see him at first, and that set me thinking. Last time we met was definitely on Skeppsholmen, wasn't it? I parked the bicycle and started to stroll through the unkempt back-yard. I didn't dare call out. I took out my mobile phone, the one only Boris called me on. No missed calls.

Someone moved on the gravel a few metres behind me. I spun round and found myself standing face to face with Boris. I couldn't stop myself from flinching when I saw the state he was in. He looked fucked. Totally fucked.

I felt marginally reassured when I realised that recent days and weeks had only taken their toll externally. His eyes hadn't lost any of their sharpness. But they had become cold and hard.

'You're not very discreet, Martin,' he said.

His voice sounded a bit hoarser than usual.

I looked around. There was no one in sight.

Boris shook his head.

'Not like that,' he said. 'You haven't brought any shadows with you. I meant the way you were strolling about here, as if you owned the place. In the middle of the day.'

He pointed behind my shoulder towards the back of a restaurant, defaced by an ugly projecting roof. That was where we had stood last time.

'I didn't see you,' I said, feeling the same need to defend myself as young children usually do.

Boris shook his head again.

'Come on,' he said.

We went and stood beneath the roof.

'Didrik Stihl mentioned your name when I was called in by the police,' I said.

'He did, did he?'

'You've cropped up in their investigation into the murder of Belle's grandparents.'

Boris took a folded piece of paper out of the inside pocket of his leather jacket. To my mind that jacket was one hell of a mistake on a lovely summer's day, but I didn't have the same need as Boris to look cool.

'Why were you called in by the police?' he said.

Without knowing why, I felt ashamed, even though it was Boris I was talking to.

'They think I murdered someone else,' I said.

Boris started to laugh.

'You really are excelling yourself these days, aren't you?' he said.

The laugh turned into a cough.

'You should quit smoking,' I said.

'Too late,' Boris said. 'For that, and for a fuck of a lot of other things.'

He straightened up and handed me the piece of paper he'd taken out of his pocket.

'I already knew you'd been called in by the police about another murder,' he said. 'And I knew they'd got some idea about me. So I'm going to lie low for a while. Leave the country until things cool down.'

I felt suddenly cold with inexplicable fear. Boris was one of my few lifelines. What would happen to me if he left the country?

'Don't look so distraught, Benner. You'll be absolutely fine without me.'

I felt like protesting. I wanted to tell him about Lucifer, about the man I'd shot. But I kept quiet. Boris was under no obligation to take care of all my problems. That was my responsibility, no one else's.

'Aren't you going to look at it?'

My fingers felt numb and clumsy as I unfolded the sheet of paper. I found myself staring at a grainy, black-and-white photocopy of a woman's face. I didn't understand, and looked from the woman to Boris.

'Do you recognise her?' he said.

I did. More than I ever wanted to. The picture had to be a few years old, but I had no trouble seeing who it was: Veronica, the woman I'd gone home with from the Press Club.

'Yes,' I said. 'I recognise her. Why are you showing me this?'

'She was a member of the same gang as Sara Texas, here in Stockholm. I received the picture yesterday. My source failed to include her picture and details in the initial bundle.'

Boris had done me an invaluable favour when I got back from Texas. Using his contacts in the police he had got hold of the names and photographs of the people around Sara Texas before she moved to the USA. Members of the gang who got their kicks beating people up at random on the streets. That was how I'd found Elias.

The news that the woman I'd gone home with from the bar knew Sara Texas shocked me.

'I thought she was older than Sara,' I said, mainly for the sake of saying something.

'She is,' Boris said. 'She turned thirty not long ago.'

'What's her name?'

'Don't you know?'

He grinned. Evidently he wasn't having any trouble figuring out how I knew the woman in the picture.

'She said her name was Veronica,' I said.

'But her real name is Rakel,' Boris said.

For a moment my heart stood still.

'Rakel?' I whispered.

'Originally Rakel Svensson. Now Rakel Minnhagen.'

17

Saying goodbye to Boris wasn't particularly emotional. I was in a state of shock and couldn't think straight. He would have liked to stay in Sweden to help me, but the way things were developing had made that hard for him. Not to say impossible. I had no idea who had given the police his name, but somehow he had popped up in the investigation into the murders of Belle's grandparents. And that was extremely unfortunate.

'Try not to be so fucking alone in all this,' was the last thing Boris said before we parted.

As if loneliness was something you chose.

'Sure,' I said.

I cycled straight home and got the hire-car out of the garage. Then I drove the short distance to the home of the woman who had called herself Veronica but whose real name was evidently Rakel Minnhagen. The same name as the woman who was supposed to have abducted Mio from his preschool. And who was also supposed to have known his mother, Sara. Why hadn't anyone mentioned her before?

Elias hadn't, Jenny hadn't, the police hadn't. And nor had Malin. I presumed that the answer to those questions was that her change of name had given her a degree of protection. That and the fact that Bobby didn't have time to track her down. If they'd met before he died, he would almost certainly have recognised her.

Boris's source had been very thorough. The document contained all the information I needed to find Rakel. She lived in a small terraced house in Solna. The house was currently empty, I discovered when I arrived. There was no answer when I rang the bell. The terrace was absurdly long. Rakel had been lucky enough to get the house at the end. I walked round to the back. The hedges that separated the little patches of garden were surprisingly tall. It was perfectly still and I couldn't hear any noises or movement in my vicinity. Like a child, I pressed my face to the glass door that was the only way in from the back. I found myself looking straight into the kitchen. It was empty.

I went from window to window along the back of the house. Apart from the last one they looked in on the kitchen. The last window belonged to what looked like a guest-room. There was a narrow, neatly made bed and a small desk. Almost like a prison cell. No pictures on the walls, no personal belongings such as clothes or shoes. I frowned and went back to the kitchen windows. That too revealed an extremely impersonal style. I had already checked the property registry. The terraced house was owned by Rakel alone, no one else. Maybe she lived somewhere other than the address where she was registered.

I liked to think that I was very rational. Goal-orientated and focused. But to be honest I was acting out of blind panic, shaken by what I'd found out during the course of the day. I thought hard. Could the house be alarmed? Or could I break one of the windows without being noticed? The thought sent shivers down my spine. If I went for it and broke into the house, I'd be crossing a boundary that I hadn't yet overstepped. I'd be breaking the law in a way that I couldn't talk my way out of afterwards. No one would take into account the pressure I'd been under, there'd be no excuses. If I got caught, I really would be fucked.

So I hesitated. It was just past lunchtime. The sun was blazing in the sky. It was a ridiculous time to choose to break into a house. That might actually offer me a degree of protection. Breaking in during the day was such an over-confident thing to do that it would seem improbable. Once I'd broken the window, I'd be able to carry on undisturbed. The whole terrace looked deserted. Whether their occupants were at work or on holiday was irrelevant. For the time being I was alone.

The thought of breaking into a house was so shocking that I felt weak at the knees. I had defended enough thieves not to do any of the things that got you caught. An infestation of unwelcome thoughts scuttled through my head. Given that I had once managed to get away with murdering another man, was I going to end up getting caught for something as simple as house-breaking?

I went back to the car and drove away. There were people who were experts at breaking into houses. People who never ran the risk of getting caught. The mobile phone felt cool in my hand when I took it out of my trouser pocket. Boris answered on the second ring.

'Yes?'

'Have you left the country yet?' I said.

'I'm leaving in an hour.'

'Have you got time to do me one last favour?'

Ordering a break-in was a new experience. A very liberating one, ironically enough. Now I was free to concentrate on other things. Such as trying to sort out my relationship with Lucy.

But first I needed to get something to eat. I was hungry enough to eat a horse, or maybe a cow, depending on what I got hold of first, so I drove to McDonald's and ordered a hamburger and a milkshake. I ate in the car.

I had both the front windows open and the car was parked in the shade. Lucy would have yelled at me if she'd seen me. McDonald's comes at the very bottom of food options for her. Not for me. That sort of snobbery is so damn unnecessary. Thankfully her objections are limited to the nutritional value of the food rather than ideologically motivated. I've never been able to understand all the noisy sods who regard McDonald's as the ultimate symbol of the damage caused to the planet by capitalism.

'I only travel to places that aren't so exploited,' is the sort of thing left-wing types are happy to come out with.

And by 'aren't so exploited' they mean places where there aren't any McDonald's. The fact that this is often a sign of a country in a state of collapse and a population that's oppressed and impoverished seems to pass these pretentious tourists by.

I called Lucy. She didn't answer. I began to feel anxious. What would I do if she'd packed her things and left when I got back to the flat? The hamburger became hard to swallow and I slurped greedily at the milkshake instead. Then I called again. Still no answer.

Did she owe me anything? It was an uncomfortable question, but it needed asking. And no, I didn't think Lucy owed me anything at all. It was remarkable that she'd put up with as much as she had. The only reason I had found out that there was something funny about Veronica was that I'd tried to get in touch with her for sex. Lucy knew that was the case, but said nothing. We kept quiet about things that weren't easy, that had always been the case. And, to be honest, what's so wrong about that? Dwelling on a relationship that was hard to define was like getting fixated on the negative impact of McDonald's on the planet. A discussion that will never be particularly worthwhile. So you might as well not bother.

One of my mobiles rang.

'It's me,' a thin voice said when I answered.

Marianne, my mother.

'Hello,' I said.

'How's Belle?'

'She's fine.'

Dressing was dripping from the hamburger. The wrapper wasn't arranged properly and the sticky sludge was oozing onto my fingers.

'Fuck,' I said as I fumbled with a napkin in an attempt to stop the sauce reaching the seat.

'How did we end up like this?' my mother said. 'With you swearing at me when I call you?'

I stiffened.

'I was swearing at a hamburger,' I said. 'It had very little to do with you.'

Marianne sighed.

'I've always been so pleased that you inherited so few of your father's bad qualities,' she said. 'But I've started to notice that you're as bad a liar as he was.'

I crumpled the napkin and threw it on the floor.

'Did you want anything in particular?' I said.

It was the wrong day to pick a fight with me. I was too tired to argue, too tired to feel guilty.

'I just wanted to know when the funeral is going to be.'

'Funeral?'

It felt like there were far too many dead people, and too many funerals. Bobby Tell had already been laid to rest. I had no idea when Fredrik Ohlander's funeral was going to be, and there was no way I could find out. But Marianne didn't know either Fredrik or Bobby. She must have been thinking of someone else.

I felt my throat tighten when I realised who she meant.

'Belle's grandparents,' I said. 'They're not being buried until two weeks from now.'

'As late as that?'

'I think there's a backlog.'

I couldn't remember exactly what Belle's aunt had told me. There had been a lot of phone calls, short and tear-filled. I regarded them as punishment for my grotesque sin. If it weren't for me, Belle's grandparents would still be alive. It was as simple as that.

'Can't I see Belle again soon?' Marianne said. 'I miss her already.'

I got out of the car and threw the rest of the food in a bin. I had no desire to see Marianne just then.

'Maybe sometime next week,' I said. 'Things are really hectic right now.'

I heard her sniff down the phone.

'We're going to have to talk everything through one day, Martin,' she said.

What for? I felt like asking. You can't just 'talk through' parental failure, or years of betrayal. It is what it is, and that's just shit.

'Sure,' I said.

'Seriously, I . . .'

I reached my limit.

'Seriously, I haven't got time for this. Stop blaming me for the problems in your life. Okay?'

Then I ended the call. And made a silent prayer that Belle would never, ever talk to me like that.

I'd driven less than a kilometre when the phone rang again.

It was death, who evidently wasn't done with me yet.

18

As a child I used to hide behind the kitchen door and listen to Marianne and her friends as they drank wine and talked rubbish. Usually they talked about their husbands. Marianne was always the loudest, the one who set the tone. She had succeeded in doing something none of the others had managed – she had met a Yank, moved all the bloody way to the USA to give birth to his child, then moved back to Sweden again as a single mother.

'He might as well be dead,' she used to say. 'You know, we never hear from him. *Never.*'

I didn't understand what she was saying, for the simple reason that I hadn't yet made the acquaintance of death. I knew that no one lived forever, but I had no concept of what that actually meant in practice.

It wasn't until I started school that the idea of death started to make sense. My friend Oliver drowned just before Christmas. We were at the swimming pool to learn how to swim, and at an unguarded moment Oliver jumped into the deep end. And couldn't get out again.

No one noticed until one little girl said: 'Oliver's floating.'

And he really was. Like a cork, his limp body was floating on the surface of the water.

The swimming teacher threw himself into the pool.

'Be careful!' my class teacher yelled. 'Be careful!'

What she actually meant was that we should move away from the edge of the pool. That was where they laid Oliver once they'd got him out of the water. I'll never forget how they tried to breathe life back into him. His lips were totally blue, his face white. Both teachers were crying. None of us children said a word. We just stood there staring. Oliver was gone, and he wasn't coming back. All of a sudden I understood how death worked. It snatched people away from under your nose.

As an adult I developed a more complex attitude towards death. Especially after I'd killed another person. There and then I learned how definitive death is. How badly the lack of any room for negotiation hurts. It's not like in films. Death doesn't want to play chess. Death is like everyone else – just wants to do his job.

'He's missing,' the woman on the phone said. 'Elias is missing. I don't know where he's gone.'

His girlfriend. We'd only met once, but that was evidently enough. She remembered me, and assumed I had some connection with whatever fate her boyfriend had met.

The moment I saw Elias outside the church I'd realised that he was having problems, something he subsequently confirmed. He was feeling frightened, thought he was being followed. I'd hoped he was just being paranoid, that his fears were unfounded.

But that wasn't the case. I'd probably already figured that

out at Bobby's funeral, but had chosen to ignore it. I didn't have room for anyone else's anxieties, and besides, there was nothing I could do about them.

'He disappeared yesterday evening,' his girlfriend said through tears. 'He set off for work but never arrived. They called to ask where he was. I reported him missing late last night. But I don't know if they're trying to find him.'

I imagined that they probably were. The police were well aware that Elias and I had been in contact with each other. I had personally managed to spoon-feed them that particular morsel of information. I felt a degree of relief that – once again – my Porsche couldn't have been involved in anything. It was still at the garage. They'd called, asking me to pick it up, but I'd squirmed and said I'd pick it up 'another day'. I had no intention of collecting it until I knew there was no longer any risk.

I avoided the word murder as I talked to Elias's girlfriend. In fact, I avoided any speculation about what might have happened. But I knew. Elias was dead. The only question was where his body would show up.

'The best thing you can do is let the police get on with their work without bothering them,' I said. 'Give them all the information they ask for. Think if anything odd has happened in the past few days. Did Elias mention any arguments, anyone he was worried about?'

'The past few days? Are you kidding? He's been weird for weeks. Hasn't been sleeping, wouldn't eat anything. He even stopped drinking beer.'

It sounded like she found this the oddest thing of all. What she told me merely confirmed my own impression – Elias definitely hadn't been in a good way.

'He was really careful to keep the door double-locked when he was home. And he closed all the curtains. He told me to make sure I wasn't being followed whenever I left the house. Really crazy stuff!'

She sniffed loudly down the line.

'Did he say who he was so scared of?' I said.

'He didn't know. That's what he said, anyway. But he did say it was to do with Sara. Sara Tell.'

I nodded silently to myself.

'Did you know Sara?' I said.

'We all did,' Elias's girlfriend said. 'We were in the same gang for years. Until she went off to the States. Then when she came home she had a kid. Most people change after that.'

A thought popped into my head and I took a gamble.

'Do you know anyone called Rakel Minnhagen?' I said. 'Or Svensson?'

My pulse rose as I said the name.

'Rakel?' Elias's girlfriend said. 'Yes, but a long time ago. She was a bit older than the rest of us.'

I made an effort not to sound too interested.

'Do you know what happened to her?' I said. 'What she's doing these days?'

'No idea. We lost touch completely when she disappeared.'

'Disappeared?'

'Left. Left the gang, I mean.'

Left the gang. A gang which had been pretty violent. Several of them ended up in prison, but not Sara. And not Rakel either, apparently.

'Where did she go?' I said, well aware that my persistence might seem provocative. 'People don't usually just vanish.'

'Of course she didn't,' Elias's girlfriend said. 'It was more like she pulled away. We – some of us got into trouble. With the police. Rakel got out in time. And then she stayed away.'

'Can I be really impertinent and ask if you were one of the ones who got into trouble with the police?' I said.

I heard her blow her nose.

'No,' she said. 'I didn't want to get involved in that sort of thing.'

'Unlike Elias.'

'He sorted himself out. He really did.'

The whole car reeked of hamburger. A thousand images exploded inside my head. There was a reason why Elias, unlike Bobby, Jenny and everyone else who had died, hadn't been found yet. If the perpetrator was finding it increasingly difficult to frame me, he was probably more likely to try to cover his tracks.

Unless Elias had simply had enough and taken off? Maybe the pressure got too much for him? But where would someone like Elias go?

'You don't have a summerhouse or anything similar?' I said. 'You, or your parents?'

'No, no, we've never been able to afford anything like that. That must be obvious, even to you.'

It probably was, but I still had to ask.

'Did Elias have any relatives or friends where he might go into hiding?' I said. 'Bearing in mind that he thought he was being followed.'

'No one I can think of.'

My heart sank. It was naïve to think that Elias had gone into hiding of his own volition. He'd been feeling under scrutiny for weeks; of course he was dead.

But how could that be?

I'd been so damn certain I wasn't being followed that night I went round to Elias's home to confront him. Who else apart from me could have figured out his role in all this?

'Exactly when did Elias start to say he thought he was being followed?' I said.

'A few days after he found out that Bobby was dead.'

'How did he find out? That Bobby had died?'

'Bobby didn't show up at a bar where they'd arranged to meet. Then he stopped answering his mobile. So Elias called Bobby's mum. She had no idea that her son was even in Stockholm, and had just found out from the police that he'd been killed in a hit-and-run.'

'And Elias concluded that Bobby had been murdered? He didn't think it could have been an accident?'

'Why would he have done? His mum told him it was murder. Because that's what the police said. They could tell from his injuries, or something.'

His injuries. Caused by a car. Which someone had taken from my locked garage the night I spent at the hospital with Belle. The forbidden thoughts returned. If it really was my car, who could drive a car out of a garage without leaving any trace on either the car or the garage?

Someone with a key.

Lucy.

Impossible.

'I need to know what's happened to him,' Elias's girlfriend said, and started crying even harder. 'How am I going to find him?'

It was a reasonable wish. But there was no way I could help her.

'I don't know,' I said. 'I'm really sorry, but I don't know.'

I didn't say that I thought Elias was dead. And outside the car the world rushed past as if nothing had happened.

Then Elias's girlfriend said something I really wasn't expecting.

'He called the police.'

'What?'

'He called the police to say he thought he was being followed. After Bobby died. But he didn't want to tell the police why, so I assume they didn't take him seriously.'

My shirt felt tight across my chest.

'Are you sure he didn't tell them everything?'

'Absolutely certain. The police told him to go back to them when he felt ready to tell them the rest of the story. Presumably they thought he was withholding information.'

'Do you know who he spoke to?'

'No. But I know he asked to speak to whoever had been in charge of investigating Sara Texas's case.'

I felt a flash of anger. What the hell were the police playing at? Bobby was dead, Jenny too. And when a third person showed up asking for help, he didn't get it. Despite his obvious connections to Sara. The peculiarities were mounting up in a way that couldn't be coincidental.

The investigation contained no photographs of Mio.

And when Elias called and asked for help, he didn't get any.

'You need to find out who Elias spoke to,' I said. 'Do you hear? It's important.'

'I'll try. I'll . . .'

'Call the police. Now. Then call me back.'

19

The flat was empty when I got home. Signe hadn't picked Belle up from preschool, and I couldn't even hazard a guess as to where Lucy was. She was refusing to answer her phone. With relief I noted that her things were still there. Everything looked exactly the way it had when we left home that morning. Even so, something felt different. My dirty laundry had been dragged out and laid bare in front of the grown-up I loved most. How the hell were Lucy and I going to move on from that?

'Baby?'

I don't know why I called out to her when it was obvious she wasn't there. In my defence, I wasn't at my most rational. I was starting to get paranoid, just like Elias. Any wrong move could have catastrophic consequences. For me, and for my nearest and dearest.

I took a long, hard look at myself. In general I thought I deserved at least a pass. The only new person I'd dragged into the shit was Madeleine. And I'd been very careful not to share everything with her. That was all I had to offer in the way of protection. I shuddered when I realised that probably wasn't good enough. Not if people inside the police were involved. That was a new and frightening thought that had emerged from my conversation with Elias's girlfriend. I didn't know who Madeleine's sources were. Nor Boris's. If the police were involved, there was a chance that Boris or Madeleine had accidentally spoken to the wrong person. Frustrated, I went over to the sink and poured myself a glass of water. I could have done with something stronger, but there was no point even thinking about that. Not just then.

I went out onto the terrace. The sky was blue, the sun warm and the wind mild. The view was vast, but I couldn't take it in. I may as well have been standing looking at a rubbish tip. All of my senses were working frantically, trying to piece together a thousand tiny fragments into a recognisable whole. It was impossible. That day was and would remain a really crap one.

My mobile rang again. It was Elias's girlfriend, phoning me back.

'I did what you said,' she said. 'I called the police and asked to speak to the same person as Elias did. They made a bit of a fuss at first, but in the end they did it. I got put through to a man called Staffan Ericsson.'

Staffan Ericsson. The plank Didrik worked with. The one who couldn't manage to look sly. It struck me that I recognised the name from the Sara Texas preliminary investigation as well. It had cropped up in a number of documents, hadn't it?

I walked back inside the flat. The boxes containing the preliminary investigation were in my study. I thanked Elias's girlfriend for calling, and made her promise to let me know as soon as she had any news about Elias.

Staffan Ericsson. I threw myself at the boxes like a wild animal and found him almost immediately. He had been one of the lead interviewers when they were questioning Sara Texas. I put the papers back in the box again. Was I losing my grip? Was I looking for ghosts in the absence of real people, real leads?

Someone inserted a key into the front door. I got to my feet and hurried into the hall. The door opened and Lucy came in. She let out a yelp of surprise when she caught sight of me.

'You're home?' she said.

'Sorry if I startled you,' I said.

I wanted to ask why it was so important that I wasn't home, but realised that she hadn't actually said that. Feeling rather desolate, I was left considering how pathetic I had become.

Lucy tossed her keys onto the hall table, kicked off her shoes and went into the kitchen.

I followed her.

'Where have you been?'

'I told you I needed to be on my own.'

She opened the fridge and took out a cola. She drank straight from the bottle.

'Baby, what I told you earlier.'

'About killing a guy and burying him in the desert?'

'I didn't murder him.'

'Of course not, you just happened to shoot him.'

I took a deep breath.

'Either way, I'm very sorry that I've never felt able to share the story with you.'

Each word came out just as I had imagined. It was more about how I had felt than about what was practically possible. Of course I could have told Lucy; she would never have shared it with anyone. But I didn't want to. I didn't want anyone – least of all Lucy – to know something so awful about me. So I buried the terrible story as deep in my memory as I possibly could. What made that sort of burial at all possible was the fact that it wasn't murder. However many times I replayed the scene in my head, I always came to the same conclusion: I couldn't have done anything different. Not there, not then. Maybe now, but not then.

Lucy put the cola down, as if she was waiting for me to go on.

'I was so frightened,' I whispered. 'So horribly fucking frightened. After that I knew I wasn't cut out to be a police officer. I didn't fit. Not then, and not later.'

Lucy looked down, unwilling to look me in the eye.

'You were out that night,' she said in a low voice. 'When Bobby and Jenny died. After what you told me about what happened in Texas ... I needed proof. I needed to know that you hadn't done what the police are claiming. That you hadn't run down and killed Bobby, Jenny and God knows who else. Because you know, things really don't look that rosy for you when you actually think about it. Who else but you could have taken your car and left the garage without leaving any sign on either the vehicle or the building?'

All these sensible people, asking such sensible questions. First Madeleine, now Lucy.

'You,' I said. 'You could have done the same thing.'

Lucy nodded and raised her head.

'Exactly what I was thinking,' she said. 'I'm the one who's

got the spare keys to the flat. And here in the flat is the spare key to the Porsche.'

I cleared my throat, worried that Lucy was going to make some ridiculous confession.

'But ... it wasn't me, Martin.'

Her voice sounded exhausted.

'It wasn't me either,' I said.

She took a deep breath.

'I want to believe you so much, you know that.'

I couldn't believe my ears. What the hell was she standing there saying?

'Lucy, look ... You've got to listen to me. I didn't murder those people. That goes without saying, surely? I mean, what would my motive have been?'

Lucy leaned on the kitchen worktop.

'That's something I've given a lot of thought to,' she said. 'If you are the murderer, what's driving you to do it?'

Time stood still, and me with it.

'I ... I wasn't in the office the afternoon Elias showed up pretending to be Bobby,' Lucy said. 'I've been wondering if that was when you started lying. If Lucifer has actually been blackmailing you ever since then, but you haven't dared say anything. And if your interest in Sara Texas's case and Mio's disappearance is an attempt to create a plausible alibi.'

I was speechless.

'So I've been lying to you all along?'

'Not because you wanted to, but because you had to. And to protect me.'

'Belle's kidnapping. How does that fit in?'

'You were obsessed with trying to find Lucifer. Presumably you wanted to escape his threats by identifying him. When we went to Texas, we got too close. So they abducted Belle to make you back off.'

The story she'd put together wasn't bad. I shook my head.

'Baby, listen to me now. Carefully. I—'

'My name is Lucy. And I've listened to you far too bloody long, Martin. Please, tell me again how you ended up going round to see the woman you met at the Press Club and had sex with. What was her name again? Veronica?'

Was this what the highway to hell looked like? Paved with shitty lies and homemade theories of how things *really* were? I tried something new. The truth.

'I went round to see her because her phone number didn't work when I tried to call her. And the reason I called her was because I wanted to have sex with her. Again.'

I had to pause and retire to one of the kitchen chairs. It felt hard and unwelcoming when I sat down on it. Lucy listened with blazing eyes.

'We've had this conversation before,' I said. 'About who I am and how I live my life. And fine, we can run through it again. But I really can't see what good that would do.'

The fire in Lucy's eyes went out and was replaced by something else. Something far more frightening. Despair and sadness.

'Because you are who you are, or what?' she said.

'Something like that.'

A single tear trickled down her cheek.

'I'm such a fucking fool for getting involved in this,' she whispered.

I felt ashamed. More than I had ever felt before in my entire life. Not so much of what I had done as of what I realised I was. And what I, to be honest, wanted to be.

I got slowly to my feet.

'What we're doing now,' I said, 'living together, being a proper couple. We've tried it before. Not officially living together, but being a couple. It didn't go very well. Playing happy families doesn't seem to be our thing. It—'

'Martin, we're not living together at the moment because we're playing happy fucking families, but because we're trying to survive a hellish situation that neither of us can understand how we ended up in!'

'Sorry,' I said. 'Sorry, sorry, sorry. You've done everything you could for me and I'm just a bastard. I'll . . .'

She held one hand up.

'No more useless promises, Martin,' she said. 'Not a single one. Okay?'

I nodded.

'Okay. I'm not going to make any promises I obviously can't keep. But I do want you to know that I love you. More than anyone. There's no one else who—'

She interrupted me again.

'Tell me it wasn't you who murdered Bobby, Jenny and all the others.'

Finally, something I could swear to.

'I promise and swear that I'm not involved in their deaths.'

It looked like she breathed out a little. I wished I could do the same. Madeleine's analysis had taken root, even though I didn't believe it.

'And you're not involved either, are you?' I said.

Quietly, embarrassed.

'Not at all.'

After that we just stood there looking at each other. For a long time. Far too long. In the end I moved closer, very cautiously. She didn't protest when I put my arms round her.

'When this is all over,' she said, 'I think we need to try something new. Or rather – I need to. Because I'm not getting anywhere, I'm just sort of stuck here with you. And that's so fucking unhealthy.'

I held her close, so close.

If she left me, I would die.

'But you'll stay until we've sorted this mess out?' I said, with my face in her hair.

'Yes. But for Belle's sake, not yours. And for my own. Lucifer's threat applies to me too. I've got nothing to gain by not being with you right now.'

It stung to hear those words. I deserved no better. But she did.

Lucy gave me a brief hug and then backed away. I let her go.

'We still don't know what she wanted. Veronica,' Lucy said.

'She might just have been trying to get information after all,' I said.

So now, apparently, we were going to talk about the nightmare we were living in.

'Did she try anything like that, then? Did it feel like she was milking you?'

Not the way I remembered it. But, on the other hand, that's probably the whole point of a good information gatherer. That the target didn't notice anything.

'Quite a few things happened after you left,' I said.

'What sort of things?'

I took a deep breath, then slowly exhaled.

'Elias Krom's girlfriend called. He's vanished. Without trace.'

Lucy opened her mouth to say something, but I went on.

'And I found out that Veronica's real name is Rakel. She was the one who snatched Mio from his preschool. Do you see? The Rakel who took Mio is the same woman I met at the Press Club.'

Lucy's chin dropped. But there was no stopping me.

'So I asked Boris for a favour. I've ordered a break-in at Rakel's house.'

Lucy closed her mouth again.

'Are you with me, baby? Are you going to stay, like you just said?'

She looked so strained. It was only a few hours since she found out that her best friend had once shot another man and then laid him to rest in the desert.

'I'm not going anywhere,' she said.

20

Evening fell. Lucy was sitting in bed reading the police report into Mio's disappearance. I had already ploughed through all the material but I didn't want to point out that what she was doing was unnecessary. Better for her to push on than stand still. As for me, I had other plans. Partly to get through a night full of bad dreams that would doubtless have been strengthened by the day's events. And partly to make an uncomfortable phone call. Discreetly I slipped one of my mobiles into my pocket and went out onto the terrace. Lucy followed me.

'Why are you standing out here?'

'I was thinking of making a call.'

'A secret one?'

I hesitated for a brief moment.

'I was thinking of calling my old boss in Houston. Because I can't bear the idea that what happened back then has got anything to do with what's happening now. I'm worried we're placing too much weight on what Bobby's girlfriend said. Maybe this is all about something else. Somehow.'

Lucy looked like she was going to ask: 'Do you really believe that?', but didn't. Because hope springs eternal, and neither of us wanted the story we were living with to become even worse than it already was.

'Have you managed to look at what I found out about the staff at Mio's preschool?' she said.

I felt ashamed. That had slipped my mind completely after Boris rang.

'Sorry,' I said. 'I just haven't had time.'

Sorry was a word that was starting to crop up far too often in our relationship. The film *Love Story* taught us that real love makes that particular word redundant. There's nothing to forgive, and nothing to ask for forgiveness for. A utopia so fucking divorced from reality that it ought to be forbidden from ever being mentioned.

'That's okay,' Lucy said.

She looked up.

'Do you want to be alone?' she said.

'Please.'

Lucy went back inside the flat and closed the terrace-door after her. I watched her through the glass as she disappeared into the bedroom. Then I took out my phone and called a man I never thought I'd have to contact again.

It was half past nine in Sweden. But in Houston it was only half past two in the afternoon. I tried to get hold of my old boss at the police station where he had worked twenty years ago. The receptionist's voice sounded bright and cheerful when he answered. That sort of thing does a lot for the confidence of the citizens. It's good for them to feel that the forces of law and order are with them, not against them.

I introduced myself with a made-up first name and explained why I was calling.

'I'd like to talk to Superintendent Josh Taylor,' I said. 'If he still works there.'

'What's it concerning?'

'Pastor Parson's funeral.'

'Sorry?'

I repeated the phrase again. The receptionist asked for my telephone number and told me that someone would call me back. Someone, but not necessarily Josh Taylor. I could hear that he believed what he was saying. Presumably it was usually the case that people who asked to speak to particular officers via the switchboard were called back by someone else entirely. But this was no usual case, and Josh Taylor would realise that if he was given my message.

After we'd buried the man I'd shot, we gave him an alias in case we ever needed to discuss what had happened. We called the dead man the Pastor. Parson's was the name of the company that had once run the oilfield where we had buried the body. The word funeral shouldn't be too difficult to interpret under the circumstances.

I sat down and waited for Taylor to call back. We hadn't had any contact since the first time I left Texas. There hadn't been any reason to be in touch. So I wasn't really sure what his role was in the police these days. I thought the receptionist had more or less indicated that he was still working there, but where he stood in the hierarchy was impossible to know.

I stood up to go in and get a glass of water. Then my mobile rang. Already? I stared at it as if bewitched, as if I couldn't for the life of me understand why it was ringing. It rang and rang and I was incapable of reaching out my hand

and making it shut up. Because what was I going to say if it was my former boss, Josh Taylor, calling? He belonged to a police force that had been corrupted by Lucifer's network. At worst, Lucifer might even be his boss. Who knew, maybe Taylor himself had gone and found salvation in the court of the great mafia boss?

But curiosity got the better of me. I answered in a hoarse voice: 'Yes?'

It wasn't possible to see who was calling, so I answered in Swedish. The voice on the line put a stop to all my doubts.

'Benner?'

It was him. The man who had once come to my rescue when I needed it most – and, to be honest, deserved it least.

'It's been a long time,' I said.

He was silent for a moment.

'I'm not too sure I'm happy to hear from you,' he said.

'Believe me, I didn't want to call.'

The terrace suddenly felt like a spaceship, separated from the rest of the world.

'Can you talk?' I said.

'Yes. But not for long.'

'I've really only got one question,' I said. 'How many people know about Pastor Parson's funeral?'

He breathed heavily down the line.

'That's a delicate question,' he said. 'I can only answer for myself. I've never breathed a word to anyone.'

My hand was slippery with sweat as I clutched the phone.

'Yet it seems as if more people than us are aware of what happened,' I said.

'Tell me,' he said.

21

It really didn't matter if Josh Taylor was part of Lucifer's network, I reasoned. For the first time since I met Fredrik Ohlander, the journalist, I told an outsider what I'd been through. Josh had said he couldn't spare me very much of his time. But he was still listening when I'd been talking for twenty minutes. That's what happens when you've committed such a serious offence together. It's not about friendship, or even friendliness: you listen for your own sake. So you can go on saving your own skin.

'They're dying now. One by one: Bobby, Jenny, Fredrik. And no doubt Elias too.'

'To stop Lucifer from being unmasked?' Taylor said. 'I don't think so.'

I shook my head frantically. I didn't believe the victims had died for Lucifer's sake either. Not for that reason alone, anyway, and certainly not in the way I suspected that Josh Taylor imagined. Taylor had left violent crime behind and was currently involved in investigating financial offences. But that didn't change the obvious fact that he, like everyone else in Texas, had heard about Lucifer and had followed his colleagues' assiduous efforts to put a stop to his activities.

'We caught Lucifer,' Taylor said. 'Admittedly, we only got him for one minor offence, but he was identified.'

I shook my head again. He was wrong there, and he needed to know it.

'No,' I said. 'You never caught Lucifer. But that doesn't matter. Because this isn't about Lucifer. Not primarily, anyway. It's about Mio.'

'Says who? You or Lucifer?'

'Says me,' I said, then added rather more quietly, 'and Lucifer.'

I heard Josh Taylor laugh almost silently down the phone. It was a peculiar laugh, devoid of all joy.

'For God's sake, Martin. You can do better than this. Surely you appreciate that you can't believe a word Lucifer says? If it is even him you've been in contact with. Permit me to have my doubts on that point.'

Josh Taylor went on: 'Either way – you must be being followed by someone incredibly skilful. Under the circumstances, murdering Jenny and Bobby seems pretty straightforward, but how did your nemesis find the others you mentioned – Fredrik, and this new guy who might be dead, Elias?'

'I haven't got a good answer to that,' I said. 'Elias got very frightened after Bobby died. And Fredrik Ohlander ... I have a feeling he didn't believe everything I'd told him, and was trying to get the story confirmed.'

'And those efforts tipped the wrong person off that he knew too much?'

'Something along those lines. It's only an idea. I don't

know for certain. But it didn't take long. Before he was killed, I mean.'

Josh Taylor murmured down the phone. I could see him in front of me. People's physical movements don't change over time, not once we're grown up. I imagined him sitting down, one leg resting on the other, in trousers that were a little too short. One hand rubbing his bearded chin repeatedly. Assuming he still had the beard. Body hair is different to movements – that does change.

'There's something else that's been bothering me,' I said.

'You don't say?'

'That several of the leads I've got can be traced back to the police.'

'I thought that when you were telling your story. To my mind, the most likely answer is that your adversary, Lucifer, is more involved than you think, and that – God knows how – he has managed to get himself some allies inside the Swedish police force.'

'According to Sara Texas, Lucifer had connections to Sweden. Personal connections.'

'I'd take that sort of information with a pinch of salt.'

I fell silent. I lacked Josh Taylor's police experience, and felt very small in the face of his warnings and corrections.

'You say Lucifer isn't the man we got convicted as a result of the raid on his network?' he said. 'Have you got any idea who he might be, then?'

That was a question I really didn't want to answer. It was also one of the details I had chosen to omit from my story. That I had found information which suggested that Lucifer could be Esteban Stiller, Houston's very own sheriff. But that had been contradicted when I finally got to see a photograph of little Mio: the boy was black. His mother was white. So his father must be dark-skinned. His father was Lucifer. And Esteban Stiller was white.

'No,' I said. 'I've got nothing to go on.'

Josh Taylor cleared his throat.

'I might be going senile, but exactly why did you call to tell me this story?'

'I never got to that,' I said. 'We started talking about other things. Do you remember me saying that Bobby told me he came to see me because he heard me talking about Sara Texas on the radio?'

'Yes?'

'That was a lie, according to his girlfriend. He came to see me because I would be able to get at Lucifer himself. Sara claimed that Lucifer and I knew each other.'

Silences that aren't awkward – but just liberating – they're very rare. But there were plenty of them when I was talking to Josh Taylor. I got the feeling that they were not only liberating but also helpful. Perhaps even productive.

'She said you'd be able to scare Satan himself?' Josh asked.

'No, not directly. She said ...'

'That you'd be able to get at him. Because he hates you. And he called you a murderer. I heard that bit. Yet it's still you that's scared. So scared that you've called me. What Bobby's girlfriend said suggests that it's you rather than Lucifer who's got the upper hand. So what are you thinking, then, Benner? That you've been dragged into this shit because of Pastor Parson's funeral?'

A small part of me hated the fact that we were still saying

Pastor Parson's funeral. The man who'd died had a name. He deserved to be called by it, and nothing else. But that was a luxury we couldn't afford. Not if either of us was being bugged. Not if we could land ourselves in the shit by mentioning his name.

'I'm not sure,' I said. 'Not sure about anything, really. Maybe I'm just being paranoid. But when Bobby's girlfriend said that ... it got me thinking. Very dark thoughts. I no longer believe in coincidence.'

Car horns blared down in the street. Several times. The Stockholm night was refusing to quieten down. I liked that.

'You said yourself that there were no witnesses to the accident,' Josh said. 'And for my part I know I decided that only the three of us should take part in the actual interment.'

The accident. I'd never been able to use that word to describe my mistake.

'And you, like me, have never talked about it to anyone,' I said.

'Exactly,' Josh said.

'Which leaves us trying to figure out if Tony talked to anyone.'

'Which will be tough, seeing as he's dead.'

Tony had been my partner. He was there the night the shot was fired. And, as I'd told Lucy, he later died.

'I didn't know him particularly well,' I said. 'But I got the impression that he was both a good man and a good police officer. Not the sort to gossip.'

'I had the same impression.'

Tony had been as shaken up as Josh and me. His face had been hard and expressionless as he stood with a spade in his hand in an abandoned oilfield and helped to bury a horribly dirty secret. I had no idea how I looked at the time. But I should have looked scared and pathetic. Because that's how I felt.

'But,' Josh said, 'some forms of talking could perhaps be categorised as something other than gossiping. Even if that might be the indirect result.'

'I don't understand,' I said.

'Have you seriously – hand on heart – not told a single person about what happened, Martin?'

I straightened my back.

'Hand on heart, Josh. Up until this morning, no one but me knew anything about what happened that night.'

'Up until this morning?'

'When I told Lucy.'

'So you held out for twenty years. Impressive. Not every-one's as tough as you.'

I was distracted by more traffic noises. This time in an annoying way. A horrible cacophony of car horns and whistles. Probably some football nonsense that had passed me by.

'What are you trying to say?' I said. 'Who have you told about it?'

'My wife.'

His reply came so quickly that I was taken by surprise. As if it was the most natural thing in the world to share everything with your beloved. Perhaps it was. Perhaps I was the one there was something wrong with.

'I see. And who has she told?'

'No one.'

'Of course. You told her because you were shocked. She

in turn was shocked, and might well have felt the need to tell someone else. I thought you said you hadn't told a soul about what happened?'

'Obviously once I'd told her what happened, there were two of us who knew. We could support each other. Trust me, she hasn't told anyone else.'

I blinked up at the dark-blue night sky.

'Tony didn't have a wife,' I said. 'If you were thinking that might be how the story could have got out.'

'No, he didn't. But he did have three brothers.'

'Three brothers,' I repeated. 'And they heard what happened?'

'I'm only speculating now, but if you're thinking someone apart from the three of us might know about Pastor Parson's funeral, that's the direction I'd be looking in if I was trying to find a leak. But I don't think you'll get anywhere. At least one of the brothers is also a police officer here in Houston. If he ever heard anything about Pastor Parson's funeral, he should have realised the importance of keeping quiet.'

Another police officer in Houston. Another possible link to Lucifer.

'What's his name?'

'The brother?'

'Yes.'

'What do you want that information for?'

'I might know him.'

'Are you kidding? You haven't lived in the USA for twenty years.'

'He could have been in the police at the same time as me.'

'No, he didn't join up until later on. Besides, he hasn't

only worked in Houston. I have a feeling he started his career in Dallas.'

'Give me his name,' I said. 'He could have had something to do with Sara.'

'You've already told me that story. With names and everything. Believe me, if you'd mentioned Tony's brother I'd have told you who he was. But I'm not going to, because you don't need to know.'

I didn't agree. Not by a long shot. Josh was wrong, and he knew it. I hadn't told him the names of everyone with a connection to Sara Texas. I specifically hadn't wanted to name the police officers I'd come across, seeing as they were colleagues of Josh.

'The other brothers, then,' I said. 'Are they police officers too?'

'No. Well, to be honest, I don't know what they are. I think one of them runs his own café. But I've no idea about the other one. If I remember what little Tony said correctly, I don't think he got on well with the rest of the family.'

'Yet you still suggested that Tony might have confided in him? That sounds pretty unlikely.'

'I didn't express myself very well. Tony had three brothers, but he was only close to two of them. The third one had let them all down. Tony's brother mentioned it when we met after Tony died. The way he put it, the third brother let the whole family down in a big way. He didn't attend the funeral, for instance.'

'How did the brother in the police take Tony's death?'

'Badly. Very badly.'

I tried to gather my thoughts. It wasn't easy. Not remotely.

'The black sheep brother. Could he have heard something before they all fell out?'

'What difference does that make, Martin? You need to let go of this.'

How do you explain the hunches you get and just have to follow? How do you explain things that aren't strictly rational?

'Tell me his name.'

'Sorry, I can't help you there. Because I don't actually know his name.'

'The other one, then. The one in the police.'

'You asked me that a minute ago. The answer is still no. Well, you're going to have to excuse me, but I've got to go. I'm due at a meeting.'

I sank onto one of the chairs.

'I'm very grateful to you for taking the time to talk,' I said.

'Don't mention it, us police officers stick together. It's as simple as that. But I'd prefer it if you didn't call again. This isn't something I want to get involved in.'

Was there a hidden criticism in those short sentences? I'd left the force, after all, abandoned my colleagues. But that betrayal was probably overshadowed by the all-pervading principle of 'once a cop, always a cop'.

I nodded to myself.

'Thank you,' I said.

I was about to end the call when I heard Josh's voice again.

'It's interesting that you haven't even considered that there could have been witnesses,' he said.

I froze.

'Witnesses to what?'

'To your mistake. The accident.'

I shook my head.

'We've already been through that,' I said. 'There were no witnesses. We were alone in the alley that night.'

'How do you know that? I'm not saying there *is* a witness. Only that there *could* be.'

My throat went dry.

'I don't see what you're getting at,' I said. 'Decades have passed. If there were any witnesses, we'd have known about it by now.'

'Would we?'

I swallowed hard.

'Thank you,' I said once more. 'Thanks for all your help.'

We ended the call. I didn't move from the terrace. There was no sign of Lucy. It was a mild evening, and if things had been different I'd have gone in to fetch her and a bottle of wine. But not this time. This time I did something completely different.

It was worth a try. Just one try, but no more than that.

I called the Houston Police again. Introduced myself with another fictitious name and explained why I was calling.

'I used to know an officer who was shot and killed in the line of duty some years back. His name was Tony Baker. Now that the anniversary is coming round again, I'd like to send flowers to his family. I understand that he had a brother in the force. I was wondering if I could have his name, to make sure that the flowers go to the right place?'

22

His name was Vincent Baker, and he worked in a police station in one of Houston's main districts. As far as I could recall, I hadn't come across anyone by the name of Baker there. My thoughts were interrupted by a knock on the terrace-door. Lucy was standing inside the flat trying to get my attention. I responded by waving her out. Energetically, to make her realise I wanted her close.

'Are you coming in soon?'

She padded out onto the terrace with bare feet. Lucy has the prettiest feet I've ever seen on a woman, no question.

'In a moment,' I said.

'Did you find out anything useful?'

I replied truthfully: 'Maybe.'

Witnesses. There couldn't have been any witnesses, could there? We searched every corner of that alley. There hadn't been anyone there. End of story.

Lucy shivered in the cool summer night.

'I'm going to go as far away from here as I can when this is all over,' she said.

'Can I come too?'

She didn't answer.

One of my phones rang. A different ringtone, a different phone. Boris's phone.

'Baby, I need to take this.'

She stayed where she was as I answered.

'Martin.'

'It's me.'

'Haven't you gone yet?'

'What's that got to do with anything? You can actually make a fucking phone call from different places.'

'You're a wise man.'

Boris let out a deep sigh. He thought I was an idiot, and I didn't try to correct him. No one has the strength to be the best all the time.

'You asked me for a favour last time we spoke,' he said.

A favour. A break-in that I didn't have the nerve to carry out myself.

'Hmm.'

'How soon can you be at Tyson's Bar? It's in Solna.'

I hesitated. I wasn't comfortable going to the same part of the city as the crime scene.

'Twenty minutes, maybe,' I said. 'Why?'

'Marie's waiting for you there.'

'Marie?'

'She was the one who carried out the aforementioned favour. And she'll be happy to tell you what she found.'

I broke out in a cold sweat. For some reason I'd imagined that the briefing would happen some other way.

'So she did find something?'

'We won't know for sure until you hear what she found

and decide if it's of any use or not. But yes – I think she's found something.'

I stood up.

'Okay, I'll be there in thirty minutes at most.'

'You said twenty minutes.'

'Maximum thirty.'

'Marie isn't a patient woman. She won't wait a second longer.'

'I'll hurry. Thanks for your help.'

'Don't mention it.'

He hung up.

'What's happening now?' Lucy said.

Was there ever going to be any time for rest and reflection? For just lazing about? For all the things I used to care about in my old life?

'I need to go out,' I said. 'Apparently they found something in Rakel's house.'

Trust is something that builds up over time. Or more quickly under very specific circumstances. A group of people who get trapped in the same lift together, for instance, start to trust each other relatively quickly if it turns out they're going to be stuck together for a while.

With Boris it was a bit like being trapped in a lift. A lift that I admittedly got stuck in of my own volition. I did have a choice, after all. I could have turned him away when he came to my office, but I chose to let him in. I could have thrown him out when I realised what he needed help with. But I let him stay. Thereby creating a bond between us that I was unable to break later. A bond that came to involve a degree of accumulated trust. So when Boris sent me off to an obscure bar in Solna, I just got in my car and went there. Brum, brum – nothing odd about that at all.

'Take care,' Lucy said.

I was tired of that phrase. After all, it didn't make any difference what I did. I was under constant threat of something bad happening.

The car rolled smoothly through the city. I played music far too loud. First Bruce Springsteen, then Iggy Pop. Music is the balm every soul needs to stay in shape. I'm trying to teach Belle things like that. Music's important, books too. Anything that takes people to an alternative reality the way books and music do has to be a good thing.

I parked the car a few blocks from the bar where I was going to meet Boris's friend Marie. I didn't know what she looked like, but assumed it didn't matter – she probably had a very good idea of who I was.

That turned out to be a correct assumption. The moment I walked into the bar, two things happened. Firstly a young woman sitting in a corner raised one hand discreetly. The second was that the bartender called out to me: 'I've already taken last orders. We're only open another half hour.'

'Thanks, I know,' I said.

Anyone who doesn't want to be remembered shouldn't stand out. Not wear ostentatious clothes, not be too noisy. Everything in that bar out in Solna was wrong. I was the only person wearing a shirt. No one else looked well-groomed. But it was too late to do anything about that by the time I'd opened the door and walked in.

The woman stood up as I approached.

'Marie,' she said, holding out her hand.

'Martin,' I said.

We sat down.

'If you weren't as important to Boris as you evidently are, I don't think you'd be alive now,' she said.

Matter-of-factly, as if she were commenting on the weather.

'Really?' I said.

'Shitty jobs like the one I did this evening are the sort of thing you do yourself or not at all. You need to be very clear about that.'

What the hell was she talking about?

'I presume you knew what I was going to find when I got inside?' she said.

I shook my head.

'That was the whole point,' I said. 'I didn't know what was inside the house. That's why I wanted someone to get in and look around. I wanted to know if there was any sign that a child had been there.'

'Any sign that a child had been there,' she repeated, jerking her head.

She had long hair, pulled up into a tight ponytail. Her face was free of makeup. Her eyelashes were so pale they were almost transparent. Her nose covered in freckles. Eyes ice-blue. Intrigued, I tried to find some explanation for the fact that she had become part of Boris's team. She didn't look like anyone else I had seen around him. She wasn't as rough round the edges, wasn't as tough. But, on the other hand, my knowledge of Boris's network was very limited.

'Okay, let's start there,' she said. 'With any sign of children.'

She took a mobile out of her handbag. She focused hard on the screen and tapped it several times.

'Here,' she said, handing me the phone. 'This is one of two indications that a child has been there.'

I looked at the screen. It showed a photograph of a packet of medication. *Stesolid – rectal solution for the treatment of various types of cramp.*

'What's that got to do with children?' I said.

'Enlarge the image,' she said curtly.

I did as she said. The picture grew larger and no longer fitted the small screen. I moved my finger around, looking at the image of the packet. Then I saw it. I read silently to myself:

Instructions:
Children 5–12kg (approx. 3 mths–2 yrs): *5mg.*
<u>**Children over 12kg (approx. 2 yrs and over):** *10mg.*</u>
Adults: *10mg.*

The penultimate line had been underlined.

'Did the child in question have epilepsy or some other illness that causes cramping?' Marie said.

'No idea,' I said.

But it was something I would try to find out as quickly as possible. Mio had been four years old when he went missing. It didn't necessarily have to be epilepsy; it could have been febrile convulsions. Belle had that once when she was two. I thought she was going to die in front of my eyes. The memory of the panic I felt at the time made me hand the mobile back quickly.

'There was no name on the pack?' I said.

'I'm afraid not. It had been torn off.'

'And the name of the doctor who wrote the prescription?'

'On the same label as the name, so that's gone as well. There were only two doses left in the box. It was on its own in the bathroom cabinet.'

'What else did you find?' I said, trying to hide the impatience in my voice. 'You said there were two things to suggest that a child had been in the house?'

She touched her phone again.

'These,' she said, showing me another picture.

It was a pair of yellow wellington boots.

I immediately remembered what the woman calling herself Susanne, the one who worked at Mio's preschool, had said. She had stood in the window and watched him being led away. The yard had been poorly lit. But in the light of the streetlamps she had recognised his yellow wellington boots.

My heart began to beat faster. For the first time I was beyond vague theories and dubious witness statements. This was firm evidence that reinforced what I had been told by a witness who hadn't even wanted to give me her real name.

'Size?' I said.

'Twenty-six. I found them right at the back of a wardrobe.'

One size bigger than Belle.

'What was the rest of the house like? Did it look like anyone lived there?'

Marie nodded.

'Oh, yes,' she said. 'There was dirty laundry in the basket, rubbish under the sink. It didn't smell, so it can't have been there for long.'

Even so, the house had been deserted when I was there at lunchtime. And at the time of the break-in.

'Were there both men's and women's clothes in the house?'

'All the clothes I saw were marked in women's sizes. There were several pairs of high-heels in the wardrobe.'

'No children's clothes?'

'Not a thing. Unless you count the boots.'

I glanced discreetly at the time. I was keen not to stay too long.

'You've got no idea what a huge help you've been,' I said. 'I'll let Boris know that you're to be properly recompensed for your work. I . . .'

'We're not finished yet.'

She said it very quietly, but also very clearly.

'Do you remember what I said when you first arrived?'

Of course I did, even if I'd chosen to ignore it.

'You mentioned something about shitty jobs,' I said.

And that I should have been dead, but I didn't repeat that.

'Did anyone know you were planning to break into the house?' Marie said. 'Be honest.'

For a moment I wondered if she was armed, but she had both hands on the table. Her nails were cut short, no varnish.

'No one at all,' I said. 'Only Boris.'

Not even Lucy, I thought to myself.

'It's impossible to break into a house without leaving some form of evidence,' Marie said. 'So I chose to do a pretty clumsy break-in. The damage was pretty severe, I wanted it to look amateurish.'

'Okay,' I said, mostly for the sake of saying something.

I wouldn't have thought of that, which was stupid, I realised. It was much better if the break-in looked like it had been committed by a junkie.

'Whereas for obvious reasons I didn't want to leave any

evidence that could be traced back to me,' Marie said. 'The police will probably react to that. The fact that someone made such a clumsy break-in but was then smart enough not to leave any fingerprints, strands of hair or anything else stupid.

She shrugged her shoulders and I nodded silently to show I was following what she said.

'Whatever,' she said. 'I did my best and it went pretty well. If you don't count the fucking unpleasant surprise that was waiting for me in the living room.'

I stared to squirm involuntarily on my chair.

'Okay.'

She leaned forward. I swear, I could have counted every last damn freckle on her nose.

'No, Martin. Not okay.'

I threw my arms out in an unnecessarily expansive gesture.

'Just tell me what went wrong, for fuck's sake!'

Marie picked her mobile up one last time. She held it close to my face.

'Anyone you recognise?'

Instinctively I threw myself backwards away from the mobile. Because on the screen was a picture of Elias Krom's pale face. A long incision ran across his throat, gaping red towards the camera.

Elias was dead.

All of a sudden I felt horribly alone.

And inside my head a new thought took shape: if everyone I'd met and collaborated with had died because they knew too much, why was I still alive?

What was it that I still hadn't understood?

PART 4

'Not hair.'

INTERVIEWER: KAREN VIKING (KV),
freelance journalist, Stockholm.

KV: Another man dead.

MB: Yes.

KV: Bloody hell. How many more were there?

MB: That depends on how you count.

KV: So, Elias lying dead in Rakel's house.
What conclusions did you draw from
that?

MB: I didn't actually know what conclusions
I could or should draw beyond the
obvious one: that Rakel was a key figure
in everything that was going on. I
felt completely outmanoeuvred. Elias
had known Rakel a long time ago. Could
he have looked her up in the hope of
getting some sort of protection, but
instead stumbled right into a hornets'
nest? I didn't know.

(Silence)

KV: That conversation with your old boss in Texas.

MB: Yes?

KV: Did it leave you any the wiser? What did you do after that?

MB: A hell of a lot of things were happening all at once. I had to try to deal with them one at a time.

KV: What did you decide to prioritise?

MB: I had been told over and over again that everything was ultimately about Mio. That if I could just find him, everything else would fall into place. But I was getting more and more dubious. Fall into place for whom, exactly? Hardly for Mio. Wherever he was.

KV: With Rakel?

MB: Possibly, but if so, where? I thought it extremely unlikely that she alone could be behind everything that had happened. After I'd had her house searched I was convinced that Mio was actually somewhere else.

KV: Together with Rakel?

MB: Together with whoever was involved in everything that had been going on.

(Silence)

KV: Let's go back to Elias, lying there with his throat cut.

MB: An extremely interesting part of the story.

KV: Because . . .?

MB: Because he went missing.

KV: Missing? He was already missing.

MB: And you know what? He went missing again.

23

THURSDAY

'What are we going to do?' Lucy asked when I told her about Elias.

'Nothing,' I said.

'Not call the police?'

'And say what? That a burglar I hired has found a body?'

She fell silent. We drank some more wine and then went to bed.

'What was he doing in Rakel's house?' Lucy said once the lights were out.

'Don't know.'

'They knew each other from before.'

'Mmm. But that was a very long time ago.'

'Do you think she killed him?'

'I ought to be shouting "Absolutely!", but it doesn't feel right.'

'I can understand that. It must be difficult, knowing you've slept with someone who's capable of murder.'

I let Lucy have the last word that night. She deserved it. I went out like a light and slept like Sleeping Beauty. I can't explain why. Maybe it was sheer exhaustion. Or shock. Or the relief that came from finally telling someone – Lucy – what happened in Texas. Only God (and possibly the Devil) knows how much I wanted to keep digging into what Bobby's girlfriend had told me. But that was impossible. Unless I wanted to risk Belle and Lucy's lives, and quite possibly my own. Besides, I had another reality that demanded all of my attention. A reality in which people I'd met turned up in empty houses with their throats cut.

I slept so soundly I didn't even hear when Belle woke up in the middle of the night, upset. Lucy told me about it in the morning.

'But it was okay,' she said. 'She went back to sleep.'

How would I have coped without Lucy? I thought about what I'd realised when we were in Texas. That Lucy wanted children. There was no space in my life just then for that thought. I had my hands full trying to keep the child I'd inherited alive.

As we ate breakfast I looked through the newspapers on my laptop. Not a word about a man being found with his throat cut in Solna. Lucy was reading over my shoulder.

'Maybe she hasn't got home and found him yet,' she muttered in my ear.

As if we could take it for granted that Rakel wasn't involved in the murder.

We glanced at Belle. She was busy trying to feed porridge to her doll and wasn't listening to us.

I shook my head.

We had to stop being stupid. Clearly it wasn't a coincidence that Elias was in her house. It was a horribly uncomfortable thought, but no less true because of that.

Lucy drove Belle to preschool. I rode my bike to the office. I scoured the online papers once more. There still wasn't anything. The anxiety was making me feel restless. It was only a matter of time before the body was found. And then the police would start looking for potential perpetrators.

Do you realise you slept with a murderer? a ghostly voice whispered in my head.

The big question was whether I was going to be blamed for what had happened. Again.

Frustrated, I called Elias's girlfriend.

'How was last night?' I said. 'Have you heard from Elias?'

Terrible but necessary questions.

'Not a word,' Elias's girlfriend said. 'I'm going crazy with worry.'

So was I, not because Elias was missing, but because I knew he was dead.

I tried to figure out how Marie had been able to find Elias, in full view, in an apparently empty house. Who had left him there? People hide bodies – they don't leave them splayed out in the living room. All I felt like doing was going out to Solna to take another look at the house. But I knew that was impossible. I had already been seen in the neighbourhood, and that was bad enough. Going back again and stomping about the garden would be as good as going to the police and confessing to the murder. No one would believe I was innocent once Elias was found.

If he's actually still in the house.

I couldn't bear it. In desperation, I called Boris to ask him to send Marie or someone else to Solna. He didn't answer. I drummed impatiently on the shiny desktop with my fingers. I was being driven mad.

Then I remembered Lucy's material about the preschool staff. I dug the envelope out of my briefcase. I'd put it in there when I left the office the previous day. My fingers felt clumsy as I opened it and pulled out the bundle of papers. Lucy had been ambitious. Using the material from the police she had managed to identify all the members of staff and had found out where they were today. No one had moved away from the area, but a number had left the preschool and were now employed elsewhere. I worked my way diligently through the pile of passport photographs. There was no picture of Mio. Of course. Sara must have taken a conscious decision not to apply for a passport for her son. To stop him being taken out of the country.

I tried to guess who the mysterious Susanne might be, but it was impossible. She could have been any one of the women staring blankly back at me from the photocopies.

The only one I recognised was Rakel Minnhagen.

'Veronica,' I said quietly. 'What the hell do you want with me?'

Lucy had checked all the staff on the national population database, including Rakel Minnhagen. The fact that she was currently registered as living in Solna was nothing new. But she had been registered at an address in Årsta havsbad the previous year. That information made me frown. Partly because she had been registered there for less than three months in late summer and autumn. And partly because Årsta havsbad primarily consisted of summer cottages that lacked running water and drains. The house she had lived in was on Arkitektvägen. My frown grew deeper. Surely I'd been to a party out in Årsta havsbad? Something like a decade, a century ago – I couldn't remember.

I called Lucy.

'Have you ever been to a party in Årsta havsbad with me?' I said.

Lucy might well have wondered why I was calling to ask such an odd question. But she didn't. We'd stopped reacting whenever the other did or said peculiar things.

'Not that I can remember,' she said. 'Actually, yes. Wasn't that where that awful friend of yours from university had a crayfish party? When all the guests were promised proper beds and you and I ended up sleeping in a hammock?'

'That's right,' I said.

It had been a terrible party. Of all the awful university friends I've got, there was none more awful than the guy Lucy was referring to: Herman Nilson. A stuck-up wanker who went on to become a very successful property lawyer. But the world needs people like that as well.

Lucy arrived at the office a little while later. She did the same as me – started by looking through the online papers.

'Still nothing,' she said.

'No,' I said stiffly.

I was terrified of Elias being found. Terrified of what that would mean for me.

Rakel Minnhagen. Could she really be behind all this? And, if so, was she alone? I didn't think that very likely. There were plenty more loose ends to look into. I had found the person who abducted Mio. I had found her home. But there was no Mio there. Only a dead Elias.

I didn't have much more to go on than the address in Årsta havsbad. I tried to work out why I was getting so hung up on that. Just because I'd once been to a party there, nine years ago (we'd figured out when it was). Without further ado I contacted the Land Registry and asked who owned the property where Rakel Minnhagen had been registered. The clerk rattled off a man's name that I didn't recognise.

'He acquired the property last December,' the clerk said.

'Can you see who owned it before him?' I said.

'Of course. The previous owner was a Herman Nilson.'

I sat for a long time in silence behind my desk. What did it mean that Rakel Minnhagen had been registered – and therefore possibly lived – at an address belonging to someone I had been at university with? Someone who had never been a particularly close friend, and whom I hadn't seen or heard from in years. I had a nagging feeling that the answer was right in front of my nose. There was something I wasn't seeing. Something I had missed. Something big.

Then my phone rang again. I didn't recognise the number and didn't feel like answering at first. Then it occurred to me that I could hardly get any more surprises on one and the same day.

'Martin Benner,' I said.

'This is Jocke from the garage. I just wanted to check when you were thinking of coming to get your car.'

I coughed and tried to make my voice sound humble and authoritative at the same time.

'It's good that you've called. I'm afraid things have got a bit hectic here. Could the Porsche stay with you until, say, Monday next week?'

I didn't want to see the car. Didn't want it anywhere near me.

'No.'

'No?'

'No, that doesn't work. It's against our policy. Cars that have been fixed have to be collected. It's to do with the insurance.'

'I understand,' I said. 'Obviously I'll be happy to pay for any extra expense. If you could just look after ...'

'You clearly don't get it. I can't help you. Can you come this afternoon?'

Only very rarely does one thing go to hell at a time. Usually it's like playing a malicious game of dominoes. If one of them falls, the rest follow. As long as they're standing close enough to each other.

'I won't forget this,' I said, making my voice sound as unfriendly as I could. 'I don't expect this sort of behaviour from a company like yours.'

'Nor we of a customer like you,' said the guy calling himself Jocke. 'The police have been here.'

I stiffened.

'Did they take the car away?'

'What? No, I'd have told you that at the start. But it was all extremely unpleasant. There were other customers in the vicinity and they looked most put out. The sooner you come and collect your Porsche the better.'

24

Jocke got his way. I went at once. The sun was blazing and the car's paint gleamed. Ordinarily I wouldn't have been able to help myself and would have started grinning the moment I saw it. Not this time. The Porsche aroused nothing but feelings of discomfort in me.

'I fixed the dent in the bonnet as well,' Jocke said.

'Great,' I said.

The dent in the bonnet. The cause of which I had absolutely no idea about.

'What did you make of that?' I said. 'The dent, I mean.'

'Tricky question,' Jocke said. 'The police asked the same thing. I assume they've got their own experts, but they wanted my opinion as well.'

'They wanted to know if the dent was caused when someone was run over?'

'He, not they. There was only one of them here. But yes, that's what he wanted to know.'

Just one police officer. Not more.

'What was his name?'

'Didrik, I think.'

Of course.

'And what did you say when he asked about the dent?'

'That I wasn't sure. That it looked as if someone had jumped up and landed on the bonnet on their butt. Something like that.'

'Big butt,' I said, and made an attempt at a relaxed laugh.

'Hmm,' Jocke said. 'Bloody big butt. But at least it no longer stinks of rotten orange. The car, I mean.'

I'd never driven so cautiously as when I pulled out onto the road. I drove straight home and parked it in the garage. I had no intention of taking it out again for a very long time. To be on the safe side I left the satnav on. Then there'd be no doubt about whether or not the car had moved, in case anyone asked.

Lucy had gone out when I got back to the office. I was disconcerted by the fact that Didrik himself had gone to the garage. He ought to have sent an underling. And then there was the fact that the unappealing Herman Nilson had lent his house to Rakel Minnhagen. There had to be a common denominator of some sort, holding all this crap together. So why was it proving so hard to find?

I leafed through Lucy's papers about the preschool again. If Herman Nilson was involved in the conspiracy I had fallen victim to, getting in touch with him would be an incredibly stupid thing to do. Incredibly stupid. That notwithstanding, however, it was unavoidable. After some hesitation I called Madeleine Rossander. Her voice sounded flat when she realised who was calling.

'Just a quick question,' I said. 'Do you remember Herman Nilson?'

'Er, yes. We worked at the same practice until a few months ago.'

Eureka.

'Excellent. If someone wanted to bump into him and make it look like a coincidence – where would they find him?'

I heard Madeleine take a deep breath.

'Why do you want to know?'

I stifled a sigh. It wasn't that I couldn't understand why she was asking. She didn't want to throw her acquaintances onto a blazing fire. Even if she didn't particularly like them.

'I need to check something with him,' I said.

My voice was much lower than normal.

'I don't like this, Martin. What is it you need to check?'

My fingers were totally dry as they touched the papers on my desk.

'He rented out his summer cottage to a woman for part of last year. Or at least she was registered at that address. I'd like to find out how he knows her.'

'And you were thinking of asking him completely out of the blue when you pretended to bump into him somewhere?'

Her voice contained so many different shades of doubt that I could feel my cheeks burn.

'I'm happy to admit that I've run out of good ideas,' I said.

I heard her laugh quietly down the phone. It was a nice laugh. I once tried to match-make between her and a friend of mine.

'What's the best thing about her?' he had asked.

'She laughs really easily,' I replied.

It had never occurred to me to try it on with Madeleine. She was far too good for me. Or too smart.

'This woman,' Madeleine said. 'Does she have a name?'

I hesitated.

'Not one that I feel like sharing right now,' I said.

'I'll buy that,' Madeleine said. 'But keep your distance from Herman. He's unreliable, towards men and women alike.'

'Feel free to elaborate on that.'

'Easy. He sleeps with any woman who comes near him, and only has a small number of male friends left, seeing as he has a tendency to exploit people in general. I was extremely surprised when he once cancelled a meeting to go and pick his godson up from preschool. In Flemingsberg of all places. Who the hell would pick someone like Herman to be a godfather?'

A godson at preschool. In Flemingsberg.

I made an effort not to sound too excited.

'How come a man like Herman Nilson would have a godson at preschool in Flemingsberg?' I said. 'I thought all his friends were as rich as him.'

No one rich would choose to live in Flemingsberg. Not if you had similar assets to Nilson.

'I'm afraid I have no answer to that particular question,' Madeleine said.

'But perhaps you know the names of the godson's parents?' I said.

'No, but if it's important I could probably find out.'

Was it important? Important enough to risk sending Madeleine out into the line of fire again? I needed to find some connections between all the little fragments of information I had.

'If you could, please.'

'I'll get back to you,' Madeleine said.

'I might do the same,' I said. 'If it turns out that I really do need to get hold of Herman Nilson.'

My office felt very quiet after Madeleine had hung up. I quickly checked the newspapers' websites again. Not a word about poor dead Elias. I was starting to feel sick. *Where was the body? And where the hell was Mio?* He'd also been in Rakel's house and had then disappeared from there.

As long as Mio wasn't dead. That thought made me feel utterly desolate. I didn't know Mio; my relationship to him was purely practical. Either I found him and everything turned out alright, or I didn't find him, in which case I might as well shoot myself. I hated being in that position. I hated the fact that I was expected to care so little about a young person.

Restlessness crept across my body like a rash. There was so much I wanted to get done, without knowing how to go about it.

I wanted to talk to the journalist Fredrik Ohlander's family, but I didn't dare contact them. Fredrik's and my collaboration had been secret. And had to remain so. Previously for both our sakes, but now for mine alone.

I also wanted to know more about who might be aware of the sin I had buried in Texas, but I didn't know who to ask.

My phone contained a short note about Stesolid. Did Mio suffer from epilepsy or febrile convulsions? His aunt or grandmother ought to be able to answer that. And that ought to have made the police try harder to find him when he went missing. I thought about what Didrik had said when we met at the Press Club. That the police were convinced

Mio had been killed by his mother before she took her own life. Had that conviction been so strong that it got in the way of any real attempt to find him? Apparently. That impression was also reinforced by the police file. There wasn't a single photograph of the boy among the material.

That couldn't be right.

I needed to talk to another police officer. Someone must have reacted to the way the investigation had been handled, must have disagreed with it. But the police were out of bounds to me; I wasn't going to get anywhere there. I found myself thinking about Susanne instead. The woman who had called in the middle of the night and wanted to remain anonymous. I didn't know her name, and I didn't know what she looked like. But I knew where she worked, and that would have to do. Having made up my mind, I stood up and went outside to the hire-car. A short while later I was on my way to Mio's preschool.

25

'Who are you and what do you want?'

Children would make excellent police officers if only they were allowed to start work before they turned ten. The little girl practically filled the doorway as she stood there with her hands on her hips.

'I'm here to see one of the teachers,' I said.

'Which one?'

'Susanne.'

'Ha! There's no one called that here.'

She turned on her heel and ran through the cloakroom into the playroom.

'There's a man here! He wants to see someone called Susanne!'

I hurried after her. In my eagerness I forgot to take my shoes off. I smiled broadly and warmly towards the horrified teacher who was staring at me from across the room. There were fewer than ten children there. Some of them were sitting drawing at a table behind the teacher. A few more were playing with a car track. And then there was the girl who had met me at the door.

'There's no one called Susanne working here,' the teacher said.

'Would you like to double-check that?' I said, still smiling. 'Because I'm quite sure. Someone here must know her.'

The teacher shook her head slowly. I took a few steps towards her and heard the sound of someone moving off to my right. An older woman was approaching, trailing yet another child.

'This man is looking for someone called Susanne,' the younger woman said.

'There's no one of that name working here,' the older teacher said.

'Perhaps in a different section?' I said.

'There's only one other room open during the summer,' the older woman said. 'There's no Susanne there either.'

'I might go and ask for myself,' I said.

'No need. I—'

I interrupted her.

'I'm sorry,' I said. 'But it really is very important. Either one of you goes over to the other room and asks if anyone either is called or knows Susanne, or I do it myself. I'm a lawyer, and I'm looking for Susanne in connection with an extremely sensitive matter.'

The older woman straightened up.

'I see,' she said. 'I can go and ask. But I can tell you now that you're mistaken.'

The children watched as she disappeared the way she had come, off down a short corridor. They were no longer drawing or lying down, just sitting quite still.

'Who's Susanne?' one boy asked another.

'No one,' the other boy whispered.

The younger teacher looked at me warily and then went over to the children who were playing with the car track. I stood where I was in the middle of the floor, as if I'd just dropped from the heavens. Perhaps I would end up regretting my excursion, but I didn't think so. The teachers seemed cool enough, and appeared to have accepted the reason for my visit. As long as the older woman wasn't calling the police. That wouldn't be good.

She came back a minute or so later. I could have shouted out loud with joy. The look of surprise on her face told me all I needed to know.

'I'm sorry,' she said. 'Apparently you're right. One of the teachers in the other room does know this Susanne you were asking about. She's waiting for you out in the playground.'

She was standing in the shade of a tree. Her face reflected a mixture of suspicion and anger. I stopped a couple of metres away from her. Relief spread through my body. I recognised her from the passport photographs Lucy had found. Short hair, side parting and a birthmark on her right cheek.

'Susanne?' I said.

I knew that wasn't her name, but I couldn't remember the name of the woman in the photograph.

'What the hell are you doing here?' she said.

Her anger gave way to another emotion just below the surface. Sheer, utter terror.

'I'm sorry to show up like this, but you wouldn't tell me your phone number. Or your name.'

She shook her head hard.

'I was very clear about why. I find it unbelievable that you can't respect that.'

Should I be feeling guilty? I didn't think so. To a very large extent she herself was responsible for the situation she was in. Besides, she bore a lot of the blame for what had happened to Mio. The more I thought about it, the harder it was to understand her decision not to go to the police.

'I don't give a damn if you find it unbelievable,' I said. 'Can't you just start by telling me your name? Or am I going to have to ask your colleagues? At the same time as I tell them about the jewellery you stole, perhaps?'

She lowered her gaze and leaned heavily against the tree-trunk. From a distance we probably looked like a couple who were in the middle of breaking up. She looked so tired she couldn't stand up, I looked so agitated I couldn't stand still.

'Nadja,' she said. 'My name is Nadja Carlsson.'

That name had been on Lucy's list, but not in the police's preliminary investigation, just as Susanne, or Nadja, had told me before.

'I've got a few more questions about Mio,' I said.

'I doubt I'll be able to help. I didn't really work with him that much.'

'But you might know if he suffers from epilepsy?'

She looked up quickly.

'Yes,' she said. 'He did. Or does. If he's alive.'

Of course he was alive.

'Did it cause him much trouble? Did he often have fits?'

'No, thank goodness. It only happened once here at pre-school, I think.'

I nodded to myself. I was wondering why whoever had removed Mio from Rakel's house had left his medication behind. Stesolid isn't the sort of thing you can just pick up from the chemist. You need a prescription, and a prescription requires a doctor. The sort of thing you'd prefer to avoid with an abducted child. A surge of anxiety was making me breathe harder. Surely the reason why we'd found the medicine couldn't be that Mio was dead? Because dead children don't have fits?

I shook my head to clear my thoughts.

'Does the name Herman Nilson mean anything to you?'

'No.'

I took my phone out and Googled a picture of him. There was one on his employer's website.

'Sure?'

She looked at the screen.

'Oh, him!'

Bloody hell.

'So you do know who he is. How come?'

'He came here to pick up his godson a few times. Extremely arrogant. All the staff used to talk about him. Handsome and horrible. It was so damn obvious that he wanted everyone to know he wasn't the sort of person who lived in Flemingsberg.'

Sad words. Did I give the same impression? I hoped not, then realised that was something I was going to have to work at.

'Did he have a relationship with Rakel?'

Nadja looked surprised.

'No, I don't think so. He'd never have been interested in anyone who worked here. Nor us in him, to be fair.'

'Whose godfather was he?'

'I think the boy was called Sebbe.'

'Sebbe. Sebastian? Surname?'

'No idea. He wasn't in my room.'

Sebbe. Sebastian. The same nagging feeling I'd had with the address in Årsta havsbad. I knew someone called Sebastian. A child. One of Belle's friends? An image of a red-haired boy at her preschool flashed through my mind. An unnecessary thought, seeing as that Sebastian could never have set foot in Mio's preschool.

'Actually, he had some ... problems too,' Susanne said.

I perked up.

'Sebastian?'

'He wasn't here long. There was some talk about why his parents had changed preschool, and how he ended up with us in Flemingsberg. He was always so tired, always seemed to have hurt himself somewhere or other. Mostly his head. He had bruises as well. I think his former preschool reported his parents. We were all convinced they used to beat him.'

When your mind doesn't have a clear thread to follow, everything becomes equally important. Or equally unimportant. Was what I'd just heard relevant? I didn't think so. Even so, I said: 'What about the staff here? What happened with the report? You must have reacted as well?'

'Oh yes, we did. But I wasn't involved. Anyway, the family moved away from the city early last autumn. By then Sebbe was in a bad way.'

'Strange,' I said.

'What's so strange about that? They must have been so ashamed.'

'Where did they move to?' I said.

'Abroad, I don't know where. It all happened very quickly. We weren't really told anything about the move. Presumably they wanted to get away from the Swedish authorities so they could go on abusing their child.'

I felt a pang in my stomach to hear her talk like that. Belle has made me soppy; I can't stand people who hit their children. Not that I used to think it was okay either – it's more that my dislike of it has been enhanced. Dramatically.

Nadja straightened up.

'I have to go back inside. The others will be wondering where I've got to.'

'How can I get hold of you in future? If you don't want to see me here again, I suggest you give me a telephone number.'

She grimaced.

'Isn't that blackmail?'

'I don't think so. But if you want to check, you can always ask the police when you go and tell them who took Mio.'

She turned as white as a sheet.

'Never,' she whispered.

I decided not to press the point. Enough people had died. No sooner had the thought occurred to me than I started looking round. If I was being followed, then I had just signed Nadja's death warrant. Which got me wondering why she was still alive. Elias had been found dead in Rakel's house. But Nadja had been left alive. I couldn't help wondering: for how long? If Rakel was the murderer, her choice of victims was inconsistent.

It isn't her, I thought. There's someone else behind her, making the decisions. And that's when it all ends in blood and death.

'Give me your phone number and you won't see me again,' I said.

She rattled off her number and then headed back towards the school.

I hesitated, but only for a moment.

'Hang on,' I said.

She turned round.

'Have you got a friend or relative outside the city you could go and stay with for a few days?'

She was just as pale as before.

'I could sign myself off sick,' she said. 'And go and visit my grandmother.'

I nodded.

'Do that,' I said.

'How long for?'

How could I answer that?

'At least a week.'

She disappeared, and I walked back to the car. The road was quiet, no traffic at all. That would make it easier for me to see if I was being tailed.

I'd just closed the car door when Lucy called.

'Martin, you need to take the Porsche back to the garage again.'

'Why?'

'It still smells terrible. A different sort of terrible, but still. I went down to get something from the glove compartment and . . .'

'You didn't drive it, did you?' I almost yelled.

'No, I just told you. I went to get something from the glove compartment. Either way – the car stinks. Take it back.'

'Later,' I said. 'I thought I'd go and collect Belle from preschool.'

'So early?'

'Mm. I might take her to the office. Or go and get an ice-cream.'

As I was driving back into the city I thought about what Lucy had said. I'd driven the Porsche back from the garage myself. It hadn't smelled then. Or had it?

Lucy's voice echoed in my head.

It still smells terrible A different sort of terrible ...

My mouth went completely dry. My hands clenched the wheel.

A different sort of terrible. Naturally, anything at all could be making the smell. But not in my car. Not in my garage. Not that day, that week.

I called Lucy.

'Meet me in the garage in fifteen minutes.'

'Why ...?'

'Just do as I say.'

'What's happened?'

I swallowed, then swallowed again, and chose my words carefully.

'I think we might have found Elias.'

26

A lot of smells are very similar, and therefore can't be told apart. The stench of a corpse is not one of those. Corpses smell like nothing else. Lucy had never smelled a dead body before. So she was unable to identify it. But I could.

The moment I stepped into the garage I knew my guess had been correct. The stench filled the confined space. Ten parking spaces, that was all the garage contained.

'Christ,' Lucy said. 'It's even worse than before.'

She was walking behind me as I slowly approached the car. Now I knew for certain that I never wanted to drive it again. It was as if it had a life of its own. With people who wished me anything but well.

I stopped in front of it. Jocke at the garage had given the car a polish before handing it back. Since then I hadn't touched any part of the exterior except the driver's door. If whoever dumped the body hadn't been careful enough, his or her fingerprints might still be on the bodywork. It would be stupid to give them any competition from mine. I didn't think the fact that Lucy had touched the car would matter. She wasn't suspected of committing a crime. I went up to the flat and fetched a pair of gloves before getting to grips with the luggage compartment. You had to open it from the driver's seat.

'Lucy, help me get it open.'

Without a word she walked past me and opened the driver's door. The lid of the trunk rose when she pressed the button. And then the stench hit us.

'Fuck,' I said, backing away quickly.

Lucy rushed out of the car and went and stood some distance away.

'Martin, we have to call the police.'

'We're going to; we just need to see who it is first.'

How had my life come to this? How had I gone from living a very comfortable life as a lawyer with the odd bit of childcare thrown in, to standing in my garage and finding a dead body in my own car?

I walked over to the Porsche again and aggressively pushed open the lid of the luggage compartment. And there lay Elias with his throat cut. In spite of the stench I couldn't take my eyes off him. He looked so damn pathetic. Lonely and frightened.

Then I shut the lid again.

'Now we can call the police,' I said.

They arrived ten minutes later. First a patrol car, then Didrik and one of his colleagues, Staffan, whom Elias had spoken to when he called the police to ask for help. Didrik's face showed no emotion when he saw Elias lying dead in my car.

I told them the story as we stood in the stinking garage.

I told them, again, about the incident with the orange and how the car ended up having to be cleaned up. I told them how I had picked it up and driven straight home.

'Feel free to take the satnav away with you,' I said.

'We'll be taking the whole car,' Didrik said grimly.

'You're welcome to it,' I said, trying not to sound generous. 'I don't want the bloody thing.'

'Really?' Staffan said.

Sticking with the cynicism.

'You'll have to come with us to headquarters,' he said.

'What for?' I said.

'We need to take a witness statement,' Didrik said. 'Isn't that obvious?'

'Maybe,' I said, sounding like a teenager.

'Maybe,' Didrik repeated. 'Alright, we'll talk more about this once we're there. Until then you can figure out how you're going to convince us that you weren't the one who put the body in the boot.'

'Easy,' I said. 'I've got an alibi.'

'For when?'

'The body must have been put in the car when it was parked here in the garage. I haven't been back since I left the Porsche here after I collected it.'

'Even if you could prove that, what does that tell us?' Staffan said. 'You could have left the body here in the garage and just waited until the Porsche was back.'

'Right,' I said. 'You don't think anyone would have raised the alarm about the smell if I'd done that? People come and go here all the time.'

'Like I said, we can talk about that back at headquarters,' Didrik said.

He began to walk towards the exit, gesturing to me to follow him.

'Lucy and I will go in our own car,' I said. 'We've got a rental.'

'You're welcome to come with us,' Didrik said, his tone of voice indicating that it was more an order than a suggestion.

But I called him out on it.

'Then you'll have to arrest me,' I said. 'Because I want to drive myself.'

'Okay,' Staffan said. 'Let's do . . .'

Didrik interrupted him.

'See you at headquarters,' he said.

His colleague glared at Didrik in surprise as he walked away. Then he seemed to realise that he too should be moving his feet. I heard him raise his voice as they left the garage.

'Why the hell aren't we taking him in?'

Perhaps because I hadn't done anything but cooperate fully with the police. Perhaps because I had called them to the garage myself. I didn't know, and I didn't care. All I did know was that I didn't trust Staffan, and very possibly not Didrik either. For that reason I didn't want to rely on them to obtain the security-camera footage. The video would clear me, and I had to make sure that it really was secured. That no one would discover that the camera was, oh-so-unfortunately, broken. The police's forensics team would find it in a matter of seconds, so I had to be quick. I practically ran out of the garage with Lucy beside me.

'Where are we going?' she said as I pressed the button for the lift. 'It's important that we go to Police Headquarters like we promised.'

'We will,' I said. 'We're just going to pay a quick home visit to someone first.'

There's one in every housing cooperative. Often the chair of the residents' committee. An angry older man who has lived in the same flat for far too long and regards the building as his own private property and the residents as his tenants. In my building that man's name is Wolfgang. He's lived at the same address for more than twenty-five years, and has been a widower for the same length of time.

Lucy looked baffled as we got out of the lift on Wolfgang's floor.

'There's a security camera in the garage,' I said. 'Didn't you notice?'

She shook her head.

I put my finger to the bell outside Wolfgang's door. The shrill noise echoed out into the stairwell. I didn't remove my finger until I heard the lock turn.

'What the hell are you doing? Is there a fire?'

Wolfgang's grey hair was sticking out in all directions and the look in his eyes was angrier than ever. Angry but also tired. Then somewhat gentler. Wolfgang has had a soft spot for me ever since I backed him up in a committee vote and helped stop the sale of our attic space to developers.

'I really am extremely sorry to disturb you like this, without any warning,' I said. 'But I'm afraid I need your help.'

Wolfgang scratched his chin. His stubble was several days old.

'Regarding what?'

'Can we come in?'

He backed away dutifully and let us over the threshold. I

closed the door behind me. Neither I nor Lucy had been in Wolfgang's flat before. I had expected a proper nest, full of old newspapers and cooking smells. But it wasn't like that at all. From what I could see from the hall, the flat was tidy and light and well maintained.

'I found a security camera in the garage,' I said.

'That's right,' Wolfgang said. 'I installed it after that business with your car. And don't imagine I haven't checked into the legality of it. The camera is perfectly legal.'

I tried to look as if I had the greatest respect for his legal competence.

'Of course,' I said. 'I wonder, could I possibly have a copy of today's footage?'

Wolfgang peered at me.

'What for?'

I took a deep breath. The police would find him within the next hour. And it was only a matter of time before journalists got wind of what had happened. He was going to find out anyway.

'Someone placed a body in the boot of my car, and I'd dearly like to know who it was.'

Wolfgang opened his mouth to speak, but couldn't get a word out.

Then he opened the door to the hall-cupboard. There was a computer on one of the shelves.

'There,' he said flatly. 'There's your footage.'

27

There wasn't a cloud in the sky as we drove from the flat to Police Headquarters on Kungsholmen. Lucy was driving while I sat and looked at the images from the security camera. Wolfgang had burned them onto no fewer than three CDs. So that there was no chance of them vanishing, as he put it. He had also promised not to mention the copies to the police unless he was asked a direct question about them.

The images weren't in perfect focus, which worried me at first. I hadn't had time to look through them in Wolfgang's flat, and had merely given him the times I was interested in. Barely three hours had passed since I parked the car in the garage. Impatiently I fast-forwarded through the jerky footage. One neighbour drove out of the garage, another one drove in. Then nothing happened for a long time. Until the garage door opened once more and a car I didn't recognise drove in.

'Bloody hell,' I whispered, leaning over the laptop.

The car was a Toyota, a model I didn't recognise. It

stopped in the middle of the garage between the two rows of parking spaces. Two people leapt out of the Toyota and ran round it. Everything happened so quickly I was sure I'd miss something if I blinked. In less than a minute they'd opened the boot of their car, helped each other to lift out a limp body, and dumped it in my Porsche. I watched with astonishment as they opened the boot. It opened easily.

'How's that possible?' I said out loud to myself.

Before they closed it, I saw the taller of the two figures do something, close to the lock on the boot of the Porsche. Then they slammed it down, got into their own car and drove off.

I shook my head and rewound the recording.

'Do you recognise anyone?' Lucy said impatiently.

I didn't. But I was pretty sure that one of them was male and the other female. The woman had short hair, whereas the man's was a bit longer. Lucy braked at a red light and looked at the screen of the laptop.

'Wigs,' she said.

'What?'

'They're wearing wigs. Can't you see, his is crooked.'

It really was, although I hadn't noticed. But what I had spotted – to my great relief – was that you could see, despite the relatively poor quality of the recording, that the man wasn't dark-skinned like me. In spite of his stupid wig and large glasses, you could see his skin was as fair as Lucy's.

'He doesn't look like me,' I said.

'No, definitely not.'

I glanced at Lucy, then at the woman in the film. There were several similarities between them. My stomach clenched once more. I wasn't looking because I seriously believed that Lucy was involved, I told myself. I was just looking to reassure myself that no one else could think that.

'Does she look like me?' Lucy said.

Her voice was hollow. A car blew its horn at us. The traffic light had changed to green. Lucy released the clutch too quickly and the car stalled.

'Shit.'

She started the engine again and put her foot down.

The woman in the film was holding Elias by his ankles as they carried him from one car to the other. At one point she looked straight at the camera. I froze the image and zoomed in. No, she didn't look like Lucy. Above all, she was much stronger. Lucy would never be able to help carry a body the size of Elias's.

'Don't worry,' I said, stroking her arm. 'You're not in this recording. Anyone could see that.'

I studied the woman's face intently. If only there was some way to improve the sharpness. And if she hadn't been wearing that ridiculous wig that gave her a low fringe.

'Is it Rakel?' Lucy said.

'That's what I can't see,' I said.

It was extremely irritating. The woman could be anyone. At best, I'd describe the portrait on the screen as a half-decent photofit picture. I pressed play again and brought the figures on the screen back to life. I watched the woman from behind as she went and sat in the car. And then I knew.

'It's her,' I said. 'It's Rakel.'

'How can you tell?' Lucy said.

I didn't really want to answer that question. I just recognised her backside and way of walking. Even though the film was jerky, I was quite certain. The woman in the recording walked exactly the same way I remembered Rakel walking. That, and the fact that Elias's body had been found in Rakel's house told me all I needed to know. The question was: who was the man? And what was the connection between them?

'So, here we are again,' Didrik said.

'Yes, here we are again,' I said.

'Last time, when we were asking about the murder of journalist Fredrik Ohlander, it turned out that your car had been in the garage for repair all night,' Staffan Ericsson said. 'Which was very practical, because we were able to dismiss you from our inquiries.'

I was starting to get annoyed just at the sound of his nasal voice. There were traces of some indefinable liquid on the table between us. Coffee or tea, perhaps. Not blood.

'Are you listening?' his colleague asked sharply.

I looked up.

'Absolutely. It's hard not to be captivated by everything you say.'

Lucy snorted but managed to stop herself laughing. When it came down to it, there was very little cause for laughter.

'After Belle's grandparents died, I'm willing to concede that we started to rethink things,' Didrik said. 'Perhaps you were the victim of a conspiracy after all. We've had trouble finding forensic evidence connecting you and your car to the earlier murders. But the fact that a dead body has just turned up in your Porsche puts things in a rather different light, wouldn't you say?'

I tilted my head to one side.

'But there was a witness,' I said.

Tension came and went so quickly across Didrik's face that at first I thought I was mistaken.

'What witness?' he said sharply.

'A witness to Jenny's murder. That should have made up for the absence of forensic evidence, surely?'

Didrik gave me a long stare. I smiled wryly. If he hadn't realised it before, he knew now. That I was aware of what a lousy false witness they had. But he wouldn't dare ask how I came by that information.

'For the time being we're focusing on this murder, not any of the others,' Didrik's colleague said.

'Quite,' Didrik said. 'We're prepared to accept the fact that you didn't have the body in the boot of your car when you drove away from the garage. We've also checked your satnav and according to it you drove straight home, like you said. But, as we mentioned before, that doesn't tell us much. So now we'd like to know what you did after you parked the Porsche in the garage.'

I drummed my fingers silently on the tabletop. I wasn't remotely inclined to sell out Nadja at Mio's preschool. I didn't actually want to say a word about what I'd been doing. But I could always string them along a bit.

'I went to check out a new preschool for Belle.'

'Really? How nice. And where is it?' Didrik said.

He was smiling, but the look in his eyes was wary.

'In Flemingsberg. It's called the Enchanted Garden.'

His smile died.

'Like hell you were there checking out a new preschool for Belle.'

'Of course I was. A friend told me it was supposed to be

really good. Go out there yourself and ask the staff. I'm sure they'll remember me.'

Didrik drank from the cup of coffee in front of him. No one had asked Lucy and me if we'd like any.

'Martin, what are you up to?' he said.

'I'm trying to get my normal life back.'

That was the truest thing I'd said to Didrik in weeks.

Didrik shook his head slowly.

'After everything that's happened,' he said. 'You're still not giving up. What the hell is driving you?'

There was no way I could answer that. Lucifer's curse was hanging like an axe above my family. I had sworn not to reveal anything else to the police, so I didn't. The fact that I was subsequently called in for questioning was hardly something I could be held responsible for.

'I think there's a fairly simple answer to the problem of the dead body in the boot of the car,' Lucy said after a few moments of silence.

Didrik raised his eyebrows.

'Really?'

Lucy looked at me uncertainly.

'Isn't there?'

I nodded in agreement.

'Absolutely,' I said. 'Because there's a camera in the garage. But perhaps you already knew that?'

It was Didrik's turn to nod.

'Yes,' he said. 'Our colleagues discovered it a few minutes after we left. They called to tell us the good news while we were in the car.'

I shrugged my shoulders.

'Well, then,' I said.

'Well, then, what?'

'Seeing as I know I didn't put the body in my car, I can only assume that the camera recording proves that. And shows someone else doing it.'

More silence.

'That might well have been the case,' Didrik said. 'If . . .'

His colleague's mobile phone rang and he left the room. I fixed my eyes on Didrik with my pulse rushing through my body.

'If what?'

'If only the recording hadn't been faulty. Well, not the recording. The camera's broken.'

I used to play chess as a child. I like to imagine that I might have become quite good at it if I'd bothered to carry on. I'm a good strategist; I don't find it hard to work out in advance which move is best. But on this occasion I felt uncertain. Both Lucy and I knew that the camera had been working perfectly well. Lucy had a copy of the recording on a CD in her handbag. We had hidden the other copies in safe places. Didrik was playing for very high stakes if he knew he was lying about the state of the camera.

I would have to talk to Wolfgang when I got home. I needed to know who had gone to his flat and asked about the camera. Assuming anyone had. They could just as easily have broken the camera in situ when they knew they weren't being watched. And then told the others it had been broken all along.

Lucy's left hand moved towards her handbag. I quickly took hold of her arm, rather too hard. She looked up in surprise. I chose not to meet her gaze. It was important that she didn't pull the recording out. Not yet.

'You look like you're thinking of saying something important,' Didrik said.

For the first time he sounded uncertain.

'No,' I said. 'I was just surprised to hear that the camera was broken.'

'Yes, it's a shame,' Didrik said. 'Do you happen to know who looks after it?'

He said it almost in passing, but I realised the question was important. Even more important was what it told me. They hadn't found Wolfgang.

I turned cold with fear. The bodies were piling up. I didn't know who I could trust, nor who would be allowed to live and who must die. But I knew I wanted to save Wolfgang if I possibly could.

I got to my feet so quickly that my chair fell backwards.

'Unless there's anything else, I'm going to leave now,' I said.

Didrik and I gauged each other's strength across the table. If he decided to charge me now, Lucy could produce the recording from the garage. If not, I was planning to walk out.

Didrik's face was dark and inscrutable.

'We'll be in touch,' he said.

'Sure,' I said.

Lucy stood up and followed me out.

'What now?' she said when we were standing in the street.

'Now we go home and save Wolfgang's life,' I said.

28

And so we did. On the way up the stairs we saw two police officers standing and talking to a neighbour who lived three floors below Wolfgang.

'A camera in the garage?' we heard him say. 'No, I don't know anything about that. You'll have to ask someone on the committee.'

Time was running out. Lucy and I tried not to draw attention to ourselves by racing up the stairs, but walking normally was a strain when we were in such a hurry. We stopped outside Wolfgang's door, but just as Lucy was about to put her finger to the doorbell I stopped her.

'Damn, we're going to have to phone him instead,' I said as quietly as I could.

The police officers in the stairwell could hear us as well as we could hear them. They'd only be curious if we started ringing on our neighbours' doorbells, all out of breath.

Quickly we ran up to my flat. Thankfully Wolfgang answered after the first ring.

'I can't hear you very well,' he said. 'I'm out shopping.'

I drew a sigh of relief.

'Listen very carefully,' I said. 'That camera in the garage. I think it could cause serious problems for you. You need to stay away for a few days. Can you do that?'

That was the second time in one day that I'd told someone to leave town and go into hiding. I had become death's tour-guide. Wolfgang protested, naturally. First he said he didn't have anywhere to go. Then he admitted that he did, but that he didn't want to go.

In the end he listened. He promised not to return to his flat. We agreed to meet up two hours later, in a car park at Kungens kurva. I promised to take a bag of clothes and other things he might need.

'It isn't the police I need to worry about, is it?' he said.

What could I say?

'I hope not. But unfortunately I don't think we can be sure of that.'

I hadn't really had time to think that through properly. Were the police involved? If so, at what level – were individual officers being paid to pass on information, or were there others who were involved to a more serious extent?

'Dear God,' Wolfgang muttered.

He was an old man. I hoped I hadn't frightened the life out of him.

'Any medication?' I said.

'I always carry it with me,' Wolfgang said.

He was that generation. The ones who lived through the Cold War and the Cuban Missile Crisis. The ones who had their cellars full of tinned food and always carried things like passports and medication with them.

'Excellent,' I said.

Lucy and I guessed that Wolfgang was about the same size as me. We packed a bag of essentials at once. I felt extremely hesitant as I folded some underwear and put it in the case. Because two men being the same size was no guarantee that they shared the same taste. Without ever having seen Wolfgang's underwear, I felt absolutely certain on that point.

'Toothbrush,' Lucy said.

'I'll have to buy one on the way.'

'If they've got you under surveillance, they're going to be hysterical when they see you going off and buying toiletries. They'll think you've gone on the run.'

'They won't,' I said. 'I'll shake them off along the way. Otherwise I may as well not bother meeting Wolfgang.'

I'd become an expert at shaking off potential followers. If it went on like that I'd soon be able to join the police again. A thought I dismissed instantly. I didn't want to remember my time as a police officer. Not the shot that was fired, nor the guy I had killed. And definitely not the heat and the hard shovel in my hands as I dug another man's grave.

Benner, we're going to bury this problem.

The nightmares had been driven out temporarily by an increasingly grim reality. But Lucifer was still there. A man who had evidently known who I was long before I heard of his existence. A man I mustn't try to find. A man Sara had said I knew.

'What is it now?' Lucy said when she saw me standing there deep in thought.

'Nothing,' I said. 'Or too much. Depending on how you choose to look at it.'

She gave me a quick kiss just as I was about to leave. The first in far too many hours.

'Shouldn't Belle be home soon?' she said.

'Yes,' I said.

I looked at my phone. No missed calls from Signe. The anxiety was ever-present. If Belle went missing again I'd go completely mad.

I hadn't got to the end of that thought before someone put a key in the lock. Belle and Signe almost tumbled into the flat when Belle pushed the door open before Signe had time to pull the key out. The relief. Impossible to put into words. But it made my eyes very moist.

Two childish hugs later I was on my way out of the flat. I was planning to cycle to a different car-hire firm. And pay cash, like any sensible criminal.

'By the way,' I said to Lucy when I was already halfway through the door. 'Do we know anyone called Sebastian? Or Sebbe?'

She tilted her head. From the kitchen I could hear the chink of porcelain. Someone was playing with the tap in the sink. Then Signe's voice: 'Belle, wash your hands like a big girl.' As if bacteria on her hands were the greatest threat to her wellbeing.

'No,' Lucy said. 'Well, I suppose we know Sebastian Berg. At the Ministry of Finance.'

I laughed.

'I'm pretty sure it's not him,' I said. 'I was thinking of a child.'

Lucy laughed too. Not because it was all that funny, but because she needed to.

'That makes it even harder,' she said. 'I can't think that Belle has a friend called Sebastian.'

Just then Belle came out into the hall.

'Or have you?' Lucy said. She has far greater confidence in Belle's ability to explain things than I do. 'Have you got a friend called Sebastian or Sebbe?'

Belle's little face turned serious.

'No,' she said. 'Not a nice one, anyway.'

Lucy and I blinked.

'Okay, not a nice one. How about one who's mean?' I said.

'Sebbe with the doggy,' Belle said.

We were getting warmer, I could feel it. Sebbe with the doggy. I searched my memory, but everything was a mess.

'Was it a real dog?' Lucy said.

'The sort you have to clap,' Belle said.

There, that was it. The memory drifted up to the surface like a secret that had been sunk in water but then pulled loose of the weights holding it down. Belle had come home very upset from a birthday party last summer. So upset that I felt I had to call the birthday-child's mother to ask what had happened. She was, it had to be said, a very courageous woman. She had freely opened her home to ten three-year-olds without asking their parents to stay. Utterly incomprehensible. When Belle has a birthday I rent a room somewhere and make sure all the parents stay.

'You clapped your hands and it moved when it heard the noise,' I said.

The memory made me giddy. How could she remember? One of the boys who was asked to the party had taken along a toy dog that reacted and moved in response to different sounds. Belle, who loves dogs but knows she's never going to have one as long as she lives with me, was extremely taken with the toy dog. And distraught when the boy hid it from her. She still talked about that dog. Every time we passed a toy shop. It was the dog rather than the boy that she remembered.

The mother I spoke to on the phone had made me laugh. Because the boy had evidently told Belle that if she didn't leave his dog alone, he'd send his dad after her. And he was a policeman.

'Perhaps you know him?' the mother had said. 'You must have plenty of dealings with the police, seeing as you're a lawyer.'

Then she had said his name, which had made me laugh even louder.

'That can't be right,' I muttered to myself as we stood in the hall.

Lucy was staring at me anxiously.

'Don't you know who the father of the boy with the dog is?' I said.

Lucy shook her head.

'I know you talked about it, but I don't remember the details.'

'Didrik,' I said. 'It was Didrik's son who took the dog to the party with him.'

I went back inside the flat. Wolfgang's bag felt heavy on my shoulder.

Lucy was holding her head.

'Hang on a moment,' she said. 'What have you got into your head now? That Didrik's son Sebbe is Herman Nilson's godson? That Didrik, of all people, had a child at the same preschool as Mio? That sounds extremely unlikely. He doesn't even live in Flemingsberg.'

Thoughts were moving through my head with the same

unstoppable force as a freight train on a straight piece of track. I thought about the bruises on the child that the pre-schools had reacted to. There was no way Didrik was the sort of man who hit his child. Was there?

'We think Rakel knew Herman Nilson,' I said slowly. 'Who in turn was godfather to a child called Sebbe. Who attended the same preschool. You might not remember, but Didrik and Herman Nilson do know each other. Didrik was at that crayfish party out in Årsta havsbad. I didn't get the impression that they knew each other well, but I know their wives spent half the night chatting in the kitchen. Maybe that's how their families are connected.'

Lucy still looked doubtful.

'I don't know what to say,' she said. 'It's too far-fetched.'

'Far-fetched? Baby, sorry, but are you crazy? This whole fucking story is far-fetched. That's the whole basis of it. But there *must* be something holding it together – there just has to be. And now there is. I met Rakel that evening I was out with Didrik. Who happens to be Sebbe's father. What more do you need?'

'So you think Didrik used to hit his son? And that's why Rebecca has moved to Denmark?'

I shook my head.

'No,' I said. 'No, no.'

But I was actually feeling quite relieved. Finally I had some sort of framework for all the disconnected thoughts I'd been fumbling with.

Belle moved closer to Lucy and wrapped her arms round her waist. When did she get that tall?

Lucy stroked Belle's hair.

'It must be possible to sort this out fairly easily,' she said.

'We can call the preschool tomorrow. Or find someone else who knows something.'

Herman Nilson. That name came back to me. He, if anyone, would know what there was to know. Possibly without realising it himself, but that was irrelevant.

'I'll get hold of Nilson tomorrow,' I said.

'Martin, that's a hell of a gamble.'

'Maybe. But this has to end somehow.'

'I'm all too aware of that. But didn't Susanne say anything else about this kid called Sebbe? What his parents' names were, for instance?'

'She didn't know.'

Lucy sighed.

'There aren't many of us who know things we ought to,' she said. 'You didn't even know that Didrik had moved to Denmark.'

I almost started to laugh again.

'That's not the sort of thing we talk about,' I said.

I'd have to explain why another time.

I winked at Belle.

'Sebbe with the doggy,' I said. 'Woof, woof.'

Lucy smiled, but Belle was serious.

'He was mean,' she whispered. 'The boy with the doggy was mean.'

29

The day seemed to never want to end. I set off to administer a dose of reassurance to Wolfgang. We met as arranged at Kungens kurva, and I was as sure as I could be that I hadn't been followed.

'The key to your flat,' I said before we parted. 'Could I have it?'

'What do you want that for?' Wolfgang said.

'I want to make sure your computer's safe,' I said.

Before someone else does, I added to myself.

Someone else. In the police? Staffan? Didrik? Both of them?

Wolfgang handed me his key without a word. He seemed to have aged several years in the hours that had passed since we last met. I had to give him credit for being so sensible. He too had gone and rented a car. When I asked where he was going to go, he said he had a summer cottage outside Strömstad. It was a long way for an elderly man to drive at that time of night. And I didn't like the fact that he was going to his own cottage. That was the first place any eventual pursuers would look. I said as much to him.

'So where should I go?' Wolfgang said with feeling.

Not a silly question, and I had no good answer.

'Do you have a relative you could go and visit?' I said. 'Or a friend? A friend would be better than family, harder to trace.'

Wolfgang looked drained as he thought about this. Then he brightened up slightly.

'My former brother-in-law,' he said. 'I haven't seen him for at least five years, but he always sends cards at Christmas and Easter. And he always says I'm welcome to go and visit whenever I want. He lives in Gävle.'

'Perfect!' I said, even if I had my suspicions as to whether this was the sort of visit the former brother-in-law had in mind when he sent those cards. 'He'll be pleased to see you.'

Late at night. For the first time in over five years.

Wolfgang nodded uncertainly.

'Okay,' he said. 'That's what I'll do.'

Then he took the bag of things I had brought him and got into his car.

'I'm sorry you've got dragged into all this,' I said honestly.

'I don't even know what it is I've been dragged into,' Wolfgang said.

There was a note of sourness in his voice. Then Wolfgang started the car and drove off. I raised my hand to wave, then got in my own car. I'd told the rental firm I'd be returning it that evening. They were open round the clock, so I could take it back whenever I wanted.

I was tired. I felt that very clearly as I drove back towards the city. But I couldn't relax. I was being tormented by too many ghosts and mysteries. If Didrik's son really had attended the same preschool as Mio, why had Didrik sent his son to a preschool in Flemingsberg? Didrik bore his aristocratic surname, Stihl, with pride. He hated suburbs that weren't populated by millionaires. His money was inherited rather than earned. I've never understood why he chose to join the police.

I had never been to Didrik's home. Our children had never played together (apart from the time they ended up at the same birthday party), and Rebecca had never been friendly with Lucy. We saw each other because of work and very occasionally met privately for a drink. There were strict boundaries to what we talked about. We talked about work. Our careers. Women. Why the police were so ineffectual. Where Didrik bought his smart suits. But never our children, and never much about our families. I had never met his son, and he had never met Belle. But he did get bonus points for knowing her name. I can never remember what other people's children are called. All I could remember about Didrik's son was that he was adopted, but I'd never given the matter any thought. Belle was also adopted, after all, albeit for different reasons.

Even so, I knew where Didrik lived. Or used to live. I didn't know if he'd moved since he and Rebecca split up. If they had actually split up. But it sounded like it when she said she'd moved to Denmark.

Didrik had inherited his maternal grandmother's house out in Djursholm. That wasn't something Didrik himself had told me, but I'd heard it from envious colleagues of his I'd encountered through work. His comet-like career in the police had put a lot of people's backs up. A lot of police officers thought, like me, that he ought to have done something else. That he didn't fit in. Which in and of itself didn't really matter to me. I hadn't fitted into the dull machinery of the police either. That actually formed something of a bond between me and Didrik. We could look at each other and know we were the same sort.

The car was practically driving itself as I passed the centre of Stockholm with no thought of actually heading home. I knew where Didrik lived because I had represented one of his neighbours a few years before: a man who had been accused of assaulting another man while drunk at a crayfish party. There was quite a lot in the papers about it. About how unusual it was for one multimillionaire to face another in court in an assault case that seemed to be more about wounded pride than physical harm. It ended with me getting my client cleared. He swore eternal gratitude to me and invited me round to drink punch on his veranda.

The thought of sitting on a veranda drinking punch made me laugh. Not much of an uproarious laugh, more one of sorrow. Punch and verandas (and clients) belonged to a past life. My present was exclusively concerned with conducting clumsy detective work and simply surviving.

Slowly I cruised past the fancy villas in the area where my client lived. His house was the last one in the road. Didrik's was the one before that. There were two cars in the drive. Both Mercedes. I stopped and looked at the garden. There was a man cutting the lawn. He wasn't at all like Didrik. A dog was running in circles around the man, barking loudly and excitedly. Did Didrik have a dog? I didn't think so. A lad in his late teens came out of the house and went over to the man with the lawnmower. They looked alike, almost certainly father and son. The man switched the mower off and took whatever the lad handed him. A phone, perhaps?

I parked at the side of the road. The man and teenager both watched me as I got out of the car and walked towards them. The man said something into the phone and then put it in his trouser pocket. Dark-green trousers, with a lot of pockets. Combat trousers, Lucy called them.

'Can I help you?' he said when I was standing by the brick wall that separated their garden from the road.

It reached just above my knees and the more rebellious part of me felt like clambering over it and rolling onto the grass.

'I'm looking for Didrik Stihl,' I said.

'I'm afraid he doesn't live here any more.'

'Oh dear. Do you know when he moved?'

'Of course I do. That's when my wife and I bought the house. Last year, early September.'

I hadn't been in touch with Didrik at the time. Again.

'Do you know where they moved to?'

The man's eyes narrowed. He was wearing a pale beige shirt that was too thick for both the evening sun and grass-cutting. Patches of sweat were spreading across his chest and under his arms.

'What business is that of yours?' he said.

Wise man. You shouldn't talk to strangers. It's stupid of us to teach children that that rule doesn't apply once they've grown up. It's just as valid all the way from the cradle to the grave. At least in the sense of being cautious. Like the man in the combat trousers was being.

I pulled out the same card as usual, did my best to look

relaxed and even managed to squeeze out an attempt at a smile.

'I'm a lawyer,' I said. 'I need to get hold of Didrik on a matter of business.'

The man's shoulders relaxed.

'Ah, I see,' he said.

He gestured to his son to take over the mowing. Without a word the lad started the mower and set off behind it.

The man cleared his throat.

'Well, if I understand correctly, the family moved to Denmark,' he said.

'Really?' I said.

'Yes, that was it,' the man said, suddenly looking very sad. 'It wasn't a particularly happy story, that move.'

I stopped myself coming out with another 'really?' and waited.

'But perhaps you already know what happened? Why they moved?'

I shook my head.

'No,' I replied honestly. 'I don't know a thing.'

The man watched his son walk back and forth across the lawn.

'It's not really my place to say,' he said.

'Was it to do with those reports?' I said.

The man stopped watching his son and looked at me. His eyes were dark with anger.

'If you've come here to talk about that rubbish, you can leave at once.'

I stared at the smart villa, unsure of what to say. Didrik and Rebecca must have ended up with several million kronor at their disposal. I remembered how Rebecca had looked when we ran into each other. How pale and tired she had seemed.

'I haven't come to talk about anything except where Didrik is these days. If you don't know, there's no need for us to continue this conversation.'

I wanted him to soften, because I felt he had something to say. Something that might explain why the Stihl family had moved abroad. Because there were big holes in the story of child abuse.

'Didrik's a police officer,' the man said. 'You can't just walk away from a job like that. So you'll probably find him somewhere in Stockholm. I think it was only the wife and son who moved to Denmark. Didrik commutes on a weekly basis.'

A gust of wind made the leaves on the fruit-trees dance. It would soon be autumn. I realised that I was looking forward to a time of year that I usually hate.

'An unusual arrangement,' I said.

'To put it mildly.'

'You're sure you don't have Didrik's contact details?'

I'd checked the population register on my way out to Djursholm, but hadn't found him. Either he was cheating, and was now registered in Denmark, or his details had been declared confidential and hidden from public view. Nothing strange about that, the same thing applied to plenty of police officers and prosecutors. I've thought about doing it myself many times, but have never got round to it.

'No, I'm afraid not,' the man said.

'He didn't give a new address on the contract of sale when you bought the house?' I said in an unassuming manner.

The man thought.

'Maybe,' he said. 'Unless they just gave the Danish address. I don't honestly remember. But if you don't mind waiting, I can go inside and check.'

Just then it felt as if I had all the time in the world. Whether it was the lush greenery of the gardens or the beautiful summer evening, or simply my own yearning for an ordinary life in which I drank punch, I don't know.

'Please, go ahead,' I said.

As the man disappeared inside his house I saw the door of my former client's villa open. A young woman emerged. I didn't recognise her. Perhaps that house had changed hands as well.

Lucy phoned.

'What's taking so long?'

'I'll be back soon. I just had to check something.'

'Okay.'

We hung up and the man came out of the house with a document in his hand. He tried to walk quickly but I could see he was limping. Trouble with his hips, maybe. But wasn't he too young for that? I had, and still have, a childish attitude towards ageing. I'm terrified that there'll come a day when I can no longer take care of myself. Not my own piss, not my own shit, and not my own hygiene. I shall die then. I can't deal with helplessness.

'Here,' he said, unable to conceal his satisfaction. 'You just need to have things in order. I keep telling my wife that.'

He handed me the document. I noted that it was the first page of a longer deed of sale. It included the details of both buyer and seller.

'Looks like he lives on Södermalm,' the man said. 'That is where that street is, isn't it?'

I didn't reply, just stared at the sheet of paper.

'Is there a problem?' the man said anxiously.

Yes.

There certainly was.

Because the address Didrik Stihl had given as his new home was where Rakel Minnhagen had taken me after we met at the Press Club.

30

I arrived home just under an hour later. From the car I called Harriet, the woman I had met when I tried to get hold of Rakel (or Veronica, as I called her at the time) at the address where we'd had our encounters. She told me there was no Didrik Stihl among the members of the housing association. But there was a man of that name renting an apartment from its official occupant. She didn't know how long that had been going on.

Bingo. But a fucking unpleasant discovery all the same.

On the way upstairs I snuck into Wolfgang's flat and removed his computer. It appeared not to have been touched, but I wouldn't know that until I started it up. I was almost certain someone must have been inside his flat by then. Someone who had cleaned up after themselves and left no sign of having been there.

Someone like Didrik?

We sat on the terrace and drank some wine. I explained what I had found out about where he was living. Lucy turned pale. I couldn't understand how Didrik, of all people, was involved in the crap I was splashing around in. Could *Didrik* have run down and killed two people in a car that resembled mine? And then gone on killing? Moving a body from a house in Solna to the boot of my car? Together with Rakel? The thought was as laughable as it was horrific. Yet it did seem to be the only plausible explanation.

Lucy started when she heard a noise coming from the street. She was like me now, always on her guard. Unable to tell what was important and what wasn't. The noise stopped and Lucy relaxed.

I made an attempt to summarise where we were: 'There was a dead man lying in the boot of my car today. A dead man who was in a house in Solna yesterday: the home of a woman I slept with, who lied about both her name and where she lived. And who also abducted Mio. I met her one evening when I was out with Didrik, who is registered as living at the address where she took me, and who therefore could have given her access to the guest-flat we used. It was Didrik who led the investigation into Sara Texas's crimes. It was his colleague, Staffan, whom Elias spoke to when he called the police and asked for help. So – Didrik and Rakel are a team. They're behind this whole story. What I can't understand is why. Or why they're trying to frame me for the whole thing.'

I could feel my throat contracting and it seemed harder to breathe. Didrik and I hadn't really been friends in any conventional sense, but I had still thought of him as an ally. Someone I could trust.

Lucy put her wineglass down. She had dark circles under her eyes. They say that a beautiful woman looks good in anything, but exhaustion isn't a good look for anyone.

'We need to try to understand what's making him do all these insane things, assuming it is him,' she said.

'Assuming it is him? Baby, it *is* him. Along with Rakel. If there was anyone else involved we'd have seen them by now.'

Lucy said nothing. Said nothing and kept thinking.

'The move to Denmark,' I said. 'I want to know more about that.'

'Does there have to be anything funny about it? Couldn't it just be that Rebecca got a new job or something?'

I pictured her before me, the way she had looked when we ran into each other on the pavement. Pale and hollow-eyed. But above all scared. I had assumed Didrik had been bad-mouthing me at home and that was why she seemed so upset. Now I was no longer so sure. She may have been frightened for other reasons. Few things make people so worried as thinking that their worst secrets are about to be uncovered.

'Maybe,' I said.

Lucy's hand shook as she reached for her wine.

'We don't know anyone else who knows Didrik,' she said. 'You aren't going to be able to find out more about the move without it looking very obvious.'

I cleared my throat.

'I know Herman Nilson.'

Lucy spilled some wine on her blouse and put the glass back on the table with a bang.

'*No, you don't,*' she said, stressing each syllable. 'Not well enough to pay him a visit and ask a load of questions about Didrik.'

'Come on, we've been to crayfish parties together.'

'You mean we were there and felt completely out of place?

He's godfather to Didrik's son. That tells you a lot about where his loyalties are going to lie. You won't have time to ask more than two questions at most before he calls Didrik, wondering what the hell you're playing at. And if Didrik isn't as caught up in it as you think, you risk getting yourself into a hell of a lot of trouble.'

As if I wasn't already. As if I wasn't already deep in the shit.

'I've got to take a few risks if I'm going to get out of this,' I said. 'It won't really do any harm if Didrik finds out I'm asking questions about him. He might even start making mistakes and give himself away. Assuming he is involved.'

I thought about the man we'd seen in the footage from Wolfgang's security camera. It was impossible to say if it was Didrik. That would need someone to enhance the image far beyond what I was capable of.

'I hate this,' Lucy said. 'I hate the fact that we know so little, that we're so exposed. I mean, for fuck's sake, we don't even know why it was so important for that Rakel to pick you up.'

She was absolutely right about that, and it was something that worried me a great deal. It was so easy to trip over all the loose ends. They were everywhere, the whole time.

I yawned so hard that I almost dislocated my jaw. I needed to sleep.

'Shall we go to bed?'

I phrased it as a question, but it sounded more like a plea. Lucy nodded.

'Definitely.'

So we moved inside and went to bed. In the same bed, under the same covers. But as physically uninterested in each other as if we were brother and sister. That was going to change when this was all over. I was going to work my backside off to get my old life back. And we would be happy again.

I found it impossible to settle. Lucy fell asleep and I lay there listening to the sound of her breathing. The list of things that were troubling me was practically endless. But two things stood out. Firstly, the question of Didrik's involvement. And secondly, why Lucifer's representative hadn't been in touch. Didn't he want to hear how things were going? Or were they keeping such a close eye on me that there was no need for telephone calls?

The thought made me shudder. I couldn't help it, I had to wake Lucy.

'Wolfgang's security-camera footage,' I said. 'We're not going to lose it, are we?'

'Martin, I checked before I got into bed. All three copies are still there.'

Feeling marginally safer, I let my head settle deeper into the pillow. At least I couldn't be convicted for having put Elias in the boot of my car. Small mercy.

I must have slept for a while. The nightmares were bubbling under the surface but never really got going. Fragments of misery flickered past. I remember dreaming about a spade. About hot soil and blood-stained clothes. But, generally speaking, you could probably say that I slept pretty well. Entirely unaware of what the following day had in store for me.

31

FRIDAY

It started with a phone call from Didrik. I didn't like his tone of voice on the phone.

'Could you come into headquarters to give us a DNA sample?'

I stiffened. A DNA sample?

'What for?' I said.

'We need it to rule you out as a suspect,' Didrik said. 'There shouldn't be any problem. After all, you haven't done anything.'

'So as a sign of my willingness to cooperate, you think I should trot round to give you a load of my saliva on a cotton-bud?'

'Something like that.'

Not a chance. My faith in the police had dwindled even further overnight. They could do anything they liked with those samples. Even frame me for the murder of Olof Palme if they felt like it.

'What sort of material have you got to compare it

against?' I said. 'I got the impression you didn't have any forensic evidence.'

'I don't know who you could have got that impression from,' Didrik said, 'but I don't feel particularly inclined to discuss my investigation with you. Are you coming?'

I didn't hesitate so much as a second.

'No,' I said. 'No, I'm not.'

I could hear Didrik's surprise even though he fought to contain it.

'Okay, you know the drill, then.'

His voice had gone from soft to hard, and that bothered me. He was firing at random and that meant I had to take care not to sound too cocky. All the same, I couldn't help feeling worried. Was he seriously implying that he was thinking of taking the matter to a prosecutor and forcing me to give a DNA sample?

'No,' I said, rather more aggressively than I would have liked. 'I don't know the drill. For which of the murders have you got DNA from the perpetrator?'

He shouldn't have answered that question. But perhaps he reasoned that I was going to find out sooner or later anyway. Besides, he had already leaked so much information that he might as well leak a bit more.

'Fredrik Ohlander's.'

Of all the names he could have said, that was the one that I was least expecting. Fredrik Ohlander. The journalist to whom I had told everything, and with whom I later denied having had any contact when Didrik asked.

'Fredrik? But . . .'

'He's dead and you knew who he was. Surely you can appreciate that that's enough for us to want to dismiss you as a suspect from the investigation. Particularly in light of what his family have said about him meeting a very secretive person with an extremely challenging story just before he died.'

It was like living under the dangling blade of a guillotine. Fredrik was supposed to have died after being run down. By a car that resembled mine. While the Porsche was in the garage reeking of rotting orange. Now there was suddenly DNA evidence instead. How convenient.

'It's an odd story, this,' I said. 'First I run him down. Then I get out of the car and dribble some DNA on his body. What have you found? A strand of hair? Two, maybe? Or perhaps some urine?'

I thought I heard Didrik laugh, but that was probably my imagination.

'Not urine, my friend. And not hair.'

'We'll be in touch,' I said, and hung up.

My stomach clenched as terror crept down my spine. They wouldn't request a DNA sample unless they had something to compare it to. If the whole thing was a trap, I could be certain that my pursuer would have done his or her very best to incriminate me, once and for all. But what sort of DNA could it be, if it wasn't loose strands of hair?

Not hair.

Not hair.

Two words I knew were crucial in this particular context. Two words that could explain something I had spent days trying to understand. The answer was right in front of my eyes. But I still couldn't see it.

*

Even though I had promised myself that I wouldn't, I felt I had no choice but to ask Madeleine Rossander for yet another favour. She was reluctant to help.

'I'm not making any progress,' I said. 'I have to get hold of Herman Nilson.'

'Only because it's you, Martin,' she said. 'And because I'm still telling myself you're a good person.'

She said I'd find Herman Nilson at the Tennstopet restaurant in Vasastan. He ate lunch there four days out of five. With or without company. And if, against all expectation, I didn't find him there, I could try getting hold of him at his office. But that would spoil the possibility of a discreet, random encounter, and he would almost certainly be busy. To be honest, I didn't really give a damn as long as I found him. I no longer had time to waste on a load of fancy footwork.

I made sure I was at Tennstopet at one o'clock. I found him sitting at a table for two. He was on his own. Seeing as his food had already arrived and he was eating, I assumed he wasn't waiting for anyone. Walking as relaxed as I could manage, I headed towards his table. He looked up and caught sight of me when I was less than a metre away. At first he didn't recognise me. Then his face lit up. His cutlery clattered to the floor as he quickly got to his feet.

'Bloody hell, it's been a while!' he said, shaking my hand.

'What a coincidence!' I said. 'I thought I'd try somewhere new for lunch, and voilà – here you are!'

Herman's reaction was so genuine that there was no way he'd been warned that I was now a terrible and dangerous person.

'Sit down, sit down!' he said, gesturing towards the empty chair at his table. 'It's good to have company!'

The waiter brought me a menu and fresh cutlery for Herman. I glanced through the menu. I had no appetite; it didn't matter what I ate. Anything would do, as long as it gave me energy. And a reason to stay at Herman's table.

'How's things?' he said.

Like you do. And I replied the way you do. Everything was fine, summer had been wonderful. Had I been away anywhere? Oh yes, I'd squeezed in a trip to Texas. But apart from that, work had taken up an unexpected amount of time.

'How about you?' I said.

'Great,' he said.

'Good, good,' I said.

And then: 'But I heard things weren't so great with Didrik and his wife.'

It was a gamble. I rarely shoot from the hip, but on this occasion I did. Fairly aimlessly, you could say.

Herman looked concerned.

'Are they having trouble again?' he said. 'I thought everything was much better now.'

While it was excellent to have confirmation that things weren't right, such a vague reply was less good. Half a fragment of information is as bad as none at all.

My food arrived. I looked down at the soup in surprise.

'Did I order this?'

'You said dish of the day. Would you rather have something else?'

The waiter looked uncertain.

'No, no, this will be fine.'

I hate soup. And porridge.

'What was it you heard about Didrik?' Herman said.

I squirmed.

'Oh, mostly just gossip,' I said. 'I'm sure you see Didrik far more often than me.'

Herman didn't answer. Some of his earlier delight had worn off now.

'Hardly at all since they moved,' he said.

'Yes, of course,' I said. 'I heard that they'd split up, him and Rebecca.'

Herman laughed. Relief spread across his face.

'Oh, that old rumour,' he said. 'No, it's not like that at all. The family moved to Denmark last year, but Didrik was planning to carry on working in Stockholm for a while, and commute on a weekly basis. He's going to start applying for jobs in Malmö soon, and commute across the bridge.'

'That's good to hear,' I said. 'But why did they move?'

Herman turned serious again.

'That's a bit of a sensitive subject,' he said. 'Might be best if you ask Didrik yourself.'

I tried a joke. After all, Herman wasn't a particularly sensitive soul.

'Come on, was he seeing someone else? Was that it?'

Herman looked up, not remotely softened up by my gambit.

'Definitely not,' he said. 'Didrik would never do a thing like that.'

Unlike men such as Herman and myself, I thought.

I tried a spoonful of the soup. It tasted disgusting.

'Okay,' I said. 'I won't pry into things that are none of my business.'

Herman's face looked even sterner.

'Like I said, I can't answer that sort of question.'

But someone would. Because now I was more curious than ever about Didrik's move to Denmark.

I decided to try one last move.

'I understand,' I said. 'But thanks for telling me about Denmark. I got a bit nervous after I heard about Flemingsberg. I almost thought Didrik had let the side down.'

I smiled at my own humour and took another spoonful of the disgusting soup.

'What, was Didrik supposed to have moved to Flemingsberg?'

Herman looked as amused by the idea as I was.

'Someone I know said his kid went to the same preschool as Didrik's. Out in Flemingsberg.'

Herman waved the waiter over and asked for the bill.

'You're right, Sebbe did go to preschool in Flemingsberg,' he said. 'But not for long. Apparently their old preschool shut down the spring before last. A good thing, if you ask me. At least the witch-hunt against Didrik calmed down a bit after that. Anyway, Rebecca was put in charge of a project for Huddinge District Council. So they thought getting him into preschool there made practical sense. I don't know how long-term they were thinking. Because of course everything changed with ... Denmark. Towards the end, Sebbe was spending a lot of time at home.'

Witch-hunt. Was that how he described the attempts of anxious preschool staff to find out why a child wasn't well?

'Why was he at home?'

My follow-up question came far too quickly, and once again I saw Herman clam up. His bill arrived and he paid.

'Like I said, I can't really talk about that. It was ...

terrible. But now things are much better. That's all you need to know.'

With those words he left me. I wasn't happy. There was something more to dig into regarding the Stihl family's move to Denmark. Something that was '. . . terrible'. I wasn't going to give up until I'd found out what.

Thoughts were swirling through my head as if they'd been stirred up by a storm. I was getting close to something that was starting to resemble the truth, I could feel it. But close wasn't good enough. Not when the threat of a DNA test that I didn't understand the background to was getting nearer.

Didrik's words were still bothering me:

Not hair.

Not hair.

That left saliva, blood and sperm. But I had neither kissed, fucked or bled on Fredrik Ohlander. If my DNA had been found on Fredrik's body, someone must have put it there. Possibly after it became clear that the Porsche was in the garage and I couldn't be connected to the crime that way.

But who could have provided them with saliva, blood or sperm, if any of those bodily fluids had actually been found on the body? I looked instinctively at my hands, and then rubbed my face. I couldn't find any cuts. In fact I couldn't even remember the last time I had actually shed any blood at all. I suppose I do spit from time to time, but who the hell would go round collecting saliva from the pavement?

Not hair.

And not blood or saliva.

So it had to be sperm. But that wasn't exactly a doddle to get hold of. Unless someone had crept into my flat and looked for stains on the sheets. Lucy's the only person I have unprotected sex with. No matter how much women beg and swear that they're on the pill, I always wear a rain-hat when I have sex, without exception.

And there it was.

The answer I had been waiting for.

Why had it been so important that I have sex with Rakel Minnhagen?

My stomach churned as I finally came up with a plausible answer: to get hold of my DNA.

32

Over the years there have been a fair number of times – more than I feel comfortable admitting – when I have been afraid that Lucy was going to leave me for good. Leave me in the sense that she wouldn't want to go on working with me, or sleeping with me. One such occasion was when I told her I'd shot a teenager and then buried his body in the desert. And another one came when I walked into her office to tell her what conclusion I had reached.

'I know what Rakel was after,' I said. 'It's not about information. She wanted my fucking sperm. Can you believe that? So fucking gross.'

I assumed she was fairly thick-skinned by then, that she wouldn't react. That sounds almost imbecilic, but it's what I thought.

The expression on Lucy's face didn't change at all. She just sat there at her desk and stared at me as if she'd suddenly realised that I was actually a Martian.

I shifted position on my chair. Lucy has such small

visitors' chairs in her office, meaning that you're always worried about slipping off them.

'How, Martin?'

'What?' I said.

'What did she do to get hold of your sperm? Because I assume you don't go round with samples in your jacket pocket.'

She leaned back and observed me with a look that could have sunk an aircraft carrier. I found that provocative.

'I don't see what the problem is,' I said. 'You know I slept with her. I ...'

'When?'

'You know that too. The day I met Didrik at the Press Club. And again a few days later.'

'That was a while ago,' Lucy said. 'Do you think she's had your sperm in the fridge since then?'

'Er, yes. How the hell should I know? The main point is that she had access to it.'

Had access to it. A deeply unfortunate choice of wording. And Lucy wasn't slow to pick up on it.

'So we're back where we started,' she said. 'How the fuck – if you'll forgive my bluntness – could she have your sperm, Martin?'

'I don't understand what you're going on about,' I said angrily. 'When I fuck, I ejaculate. Is that such a sodding surprise?'

'Not at all. But the fact that you're so fucking stupid that you don't wear a condom is!'

Lucy very rarely shouts at me, but this time she did. Without any justification, I felt.

'Is that really what you think of me?' I said. 'Of course I use condoms.'

Lucy looked taken aback at first. Then it looked as if she was about to start laughing. I couldn't decide which I found worst.

'Are you fourteen years old or something?' she said. 'Please tell me you don't just dump your condoms on the floor. Because if you do I shall lose all respect for you.'

I was gratified to hear that she still had some respect for me to lose, but apart from that the situation was grim. I paused to think before replying. Asking what I'd done with the condom was like asking me what I had for breakfast on the first Saturday in September in the year I turned ten. There are plenty of places to get rid of a condom. It was a detail I hadn't given any thought to. I'm happy to admit that I occasionally behave like a pig, but I'm rarely unhygienic. Had I really left the condom somewhere she could pick it up? That didn't really sound like me.

'She told me not to flush it away,' I said slowly. 'I mean, I know you're not supposed to anyway, but sometimes it happens. The first time she was too late, I'd already dropped it in the toilet before she told me not to. But the second time ... She said she'd had one that got stuck in the pipes and caused a blockage. So I had to put it in a little pedal-bin on the floor. I didn't react to it at the time.'

Lucy was looking at me in a new way. Her eyes were full of sympathy, the way you look at someone with learning difficulties when they do something silly.

'Don't look at me like that,' I said, folding my arms over my chest.

'I'm looking at you the way you deserve,' Lucy said.

I sighed.

'This doesn't feel good,' I said.

Lucy reached the same conclusion. She looked deflated.

'If it really is as bad as you think,' she said slowly, 'how are you going to get yourself out of this?'

It was a question I'd been asking myself, and it terrified the life out of me. Because I was fucked if they had DNA.

'Wasn't Fredrik gay?' Lucy said.

'Yes,' I said.

'Whereas you aren't,' Lucy said.

'If the evidence says I had sex with him right before he died, then I did.'

'But isn't it possible to tell if sperm has been frozen or chilled? We ought to be able to find someone who knows.'

My chest felt tight.

'Lucy, if they pull me in with that evidence, I'm finished. Okay?'

I said it quietly, as if to soften the implications of what I was saying.

She picked at one of her cuticles before she replied.

'I think we've reached the end of the road,' she said. 'You won't be able to wriggle out of this one. You need to go to ground, Martin. Get yourself a good lawyer, someone you trust, and then vanish.'

The thought was dizzying. I'm not the sort of person who goes to ground. I'm far too fond of my comforts, far too lazy. Besides, I'm responsible for Belle. That limits my options.

'I already have a good lawyer I trust,' I said.

She shook her head.

'This isn't my area, and you know that.'

She was right, but still wrong. I had no desire to find someone new to represent me. Besides, I was starting to think it didn't really matter who I had representing me.

DNA has revolutionised our entire legal system. It offers indisputable evidence, far stronger, for instance, than some feeble witness who says she saw a Porsche at a crime scene. Which got me thinking about something that had previously passed me by.

'They must have found another fake witness,' I said. 'To Fredrik's murder. Because someone said they saw a Porsche run him down.'

'Christ,' Lucy said. 'You have no idea how happy I am right now about that whole thing with the orange.'

I allowed myself a brief smile. But the incident with the orange brought up other thoughts that lowered my mood again.

'Belle,' I said.

'I can look after her.'

'Good,' I said. 'Good. Thank you.'

I should have been in tears. I know that, but I couldn't. Not just then.

'We've still got one trump card,' I said. 'The footage from Wolfgang's security camera.'

'Exactly,' Lucy said. 'I'll let the police have a copy when I judge the time is right.'

Neither of us felt like saying anything else. We just sat there in our chairs waiting for time to stop or for the sky to fall in.

'When are you going to leave?' Lucy said.

As if I already had a plan.

'In the next few hours, I suppose,' I said.

'Where will you go?'

I did have an answer to that question.

'I'm going to get hold of a car and then pay someone a visit.'

Lucy looked quizzical.

'Who?'

'Didrik. In Denmark.'

And with that it was settled. For the first time in my life I was going to run away. From the forces of law and order, and from an enemy with no name. I thought I had a bit of time. A few hours. But in the middle of my conversation with Lucy, the doorbell rang. I didn't have hours.

Only a matter of seconds.

PART 5

'What happened to Mio?'

TRANSCRIPT OF INTERVIEW WITH
MARTIN BENNER (MB).

INTERVIEWER: KAREN VIKING (KV),
freelance journalist, Stockholm.

KV: Tarantino.

MB: Sorry?

KV: This story – it's so convoluted it feels like a Tarantino film.

MB: Hmm. Or Woody Allen.

KV: A bedroom farce?

MB: A farce? Allen doesn't do those, does he? No, I was thinking more neurotic, chaotic relationships.

KV: Tarantino would be better, then.

MB: Who cares? Are you following it so far?

KV: The story? Oh yes, I am. And now I'm seriously curious. Did you get confirmation that it was sperm they had found?

MB: I'm getting to that.

KV: But to sum up the situation you

were in, things weren't looking too
bright?

MB: That's a pretty fair summary. The net
was drawing in just as I was getting
closer to the truth. It was right in
front of my nose. But I could never
have imagined it looked the way it did.

KV: I have to admit, I have my suspicions
about how it's going to end.

MB: So did I. It's safe to say that I was
surprised. You will be, too.

(Silence)

KV: It disgusts me. That they went on
hurting Fredrik after he was dead. That
business of planting your DNA on him.
That's just appalling.

MB: I think . . . or rather, I know . . .
that by that point the whole thing
had slipped beyond the control of the
people behind it. No one was in control
any more. That was the most alarming
thing of all.

KV: No one was in control?

MB: No, not in the way I had imagined. And
that was very unsettling. Very, very
unsettling.

KV: But you did head off to Denmark? Did
you find what you were looking for?

MB: I don't know how to answer that.

KV: But you must be able to say something about what you found?

(Silence)

MB: Something completely unexpected.

33

It was Boris who taught me that I ought to have an extra shithole.

'You're a lawyer, for fuck's sake,' he said, the first and only time he ever came to my office. 'Sooner or later you're going to piss off a client. Piss them off really badly. At which point you'll need a way out.'

I didn't understand what he was talking about.

'You think I might have to jump out of the window? I don't think my clients are that dangerous.'

Boris groaned.

'Jump out of the window? No, Christ, that's exactly what you shouldn't have to do. Seeing as your office is on the tenth floor. How much do you know about the dark sides of your clients? You should have somewhere to hide if some crazy fuck shows up here with an axe or a pistol or some other bollocks.'

The thought made me chuckle.

'You can laugh,' Boris said. 'But what you need is an extra shithole.'

An extra shithole. A place to hide, the sort that little kids dream about. A hidden compartment behind a bookcase. Or a magic trapdoor in the ceiling. Or, in Lucy's and my case, a horribly cramped space behind a fake wall at the back of the store-cupboard. Not even our assistant, Helmer, knows it's there.

We hadn't ever had to use the shithole. Well, actually, we had. To have sex in. But that didn't count. There had never been any sort of emergency at our office. Not until the doorbell rang that day.

'I'll get it,' Lucy said when we heard it ring. 'You go and hide.'

'Come off it, what for?' I said.

'Because it might be the police,' Lucy said.

Neither of us thought she was right, but she was. She didn't open the door until I'd sorted myself out behind the fake wall. I felt truly pathetic as I stood there in the darkness. Boris would have despised me if he knew what my shithole looked like. Far smaller than he had in mind, and completely unfurnished. It wasn't designed to be used for more than a few minutes at a time. And the police's visit lasted no longer than that.

I didn't recognise any of the visitors' voices. There were two of them, a man and a woman.

'I'm afraid he isn't here,' Lucy said.

'Do you know where we can get hold of him?'

'I'm afraid not.'

'Perhaps you can let him know we're looking for him? The prosecutor has decided that he needs to give a DNA sample. We'll expect to see him before this evening.'

Lucy promised to tell me. I held my breath and waited for

the police officers to leave. They didn't. They wanted to look round first. I didn't dare move a muscle while they poked about our premises. One of them admired the design and Lucy said something about the company we'd used.

'Tell Benner this is serious now,' was the last thing they said.

'Of course,' Lucy said.

Once they had gone she went and sat in her office. I waited in the shithole. Minutes passed. We waited for the police to return, but they didn't. Eventually I dared to emerge.

'Maybe I should come with you?' Lucy said as we were picking out the things I wanted to take with me from the office.

'Not a good idea, baby,' I said. 'Someone needs to look after Belle.'

'Will you have time to see her before you leave?'

'No, but that doesn't matter too much. I'm expecting to be back tomorrow or Sunday, then I'll go to ground here in Stockholm. I'm going to hire a car that they'll easily be able to trace, and drive it over the bridge to Copenhagen. I'll check into a hotel. Then I'll leave the car there and take the train back. That'll win me a bit of time.'

'Are they that easy to fool?' Lucy said.

'Believe me, things will start to move in our favour, as long as I can get away from here. Today's Friday. If we've got it right, Didrik will go back to see his family for the weekend. He's going to tell me everything he knows. And lead me to Rakel, so I can find out what happened to Mio.'

Lucy didn't raise any further objections. People who don't have any better suggestions usually go quiet.

Then Madeleine Rossander called.

'Can you talk?' she said.

I thought I could.

'My source in the police has just called,' she said. 'He said something I need to tell you.'

I sank onto the chair beside my desk and waited. I wanted to tell her not to take any risks, but she was already far too involved. I had to learn to differentiate between what she and I were each responsible for. She was an adult, and she was aware of the risks. If she continued to supply me with information, I had to trust that she knew what she was doing.

'He said he'd seen something funny in the preliminary investigation into Jenny's death,' Madeleine said.

'Okay.'

'There's another witness, Martin.'

The hairs on the back of my neck stood up.

'Someone apart from that woman who saw Jenny murdered? The one who was upset because I represented a suspected rapist?'

'Yes,' Madeleine said, and I could hear the excitement in her voice. 'Another young woman. She sat with Jenny until the ambulance and police arrived.'

I was clutching the phone far too tightly, waiting for her to go on.

'She said Jenny had been run down by a black Volvo.'

'A Volvo? There's a hell of a difference between that and a Porsche. How ...'

'The police questioned her, but she was later dismissed as being of no interest once the other witness came forward. There's a note saying that she was drunk and confused, and therefore unreliable.'

I shook my head slowly. Someone who identified a specific make of car, not just 'a black car', was in pretty good command of their faculties.

'No way was she drunk,' I said. 'Have you got a name and address? Assuming she's still alive. Is she?'

I blurted out that last question. Madeleine answered as if there was nothing odd about it.

'Yes. But she's moved to Malmö since Jenny died. Her name's Viola Benson. I couldn't resist checking her out. Looks like she does a lot of work abroad; she's a member of a dance group.'

Malmö. On the way to Copenhagen. A lot of work abroad, so possibly not home at the moment. But still worth a try.

I asked for her address and wrote it down carefully.

'I'm starting to get seriously worried for your sake,' Madeleine said.

'And I am for yours,' I said. 'Promise not to dig about in this any further.'

'That's a promise I'll be only too happy to keep,' Madeleine said. 'But I did find out the other thing you asked about: whose child Herman is godfather to.'

'Didrik Stihl's,' I said.

'Precisely. So you already knew that, then?'

'Yes,' I said. 'But it's good to have it confirmed.'

'Don't worry. I can imagine you've got more than enough to think about.'

I glanced at the time. She couldn't imagine how right she was. I didn't know how much I should tell her. The general rule is that someone in possession of a lot of information has the advantage over someone who knows less. But that wasn't the case this time. Not if the information was about me and all the shit I'd been subjected to. It was best to know as little as possible. Otherwise you were dead.

'You know this Didrik, don't you?' Madeleine said.

'Yes,' I said, beginning to pack the rest of the things I wanted to take with me. 'I do.'

At that precise moment I could hardly remember how we knew each other. It must have been as a result of some case we were both working on, him as a police officer and me as a lawyer. But which case? I couldn't remember. There was only room in my head for what was happening now, and in that context how Didrik and I met hardly seemed relevant.

'I must say, I did rather well with my intelligence-gathering,' Madeleine said. 'It turned out that my friend knew Herman Nilson much better than I thought she did. She even had pictures of all the kids on her mobile.'

'All the kids?' I repeated.

'Her own and Herman's. Apparently they play together a lot – that was how the parents got to know each other. Didrik's son used to be part of the group too, but they seem to have moved away from the city last year.'

'They moved to Denmark,' I said automatically.

'Oh, so you know about that as well? What a dreadful story. Poor parents.'

Something in the way she said that made me stand still. Lucy had started shooting impatient glances at me, keen for me to end the conversation.

'Poor parents? You mean the accusations that were levelled at them?'

Madeleine fell silent.

'No,' she said hesitantly. 'No, what accusations?'

'I heard they moved because they were accused of abusing their son.'

'How odd, my friend didn't mention that at all. I didn't want to pry too much into that part of the story. She just said that the boy had been very ill, and that's why they moved. To receive better treatment than they could get in Sweden.'

I froze. Was that why Herman Nilson had been so edgy? Because he was trying to protect his sick godson, and not Didrik, as I had thought?

'What illness was it?' I said.

'Don't know. I didn't think that was important.'

I had stopped filtering what was important from what was irrelevant. I was like a vacuum-cleaner, sucking up everything that came my way.

'What sort of treatment would they have in Denmark but not in Sweden?'

'Martin, there was absolutely no way I could have guessed this would be what you were most interested in. I've got no idea what illness it was, or what sort of treatment. My friend mentioned something about a transplant, but she didn't sound at all sure.'

'A transplant?' I said.

'Maybe from one of the parents to the boy,' Madeleine said.

'I doubt that,' I said. 'Sebbe was adopted. He came to Sweden as a baby, around the same time I started to look after Belle.'

'Do you think the illness is important? I'm not sure if I can find out any more, but I can ...'

'No,' I said quickly. 'No, definitely not. Your investigations stop right here, Madeleine. Is that understood?'

She was silent for a moment.

'Okay, understood,' she said eventually.

'Good,' I said.

My pulse was racing.

There was no way the illness could be relevant.

I looked helplessly at Lucy after I'd ended the call.

Could it?

'I don't know,' she said. 'I don't know anything any more.'

34

If there's one word I really like, it's roadtrip. It has no Swedish equivalent, which is a shame – the direct translation makes it sound incredibly dull. My last proper roadtrip had been through Texas. That was the last time I went to the States, in an attempt to be reconciled with my dad. It ended with me punching him. We never saw each other after that.

The roadtrip I had ahead of me now would take me from Stockholm to Denmark, with a stop in Malmö. To be honest, the word roadtrip was far too positive under the circumstances. This was more like going into exile. I was on the run in a new hire-car. I longed for the day when I wouldn't have to keep switching cars and phones. I longed for a day when everything would feel calm again.

The police are hardly ever as quick to react as they are in films. It would take them at least a day to realise that I'd disappeared. By that time I'd be across the Öresund Bridge, which itself would make it easy for the police to figure out where I was going. Always assuming that they managed to find the firm I had rented the car from. I jumped involuntarily every time I saw a police car on the road. I was terrified of not making it, of getting stopped before I had done what needed doing.

I had to get to Malmö.

I had to get to Denmark.

It's roughly six hundred kilometres from Stockholm to Malmö. I didn't want to draw attention to myself by driving too fast, so I stuck to the speed limit much more carefully than I usually do. Hour after hour I drove on and on through our elongated country. I passed towns I'd never been to and about which I felt not the slightest curiosity. I hate small towns. I remember one summer when I was a child. Marianne had hired a caravan. She, my sister and I meandered from campsite to campsite for at least two weeks. I remember it as a relatively untroubled time. Because Marianne was driving, she was forced to drink less than usual. But apart from that there wasn't much about that holiday that was fun. But Marianne did pretty well just by keeping herself sober.

I had an evening meal at a roadside diner. I joined the truck-drivers at the long tables and ate meatballs that tasted rubbery. I bought a bag of liquorice from the kiosk and got back in the car. Lucy loves chocolate, but I find liquorice far superior. So does Belle. Possibly just because I do, but I like the fact that we have something like that in common.

I called home to check that everything was alright and to say goodnight to Belle. Lucy sounded breathless when she picked up. Her voice was full of laughter.

'Crazy bedtime tonight?' I said.

'We've been messing about,' Lucy said. 'We needed it.'

I could have done with it too. I heard Belle sweeping

through the flat like a tornado in the background. It was a wonderful thing to hear.

'I just wanted to say goodnight,' I said.

Lucy gave the phone to Belle, but she wasn't really interested in talking to me. She hadn't sounded that happy in ages.

My heart felt lighter when I ended the call. As long as I knew Belle and Lucy were okay, I could concentrate fully on what lay ahead of me. First a stop in Malmö. Then another in Denmark. After that I would head home. And remain in hiding until everything was sorted out.

But things didn't turn out the way I had imagined. Perhaps I shouldn't have been surprised. Fate really hadn't been on my side over the previous few weeks. Even so, I felt disappointed as I stood outside our newfound witness's door and no one came to open it. I waited on the pavement outside for a long time, hoping that I might see movement in one of the windows. Maybe she was home, but was scared of being seen? Scared to open the door because she had no way of knowing if the person knocking was friend or foe? Unless she was abroad.

Damn.

I thought about the people I had told to leave Stockholm: Susanne, whose real name was Nadja; and Wolfgang. They had got away, hadn't they? I had to believe that, or I'd go mad.

It started to rain. That pretty much fits my image of the far south of Sweden, that it's always raining there. There and in Gothenburg. Lucy thinks I exaggerate, whereas I maintain I'm just saying what I see. It was almost half past eight. I hadn't booked a hotel in Denmark. I managed to get a room in a place on the motorway between Copenhagen and Roskilde. It was perfect. The following morning I would drive to Sjællands Odde and take the boat from there to Ebeltoft in Jutland, where Rebecca and Didrik lived. I was going to take the car with me. I ought to reach the Stihl family at around ten o'clock in the morning. Once I knew what I was looking for, it had been easy to track them down. Rebecca was a registered property-owner in Denmark, and there was no problem getting the address from the Danish authorities. Ebeltoft, fifty kilometres from Aarhus, a bizarre choice of location. Why not Copenhagen? That would have made Didrik's commute much easier.

It was just after midnight when I switched off the bedside lamp. I closed my eyes, lay back on the pillow and waited for sleep, without really believing that it was going to come.

35

SATURDAY–SUNDAY

How wrong I was. To my surprise, I fell asleep at once. And with sleep the nightmares came back. Worse than ever. This time I was being hunted like an animal through the pouring rain in an abandoned part of town. With every step I grew wearier and more scared. I knew I couldn't get away. I knew I was going to be shot.

I screamed when the shot was fired. That isn't what happened when I shot someone in real life. The bullet silenced him and he didn't make a sound. But in the dream I screamed. Loudly, desperately. Once again I was dragged through a grimy industrial wasteland. Once again I was buried alive. And once again I woke up in a cold sweat with a scream catching in my throat.

I'm never going to be whole again, I thought, as I kicked off the covers and went into the bathroom. Not as long as I fucking live.

The past kept me awake at night, and the present during the day. When the alarm-clock rang a few hours later I was lying wide awake, staring at the ceiling. My actions came automatically. I got in the shower. Turned the water on. Washed and dried myself. Found my shaving gear in the washbag. Brushed my teeth. Got dressed, left the room and paid at reception when I checked out.

'Has everything been okay?'

'Absolutely. I'd be happy to come back again.'

I would never come back. It wasn't the sort of hotel I usually stayed in, and it certainly wasn't in a location I passed particularly often. But I could hardly blame the guy in reception for that, so I kept my thoughts to myself. Instead I did what I guessed all his other guests did: paid and went on my way. Got in the car and drove off.

It was eighty kilometres to Sjællands Odde. I don't remember what I thought on the way there. Perhaps I reflected upon the fact that the first part of the journey passed quickly on a wide motorway, but that the later stretch, on narrow roads, took much longer. Perhaps I thought about the sun, which was only intermittently visible, and when it did appear the grass became much greener, the sea much bluer, the road greyer. Or perhaps I didn't think about anything at all. I had ended up in an intellectual dead-end. A Gordian knot of the mind. I gave up trying to disentangle any further thoughts and theories. Didrik could take over and do the groundwork, voluntarily or under duress. I wasn't going to give up until he told me what he knew. What he was up to.

And not until I had found Mio, who had been taken from his preschool by Rakel, a former friend of his mother's. How the hell had she dodged being dragged into the investigations into both Mio's disappearance and Sara's escape? Everyone else seemed to have been included.

There was a brisk wind blowing as I made the brief crossing from Sjællands Odde to Ebeltoft. The catamaran swayed back and forth. People queued for coffee and sandwiches, but I just sat in my seat looking out at the sea. Belle would have loved it. She loves any sort of boat, and is at her happiest at sea. Her grandfather used to say he'd never met a child with such a lack of fear for water. My heart ached at the thought of Belle's grandfather. He had been the only member of my brother-in-law's family that I liked. I would keep his memory alive for Belle. Tell her what he did with his life, and what made him such a good person.

We docked and I drove off the boat. Didrik's house was on the coast, a few kilometres from the centre of Ebeltoft. It didn't take more than five minutes to drive there from the harbour. Although I don't really remember much about what I was thinking as I approached his house, I'm very sure of how I felt.

My whole body was shaking and my hands were slippery with sweat. I stopped the car a few houses away. On one side of the road a large, beautiful meadow spread out. On the other was a row of houses. Didrik's was the last one.

Was he there? Was *anyone* there? I had met Rebecca in Stockholm earlier that week, after all. Perhaps the house was empty. Perhaps the whole family was in Stockholm.

My heart was pounding so hard it was hitting my ribs. It was a deeply unpleasant feeling and for a moment I thought I was going to have a full-blown heart attack. It felt like a bad strategic move to have no one but Didrik to rely on if that was indeed the case. I fumbled with clumsy fingers through my stock of mobile phones to find one I could call Lucy on.

I'm dying, baby. Look after Belle.

That made me pull myself together. I beat my hands against the steering-wheel, angry and upset at my own weakness. Like hell was I going to die sitting in a car in the middle of the Danish countryside. Like hell was I going to die before I'd found out what Didrik was hiding. Perhaps I'd been completely misinformed. Perhaps Didrik was nowhere near as significant a figure as I imagined. But he must have something to say. Because otherwise I had no one left to turn to. Rakel had vanished, and the rest were dead.

It was those words, those thoughts that finally made me open the car door and get out. I wasn't having a heart attack. My pulse rate sank, the palms of my hands dried out. With a firm gesture I closed the car door and pressed the button on the key to lock it. I like to think that my back and neck were upright as I walked towards Didrik's house. And I know I thought I was ready for whatever I was going to see or find out. I even thought there was no way I was going to be surprised.

Stupid. Very stupid.

The house was a traditional red wooden building. It had white detailing and a hipped roof. The walls of the ground floor were full of large windows. That was how I first caught sight of them from the road. I could see them right through the house. They were sitting at the back eating breakfast. The sun was shining and the wind was nowhere near as blustery as it had been out at sea. Didrik and Rebecca were seated opposite each other, each peeling an egg. Next to them, and opposite one another, sat two people I didn't recognise. They seemed to be roughly the same age as me. Visiting friends? Or neighbours?

It was such an idyllic day. I couldn't see anyone else about. That both pleased and troubled me. Seclusion was good. But sadly not only for me, but also for Didrik.

The moment had arrived. It couldn't be put off any longer. And, like the fighter I had become, armed with nothing stronger than my own intellect, I marched straight into Didrik's garden. There was no hesitation in my stride. I just walked, like a machine. As I walked round the house, Rebecca was in the middle of saying something that seemed to amuse the others at the table. She had her back to me, and therefore didn't see me approach. But Didrik did. The expression on his face changed so abruptly that I had to force myself to carry on walking, as if nothing had happened. First, a look that clearly showed he was so shocked to see me that he didn't actually recognise me. Then astonishment and surprise. And finally fury. But I just kept walking.

'Hello,' I said. 'Sorry to intrude on a Saturday morning like this.'

Rebecca got to her feet almost unbelievably fast. I smiled at her apologetically, then took my time looking around me.

'Lovely place you've got here.'

It was a huge garden, at least one hundred metres long. It stretched all the way to the sea.

The other couple at the table were staring at me in silence, unsure how to interpret their hosts' reaction. I helped them.

'Sorry,' I said. 'I should have introduced myself. My name's Martin Benner, I'm an old acquaintance of Didrik and Rebecca.'

I shook hands with the woman first, then the man. They both smiled warmly. They spoke unusually intelligible

Danish, presumably tailored to an audience of Swedes. They said it was nice to meet me. I reciprocated. Then Didrik tried to interrupt my charade.

'Martin, what can we do for you?'

'Quite a lot,' I said.

I raised my eyebrows pointedly.

'Perhaps we should go inside?' Didrik said.

'Don't bother on my account,' I said.

We were interrupted by children's voices. They were both talking Danish, but one had a Swedish accent. One was a boy, the other a girl. They came racing out of the bushes beneath a large apple tree some distance away. The girl was running first, dressed up as an Indian. The boy, the same colour as me, raced after her. Sebbe. He didn't look like there was anything wrong with him. I felt a wave of relief. Didrik didn't beat his child. And the boy didn't look ill, either. Everything seemed fine.

'It's fantastic,' the Danish woman said with a broad smile. 'He looks so well!'

I looked at Didrik and Rebecca with concern.

'Has he been unwell?' I said. 'I'm sorry to hear that, I didn't know.'

'Martin, let's go inside now.'

It was only for the neighbours' sake that he didn't raise his voice. I didn't move a muscle. I just stared at the running children, racing through the park-like garden like rockets. The boy's steps were quick and lithe.

'I'm going to get you now!' he cried to the girl.

But he didn't. In fact he missed her by several metres.

'Ha!' the girl said, and turned round.

She was running back towards the water now. Sebbe set

off after her. No one runs faster than a man who's been humiliated.

And no one takes greater risks than someone who hasn't got much to lose. I saw his feet pound the grass, his blue shirt blowing in the wind. And I just knew.

'Mio!' I shouted. 'Mio!'

He stopped abruptly. So suddenly that he fell down. Slowly he turned round and looked at me. His eyes were big and wide-open.

'Daddy?' he said.

36

'Christ, Martin, that's enough!'

Didrik's voice was a warning, so loud and clear that no one could possibly mistake it. Not even the children. The girl stopped running and turned to look at the adults.

Didrik waved to them.

'It's okay,' he said, and tried to smile. 'We've just got a grown-up thing to sort out here.'

But the boy was already on his way over to us.

'Are you my daddy?' he said. 'Are you?'

His words breathed life into some terrible childhood memories. I didn't see my father once when I was growing up. I lived with my very blonde mother and my equally blonde sister, and every time I saw a black man in the street I thought: Could that be him? Until I reached the age of ten I was obsessed by the idea that my dad was out there somewhere, that I could find him if I just made enough of an effort. It never happened. No matter how hard I looked, or however many people I asked, I never found him.

Rebecca ran to meet the boy.

'Sebbe, he's just a man we know. He isn't your daddy.'

The neighbours stared from Didrik to Rebecca with their mouths gaping. Didrik tried to explain what they'd just seen.

'Of course you know he's adopted,' he said. 'He's clearly at the age where he wants to know more about his background.'

'And his name,' I said.

If looks could kill, I'd have reached my last breath several seconds ago. My heart was pounding like a steam-hammer, but I was still alive.

'Mummy, what's going on?' the girl asked.

'Nothing, I think,' the woman said, and glanced anxiously at Didrik.

'Absolutely nothing,' Didrik said in the same tone of voice he had just used on me.

His tone caused a reaction in his visitors. No one likes feeling threatened. The man stood up.

'I think we'll be going now,' he said. 'Thanks for the coffee.'

The woman stood up as well. The girl ran over to her and took her hand. Rebecca was still standing on the grass with her arms round Mio. She looked horrified.

The neighbours thanked her. I wondered if they'd ever come back.

'I'll explain another day,' Didrik said.

He was evidently more optimistic than me.

The neighbours disappeared. As did Rebecca. Holding the boy by the hand, she vanished into the house.

'What are you going to explain, Didrik?' I said when we were alone. 'Because, speaking purely for myself, I'd much rather not wait until another day.'

Didrik was standing motionless with his hands in his trouser pockets. His gaze was fixed on a point far out in the water. His ribcage rose and fell in time with his breathing. In and out, in and out. He looked the way he always did. Like a pleasant, affluent man in the prime of life. Warm and open. Not like a sadistic child-beater, or a murderer.

I didn't like the silence that had arisen.

'That wasn't Sebbe,' I said, to break it.

At last Didrik looked away from the sea.

'What do you know about that? You don't give a damn about children. You hardly care about your own.'

I let the insult pass.

'True,' I said. 'I don't know what Sebbe looks like. But I have, despite your efforts to prevent it, seen pictures of Mio. And unlike other people, I can tell one black child from the other. That lad on the grass was Sara Texas's son. So what have you done with your own?' The clicking sound came from the left, from inside the house. I had no trouble recognising it, and I knew exactly what I was going to see when I instinctively turned my head.

'You need to leave now.'

Rebecca was standing in the doorway with a rifle in her hand. She was remarkably calm. So, to my immense surprise, was I.

'Are you stupid?' I said. 'You're going to shoot me here? Unarmed? Sober and in daylight, in the middle of a residential area?'

I shook my head and before she had time to think about what I was doing, I sat down on one of the chairs at the table. It had a high back that reached all the way to the hair on the back of my head. I leaned back comfortably.

'Go on, then,' I said. 'Shoot me as I sit here. But you'll have to explain it to the police afterwards. Why you shot me while I was sitting at your breakfast table.'

'They won't find you.'

She came closer. Didrik watched what was going on without intervening. But I could see that he was far from sure if he liked the turn things had taken.

I thought about everyone else who had died. Sooner or later they had turned up, and so would I. Rebecca took a few more steps towards me. There was no sign of the boy. I sat calmly where I was.

'It's probably best if you stop now,' I said. 'You'll never be able to explain to the police why you shot me with a rifle from a distance of less than a metre.'

Then Didrik walked over to Rebecca. Gently he put one hand on her shoulder.

'That's enough. I'll take care of this.'

'I don't think so.'

Her words provoked Didrik. Quickly and roughly, he tried to grab the rifle. She refused to let go, and went with him. Her scream echoed across the neighbourhood.

'Let go of me! Damn it, let go of me!'

Then the boy appeared again. He was standing in the doorway with tears running down his cheeks. I felt a pang in my chest. It was Mio, alright. There was no doubt about it.

Rebecca caught sight of him too.

'Hello, sweetie, I thought I told you to wait indoors.'

At last she let go of the weapon. Didrik tried to hide it behind his back. Completely idiotic. You can't fool children with silly tricks like that. They see what there is to see, then demand an explanation.

Rebecca's eyes were full of tears as she walked back into the house. She picked the boy up in her arms and he sobbed silently against her shoulder.

Didrik and I were left alone again. With the minor difference that he was now armed. I'm happy to admit that it bothered me.

'Aren't you going to sit down?' I said.

'Rebecca was right. You need to leave now. And I need to call the police.'

'Really?' I said.

I said it more quietly than I had imagined. Did he really think they could get away with this?

'No one's going to believe you,' Didrik said, as if he could read my mind. 'No one.'

I couldn't understand his reasoning, because I had proof. There were pictures of Mio. And there were DNA tests. There'd be no problem proving that Mio was Sara Texas's son. I said as much to Didrik.

'And there's also his father,' I concluded.

Those words made Didrik start.

'He doesn't want him.'

'Yes – he does. That's why I'm here.'

Didrik laughed.

'You don't know what you're talking about, Martin.'

He sat down with the rifle across his lap.

He rubbed his face with his hands. People have done that for aeons. Tried to massage tiredness away by rubbing their face. It doesn't work.

It was a bewildering scene to take in. We were sitting in a delightful garden with the sea in the background. It could have been idyllic. But it was actually hell.

'Did you kill your own son, Didrik?' I said.

He jerked as if I'd punched him in the face.

'What the hell are you talking about?'

I held my arms out. I wasn't sure of anything. Maybe Didrik did hit children.

'I know everything,' I said. 'I know you moved because you'd been reported to Social Services. I know about the terrible bruises. And how happy you were when you changed preschools. And then you moved here.'

Didrik's jaw dropped. He opened and closed his mouth several times before he managed to say anything sensible.

'Is that what people are saying?' he said. 'Is that what you've heard?'

'Yes,' I said. 'And that's not all I've heard. Someone told me Sebbe was ill. Seriously ill.'

'Who said that?'

'I've talked to a number of different people. Discreetly, to stop anyone else having to die. I talked to Sebbe's own godfather, for instance. Your best friend.'

It was a ridiculous gambit. Herman hadn't said a word about Didrik's alleged abuse of Sebastian.

'He's not my best friend. But his wife used to be Rebecca's. Until she fell for the same crazy stories as you. Of course she changed her mind when she found out how ill Sebbe was, but by then we'd already cut off all contact. Herman probably never really understood that, sadly. I'm sure he still thinks of me as a good friend. He and his wife live what one might call separate lives.'

I leaned forward and rested my elbows on the cool tabletop.

'So tell me, then,' I said. 'Where's Sebbe?'

Didrik could no longer look me in the eye. He looked at the trees, the grass, the sky, but not at me.

'He died.'

'You killed him?'

'Are you really that stupid?'

Didrik got to his feet with a roar. The rifle fell to the ground. I forced myself not to move. So it was true, what Madeleine had said: Sebbe had been ill, not abused.

'I didn't kill my own son,' Didrik whispered.

He was panting as if he'd run a marathon in stifling heat.

'And I didn't kill Jenny, Bobby, Fredrik or Elias,' I said. 'Or anyone else.'

I tried to hold my voice steady.

Didrik shook his head.

'Sebbe was suffering from an extremely aggressive form of cancer, which was diagnosed far, far too late. In Sweden they didn't even want to try to treat him with anything other than palliative care.'

I don't know what I'd expected to hear, but this wasn't it. Astonished, I listened to a story I had little reason to doubt.

'They take a different view here in Denmark,' Didrik said. 'They had some new medication that was still at the trial stage, and they were willing to test it on him.'

'So you sold your house to fund the treatment?'

'The Swedish authorities weren't prepared to pay for it. We didn't have time to persuade them to change their minds. And of course we knew we could actually get hold of the money.'

'Couldn't you just mortgage the house?'

Didrik looked away.

'No. We knew we'd be staying in Denmark ... for a while. To start with we lived in Copenhagen, where Sebbe received his treatment. Then we moved here. Rebecca lived in Aarhus for several years at the start of her career. That's why the Danish authorities accepted her as a property-owner.'

'Where did he die?'

'Here in Ebeltoft.'

'When?'

'In November. Only a few months after we found out he was sick. By then he'd already been unwell for a while, but everything was delayed by the bizarre distraction of those claims that his problems weren't the result of illness but because his parents were monsters.'

I didn't know where to start. This was too big, too implausible. Implausible was the word that stayed with me. Sebbe had died in November. The same month Sara Texas took her own life and her son disappeared.

'You replaced one child with another. Do you have any idea how sick that is?'

Didrik slumped in his chair.

'You really don't have a very high opinion of me, do you?' he said.

I swallowed hard.

'You've kidnapped a child. Murdered at least four people. How high should my opinion of you be?'

Didrik took his time before he replied. Perhaps he didn't have a very high opinion of himself any more. A sleepy wasp mounted an attack on us. I knocked it aside with my hand and saw it fall to the ground. Tired fighters fall fast, I concluded.

'I didn't kidnap him.'

The words were so light, weighed absolutely nothing individually. But together they were dynamite.

'Sorry?'

He looked me right in the eye.

'I made a promise to save him. A promise that was actually forced upon me, but that no longer matters. Never in my worst nightmares could I have imagined that everything would turn out like this.'

My mouth felt dry as dust.

'Who was it, Didrik? Who the hell made you promise to save Mio?'

His voice was barely audible when he replied.

'Sara. I promised his mother, Sara.'

37

It's often said that grown men like to do things together. That we find loneliness harder than women. Didrik and I left his wonderful garden and walked down to the shore. And there we took a walk. Like two people who didn't want to be alone.

'Sara came round to our house,' Didrik said. 'Back when everything was just starting, after my colleagues and I had been contacted by the Americans and we'd held our first interview with her. It was evening, and it was raining. She banged so hard on the door that I thought she was going to break it in. When I opened it she was standing there on the step with the boy's hand in hers. "I'm going to end up in prison," she said. "And someone has to look after my son."'

'Pretty epic,' I said.

Didrik went on: 'That sort of move isn't exactly common. There was also one rather sensitive detail that I had thus far managed to keep hidden from my esteemed colleagues.'

'That Sebbe and Mio went to the same preschool.'

'Exactly. Rebecca did most of the dropping off and

picking up in Flemingsberg, but I went a few times. We'd bumped into Sara, even though our children weren't in the same class. It's a ruddy big preschool, loads of kids. Mio and Sebbe were the same age, but in different groups. We thought that was a shame, because Sebbe used to talk about Mio at home. They used to play together when all the children were outside. We tried to invite Sara and Mio round to ours several times, but it was always so hard to pin her down. There was work and studying and laundry and God knows what else.'

'Her life was chaotic?'

'No, more just unfocused. We understood that something wasn't right, but to be honest our guesses came nowhere close to the truth, I can tell you.'

My feet sank into the sand. It was getting harder and harder to walk.

'The truth, you say,' I said.

'Yes. Do you think you know anything about that?'

'I'm pretty sure I do, so I'd have to say yes.'

Didrik brushed his rather too long fringe from his eyes. That's one downside of having a fancy haircut based on the idea of it always being exactly the right length. It loses its elegance after just a week or so.

'So, tell me,' Didrik said. 'Tell me how far you've got.'

'I'm afraid I can't. I had to swear not to reveal anything to the police. I don't think the person who extracted that promise would care to differentiate between talking to the police and what I'm doing now.'

'Interesting. Who did you make such a stupid promise to?'

His voice was calmer now, his earlier agitation had almost literally blown away.

'It's rather in the nature of the beast that I can't reveal that either.'

Didrik sighed.

'Let me guess. Lucifer?'

I stopped. Didrik nodded and carried on walking. I hurried after him.

'If you know who Lucifer is, then you also know that Sara didn't commit those murders.'

'Of course,' Didrik said.

'So why not reveal what he's been doing? Is it because of Mio? If only you'd left me alone and hadn't tried to frame me for those murders. Then you'd have had the case solved. You'd ...'

'Yeah, why not keep telling me what else I could have done? You fucking idiot. What makes you think that you and I are in fundamentally different positions, and that I don't know what you know?'

I couldn't walk another metre. Like a child, I sat down on my backside in the sand.

Didrik followed my example, but far more smoothly than I had just done. That was always one of the differences between us. He wasn't just elegant on the surface like I was. Didrik was the real deal. Stylish, down to his very marrow.

'Let's take it from the start,' I said. 'Sara came to see you after that first interview. She knew she was going to be found guilty of murder and she wanted to find a solution for Mio. Is that how I should understand what you're saying?'

'Yes. I assumed she came to see me because I was in the police, because Rebecca and I had been kind to her, and because I conducted that first interview with her. She realised I was going to be along for the rest of the ride as well.

She believed that Rebecca and I would be both willing and in a position to help her son.'

'So you said straight away that you and Rebecca could take him? How noble.'

'It's difficult to summarise the story so long afterwards. Sara had no idea of the position we were in, that Sebbe wasn't well and that we were fighting tooth and nail to get him treated. She stayed with us until early the next morning, talking and talking. I told her she was foolish to be so frightened. If she was innocent, she wouldn't be convicted. The story she told us, dear God, I'd never heard anything like it.'

'But you believed her?'

'No, I didn't. But I realised that she was very, very upset. I even toyed with the idea that she might be guilty. That that was why she had come to see me, so that afterwards, if the evidence changed, she'd be able to say: "I told you this would happen." Then everything unfolded horribly quickly. Overnight there was suddenly a mountain of evidence, and at the same time she made her confession. She was charged and remanded in custody, and Mio was placed with foster parents.'

He fell silent.

'Tell me how you went from thinking Sara was lying to believing her, and then also taking responsibility for her son.'

Didrik swallowed.

'That ... that may not have been entirely voluntary,' he said. 'Not to start with. Look, Rebecca and I have never been able to have children. We used to dream of having four kids, but we weren't able to have a single one. It took years to adopt Sebbe. We both turned forty a couple of years ago.

If we'd wanted to adopt another child, we were starting to run out of time. Early last year we tried to get going with another adoption application. But then that fucking report of abuse appeared out of nowhere just a month or so later. I feel nothing but contempt towards an awful lot of people involved in that. The preschool staff who wouldn't listen, the doctors who didn't take us seriously when we asked for help. Because of course we knew we hadn't hit Sebbe, that there was something else wrong. He was tired, in pain, and there were those marks on his skin that the preschool staff said were bruises. But the weeks passed and we didn't get any help. It was a seriously fucking thin silver lining when the doctors here in Denmark told us that there had never been any "in time" for Sebbe. We might have been able to get a few more months with him, but there was never any chance of anything better than that.'

Didrik stopped to catch his breath, take a pause in the story of how his life fell apart.

'Sara came and asked for help just after we found out that Sebbe was sick. I didn't believe her. Not until she was remanded in custody, and there was another knock on our door.'

'Jenny or Bobby came to see you,' I said.

'Wrong. Lucifer.'

It was like falling through ice and finding yourself in astonishingly cold water.

'Sorry?' I said. 'I can't believe that. Lucifer would never come in person. He'd send an envoy.'

'You'd think so. But not on that occasion. I don't have much reason to think that I misunderstood something as important as that. But I did make the mistake of reacting the same way as you at first. Seeing as he was armed, I had to let him in. He was standing on the front step with a gun in his hand. I was alone in the house. We sat down in the living room. He explained how he wanted everything to play out, and warned me against involving my colleagues in what I had heard and what was coming my way. It was Sara who led him to me. She didn't realise how closely he was watching her at the time. After that first interview with the police she never took another step without being watched.'

'What exactly did Lucifer want?'

'For me to take care of Mio.'

'But . . .'

'I refused, said it couldn't happen the way he wanted. He'd worked out that it would be impossible to take Mio back to the USA, and was therefore asking for my help. First I was to abduct him. Then hide him. And then, once everything had calmed down, fly to the States with him and hand him over to Lucifer.'

'You refused, of course?'

'Obviously. I pointed out that it was impossible to travel anywhere with a child who was the subject of a nationwide search. But as you know by now, not much is voluntary when it comes to Lucifer. He thought Mio could travel on Sebbe's passport, more or less the way people-traffickers work. You travel using the passport of someone you resemble. When I said I wasn't going to cooperate with him, he asked me where Rebecca and Sebbe were. I said something vague, like "Out doing something". In actual fact they were at the doctor's. Lucifer grinned and said, "Call them". So I did.'

Dark clouds were rolling towards us from the sea. There

was rain on the way, possibly even a storm. I was freezing, but couldn't have cared less.

'They didn't answer,' I said quietly.

'Oh, but they did. Rebecca was crying like a child and Sebbe was screaming in the background. Lucifer took the phone from me and told me he'd be back in three days. By then I needed to decide what I was going to do, whether I was going to cooperate or not. If not, Rebecca and Sebbe would die. And if I accepted, I would get them back the same day. I was utterly fucking terrified. I demanded their immediate return, said he could have everything he wanted. He refused to negotiate. I would be without my family for three days, no more, no less. It was a complete nightmare. I had the sense that he was absolutely everywhere, that he knew everyone. Obviously I know what you're supposed to do if you're blackmailed. Always, always contact the police. But that simply wasn't possible. Because I knew he wasn't messing about. If it came to it, he wouldn't hesitate for a second to murder my wife and child. And he'd get away with it. I realised that from what Sara had told me. Not that I ever shared her story with anyone else.'

Didrik's eyes were dark as he looked at me.

'Those days without Rebecca and Sebbe were the longest in my life. When Lucifer called to ask what I wanted to do, I would have given him anything. I shouted down the phone that I'd do everything he wanted if I could just have Rebecca and Sebbe back. They were dumped at a rest area on the motorway just north of Stockholm. Rebecca couldn't walk. She'd been beaten black and blue. I took her to A&E and said she'd been attacked in the city. But of course the doctors could see that some of the injuries were several days old. So they reported me for abuse. There was an investigation, but it was dropped. Rebecca said she'd fallen down the stairs. Caught her hand in the car door. Got attacked in the street. By then we'd already started planning our move to Denmark. It was only a matter of weeks before we were off; having cash from the sale of the house worked miracles. In Sweden, Sara's case rumbled on. Under any other circumstances I'd have abandoned work and taken some time off to be with my family. But after Lucifer's visit I didn't dare to; I needed to keep an eye on how Sara's case developed. I didn't know she was planning to run. She called me from a phone that came up as unidentified: it later turned out to be a pay-as-you-go mobile. "Can you take Mio?" she sobbed. "You have to take him! To stop his father finding him.'"

The memories seemed to overwhelm Didrik, and he started to cry. I hadn't had any idea that he had also been accused of wife-beating.

'She didn't know Lucifer had contacted you?' I said, astonished at what I was hearing.

'No, and I spared her from that. I said she had to hand herself in to the police, but obviously she wasn't interested in doing that. Her life was over, finished. The only thing she wanted, all she needed to know, was that Mio would be safe. So I gave her my word. I promised to do my best.'

'I heard that Sara's friend Jenny had travelled to Sweden to look after Mio,' I said.

'That may be so, but if she did it was without Sara's knowledge.'

'As I understand it, it was a plan they'd come up with together.'

'I'm not sure I can believe that.'

So Lucifer's envoy had filled my head with shit when he called to give me the task of finding Mio. Not that there was anything odd about that, seeing as he'd lied about everything else.

'Okay, so you promised to do your best. Together with Rakel?'

He looked surprised when I mentioned Rakel's name.

'Yes,' he said. 'She was a friend of Sara's, and it was Sara's idea that she should help. After she abducted Mio she looked after him for a few days. I think she wanted him for herself. But that was never an option. She wouldn't have been able to protect him.'

I remembered my own encounters with Rakel. Remembered the sex.

'She was a very loyal friend to Sara, that Rakel,' I said.

'You have your weaknesses,' Didrik said.

'Were you worried the stuff about the Porsche wouldn't be enough? Was that why you needed my DNA?'

I refused to say the word sperm. Refused.

'The first time it was just about finding out how much you knew,' Didrik said. 'Rakel was already up to her eyes in shit – it didn't take much to persuade her to do what she had to do. But things had changed before the second time you met a few days later. Basically, it was absolutely vital that you got caught. So getting hold of some of your DNA was a good idea.'

Madness, I thought. As well as repugnant.

'And you had to drag Herman into this mess as well?'

'Herman is a man with very few friends. Rakel needed somewhere else to stay, and his little summer cottage was ideal. At first we thought we'd be able to hide Mio there when the time came, but that plan soon fell apart. Herman wanted the house back so he could sell it.'

'So Rakel got the terraced house in Solna instead?'

'I don't know about "got". She was already looking for a place when she was staying out in Årsta havsbad. A summer cottage with so-called "summer water" and a chemical toilet is hardly a permanent solution, after all.'

I changed tack.

'You snatched Mio the same day Sara disappeared,' I said.

Didrik nodded.

'That wasn't the plan, originally, but all the commotion meant that it was a good opportunity. That was a terrible, terrible day.'

Didrik rubbed his chin with his hand. It started to rain and we stood up. We were walking into the wind as we headed back towards Didrik's house.

'And then Sebbe died,' I said.

'Yes.'

'And Mio became Sebbe? Because no one would notice if you replaced one black kid with another?'

Didrik snorted.

'Of course they would. That was why we had to stay here, where no one knows us. Mio needed a new identity, so he assumed Sebbe's. That was the simplest solution.'

I didn't buy that. There was something Didrik wasn't telling me.

'But didn't Sebbe have grandparents who'd want to see their grandson regularly?' I said. 'Or other relatives?'

'I haven't actually had any contact with my parents since I inherited my grandmother's amazing house,' Didrik said. 'Rebecca's father is dead, and her mum had a stroke just over a year ago. She hasn't been right since then. We've both got brothers and sisters, but we fell out with them, partly on purpose, when we moved to Denmark. They seriously thought we should give up the dream of saving Sebbe. Because of course the doctors were all saying it was hopeless, so we were only prolonging his suffering by trying to find new solutions abroad.'

'Siblings can be bastards,' I said helpfully, even though I had never thought of my sister in those terms. Her husband was a different story, though.

'True,' Didrik said.

But I still didn't understand.

'Why turn Mio into Sebbe? I mean, you knew – still know – that Lucifer will demand to have him back. Is he going to – and I'm sorry for the choice of words – die again? Really? Wouldn't it have been easier to give him a different name? Besides, here in Denmark Sebbe is officially dead.'

'You've got a lot of questions,' Didrik said. 'Rebecca and Sebbe are registered at an address in Malmö, mostly to keep the Danish authorities and Stockholm Council off our backs. You see, Sebbe isn't officially dead in either Denmark or Sweden. He died at home, here in Ebeltoft, and we never registered his death. We told the hospital in Copenhagen that we'd taken him home to Sweden once it was clear that their treatment wasn't helping him. And we told the hospital in Stockholm that Sebbe was still being treated in Denmark. But we stayed here and let him die in his new home. That was the only way for Mio to assume his identity. By keeping Sebbe's death a secret.'

As a plan it was so full of holes that it could have capsized at any moment. All the same, it evidently hadn't done so.

Didrik carried on with life in Stockholm while Rebecca lived in Denmark as a full-time mum, initially to a dying child, then to a child who had made a miraculous recovery.

'Doesn't Mio suffer from epilepsy?' I said.

'Yes. We've found a doctor here who prescribes his medication. It's pretty straightforward.'

I stopped. The rain stung my face. I needed to gather my thoughts. Didrik's torrent of words and information contained something that had passed me by completely.

Something crucial.

Didrik had taken Mio because Lucifer forced him to.

So why the hell had I been told to find the missing child?

'Lucifer,' I said hoarsely. 'It sounds like you've had plenty of contact with him.'

'More than I'd like.'

'So he knows where you live? He knows where Mio is?'

'Yes.'

I shook my head. This was a whole new level of madness. It didn't make sense. It *mustn't* make sense.

'You're going to have to hand him back,' I said.

'No, Martin, we're not going to do that. We've bought our freedom.'

'How the fuck have you done that, if you don't mind me asking?'

Didrik looked out over the sea. His face was pale and taut.

'I picked up Mio in Stockholm one week before Sebbe died,' he said. 'Seven days from hell. By then we'd left Copenhagen and moved into this house. We hid Mio and Sebbe from the outside world. I can't even begin to describe how lonely Mio must have felt then. Because of course

Rebecca and I were fully occupied with Sebbe. It was terrible. Terrible! We sat up all night after Sebbe died, talking about what to do. You have no idea ... you can't even begin to imagine ... the extent of the self-loathing ... and the grief ... nothing but absolute blackness. And, in the midst of all that: Mio. It ... it was Lucifer who forced us to give him Sebbe's identity. To make it easier to move him, so to speak. In spite of all the new problems that caused. We relented, after a lot of anguish. Today I'm quite pleased it turned out that way. It was an opportunity that was never going to come again, if I can put it like that.'

So Lucifer was the brains behind the idea of turning Mio into Sebbe. I should have realised.

Over the previous few weeks I had told anyone who was prepared to listen that I didn't know Didrik very well. I barely knew his son's name, I'd never been to his home. But the word 'know' has many meanings. I thought I knew Didrik in the sense that he was predictable. Now I knew that wasn't the case. There were so many aspects of his story that I wanted to talk about that I hardly knew where to start.

'Where did you bury him?'

Didrik shivered when he replied.

'In the garden. Under the apple tree,' he said.

His voice was only a whisper away from cracking.

I didn't want to hear any more. It was the notion of it being 'an opportunity' that was the problem. I had missed something in Didrik's story. Something he had already said. 'We're not going to hand him back.'

'Lucifer was in no rush to have Mio,' Didrik said. 'Not at first. Several months passed, and spring came. Then he began to get impatient, and wanted his son. I kept coming

38

It was hard to get Didrik to say what 'he wants you' meant in definite terms. But I did at least realise that from the moment I first showed up on their radar, Didrik's task had been to put a stop to me, and try to tie me to the crimes that Sara had been accused of committing. As he himself put it: 'It wouldn't have been difficult to persuade a prosecutor that Sara hadn't committed those crimes on her own.'

I assumed it would have happened the same way Sara had been framed before me, with fake evidence and forced confessions. But then, almost immediately, completely new crimes popped up that I could be framed for. Bobby and Jenny's murders changed everything. But that was a conclusion I drew for myself. Didrik talked less about what he had actually done, and rather more about what he thought Lucifer and I had done.

Neither Lucifer nor his representative had called me so much as one single time since I started to look for Mio. And I had no way of contacting them. But Didrik did. When we got back to the house I wasn't keen to go inside.

'Don't worry,' Didrik said. 'Killing you isn't part of our task.'

'No? You've already killed plenty of other people,' I said.

Didrik looked away and stepped aside as if to let me go past, into the house. But I stayed where I was.

'Okay, in that case I'll make the call,' he said.

'Who to?'

'Lucifer. I'm supposed to call him if and when you showed up.'

But he didn't make the call. Instead he said: 'You do realise why you were instructed to look for Mio, don't you? You needed to be kept active; the police's preliminary investigation needed new fuel. So that I had something to pin you down for.'

I stood there paralysed. *If I could only realise how Lucifer and I knew each other.* Pastor Parson's burial flashed past. I was convinced that played an important role. *But in what way?*

'Are you going to stand out there in the rain, or are you coming in?'

Reluctantly I went inside with him.

'What happens now?' I said.

'I have to call him,' Didrik said. 'I have to.'

He took out a mobile phone and started fiddling with it.

'Don't do it,' I said.

'Sorry, but . . .'

'I'm sorry too,' I said. 'Fucking sorry, even. But you're not calling Lucifer to tell him I'm here. That I've found Mio. Don't you understand that it's over for all of us if you do?'

I was clutching for the feeblest of straws now, but what choice did I have?

'If you make that call, I'm finished,' I said. 'And so are you. The plan is either that we both end up in prison, or else you're signing our death warrants by telling him I've succeeded in what I was forced to do – finding Mio, and whoever was trying to frame me for murder. This is a game. Don't you realise that? He's got us both.'

'My deal with Lucifer is done,' Didrik said. 'I've got nothing to worry about.'

But that didn't seem to be entirely true, because he was still hesitating.

'Go on, then, call!' a voice said behind him.

Rebecca stepped out from the shadows.

'Make the call,' she said. 'Now!'

'Keen to put an end to this, Rebecca?' I said.

'More than anything.'

'There is no end!' I shouted as loudly as my lungs would let me. 'Don't either of you get it? How can you live a normal life after all that's happened? How can you live with everything Didrik's done? Sorry, Rebecca, but if you haven't worked it out, your husband's the one who carried out all the murders he's trying to pin on me.'

Rebecca pulled her kaftan tight around her.

'No, he isn't,' she said.

'How interesting,' I said. 'So who killed them, then? Lucifer?'

The silence that arose was more fragile that antique porcelain. I had no response to the answer I got.

'I did,' Rebecca said.

'You?'

She nodded.

'I was the one who started it all. So it's my fault that Didrik had to carry on.'

Her face was paler and more haggard than any I had ever seen. The same could almost be said about Didrik's. The things our lies do to us. I thought I knew a fair bit about that, but Rebecca and Didrik knew infinitely more. Everything had slipped from their grasp. The life they had known was gone, in the past. Things would never be the same again.

'It was an accident,' Didrik said.

Rebecca nodded frenetically.

'It was,' she said. 'It was.'

I almost burst out laughing.

'For fuck's sake, you can't call murdering four people "an accident"? They didn't even die at the same bloody time!'

Rebecca clapped her hands over her face and turned away.

'I'm sorry, but I can't handle this right now,' she said.

She ran upstairs and disappeared into one of the rooms. A door slammed shut.

'Perhaps you can manage a bit better?' I said to Didrik. 'Let's talk about something easy. Exactly when were you told by Lucifer to stop me poking about for the truth about Sara Texas?'

'I can probably manage, but I'm not sure I really want to. The same day you called me and wanted to meet up to talk about Sara. That was pretty much the last conversation on the planet I wanted to have with anyone. And that you of all people should have started thinking about Sara's fate . . . Lucifer had given me a number to call in emergencies, if there was ever a problem concerning him or Mio. I called it as soon as I'd spoken to you. It would have been disastrous if he'd found out afterwards and it looked like I'd gone behind his back.'

'Of course,' I said. 'Good that you know where your loyalties lie.'

Didrik went on: 'You're clever, Martin. Smart. So I started to keep an eye on what you were up to. You and everyone else I was worried about. When Jenny showed up it was pretty much time to act. I kept Rebecca informed of what was going on. Big fucking mistake. I hadn't really understood how damaged she was. Or how scared. I had enough on my hands dealing with my own grief, my own terror. Those were things I . . . we couldn't share. I contacted Bobby and Jenny later that evening and arranged to meet them a few hours later, in the middle of the night. I didn't have any trouble persuading them; we'd been in touch before when I was in charge of the Sara Texas case and I let them think something had happened that radically altered the police's view of what had taken place. The fact that I refused to answer any questions over the phone and implied that we had to meet at night only made them even more eager. My plan was to lay more or less all my cards on the table when we actually met. Tell them Mio was okay, that I knew Sara had been innocent, but that there was nothing I could have done about that. That it would be best for Mio if they left him alone. I was extremely unsure of how far my plan would get me, but it was worth a try.'

'But Rebecca didn't agree with it?' I said.

'Not at all,' Didrik said. 'She was in Stockholm at the time. She decided to intercept Jenny first, then Bobby, on the way to our meeting. She was planning to give them a fright. A serious one. Make out she was part of the conspiracy against Sara, and that Bobby and Jenny would come to a sticky end if they didn't keep out of the way. She hadn't thought it through very well. Or at all, really. She's never been much good at driving, either. The idea was presumably to swerve before she hit them, but she misjudged Jenny's movements and ended up running her down instead. She didn't know she'd killed her until she got out of the car. Jenny didn't die from the actual impact. She died because she fell and broke her neck when she hit the edge of the pavement. No defence for what Rebecca did, obviously, but that was what happened.'

My rain-soaked shirt was sticking to my skin. The cold was corrosive, a long way from how you usually think of summer rain. I could feel myself shaking. Not just from the cold, but also from shock and rage.

'What about Bobby, then?' I said.

'Rebecca panicked. If Jenny was dead, Bobby had to die as well.'

'Why?'

'You can see why! If Bobby had lived, he'd have been able to tell the police where he and Jenny had been going that night. Who they were going to meet. How long do you think it would have taken the police to figure out who had known Jenny was going to be out at that time of night?'

I tried to swallow the lump in my throat.

'So you decided to pin the blame on me?'

'It was easy to prove that you'd been in contact with them both.'

'And the dent in the bonnet of the Porsche?'

'Not hard to make.'

'You went to the garage yourself after the incident with the orange. Why?'

'I wanted to check if the car had the alibi you were

claiming for it. And I wanted to get a second opinion about that dent.'

'You were worried that the imprint left by your backside wouldn't be enough for Forensics to say the car had been involved in two murders?'

Didrik didn't answer.

I started to walk around the room, driven by demons I was wondering if I was ever going to be rid of.

'You can't begin to imagine what our lives are like,' Didrik said. 'Sebbe died last autumn. And we were left out here in the Danish countryside, so alone. I can't find the words to describe how terrible it was, what wrecks we both were. Those neighbours you met when you arrived – they're pretty much the only people we socialise with here. Them and two or three others.'

He sat down heavily on one of the armchairs with the phone in his hand.

'So you raised the subject of Mio's future when you called to tell Lucifer about me?'

'Yes. It was Lucifer's idea. He said he assumed we were already very attached to Mio. Like I've said several times now: we get to keep him if we can put a stop to you looking and get you out of the way.'

'So you don't think I'll talk if you put me in prison?'

Didrik swallowed hard.

'Not if you know it would cost Belle her life.'

When he saw my reaction he quickly added: 'Lucifer's words, not mine.'

I took several deep breaths.

'You do understand he's going to blow us both out, Didrik? You understand that the *instant* I'm behind bars, he'll come and get Mio? And you'll never be able to say a word. You kidnapped a child and gave him your own deceased child's identity. If you need a hand to work out how many laws you've broken, I'd be happy to help you count.'

Didrik sat motionless in the armchair. For a while it looked as if he was going to fall asleep. The phone was in his hand. He seriously believed he had a deal with Lucifer. Was that the sort of damage you suffered when you lost a child? Were you left believing in stories and fairytales?

'How else do we solve this, Martin?' Didrik said. 'How do we both manage to escape from this nightmare?'

39

The rain drummed against the window. I stood in the middle of the floor, as speechless as if carved from stone. Didrik was talking about escape, when, just moments before, he had told me that his wife had run down and killed two people who wanted nothing more than to put things right.

'Who murdered Elias and Fredrik?' I said. 'Was that Rebecca as well?'

Didrik put his phone down.

'That's something you don't need to know,' he said. 'Whether it was me or Rebecca, I mean. That stays between the two of us.'

So the wavering husband was now retreating, worried he'd already said too much.

'Elias called the police to get protection,' I said hoarsely.

'In a way you could say that he got it,' Didrik said with a grimace. 'Staffan told me he'd been in touch. Elias had evidently got it into his head that he was being followed, got paranoid after Bobby died. Completely unnecessary.'

Staffan, the useless fucking pile of shite.

'Yes, so unnecessary,' I said. 'And such a nuisance for Rakel to be left with a dead body in her living room.'

Didrik looked astonished.

'Was that *you*?'

It was my turn to say nothing.

Didrik almost looked relieved.

'We assumed it was a run-of-the-mill burglar who'd broken into the house, seen ... well, you know, and ran off in panic. Nice work, Benner.'

There's a limit to how much garbage you can bear to listen to at any one time. I had definitely reached mine. I couldn't summon up the energy to ask why Elias had been lying in Rakel's living room. Waiting for onward transportation to my car, perhaps, or something else altogether. Either way, he hadn't stayed there long.

'And Fredrik?' I said.

'He got in touch and asked a load of awkward questions,' Didrik said. 'Not particularly discreetly, sadly.'

My entire body felt like it was in uproar. You didn't act like this. Not under any fucking circumstances. The awful thing was that it wasn't Lucifer who had kicked Didrik, the murder-machine, into action. He had done that himself, and then come up with the idea of pinning the blame for it all on me. I still didn't understand why Lucifer thought it was such a brilliant plan. I still didn't understand why he thought my sacrifice was worth so much.

'How did you manage to silence all the leaks from Police Headquarters?' I said. 'There's hardly been anything in the papers.'

Didrik avoided my gaze.

'I suppose people listen to me,' he said, as if that was a good enough answer.

'Speaking of listening,' I said. 'Are you monitoring my phones?'

'We were until Belle's grandparents were murdered. Then the prosecutor objected. Until there was more evidence. Then we got permission again. I don't know how many phones we're monitoring at the moment.'

'And surveillance?'

Didrik smiled wryly.

'Sometimes. You're a bloody hard man to keep track of, you know.'

I thought about the people who had died. Then about those who had survived. Madeleine. And Nadja. It said something that the only witness to Mio's abduction was still alive. Even though Rakel had seen her. Didrik didn't have the complete picture. And Rakel wasn't one hundred per cent bad. She probably hadn't even told Didrik that Nadja had seen Mio being taken, out of fear for what it might lead to.

Didrik's the one doing all the killing, I thought. Rakel is just going along with it.

I didn't know what to say, so I kept quiet. We had to put a stop to this madness. We had to get rid of the architect of this nightmare: Lucifer. If the price for my own freedom was helping Didrik and Rebecca, then so be it. If we could get rid of the threat from Lucifer – however the hell that was going to happen – the rest could be sorted out.

And I said as much to Didrik.

'Who is he?' I said. 'You've met him. What's his name?'

'No fucking idea.'

'Stop it. You must have . . .'

'Yes, you'd think so, but I don't actually know. But I do know two things, and they're enough to make me doubt your idea of rendering him harmless.'

I sat down on one of the kitchen chairs and waited.

'Firstly, he has a network that's so comprehensive and close-knit that you'd never get near him. Never.'

How many times had I heard that when I was in Texas with Lucy? A hundred or more? I didn't care.

'Bollocks,' I said. 'Everyone can be reached. What's the other thing you think you know?'

The look in Didrik's eyes grew sharper.

'That he hates you.'

'Has he said that?'

'Yes. And I know you lied. When you said you'd never killed anyone.'

The words were so harsh and implacable. Someone else who knew about my secret. Someone else who had learned of it from Lucifer. It was indescribably unsettling.

I asked the question to which I had to have an answer.

'Is that why he hates me?'

Didrik seemed to hesitate, and I could hardly breathe. 'Yes,' he said. 'At least that's how I understood it.'

It was the confirmation I had been looking for. Confirmation that Lucifer and I had some sort of unresolved issue dating back to the time I shot an unarmed man and then buried him out in the desert.

Didrik watched me with ill-concealed satisfaction. 'Look at that. I honestly thought he was lying, but now I can see he wasn't.'

I ignored him. I was frightened and angry, stressed and tormented. What the hell was I going to do?

'Give me three days,' I said.

'To do what?'

'To go to the States and put a stop to this. Once and for all.'

'Not a chance.'

'Why not?'

'If Lucifer finds out you've been here without me telling him, my family are dead. It's impossible.'

'And how would he find out?' I said.

Didrik lowered his gaze.

'It feels like he's everywhere.'

'Rubbish. You know he isn't.'

Silence spread through the room.

'Three days,' I said. 'Three fucking days, that's all. Make sure my passport hasn't been blocked. I need to be able to travel without getting caught.'

Didrik thought for a long while.

'Three days,' he said. 'The countdown starts now.'

A glimpse of the Didrik I used to know. Factual and nuanced. So much that had been lost.

I stood up and walked over to him. Then I slowly held out my hand.

'I want us to agree on one thing,' I said. 'If I manage to sort out Lucifer and you get to keep Mio, you'll make sure that the charges against me are dropped.'

Didrik got to his feet and took my hand.

'If you see to it that Lucifer disappears, I'll take care of the rest.'

40

My flight left that evening. I told Lucy I needed to stay in Denmark for a few more days.

'What have you found?' she said.

'Nothing, so far,' I said.

'But you went to see Didrik?'

'Yes.'

'And?'

'The house was empty, baby. So I'm going to stay and wait for them for a bit.'

'You were supposed to be coming back to Sweden again. Tomorrow.'

The rules of the game had changed. The truth was now a luxury I couldn't afford. I would tell Lucy everything afterwards. And nothing beforehand. Because I didn't want any debate. But mostly because I wanted to protect her.

'I'll be back. Just a bit later than I said.'

'Where are you now?'

I was sitting in the car outside Kastrup Airport.

'In my hotel room.'

'Okay.'

We fell silent. That wasn't a good sign. Lucy is the only person I've ever met whom I always have something to say to.

'I'll be in touch,' I said.

'Don't you want to talk to Belle?'

My heart ached. Of course I did. But could I bear to?

'Sure.'

Lucy called Belle, who came to the phone.

'Martin?'

My heart stopped aching, and stopped beating instead. When had she stopped calling me Daddy and started saying Martin again?

'Hello. Are you having a nice time?'

I ask Belle questions I'd never dream of asking an adult.

'Really nice! Lucy's given me lipspit!'

'You mean lipstick.'

'No.'

It sounded like she dropped something.

'I can't talk any more,' she said, and let go of the phone. Lucy picked it up.

'We're playing models and cowboys,' she said apologetically.

'Models and cowboys – how many of you are there?'

'Just two. Belle's a model, I'm a cowboy.'

'Sounds like fun, baby.'

She laughed loudly down the phone.

'You should see Belle now. She's stuck one of the plastic pistols in the lining of her skirt and is wearing a fancy hat. She's going to go far!'

I wondered which of us had bought the plastic pistols for

Belle. Probably me, seeing as I was keen for her not to grow up to be a girly girl. But at that moment I regretted it bitterly. Children shouldn't play with guns, no matter whether they're girls or boys.

'I miss you,' Lucy said.

'Me too.'

I had to go, otherwise I'd miss my plane. Another trip to Texas. Last time I'd had Lucy at my side. Now I was travelling alone. If that sheriff in Houston, Esteban Stiller, had managed to block my passport I would find myself in serious trouble, with both the American and Swedish authorities.

'Got to go,' I said. 'I'll be in touch.'

'Be careful,' Lucy said.

'Always, baby.'

Then she was gone. She and my daughter. I put the mobile in the inside pocket of my jacket. I'd have preferred to travel in shorts and a t-shirt, but it's important to look smart. Especially when you're in the shit.

I'd had to take a decision about all the mobiles I was dragging around. It wouldn't do to look like I was running some sort of smuggling operation. So I'd made my selection and was only taking four. If I needed more I could always buy them when I was there. I had given Didrik a number he could call if necessary. I wasn't planning to use that particular phone to call anyone else.

My plane took off on time. I was flying first class, and was deluged with offers of everything from snacks to alcohol. I turned down everything except the evening meal. Then I leaned back and closed my eyes.

In my dream I was chased by new horrors. Once again I

was buried alive, standing up, but in Didrik's back garden this time. Mio was holding the spade.

'I want to stay here!' he was howling. 'I want to stay here!'

'You can!' I shouted back. 'I promise! No one's going to force you to live with your real dad!'

When the stewardess woke me I was in a cold sweat.

'Are you okay?' she said. 'We're about to land.'

I nodded. Everything was okay; nothing was okay.

Little Mio's plea to be allowed to stay with Rebecca and Didrik was throbbing in my head. Rebecca and Didrik seemed to imagine that there would come a day when Mio no longer remembered his name was Mio. I thought about Belle. She was the same age as Mio. No way was her memory so fragile and short that she could forget who she was? That would be like forgetting a large part of her childhood. But on the other hand, I couldn't help noticing how her memory worked. She didn't seem able to absorb the fact that her grandparents were gone for good. And she didn't really seem to have much idea of when they died. If anyone asked her, she didn't know how a week related to a year. Children don't define time the way adults do. And when I ransacked my own memory I realised that I couldn't remember a single thing before I was six.

They murdered four people, I reminded myself. They have absolutely no right to keep Mio.

But perhaps this wasn't about Rebecca and Didrik's rights. Perhaps it was more about Mio's. Where would he end up if he lost Rebecca and Didrik? It was obvious that he'd developed a close bond to them both. Moving him would only add to the traumas he had already suffered.

What sort of man would he grow up to become? I didn't want to think about that. Rebecca and Didrik may well be right about him forgetting who he had once been. But that didn't mean that the loss of his mother, Sara, whom he hadn't even been allowed to grieve for properly, wouldn't leave lifelong scars.

I thought about all this while I was standing with my passport in my hand, approaching border control. I carefully avoided asking myself what I would have done if I'd been in Rebecca and Didrik's situation. Would I have lost my grip and started killing people? I wanted to say I wouldn't. But the truth is that I didn't know.

The passport queue slowly shrank. I was confronted by more immediate problems. What would happen if I got picked up at the border? Would I be put in jail? Or just placed on the next flight back to Sweden?

'Next.'

I hurried forward to the woman behind the desk. My heart began to beat faster and sweat was making my hands slippery.

'What's the purpose of your visit to the USA?' the woman said as she studied my passport.

I'm here to find a serial killer and mafia boss.

I didn't say that.

'Just a holiday,' I said.

'It's not long since you were last here,' she said.

There was no hint of accusation in her words. More a simple statement.

'The USA is a fine country,' I said.

The woman stopped and looked at me. I forced a smile and hoped I didn't look too panic-stricken.

A man behind me said loudly: 'Why does it always have to take so damn long!'

He was dressed in a suit, and looked stressed the way only a certain type of businessman does (the ones who never make it as far as they would have liked).

The woman behind the desk shook her head at him. Then she took my fingerprints, got me to stare straight into a camera, then stamped my passport.

'Welcome to Texas, sir.'

Barely three weeks had passed since the last time I was in Texas. Back then Lucy and I had thought it was extremely hot. Now it was unbearable. Lucy and I had joked that it felt like the tarmac was melting. Now it was no longer a joke but a fact. Not everywhere, but in places. I couldn't bear the heat for more than a minute or two at a time. I rented a car as quickly as I could and drove towards downtown Houston. I picked a different hotel to last time. But apart from that I didn't go to much effort to cover my tracks. I had neither the time nor the inclination.

I'm happy to admit that I was afraid. Mainly because I was breaking the most important part of my agreement with Lucifer: that under no circumstances would I try to find out more about him, or – still worse – try to find him. I was also worried that he would discover that I had fulfilled my task but hadn't told him. That I had found Mio without actually reuniting him with his biological father. Who, admittedly, already knew where he was, but that didn't seem to be the point. Just as I suspected that it didn't matter that I had no telephone number for Lucifer. I was simply expected to solve things like that.

I was deeply uncomfortable about the fact that I was having to trust Didrik so much. Didrik had served up an almost unbelievable story. But on the other hand, everything – *everything* – that had happened in recent weeks could only be described as unbelievable. If someone had come up to me at that point and told me the world was flat, I'd have believed them. Without question.

My hotel welcomed me with open arms. They usually do, as long as you're staying in a good enough room. I'd booked into one of their finest rooms on the second from top floor.

'Hope you enjoy your stay,' the receptionist said, handing over my key-card.

'Thanks, I'm sure I will.'

It was certainly a fine room. Spacious and light. Good air-conditioning and the obligatory basket of fruit and wine on the coffee table.

The view was vast.

'You can see all the way to Mariannelund,' I heard myself mutter as I later stood alone by the window.

My suitcase lay open over in one corner. In my hand I was holding a glass of water. All around me was nothing but silence and emptiness. You are never so alone as when you're alone in a hotel room. I was a soldier without allies. Without weapons. Without the answers to vital questions. But I had the name of a person who might be able to help me.

His name was Vincent Baker. And he was the brother of the man who was with me when we buried the guy I had shot and killed by accident more than twenty years ago.

I prayed to a higher power that he might have in his possession some of the pieces of the puzzle I so desperately needed.

41

MONDAY

If we'd been in Sweden it would have taken me a matter of seconds to find Vincent Baker. As long as his details hadn't been declared confidential, which most people's hadn't. Things are different in the USA. There's no magical population database that you can do whatever you like with. So finding someone who doesn't want to be found is difficult.

I didn't have time to try to orientate myself in American bureaucracy. I had simple questions, and I wanted simple answers.

Where did Vincent Baker live?

And when could I see him?

Obviously no official could answer this second question. But I could investigate that myself if only I could get hold of his address.

I took the quickest shortcut I could think of, playing for high stakes. It wasn't especially speedy. All of Sunday was lost before I could get to work. On Monday I went to the police station where I knew he worked. Someone there would be able to help me. More or less voluntarily.

I saw her the moment I walked through the glass doors: the young woman who was sitting behind the reception desk. In front of the desk were several rows of chairs. They were all made of black painted metal and bolted to the floor. Clearly not a place where anyone would be tempted to spend a lot of time.

I caught the young woman's eye, and for a short while I was back to my old self again. The flirtatious man who stands or falls on his charm. I sauntered over to the reception desk and leaned my elbows on it.

'Vincent Baker,' I said. 'Is he available?'

I didn't actually want to see Vincent Baker. Not just then, and certainly not at his place of work.

'I'm sorry, all meetings have to be arranged in advance. What's it concerning?'

She smiled broadly at me. The best of combinations: sensual but professional. Damn. I'd been hoping she'd only be one of those.

'I'm afraid I can't say.'

I adopted a serious expression and she automatically did the same.

'It's about his brother, who died a number of years ago now,' I said, well aware of the risk that Vincent Baker would later hear exactly what I had said.

The young woman shook her head.

'I've never heard of him,' she said.

No, I thought. Because you can't have been more than five years old when it happened.

'I'm a lawyer,' I said. 'Some fresh information has emerged that I think he'd be interested in hearing. There's no home address I could try to reach him at?'

I'd have been disappointed if I'd got it. It would have been a serious dereliction of duty, and she didn't seem the sort to make that kind of mistake.

'I'm terribly sorry,' she said. 'I can't help you there. If you'd like to leave a message for Superintendent Baker, obviously that would be fine, but I'm afraid I can't give out his address or phone number.'

Damn. My ideas of 'more or less voluntarily' vanished. I was a paper tiger, there was no point pretending otherwise. I'd have to retreat and try a different way. This wasn't the place where I was going to get hold of Vincent Baker's home address.

I nodded and assumed a different facial expression. Now I looked understanding.

'Of course,' I said. 'Obviously I understand the rules. You know, I reckon I'm going to have a think about what to do next. But do tell him I stopped by.'

The young woman seemed relieved, as if she'd been expecting me to argue with her.

'What was your name?' she said.

I hesitated. I had no evidence that Vincent Baker had any conflict with me, or that he even knew who I was.

Even so, I heard myself say: 'You know, just say hi from Lucifer. He knows who I am.'

Lucifer. A name you can say to any cop in Texas and be sure that the person you're talking to knows who you mean. The receptionist looked bemused when I said Lucifer's name, but she didn't remark upon it.

'Okay,' she said simply.

'Okay,' I said.

Then I thanked her for her help and left. It was just past

eleven o'clock in the morning and I had the distinct feeling that I had just declared war on a complete stranger.

At that point there weren't very many people in the world I could trust. Hardly any at all. If I'd been four years old, like Belle, I'd have yelled: 'I'm so lonely!' But I wasn't four years old, and that was just as well. Standing on the pavement screaming really wasn't an option. I had to keep moving: forward, onward. I couldn't carry on without allies. So I had to identify someone I could trust. Someone I didn't think would blow me out the minute he or she got the chance. In Houston there was pretty much no one in whom I had the slightest confidence at all.

With one exception: my former boss, Josh Taylor.

I'd trusted him the time I called to talk about what we called Pastor Parson's funeral, and I would have to trust him again. Even though he'd said he didn't want to hear from me any time soon.

I decided not to call him. I showed up at his place of work instead. A different police station, a different part of Houston. This time asking for him at reception worked fine.

'I'm not sure he's available,' said the man I was talking to.

'Tell him Martin Benner would like to see him,' I said. 'I think he'll have time.'

And sure enough, just minutes later he was standing in reception. He wasn't happy.

'Sorry to bother you,' I said.

To my own surprise I felt myself shrink as I greeted him. Josh Taylor was twenty years older, but I seemed to have got younger. I was a boy, standing there shuffling my feet, aware that I'd done something really, really stupid.

'Come with me,' Taylor said.

He led me into a corridor behind the reception area. The walls were adorned with portraits of former police chiefs. The floor was covered by a worn carpet. The wallpaper was coming loose. Houston's police force wasn't exactly awash with resources.

Taylor opened the door to a small meeting room.

'In you go,' he said.

He looked round to see if anyone was watching us. As far as I could tell, no one was.

He had barely shut the door before he started.

'What the hell are you thinking, showing up here and asking to see me? Have you lost your mind?'

Getting a serious telling-off happens so rarely when you're grown-up that you don't really know how to react.

'I need your help,' I said, embarrassed that I was stammering.

'Yes, I figured that out when you phoned. But I have no memory of telling you to come and stir things up here. Or did I?'

Twenty years ago Josh Taylor had been one of the rising stars in the police firmament. One of his strengths had been his quick-fire rhetoric, his inexhaustible energy. He was the finest interviewer in the district, as well as being an excellent boss. He could have gone far. But he hadn't. I could see that clearly enough.

'What happened?' I said.

He lost his thread.

'When?'

'With you,' I said. 'How did this happen?'

Americans are a proud people. They don't tolerate anyone

pissing on their successes or their failures. It wasn't that Taylor had been downgraded, because he hadn't been. No, what surprised me was that he hadn't risen even further. Twenty years ago people said he had the potential to become a sheriff. Now those thoughts seemed very distant.

'I changed,' Taylor said in a gruff voice. 'Didn't you, Benner?'

I was so young back when we stood in the desert and buried a man I had shot. Of course I'd bloody changed. But not in the sense that I'd got weaker. Quite the reverse. With every swing of the shovel, my conviction that I needed to do something else with my life grew. That was my only hope of redemption.

'I know Tony's brother's name is Vincent Baker. I know where he works, and yes, I have been there.'

'You stupid bastard.'

'I need his address,' I said. 'You weren't willing to tell me his name so I found that out for myself. But I can't get hold of his address. You'll have to check your internal register.'

Josh Taylor's eyes had become black as coal.

'I don't have to do anything,' he said calmly. 'You're the one who owes me, Benner. Not the other way round.'

We stood in silence for a long while in that little meeting room.

'I know you don't owe me anything,' I said. 'I'm sorry if it sounded that way. It's just that . . . There aren't many people I can ask. You can't begin to imagine what my life is like. What I'm facing.'

'I think I probably can. You told me yourself over the phone. You've ended up in conflict with Lucifer. How you've managed a thing like that is way beyond me.'

I took a deep breath.

'The conflict is about Pastor Parson's funeral,' I said. 'And that concerns you too. So for God's sake, help me.'

Taylor stared at me long and hard.

'There's no question that your conflict is related to the Pastor?'

'I'm completely certain. I got final confirmation of that in Denmark the day before yesterday.'

'In Denmark?'

There was no point holding back. I told Taylor what I'd found out from Didrik. For the first time since we met, I saw him grow uncertain.

'You're out on damn thin ice, Benner,' he said.

'Do you think I don't know that?'

Taylor began to walk up and down in the little room. I hate it when people do that. Move around anxiously in small spaces, filling up all the room.

'If you drag me down with you I'll never forgive you. Do you understand? Never!'

He roared so loudly I was sure it could be heard outside.

'Give me Vincent Baker's address,' I said in a subdued voice. 'I understand that you weren't willing to help me when I wasn't certain if Pastor Parson's funeral was relevant, but now everything's changed. Help me. Please.'

The English word *please* is much better than the Swedish equivalent. More worthy. Sturdier.

Taylor stopped at last. He let out a deep sigh.

'And then what happens?' he said. 'What are you going to do with Vincent Baker?'

I straightened up.

'Find out if he can direct me towards Lucifer.' I cleared

my throat and went on: 'Who knows, maybe he's the big mafia boss himself?'

I felt ashamed at my choice of words, hardly knew where they'd come from. It sounded so heavy, such a long shot.

Taylor came so close that I could smell the tobacco on his breath.

'Have you lost your mind completely? You think Vincent Baker, a totally fucking average police officer, could be Lucifer? Or even know where he is?'

I backed away, and Taylor followed me.

'I ... I don't know. But I have to start somewhere.'

Taylor shook his head.

'Okay, then what? What are you going to do if he does turn out to be Lucifer?'

I didn't yet have an answer to that question, and Taylor should have known that. I had tried to imagine at least a hundred times what I'd do if I did manage to find Lucifer. I failed every time. All I knew for certain were two measly facts:

I would never have peace until my conflict with Lucifer was over.

And I wouldn't be able to kill him.

As if he could read my mind, Taylor said: 'Martin, you're never going to be able to make him see sense. You do realise that, don't you?'

'I know,' I said. 'I know.'

But I didn't, not at all. In my world the right way of talking can achieve almost anything.

'So what are you going to do?' Taylor said, folding his arms over his chest. 'Another funeral conducted by Pastor Parson?'

I shook my head.

'I could never do anything like that.'

Josh Taylor gazed at me with what looked almost like sympathy.

'And if he isn't Lucifer, and doesn't know where he is either, which has to be the most likely outcome, what do you do then?'

I had to blink several times, because my eyes were stinging badly.

'I don't know,' I whispered. 'Go on looking, I suppose. Because he must be here somewhere.'

Taylor's eyes softened. He looked more sad than anything.

'Have you thought about what I said, about possible witnesses?'

'There weren't any,' I said firmly. 'Not a chance. This all fits together somehow.'

My shoulders slumped. Taylor backed away from me. He couldn't bear to see me looking so wretched and, to be honest, neither could I.

'I'll get you the address,' Taylor said. 'Then you disappear from here and do me and yourself a great big fucking favour.'

'What?'

Taylor's eyes were hard as they met mine.

'You don't approach anyone you think might be Lucifer without having a plan.'

42

That was how I came to find myself sitting in the car driving to the home of a man I didn't know. The promise my old boss had extracted from me, not to do anything I hadn't thought through, vanished in the exhaust fumes of the car. There was no time to think, I told myself. People talk about houses of cards collapsing. In my case that had already happened. At that moment I was lying beneath the pile of cards, waiting for the bulldozer to come and put an end to the misery by obliterating them.

Vincent Baker lived just twenty minutes' drive from downtown. In Houston that counts as a central residential area. Nothing but smart, middle-class houses. No ramshackle plots, no extravagant cars. There were plenty of women with buggies. If they looked young, I assumed they were au pairs. If they looked older, housewives. The majority of the people I saw were white. Vincent Baker was black. At least I assumed he was, because his brother Tony had been. But that could be a miscalculation, of course. Like me and my sister. No one who ever saw us together believed we were brother and sister.

There was a pickup parked in the drive of Baker's house. A man was standing on the back, moving things. His white shirt was shiny with sweat and sticking to his back. His black trousers can't have helped. I pulled up and parked by the pavement. He didn't seem to notice me, just went on with what he was doing. I swallowed several times, my heart pounding like a steam-hammer. Slowly I got out of the car and closed the door behind me.

The man on the pickup looked pretty carefree. I had almost reached the vehicle by the time he noticed me. He smiled in my direction.

'Can I help you?'

He was wearing a red bowtie and a name-badge. Josh Taylor had said that Tony's older brother owned a café. This must be him.

Could he be Lucifer?

I looked at his disarming manner and thought to myself, like hell he could. I needed to pull myself together and not start seeing things that simply weren't there.

I smiled back, and just about managed to hide my nervousness.

'I'm looking for Vincent Baker,' I said.

The man on the pickup shaded his eyes with one hand.

'Who should I say is here?'

'Martin Benner.' I had to stop and take a deep breath, because I was about to stake everything I had on one card. 'I used to work with his brother, Tony.'

The smile on the man's face faded. Slowly he brushed the dust from his bare lower-arms. His white shirt-sleeves were rolled up in such a way as to make it impossible to roll them down again. They'd be far too creased.

'In which case you used to work with my brother too,' he said. 'My name's Simon.'

'I'm sorry,' I said. 'I had no idea Tony had another brother as well as Vincent.'

A lie, but Vincent's brother wasn't to know that. He jumped down from the back of the pickup and landed less than a metre from me.

'What do you want?'

The carefree attitude was gone, replaced by sheer, unadulterated fury. The change took me by surprise. This wasn't a situation I'd been prepared for.

Tony's brother tilted his head.

'Benner, you said?'

'Yes.'

'Then I know who you are.'

He didn't need to explain what he meant. Or so I thought. Every part of his face told me he knew what I had done, and that he hated me for it. Or so I thought. And this was where it got incomprehensible. Or so I thought. Because how could my fatal shooting of a teenager affect my relationship with my former partner's family? Tony had been almost as guilty as I was for what had happened. He'd said as much that night. That he was so sorry about what had happened. That if I hadn't fired, he would have done.

'You ran away,' Simon said. 'You don't do that.'

What was he talking about?

'I didn't run away,' I said, unsure of what he meant, and unwilling to give him more information than he already had.

He came a step closer. I forced myself not to back away.

'Of course you did. You left Tony when he was feeling so fucking bad. What do you want with Vincent? He doesn't give a damn about you, and neither do I. No one in this family wants anything to do with you. If you couldn't be bothered to come earlier, you needn't have bothered coming now.'

I stood speechless in the face of the torrent of words pouring out of him. *No one in this family wants anything to do with you.* So they'd talked about me. And had agreed that I wasn't welcome. There was something implicit in the reasoning that I didn't understand. *No one in this family.* What was it that I wasn't getting?

'I'm very sorry,' I said. 'I didn't know Tony had been feeling bad.'

What else could I say? Had there been any way I could have realised that Tony felt like shit? After all, he'd requested a transfer after the fatal shooting. And we'd never been friends outside work.

'Crap, everyone knew. You, too.'

He put his hands in his trouser pocket and pulled out a keyring.

'I've got to go now. You should leave too. For good. No one here wants to meet you.'

For good. *No one in this family.*

'Can you tell Vincent that I'm looking for him?'

'Sure, but he won't contact you. He hates you just as much as the rest of us.'

It was my turn to take a step closer, driven by frustration.

'Excuse me, but what are you talking about? "He hates you just as much as the rest of us." What "rest of us"? I don't know you. And you sure as hell don't know me.'

That fucking heat. It felt like the pair of us were melting, dissolving into the tarmac. Your brain doesn't work well in those circumstances. We stood there staring at each other, raw and upset. And neither of us capable of saying anything sensible.

I tried a gentler tone. Gentler, but still factual.

'I'm really sorry about what happened,' I said. 'But ... you need to know it was a tragic fucking mistake. I ... I never meant him to die. We were standing in the pouring rain and he pulled a damn pistol – or rather he didn't, but I thought he did – and I just ...'

'Sorry, but what are you talking about?'

This man, Vincent and Tony's brother, looked utterly uncomprehending.

'What happened,' I began. 'Why, what were you talking about?'

We were interrupted by a ringtone. His, not mine.

'You're not right in the head,' he said, and walked round the car to get in the driver's seat.

I followed, keen not to have to drive away with more questions than I had arrived with.

'Sorry, but I don't get it,' I said. 'What exactly does your family hold me responsible for? I didn't know Tony was feeling bad. All I know is that he requested a transfer, and ...'

Simon got in the pickup and closed the door. The window was down.

'Yeah, and why do you think he did that? Requested a transfer?'

'Because of what had happened?' I said.

I felt stupid. Words like 'what had happened' clearly meant something different to me than they did to Tony's relatives.

'I don't know what you mean by "what had happened",'

Simon said, as if to confirm what I'd just been thinking. 'The rest of us would probably say: "what you did". Tony requested a transfer because of what you did, you fraudulent bastard.'

I shook my head. He started the engine and began to reverse.

'I'm really sorry,' I repeated. 'If you explain, if you tell me what you think I've done, maybe we can work this out. Because I'm quite sure there's some massive misunderstanding, and ...'

The truck swung out into the road.

'There's no misunderstanding. Stay away from us.'

I was like a child, impossible for him to shake off. I ran alongside the pickup as he pulled away.

'Tell Vincent I want to get hold of him!' I yelled, and dropped a piece of paper with my phone number on it inside the cab.

He responded by putting his foot down, then he was gone.

43

I got what I wanted. That's the way things usually end. With me getting my way. But first Josh Taylor called.

'Can you talk?' he said.

'I'm pretty sure I can,' I said, to indicate that there was a microscopic chance that we were being monitored.

'Pretty sure will have to do,' Taylor said. 'Your arrival in the city seems to have kicked up a huge stink.'

'Seriously?'

'Seriously. So be careful. That's all I wanted to say.'

'Hang on a minute. Who should I be watching out for? The police? Lucifer's guys?'

'There are a number of police officers who remember your last visit, Benner. You were told to go home and not come back. And now you're disobeying that advice. That's enough.'

'How do they even know I'm here? I . . .'

'You had no problem getting into the country because your passport hadn't been blocked. But it had been flagged. The sheriff was told you'd arrived less than fifteen minutes after you passed through customs.'

I started to sweat.

'From a purely legal point of view, they can't stop me. From a purely ...'

'From a purely legal point of view, you're a fucking idiot. Be careful. You've got people after you.'

He hung up and was gone. I thought about what he'd said. That I had people after me, in all likelihood. I sat in my hotel room with far too much energy and my head full of thoughts. Restless, I walked over to the window. I was too high up, too far away, to see anyone or anything interesting. If I had shadows tailing me on the ground, I couldn't see them.

I sat down on the bed. Maybe it was time to call Lucy. She had had to make do with texts up until then. It was only a matter of time before she phoned me. But the idea of calling Lucy got no further than that, because at that moment I received a text that changed the game completely.

> Heard you came to my home looking for me. Bad move. Cocky. But have it your way. Meet tonight at Pastor Parson's grave. 9 p.m. Come alone.

I read the message over and over again. My pulse went up, up, up, then plummeted. I slid onto the floor and felt the hands holding the phone shake.

The text was evidently from Vincent. But he hadn't sent it to the number I gave his brother. No, it was sent to the mobile on which I had previously heard from Lucifer. Terror spread through my body in less than a second.

I read those short lines once more.

Vincent Baker ...

... *was* Lucifer.

I couldn't draw any other conclusion. Well, there was a chance that Baker was just one of Lucifer's acolytes. That that was how he had got my number, as well as permission to use it. But that was too far-fetched. I read the message again. Vincent Baker, who I assumed had sent those brief lines, had – unlike his brother – no problem referring to the fatal shooting which I assumed was the reason for my dispute with Lucifer (and evidently the whole of Tony's family). It bothered me that he used our private term for what had happened. Pastor Parson's funeral. Even if I had a certain sympathy for the fact that Tony might have felt a need to tell his brother about what had happened; I couldn't understand why he had revealed our codename.

But that was only a tiny detail. I mustn't let my shock get the upper hand. This was what I had come for, after all. This was what I had wanted, even though I knew it was dangerous. I needed to decide how I felt about the cryptic invitation. There was an obvious threat in the demand that I come alone. To a place where I had once buried a man I had shot. The recurring nightmares that had tormented me since I got home from Texas had become genuine premonitions. I had received warning after warning. Was I going to dare to defy them? Alone and unprotected?

It struck me that I didn't even know what the old oilfield looked like now. Americans are industrious; they could have whacked up a whole new city out there. It was approaching four o'clock. I had five hours to prepare for the evening.

I knew I ought to get some rest. But I also knew that there wasn't a hope in hell that I'd fall asleep. So I did what I often do when I'm tired and stressed: I acted on pure impulse. I needed to see that damn burial site again. Simple as that.

Otherwise I would never manage to meet Lucifer there. It was roughly an hour's drive away. I would have plenty of time to get there and back, and then drive out there again. If I went any later I risked Lucifer thinking the same thing as me and getting there too early. But if I went right away I could be almost certain of being alone.

I took the lift down to the garage of the hotel and got in the car. I set the air-con going and drove out of the garage. Lucy called just as I was pulling out onto the street. I decided that was good. We needed to talk. More than ever.

'Where are you?' she said.

Her voice was tight as a violin string.

No more bad news now.

Not Belle, I thought, with my body and soul numb with fear. Not Belle. Not again.

'Out driving,' I said. 'What's happened?'

'Martin, stop talking crap. *Where are you?*'

How much should I tell her? What did I want her to know? Everything, really. If I died in the desert that night, someone needed to know where I was going. It seemed reasonable that Lucy should know rather than anyone else.

When I took my time replying, she said: 'The police have been here. An arrest warrant had been issued in your absence, Martin.'

'An arrest warrant?'

'Apparently there are new witnesses.'

My eyes flickered. I thought I'd had a deal with Didrik. That I'd bought myself some time to act.

'That's bullshit and you know it,' I said in a voice so sharp that it echoed down the line. 'There aren't any witnesses. Have you given them the recording from the garage?'

'Yes, and I've let them know there are copies, in case someone manages to lose it by accident.'

I could hear from Lucy's voice that she wasn't telling me everything. If someone had offered me some heroin just then, I'd probably have taken it just to calm myself down.

'What else is it, baby?'

Her voice was trembling when she replied.

'They're saying I must have been involved in this, so they've contacted Social Services. Martin, they're talking about taking Belle away.'

I couldn't handle those words just then.

'They haven't taken her already?'

'Martin, I . . .'

'They haven't already taken her?'

I was shouting so loudly it must have been audible outside the car.

'No, no. They said that bit about Social Services when they came back to the office to get hold of you. They probably thought Social Services had already acted, but I managed to call the preschool after they left and Belle was still there. I was afraid I was being followed so I called Signe and got her to drop everything and pick Belle up at once.'

My heart began to slow down.

'And where are you now?'

'We're on our way to Madeleine Rossander's summerhouse, which is empty at the moment. Sorry, but I didn't know who I could trust. She really didn't want to be dragged into it, but . . .'

'You did the right thing, Lucy, absolutely the right thing.'

I didn't give a damn about Madeleine Rossander's safety and whatever price she might have to pay for helping us.

All I cared about was Belle and Lucy. And Madeleine knew that. If she hadn't wanted to, she would never have helped Lucy.

'Are you being followed?' I said.

'Don't think so. I must have cycled through red lights and gone the wrong way down one-way streets a hundred times before I got to Signe's.'

'So you haven't been back to the flat? Just to Signe's?'

'Yes.'

I felt like crying with relief.

'Martin, you've got to come home. This can't go on.'

I tried to formulate a good response to her plea.

'I'll be home in a couple of days at the latest.'

'Two days? Martin, we haven't got that long. You need to confront Didrik, wherever he is. And if that house in Denmark is empty, you need to start looking in other places. Here in Stockholm, for instance.'

'Baby, the house wasn't empty.'

'What?'

'I've already met and confronted Didrik. I thought I'd bought myself three days to sort this crap out. Sorry about that.'

'Sorry about that' was pretty feeble given the circumstances. Lucy thought so too.

'You're fucking unbelievable. You lied. To me. Again. After everything that's happened. After the talk we had after you called your old shag and just had to have another fuck, even though we were living together. *Do you know how much it hurts to hear this bullshit?*'

Oh yes, I did. Fear of losing Lucy got the better of me and I started babbling.

'It was to protect you and Belle. Don't you get that? I didn't want you to know too much in case the police started asking questions.'

'You're so fucking considerate! Where are you? Give me a proper answer, and don't lie.'

I braked for a red light.

'I'm in Houston.'

The phone went completely silent.

'Lucy?'

I heard Belle say something in the background. It sounded like Lucy was snorting. She does that when she cries.

'Sorry, baby. Sorry.'

'Don't call me baby. You went without us. Without even telling us. You fucking bastard.'

She was crying. No doubt about it.

'I wanted to tell you, but I couldn't.'

'Why not?'

'I just said. So that you'd know as little as possible if the police asked. Because I was worried we'd start arguing. I couldn't bear that. But I was going to call, Lucy, later this evening. I swear, I wasn't going to carry on lying.'

'Very generous of you.'

Red turned to green and I drove off. Towards hell, towards my oh-so-neatly buried sins that had now found their way up to the surface.

'There's a very logical reason for why I'm here. Didrik told me things that made the situation untenable. There was never any intention of letting me get out of this. Lucifer already knew where Mio was before he asked me to look for him. Don't you see? He's been leading us in circles, me and Didrik. But Didrik, the stupid bastard, still thinks he can trust him. He thinks he'll be allowed to keep Mio if he can just get me out of the way.'

'Didrik's got Mio? Have you seen Mio?'

The memory overwhelmed me. Mio running in the garden. Mio asking if I was his daddy.

'Yes.'

More silence. This time I didn't press Lucy to say anything. When she finally spoke, I wished I'd hung up instead.

'I don't think I can forgive this, Martin.'

An icy chill in my chest.

'Lucy, you have to believe me when I say I had no option but to lie to you.'

'Like when you neglected to tell me you'd killed another person?'

I hated it when she said things like that when Belle could hear her. And I was very close to panicking at the thought that she was slipping away from me in such a definitive way, just as I was preparing for the most important encounter of my life.

'Listen to me,' I said. 'I understand that you're angry. Just like I understood that you were angry when I called Veronica, or Rakel, for sex. I ... I got it wrong. Over and over again. But this time I really did think I was doing the right thing. I wanted to protect you. Not hurt you. And ... and I love you, for looking after Belle. For being by my side throughout this nightmare.'

I had to pause there, because the sob in my throat was making it hard to speak. We hardly ever said we loved each other. Me because I thought it was understood, and Lucy because ... Well, I hadn't really given much thought to her reasons. Which in itself was frightening.

'Do you hear me, Lucy? I love you.'

She started to cry again.

'That's not enough, don't you see? Not when you behave like this.'

I started to cry too. Hot tears made my eyes sting.

'I'm meeting Lucifer this evening,' I said.

'You're mad.'

'I haven't got a choice. I—'

'You're completely fucking mad. If you go to that meeting, it's over, Martin. Over. Do you hear?'

Yes, so you just said.

'I haven't got a choice,' I said.

'Of course you have. Come home. Hand yourself over to the police. It'll take me less than a week to sort out the investigation, to get the police to see what Didrik's done.'

She probably believed what she was saying, and I can hardly blame her for that. But she was fundamentally wrong.

'That won't solve the problem of Lucifer,' I said. 'As long as he's still out there, none of us will be safe.'

'What are you going to do? Murder him as well?'

That 'as well' was unnecessary. It stung like the crack of a whip across my back.

'The first one wasn't murder,' I said. Or muttered, the way you do when you're ashamed.

'Anyway, how did you even manage to find Lucifer? You haven't been gone more than a day yet.'

Finally I was able to say something sensible.

'I don't honestly know if it is Lucifer. Not one hundred per cent. But ninety-eight. That'll have to do. Remember this, Lucy: his name is Vincent Baker. He's a police officer in Houston, the brother of Tony Baker, who was my partner that night when I shot a guy I thought was a drug-dealer.'

'You mean he's the brother of the man you shot?'

'No, I mean exactly what I said. He's the brother of my former partner.'

The words of the third brother, Simon, were ringing in my head, still just as incomprehensible. No one in the family wanted anything to do with me. No one could forgive what I'd done. Not what had happened – *what I'd done*.

I heard Lucy say something to Belle.

'I have to go now,' she said. 'Belle's tired and hungry.'

It occurred to me that it was the middle of the night in Stockholm.

'How long have you been driving?' I said.

'A long time,' Lucy said. 'Madeleine's summerhouse isn't exactly in the archipelago.'

'Drive carefully,' I said. 'Look after Belle. I'll be in touch.'

I said those last words in a muted voice.

'You'd better, Benner.'

And with those words she ended the call. I was more alone than ever.

44

It was still light when I arrived. I'd stopped on the way and forced down a hamburger. Not as nutrition, just fuel. The closer I got, the slower I drove. And the harder it got to breathe. The pressure in my chest was immense as I first turned off from the motorway, and then the side-road. The road-signs looked exactly as they had done when I had driven the same route for an entirely different reason. To my surprise, the whole area looked unchanged. I drove the last ten kilometres, now as then, on a gravel track. The landscape around me was open, barren and uninhabited. The Yanks love building and settling and exploiting. Why had they forgotten about these square kilometres?

Last time I had a heavy load in the trunk of the car. For that reason I had driven off the gravel track, straight across the desert to where the burial later took place. This time I pulled over at the side of the track and walked the last bit. What I was going to do when I came back a few hours later to meet the man who might be Lucifer seemed fairly self-evident: I would drive all the way.

It was as hot as hell. The sun showed no mercy whatsoever, and was busy trying to fry me alive. I couldn't believe where I was going. I couldn't believe how the past had caught up with me in such a brutal way. Had I not lived a sufficiently good life? Had I not played my cards right? Like when my sister died and I took care of Belle. Or all the times I had helped clients deal with problems.

Boris's face drifted up to the surface of my memory. Perhaps I hadn't done my best. Perhaps I had behaved questionably. Towards Lucy and my family and society in general. Lucy had called me the most egotistical man in the world on more than one occasion. She was probably right about that.

Better a sinner who repents, as the saying goes. And I can say without the slightest hesitation that I repented as I walked my own path to Calvary from the car to the site of the grave. It wasn't marked, but even so I knew exactly where it was. Just below a slight hummock.

I stopped right by the grave. This was where we would be meeting in a few hours' time to resolve things. I looked around. No one and nothing in sight. Just some derelict old barracks. The massive oil wells had all been removed.

This is impossible, I thought. I'm not going to get out of here alive.

Obviously that thought had occurred to me before, but it hadn't really sunk in and taken root until I was actually there. I also suspected that there wasn't merely a chance that I might die – it was a certainty. The only question that remained was: why?

I crouched down to pick up a handful of sand, and let it run through my fingers. I thought about time, and how little

I had left, and I thought about Belle. She was going to be left an orphan again. If Lucy was charged with conspiracy to commit the crimes I hadn't committed, Belle would end up with foster parents. Without ever knowing why.

If she was even allowed to live.

Lucifer had threatened to kill Belle and Lucy before, and would no doubt do so again if he had to, or felt like it. I realised I wouldn't be able to turn to the local police to ask for help. If I did, not only was I dead, but so were Belle and Lucy.

I stood up quickly and wiped my hand on my trousers. I couldn't let it end like that. No fucking way. I owed Belle – and Lucy – something other than that. Something better. I walked back to the car with long strides. Lucy had convinced me that she had things under control. She was smart; she'd be able to stay hidden for as long as it took. Both herself and Belle. What responsibility I had left concerned myself, not them. Vincent Baker, or Lucifer, could go fuck himself. There was nothing he could do to me that mattered, as long as Belle and Lucy were okay.

He could burn my office down.

Destroy my career and strip me of my fortune.

Hell, he could even go after my mother, even if I dearly hoped he wouldn't.

He could do whatever he wanted – because I no longer had anything to lose.

I took out my mobile and brought up his text. Naturally he had sent it from a concealed number. What a shame. He'd have no way of knowing that we were going to meet up somewhere else.

The car had turned into an oven by the time I got back

inside it. I revved the engine and drove down the gravel track to the road that would take me back to the motorway. My encounter with Simon was still lingering in my overheated head. I couldn't shake off what he had said. Nor could I understand why he had looked so baffled when I started talking about the fatal shooting. If it wasn't about that, what the hell could possibly be the cause of any conflict between me and those people?

He'd said that Tony had felt bad. I had no memory of that. Or, to be more accurate: Tony was the sort of person who was always a bit low. Never on a high. Never full of energy. I had assumed it was part of his nature, being a bit subdued, and I liked the fact that he was the way he was. So many of our colleagues were driven by pure adrenalin. They marauded down the streets like gorillas on speed and I always had the uncomfortable feeling that if they hadn't joined the police they would have become criminals themselves.

We hadn't had any contact after he requested a transfer. The only information I heard about him was through other people. When I moved away from Texas, the flow of information got even more sporadic. I was only in touch with a very small number of my former colleagues, and only for a few years. Long enough to hear that Tony had died. He had been shot while on duty and hadn't been found by his fellow officers until a few hours later. I considered going to the funeral, but it didn't happen. There was no compelling reason to go, and it would only have aroused a whole load of awkward questions.

During the drive back to Houston a plan began to take shape. Well, calling it a plan would be a bit of an exaggeration. It was more a strategic thought. I knew too little, and that made me vulnerable. There wasn't much time and I really didn't have many good ideas. Seeing as I couldn't contact Vincent Baker, I decided to go on the offensive again. I was going to pay a visit to his brother Simon's café. Because I didn't have any other way in to the family, and because I had to get closer to them.

I remembered what it had said on the name-badge he had been wearing: Simon Baker, Baker's Café. It didn't take me long to get hold of the address. It turned out to be a chain, with all of the branches located in Houston. The chain consisted of a total of five cafés. An excellent way to launder money, if need be. If Vincent Baker was indeed Lucifer, I suspected that there was probably quite a pressing need. And like the loyal brother he no doubt was, Simon would be only too happy to help.

I didn't know what I was looking for. That's all too often the case. We don't know what we're looking for until we see it. All the cafés were in so-called good locations. Good in the sense that they weren't in shady backstreets, but the more central parts of Houston. They were fairly small, not unlike Starbucks. I didn't go into the first one I visited. I just stood outside looking in through the large windows. There were two Latino guys behind the counter, making coffee for a long queue of customers. They were wearing the same uniform that Simon had been wearing: white shirt, black trousers, red bowtie. There was nothing and no one there that caught my attention.

Same thing at the next one. A few employees, a queue. The smell of coffee brought my caffeine addiction to life. I went back to the car and drove to the third café. This time

I was going to go in. If I didn't see anything interesting, at least I could get a coffee to take out. I parked ten metres from the door. That's one of the best – and worst – things about the USA. That the car has such an unquestioned place in society. You never need to drive round looking for a free parking space. I pulled in and locked the car. Then I went into Baker's Café.

It was a bit bigger than the others I had seen. More staff, similarly long queue. Baker's Café was clearly a popular brand. I looked out for Simon Baker. He had looked as if he actually worked in one of his own cafés. The question was, which one?

I joined the queue. There were two men in suits in front of me. They were having a quiet conversation about a newly established oil company.

'They'll be gone in two years,' one of them said. 'They'll never be able to cope with the competition.'

That was all I took in of their conversation. Oil, money, desert and sand. I couldn't have cared less.

The queue shrank. I was closer to the till now. Then it was my turn.

'What can I get you, sir?'

The girl behind the counter smiled broadly at me.

I pointed at the menu.

'I'll try that.'

I barely knew what I was ordering. They called it 'offer of the week', and anything labelled as that tends not to be great.

'Excellent choice! That'll be four dollars and fifty cents.'

As I was paying I caught sight of Simon. He was standing with his back to me, halfway through a door I assumed led to the kitchen or something similar. I took my coffee grate-fully and moved in his direction. No grand gestures, no loud noises. Just discretion and the minuscule amount of sense that was left in my body. Soon I was close enough to hear what he was saying. He sounded upset. He was talking to someone I couldn't see.

'I've already told him we don't want anything to do with him. Turning up out of the blue like that. Completely fuck-ing unbelievable.'

The voice that replied was considerably calmer.

'I think you may have misunderstood why he came to see us. In fact, I'm absolutely certain of it.'

'How come? He started going on about someone who'd been shot, but I interrupted and said I didn't know what he was talking about. Do you?'

'I don't want to go into that now. But you're right that the murder had nothing to do with anything. It's good that you let it go.'

'Who died, then?'

'Some nobody. Just let it go.'

'There's a lot I'm supposed to just let go, Vincent.'

Vincent.

Then silence. Perhaps they realised they were discuss-ing sensitive matters in public. Admittedly, I was the only person listening, but that was enough. I sat down at one of the few tables in the café. I huddled over my disposable mug of coffee and sipped the hot liquid. My ears rushed and the blood bubbled in my veins.

Simon came out and stood behind the counter. With a smile that refused to reach his eyes, he welcomed the next customer. He was totally absorbed in his own thoughts and work. He wouldn't have seen me even if I'd been standing right in front of him. Discreetly I tried to look through the doorway. Vincent was back there somewhere. It would be worth a fortune to know what he looked like.

And once again my wish was granted. The man who had to be Vincent Baker slipped out into the café. At first I only saw him from the side, with his face lowered, fully occupied with the phone in his hand. Trying to control your own impulses is very interesting. I tried to make myself as nondescript as possible as I sat there. As if I hung out there every day. As if I wasn't simultaneously both the quarry and the hunter.

I think I managed it for a little while. Long enough, at least, to stifle the exclamation that bubbled up in my throat when he finally took his eyes off his phone, straightened up and glanced momentarily in my direction. One second. That's all it took for all the pieces of the puzzle – the pieces I had been searching for so desperately – to fall into place. It was as if they'd fallen from the sky. Just crashed down to where I was sitting and landed on the table beside my mug of coffee. And formed the clearest of pictures.

How had I not realised?

Vincent's face. I'd seen it before. I'd punched it. The only face I had ever tried to harm with my bare hands. Now on someone else. Someone younger.

Josh Taylor had said that Tony had three brothers. One who was in the police, one who ran a café, and one who took off. How had I not realised before now?

I was the third brother.

45

Families are terrible things. I even hate the word. Family members are the only people we don't choose for ourselves. And they're the only people we are expected to love, and – on top of all the other crap – actually spend time with. Even if we don't have anything in common. Even if we don't like each other.

I've never felt so alienated from the whole concept of family as that day when I sat drinking coffee in a café in Houston – and, completely out of the blue, saw my brother standing less than four metres away. I knew that was who he was. Because he was a carbon copy of the father we shared. I couldn't stop my eyes from roaming. They settled on Simon, who was absorbed in his work behind the counter. He didn't look anything like the man who had been my father. Nor had Tony. They must have taken after their mother. I drank my coffee. Looked up again. And found myself gazing straight into Vincent's dark eyes.

The charade was over. Neither of us said anything. But my senses have never been more receptive to impressions than they were at that moment. There wasn't a single change in colour, a single detail, a single sound or a single smell that I didn't register. I soaked it all up, and I can remember all of it. From the corner of my eye I saw that Simon's pattern of movement had changed. He'd stopped when he caught sight of me and his brother.

'Vincent?' he said.

No one seemed to react. The customers went on placing their orders, the staff went on serving them. But not Simon. And not Vincent. And not me.

'Vincent?' Simon repeated.

He was the younger brother, that was all too obvious. The one who didn't know how to deal with problems he was faced with. The one who always turned to his older brother for advice.

'It's okay,' Vincent said. 'I'll deal with this.'

He didn't take his eyes off me for a second.

'Okay,' Simon said, still unsure of what he was expected to do.

'But not here,' Vincent said, and now he was talking to me.

I didn't move from my chair, with my elbows on the table and the mug of coffee in my hand. I should have been scared, but that and every other emotion was consumed by the overwhelming sense of surprise. At once, every word that Simon had uttered made sense.

Their family didn't want anything to do with me.

It was no more complicated than that. And it needn't have become any more complicated, because I didn't want anything to do with them either. Was I going to have to die for such a simple reason? I couldn't understand how that could be the case.

During the time I lived in Texas I had met my father a handful of times. He never invited me home. I had dug out his address for myself and seen where he lived. I slid past his house countless times, and knew I'd seen family members come and go. An angry woman and young men of my own age. He'd worked hard, my dad. Had four sons with two different women in the space of five years. His new family had been a fact even by the time my mother left the USA. But we didn't realise that until much later. During our few meetings he led me to understand that his new woman had known about me and Marianne all along. The reason why she still decided to make a go of their relationship was that Dad had promised that we – my mother and I – would soon be out of his life. Which of course turned out to be true.

'I didn't know who you were,' I said to Vincent. 'I didn't know Tony was my brother.'

I still didn't understand the ramifications of that. *What did they hold me responsible for?* What did they think I had done to my brother that was so unforgivable? After all, it was Vincent and his brothers and mother who had drawn the winning ticket. They'd had a father who was present in their family as a father and husband.

'Not here, I said,' Vincent said. 'We were supposed to meet later. Couldn't you wait?'

I chose not to answer his question. I assumed he was armed, but that didn't matter. He wasn't going to shoot me in the head in front of all the customers, that much was certain.

'Come with me,' he said.

He nodded to get me to stand up. I did so slowly, leaving the coffee on the table.

'Where?' I said.

'Outside,' he said.

He indicated that I should walk out of the café ahead of him. The pavement was now in the shade, and that was the only good thing about the situation I found myself in.

We stopped a short distance apart. Not far, but not close enough to be able to touch each other. If I stretched out my hand I wouldn't quite have reached him.

'It's seven o'clock now,' Vincent said. 'I suggest you go and have a nice meal, then we'll meet as planned at nine o'clock.'

'No,' I said.

I didn't like the way he said I should 'go and have a nice meal'. As if he was offering me a last meal.

Vincent's eyes flashed.

'Are you so fucking stupid that you still think you have a choice?'

There were more answers to that question than he could possibly count.

'Yes, I'm afraid I probably am,' I said.

Vincent snorted with derision.

'You must have had a really shit mother. So little love and respect you feel for your own family.'

He crossed a boundary there. The fact that I think Marianne was a fucking useless mother was one thing. Other people thinking it is another matter altogether. If it weren't for the anxiety his second sentence prompted, I'd probably have gone on the attack. But I managed to stay calm enough to respond rationally. What did he mean by 'my own family'? He could hardly mean himself and Simon. So presumably he meant Belle and Lucy.

Was he threatening them?

It sounded like it.

'There's not much you can teach me about love and respect,' I said.

'We can discuss that later. Nine o'clock. Where Pastor Parson was buried. Exactly as planned.'

'I said no,' I said.

'Then Lucy and Belle will die. Your choice.'

And with that I knew for sure. Any last fragile doubts that Vincent might not be Lucifer but one of his agents vanished. Vincent was Lucifer. An ordinary middle-class American who had done reasonably well for himself in the police force, someone who didn't stand out in any way. But, more than anything, Lucifer was my own brother.

'You're thinking of killing your own niece,' I said. 'You fucking bastard, who the hell are you to lecture me about family love?'

'Unless I've been wrongly informed, Belle isn't my niece. She's yours. And I'm not related to your sister at all. Or am I wrong?'

'That depends how you define parenthood,' I said, feeling my courage waver. 'Belle has been my daughter since she was a baby. She has no parents apart from me.'

Vincent laughed.

'Poor kid,' he said.

Then he became serious again.

'We'll meet at nine o'clock,' he said. 'Don't be late.'

He turned to go.

'I said no,' I said in a raised voice.

My words made a few other people on the pavement react. As did Vincent. He froze mid-stride. He turned round slowly.

'You wouldn't dare behave like that unless you thought Lucy and Belle were okay,' he said. 'So let me simplify things for you: I know exactly where they are. And I can kill them both in less than – let's say – ten minutes.'

'You're lying,' I said.

'It's the truth,' he said.

Then he took out his mobile and called someone who answered remarkably quickly.

'Where are you?' I heard him say.

My stomach contracted with fear.

'You just got there? I see, that's useful. And you're ...? What was her name? I see, excellent. Madeleine Rossander's house. Belle is wearing her pink jacket and is asleep. Lucy is carrying her from the car.'

The ground opened up beneath my feet and I fell.

Vincent watched me with intense interest. He put the phone back in his trouser pocket again.

'You know what? Why not call and warn your loved ones?' he said. 'It's great when people try to escape into the darkness.'

I didn't answer. It was night in Sweden. Lucy, probably exhausted, was carrying Belle from the car, fumbling with the keys and going to ground in Madeleine Rossander's summer cottage. With the enemy right outside.

This was way beyond fucked up.

Vincent tilted his head to one side.

'So we'll meet at nine o'clock, as arranged?'

I nodded. Beaten and defeated, beyond salvation.

I said: 'And then you'll leave Lucy and Belle alone? If you get me instead?'

He said: 'Of course.'

That did it. I was going to die, and Belle and Lucy would be allowed to live. The realisation left me feeling numb.

Of course.

Vincent sounded genuinely surprised when he answered my question. As if he couldn't understand how I could think he was going to deceive me about a thing like that. What they say is true. There's a gentleman hidden inside every bastard.

He turned round one last time before we went our separate ways.

'By the way, don't even think about calling your friend Didrik, or anyone else.'

He didn't have to worry about that.

'Of course not,' I said.

'Especially not Didrik. Because you won't get any joy from him.'

I'd realised that.

'Thanks, I already know that,' I said.

His eyes darkened.

'So you already know?'

'What?'

'That he's dead.'

I didn't know where to turn. Death was everywhere. I managed to think that I must have been followed when I drove from Stockholm to Malmö. That Vincent had found out that Didrik and I were plotting against him.

Vincent was Lucifer.

Lucifer was my own brother.

'He died in a car crash.'

'Really?'

I didn't know what to say. There are an infinite number of ways you can kill a person.

But then Vincent said: 'It pained me to hear that. He deserved a better fate.'

'So you didn't kill him?'

The words came out by themselves, I couldn't stop them, still less take them back.

'No, certainly not. I had other plans for him. He and Rebecca died instantly. A tragedy for all concerned. And evidently you still trusted him, in spite of everything he'd done to you?'

That last sentence made me blink.

'I don't know that I'd call it trust,' I said. 'I—'

'You thought you had a deal. Sadly Didrik couldn't handle the pressure. He realised, of course, that I'd find out sooner or later, so he called and told me everything. That you'd showed up and had found Mio. Sad, isn't it?'

Sad was the word.

He put on a pair of sunglasses and brushed something from the sleeve of his jacket. He was evidently about to go. I had one more question I wanted an answer to.

'What about Mio?' I said. 'What happened to him?'

Vincent fixed his gaze on something far behind me.

'That seems to be the eternal question, doesn't it? What happened to Mio?'

Then he turned and walked away.

46

Dusk was falling when I got in the car and set off towards the old oilfield one last time. After my encounter with Vincent I had spent barely half an hour in my hotel room, lying on my back on the bed. There was no one I could call, no one I could ask for help. Josh Taylor's name flickered past as a possibility, but I daren't defy the order I had been given. If I did, Lucy and Belle would be gone forever. And I would have to live my last hours in the knowledge that I had killed them.

I thought about calling Lucy. Just to say goodbye, and to thank her for everything. I wanted to hear her voice before I died. That was all. And surely every man or woman under sentence of death had the right to one last wish? I concluded that it was an impossible wish. There was absolutely zero chance of me being able to tell Lucy that I was on my way to my own execution without her reacting in a way that would cost her her life.

Anguish is one of the worst things in the world. Most people use the word wrongly. Anguish is a force as strong as the torrent of water from a burst dam. It's unstoppable, uncontrollable. No sane person who knows they're going to die can face their last hours of life with any degree of calmness. I've always known that I love being alive. Even when everything was terrible – like the first year after my sister's death, when I rapidly and reluctantly found myself a father – my lust for life was undiminished. It has always, always been there. Not once have I ever considered death as the solution to any problem I have faced. So the anguish that took over my body and mind during the hours after Vincent and I parted was unlike anything I had ever encountered before. Up to the moment where we were standing eye to eye, I had somehow imagined that I would be able to negotiate my way out of the situation. That there would be something I could say or do to put everything right. But that wasn't the case, and I knew that now.

There was no way back.

And there was no way forward.

When I got in the car, it felt like I was shivering with fever. It took me several minutes before I was able to pull myself together enough to dare to start it and drive off. I know I was crying, and I remember thinking that it didn't matter. People who know they're going to die can do what the hell they like.

When I had been driving for half an hour one of my mobiles rang. The oldest one. I glanced at the screen, convinced that if I looked away from the road for as much as a second, the last thing I did would be to run down and kill someone.

It was Marianne. The woman who had once given birth to me, and who I refused to call Mum. Of all the people who could have called just then, she was the last one I wanted to talk to. Not because I had nothing to say to her, but quite the opposite. We had far too many unresolved issues for a final conversation to serve any useful purpose. What could we discuss in a few short minutes – all I was prepared to give her – that could sort out all the shit that lay there festering between us, just in time for me to die?

I rejected the call. And if I had to identify the one thing I've done that I regret most, that would be it. The fact that when I was sitting in a car and driving to what I knew was my own execution, I didn't answer the phone when my mum called.

There aren't many people who know in advance when they are going to die. And not many people who ever know why. I dearly wanted to be the exception to that rule. I wanted to know why I didn't deserve to live.

For the second time in one day, I turned off the motorway and carried on along the deserted side-road, then onto the even more desolate gravel track. The gravel track was, or rather is, absolutely straight except for a bend just before it reaches the abandoned oilfield. It wasn't until I got past it that I saw my welcoming committee. I counted six of them: five men and one woman. There were two cars parked up behind the little group of people. Their headlights lit up the whole of the meeting place. Vincent, my newfound brother, was sitting on the bonnet of one of the cars. He exuded all the arrogance I expected from a man in his bizarre position.

One of the other men gestured to me to park a short distance away. I followed his instructions and got out of the car. Well, I didn't, actually. First I had to sit in the car with the engine switched off for a minute or so before I opened the door and got out. I also sent Lucy a text. The shortest ever, and the most important.

How I wish I could have met my death with dignity. That I could have been as cool as people in films when they're about to die. Straight-backed, smiling, with some razor-sharp quip at the ready. And with at least seven automatic weapons hidden inside my jacket.

I'd thought about getting hold of a gun to take with me, before realising that was a bad idea. I'm a crap shot, and I hadn't fired a gun since I hit another man by mistake. There was no way I'd ever be able to shoot my way out of the situation I found myself in. In which case it was best to come the way I'd been instructed: unarmed, defenceless, and alone.

Sweat was running down my back as I walked the last steps towards the gang; the only member I recognised was Vincent. He nodded in greeting and slid off the car's bonnet. To my left someone had dug a deep hole in the hard ground. The shovel lay alongside it.

'Good that we can meet like this, without too many pre-liminaries,' Vincent said, sounding genuinely grateful.

I thought about the last time I'd been in Texas. Lucy and I had met Sara Texas's friend in Galveston, and found out that Lucifer had a connection to Sweden. I'd spent a lot of time thinking about that connection. Now I knew. He had a Swedish brother. Who he hated so much he wanted to see him dead.

I wasn't interested in a load of theatrical nonsense. I was angry and terrified, and I wanted to understand what this was all about.

'You asked me to find Mio,' I said. 'Even though you knew that Didrik had him.'

Vincent came a few steps closer.

'I don't remember ever asking you to do anything,' he said.

'Not in person. You told me via one of your messengers.'

'We all communicate in different ways.'

'I don't give a shit how you communicate. I'm just wondering what was the point of me floundering about looking for a child who was never missing. To keep the police interested in me?'

'Exactly. After I had Belle abducted, and everything that happened in conjunction with that, I was worried the police would fall for your nonsense about being the victim of a conspiracy. Didrik wouldn't have been able to influence his colleagues if that happened. So I gave you a task that meant you'd carry on contacting a whole load of people I guessed that dear Didrik was already watching and would be stressed out by it.'

'So that more people would have to die and I'd be accused of even more murders?'

I could feel that I was breathing far too heavily. My vision was also affected. Everything looked a bit fuzzy round the edges, and I was distracted by little flashes of lightning that kept crossing my eyes. My head ached and my mouth felt swollen.

'You need to appreciate what I got from the deal,' Vincent said. 'To be brutally honest, those people needed to die sooner or later. And the lengths Didrik was prepared to go to in order to protect his family were pretty damn impressive. I mean, really, I take my hat off to him. Rebecca wasn't bad either, but Didrik is obviously the hero. Which in itself was a bonus. I had any number of things I could use to put pressure on him. Not that I needed that many, but I had to have something in reserve for when I took Mio away from him.'

Didrik, Didrik, Didrik. What would Lucifer have done without Didrik's drive and desperation?

'So you were never thinking of letting him keep Mio?'

'Are you mad? Not a fucking chance. But Didrik was like you. He didn't understand the whole family thing.'

'You just praised him for the strength of his love for his own family.'

'His own, yes. But he totally misjudged how I feel about my son. My only son, at that. God help anyone who tries to take him from me.'

I had a thousand remarks on the tip of my tongue, but swallowed them all. If Vincent had felt an ounce of love for his son, he should have started by never separating him from his mother.

Vincent took a deep breath and his eyes flickered uncertainly as he looked round. One of his men spat in the sand, and another reached for the spade that lay on the ground.

'I made up my mind many years ago that I was going to force you to take some responsibility,' Vincent said. 'To give you the punishment you deserve. Even in my wildest dreams I could never have imagined that Sara would provide me with the opportunity. That she would drag you into this – after her own death, no less – and provide me with such a fantastic opportunity to put everything right. If I'm honest, that still bothers me. The fact that it's taken so little effort. All the shit you've been wading through in the past few weeks is the result of an operation I originally set up to punish Sara, not you. It had all been abandoned, it had served its purpose. But then you of all people popped up. I'd have liked to see you cost me more effort. But on the other hand … Let's not forget that it's thanks to Sara and Didrik that I was able to turn your life into such a nightmare. If it hadn't been for them, my revenge on you would have looked very different.'

He shook his head.

I blinked a few times. My vision really wasn't working the way it should, and I was starting to have trouble absorbing all the words that were reaching me. All the nuances vanished, leaving just the core message: nothing I had suffered during the past few weeks originally had anything to do with me. I just happened to get dragged into it. And that suited Lucifer just fine. Absolutely fucking fine.

'Why was I told to find the person who was trying to frame me for two murders? I get the bit about finding Mio, but the other bit is … harder to understand.'

Vincent tilted his head.

'What do you see when you think of Didrik?' he said.

I didn't feel up to replying, so he did so himself.

'You see one hell of an honourable man. The sort who never does the wrong thing, always does what's right. I could hardly believe it when he took responsibility for Bobby and Jenny's deaths. There was a risk that everything had grown more complex than I was able to easily understand from here in Texas. So I wanted to be sure. But that doesn't feel terribly important any more. You're here, and you're going to get your punishment. That's all that matters.'

All that matters. More, even, than the fact that Mio was missing?

I tried to gain some time.

'Did Sara know that you and I had the same dad?'

I could have framed the question differently. I could have asked if Sara knew we were brothers. But that was too strong a word.

'She knew I had a connection to Sweden. And she knew that I really, really didn't like you. It was stupid of me to volunteer that little detail, but I'm only human. If you hate someone as much as I hate you, there's always a risk that it will show.'

Hate. That burning, red-hot hatred. I had to know what that was all about. Before it was all over, before I was dead.

'Why?' I said.

The word emerged as I was breathing out, and turned into a whisper. My left shoulder was beginning to ache. I tried rolling it back and forth. It didn't help.

'Because of your betrayal!'

His bellow hit me like a punch in the face. I couldn't help staggering back.

'For fuck's sake, what betrayal? Do you mean Tony? I had no fucking idea he was even my brother.'

'*Do you expect me to believe that?* Do you expect me to believe it was a coincidence that you came back to Texas, trained to become a cop, and then ended up as your own brother's partner?'

His voice was a roar that risked deafening me. I tried to fend him off by wrapping my arms round my head, but quickly lowered them again. The pain in my shoulder was now shooting straight down my left arm.

'Of course it wasn't a fucking coincidence. I came here because I wanted to meet my father. Get to know him. You too, maybe. I knew you existed. I knew we were the same age. But you know what? He refused. He didn't want me to meet you. He didn't ask me back to your home one single fucking time. I had to find out where you lived for myself. So how the hell can you believe that I knew Tony was my brother? He didn't even have his father's surname – just like you don't.'

I was exhausted by my speech, and had to stand still and catch my breath.

'No, we've got our mum's name.'

'You've certainly chosen a brilliant way of honouring your father,' I said through gritted teeth. 'By becoming a fucking mafia boss who trades in women and drugs, and goes around murdering people the whole time. *Do you think he'd have been proud of that?*'

I don't know where I got the strength to raise my voice. My eyes were flickering and I sank to my knees just in time to connect with Vincent's kick to my head. I collapsed on the sand and stayed there. Vincent loomed over me, feet planted far apart.

'You don't get to tell me about making Dad proud,' he said. 'If it hadn't been for me, Mum and Simon would never have coped after Dad died. Did you know he killed himself?'

I didn't know that. I was just told that he had died, and that was that.

'Dad was weak,' Vincent said. 'Just like Tony. Don't imagine they could help it, because they couldn't. But the rest of us did what we could. *And that's what you should have done too.* We knew who you were all along. And we know that you knew who we were.'

I slowly moved my head in the sand. I was on my way now, I could feel it.

'That's not true,' I whispered. 'Tony was a year younger than me. It never crossed my mind that ...'

'Don't lie!'

Vincent's next kick hit me in the crotch.

'Don't lie! Dad said he'd told you about us! Tony liked you. He told the rest of us that if we just gave you time, you'd come clean about who you were. But you never did. Not even after Tony backed you up that fucking night when you shot a teenager. *How fucking cruel can anyone be?*'

I thought I was about to be kicked again and curled up. But nothing came, no kicks or punches.

'Tony couldn't bear to go on working with you after that. He requested a transfer, but believe me, he never stopped hoping. And then you did the most incomprehensible thing of all. You just left. You resigned and went home. You fucking coward! After that, Dad started drinking. Then Tony died, and after that everything was finished. Dad never got over it. Don't you realise that you destroyed our family?'

I understood what he was saying, but I couldn't take it in. Because I had no reason to believe he was lying. No doubt my dad had said all those things, pretending everything was my fault when his life fell apart. But I – and my mum – knew the truth.

'It was your dad who destroyed my family,' I said. 'Not the other way round, Vincent.'

'Our dad!' Vincent roared. '*Ours! Not mine!*'

I felt like screaming. Partly from the pain in my arm, and partly in protest. I had no father that I cared to acknowledge. Far from it. And I wasn't going to let any other bastard force one down my throat. But I didn't manage to get a single word out.

'I was the one who had to sort everything out when Dad was gone. For Mum and Simon ... Simon's a great guy. But he's not very smart. He's got his cafés, but that's as far as it goes. He never knew what happened out here, for instance. He would have talked. Not out of malice, but because he couldn't handle it. You can despise what I've become all you like, but I've still managed something that you'll never get anywhere close to: I've made myself immune to any more fucking accidents. I govern the piece of the world that belongs to me just as I like. Do you get it? *Do you get it? You can't touch me or the people I care for.*'

But he had lost Mio. His own son. If only Sara had known what forces she was setting herself up against. There's no one more dangerous than people who are driven by private – and sick – motives. Because they're not open to compromise. That was why I was now lying in the sand with death just a few metres from my face. The only question was what variety of death was going to get me first. My left arm had gone numb. I was quite certain I was having a heart attack. Yet another weak brother in the family. But not one to whom Vincent would show any mercy, that much was obvious.

Without any elaborate gestures, he pulled a large revolver from a holster concealed beneath his jacket. I had left my own jacket in the hotel. I'm happiest in just my shirt-sleeves.

'Do you know how Tony died?'

I didn't answer.

According to Josh Taylor, he'd been shot while on duty.

'They wrote in the report that he'd been shot, that he walked into an ambush. They never found the man who did it. Do you know why?'

I tried to shake my head.

'No,' I whispered.

'Because I took care of the bastard. Simon didn't want to know, nor did Mum. I put everything right. But before I shot him, guess what he told me?'

My brain had turned to mush. Making wild guesses was the last thing I had energy for. Vincent came so close that I could see the thin lines around his eyes.

'That he was the brother of the guy you shot and then buried out here.'

I blinked. Impossible. That was completely impossible.

'I see you're surprised,' Vincent said. 'So was I. Because of course Tony had told me about your fucked-up shooting, and how you'd made sure no one had seen what happened. It's a shame you did such a fucking useless job. The brother of the guy you shot was sitting inside one of the abandoned old workshops, and he saw everything. Fourteen years old. You can imagine what that would do to a person.'

My neck felt tight and my vision was blurring. That couldn't be right. There was no way that could be right.

'By the time the kid was old enough to take revenge you'd already run away,' Vincent said, breathing hard. 'Leaving no one but Tony behind, so he had to pay the whole bill himself. Do you understand now, Martin? Making your brother miserable wasn't enough for you – you killed him as well!'

So that was why I had to die. That was why I had to be crushed. Like some Old Testament drama: the finale to a dispute between two brothers.

The sky was still dark blue. A crescent moon shone yellow against all the blue. I wondered how Lucy and Belle were. If they'd be allowed to live. I thought they would. I had to believe they would.

'Sorry,' I whispered. 'But it wasn't my fault.'

The words came out in fits and starts. The pain in my chest was so immense that I could hardly think of anything else. I was struck by one last thought about the irony of the fate I was now facing: I was going to die without knowing what had happened to Mio. Mio, the ghost no one could catch.

'It's all your fault,' Vincent said, and pressed the narrow barrel of the revolver to my forehead.

'Not Belle and Lucy,' I whispered.

'Of course not. This is enough.'

And then a shot rang out. And another one. And then more than I could count. I heard agitated voices and screaming, felt everyone around me spring into motion. In the distance I heard a great number of sirens, and somewhere in the distance a helicopter was approaching. By the time it landed I was already gone.

47

AFTERWARDS

The first shot was fired from a revolver in Sheriff Esteban Stiller's hand. It hit Lucifer in the back of the head, killing him instantly. Who died after that, I don't know. But a wild fire-fight broke out between Lucifer's men and the army of police who in some unfathomable way had managed to conceal themselves nearby. They had followed me the first time I drove out there. And apparently they hadn't driven away again.

'Gut instinct,' Stiller said later when we talked about it. 'I thought you went out there to do some reconnaissance and I was right.'

Stiller's instinct had got him a long way. He'd had his eye on Vincent for years, convinced that he was in the pay of Lucifer's network. He didn't know we were brothers. He didn't know that Vincent was Lucifer. But he didn't need to know any of that once he was there.

'When I realised he was about to blow your head off, it was time to act,' he said.

But he neglected to tell me that the real hero was Josh

Taylor. He had called to tell Stiller that he should be keeping a very close eye on me. Because if he got lucky, I might be able to lead him to Lucifer himself. Stiller had already been informed that I had entered the country, but hadn't done anything much about it. Not until Taylor contacted him. At the same time as he contacted me to let me know I had half the police in Texas after me.

'So you didn't do anything stupid and end up acting like the criminal Stiller thought you were all along,' he explained.

The doctors said I was dead for twelve minutes. Then I spent three weeks in a coma. Three weeks was also how long it took Lucy to persuade the Swedish and American police that I was a victim of crime, and not actually involved in any criminal activity in either Sweden or the USA. The Americans managed to sort out the footage from Wolfgang's security camera and improved the focus to the point where it was possible to see that it was Didrik who was moving Elias's body into my car. The woman, however, remained unidentified, which didn't really bother me too much. She obviously wasn't me, and that was the important thing. Lucy also managed to prove that the witness who claimed she'd seen a Porsche run down and kill Jenny had been bribed by Didrik. After that, things looked considerably brighter for me.

The last text message I sent Lucy proved conclusive for the police.

'Lucifer is my own brother.'

That's exactly what I wrote. No more, no less. It was enough to blow the story open. Unfortunately that now happened in full view of the public. Until then there had been forces holding the media back, plugging any leaks. But now those forces had gone. When Vincent died, his network imploded. Some of its members chose to run, others handed themselves in, and negotiated shorter sentences by informing on their friends. The media in more countries than I care to list wrote hundreds, thousands of articles during the three weeks I was gone. The only detail that Stiller did manage to keep quiet, with vague references to a serious threat against me, was my name. So I came to be known as Coma Man in the media. And the day I woke up, Islamic terrorists blew up the American Embassy in Jordan. Coma Man's reawakening was overshadowed by this new atrocity and I didn't end up the global celebrity Lucy was sure I was going to become.

Coma Man. A name that made Lucy cry at first, then laugh, once I'd woken up and demonstrated that I wasn't a cabbage. The doctors hadn't been particularly optimistic. I'd been gone a long time and my brain could have been severely damaged.

'In that case, you need to let him die,' Lucy said seriously.

'Never,' the doctor said. 'In this country we let the living live. Even if they're broken. If he wants to die, he'll have to commit suicide.'

I'm not even going to try to describe what it was like, waking up after being unconscious for so long. It would be hopeless. I'll just say that it's the worst thing I've ever been through. Doctors are very fond of using the word 'discomfort' to describe things that are absolutely terrifying. I prefer to call a spade a spade. Appalling is a good word. Fucking shite would also do.

It wasn't like I could just get up and go home. I could

hardly move at all. And things weren't quite sorted out with the police, either. Lucy had done a hell of a good job, but I had to sort out the remaining problems myself. My memory got better day by day, at roughly the same rate as I became capable of movement again. Lying in hospital is a never-ending humiliation. And having your credibility questioned by the police is pretty much the same.

'Why did you meet up at that particular abandoned oil-field?' Sheriff Stiller wanted to know.

I said I didn't know. Josh Taylor was present at that interview. He lowered his gaze when the oilfield was mentioned.

Lucy was there for me the whole time. Belle too. Lucy had travelled to Houston together with my daughter and Signe, the au pair. Belle was her usual bubbly self, and charmed everyone who crossed her path. One of the doctors at the hospital removed her plaster-cast. That was the first thing she showed me when I came round.

'Look! Just a normal arm!' Lucy was talking to the doctor, organising my care.

She's good at sorting things out, Lucy.

We landed back at Arlanda on a Tuesday. By then it was September, pouring with rain, and I tried not to think what my stay in hospital must have cost my insurance company. Autumn lay ahead of me like an endless stretch of straight road. The doctors had recommended at least eight weeks' sick-leave. I promised to follow their advice. I'm not so stupid that I don't know when to listen to other people. If you have your first heart attack – and such a bad one – before the age of forty-five, you need to be careful.

'I'm going to start exercising,' I told Lucy in the taxi on

the way from the airport. 'Eat better, maybe go to one of those nutritional experts.'

The three of us were all sitting in the back-seat, Belle in the middle. She'd fallen asleep with her head on my arm. Lucy was very quiet, looking out through the rain-streaked window. I reached out my hand and touched her cheek. Belle fell onto my chest when I moved my arm.

'Are you okay, baby?'

And she replied in the only reasonable way. The only way I expected her to.

'No.'

Then she went on: 'It's over now. Okay? It's over, Martin.'

How can I begin to describe the shockwaves that ran through me? They terrified me, left me more frightened than I had been when I woke from the coma. Not that I had forgotten our earlier arguments. But I thought those weeks in Texas had changed everything. That we had grown closer. It felt like that, anyway. All the way through my aching body.

'You came to Texas. You ...'

She silenced me by gently putting a finger to my lips.

'I love you.' She started to cry. 'Okay? I love you. More than anyone. But that's not enough, Martin. What we've got, it isn't a proper relationship. And, to be fair, you never promised me that. But you know – this isn't what I want. Don't tell me you can change, because you can't. And you won't. Okay? I love you. But that's not enough. Because you don't love me the same way.'

I started to panic. Much worse than when I thought I was going to be shot. I tried to find the words to tell her how much I loved her, how much I needed her. I wanted to say I wasn't complete without her by my side, that I had no better friend than her.

But I didn't say a word. Because I was thinking about everything I knew she wanted beyond that.

A faithful lover.

A shared home.

Shared children too, maybe.

And then the tears came, because of course Lucy was right. Just like she always was. I couldn't give her any of those things. Well, maybe I could, there and then. Being ill and then getting better makes you very humble. There had been moments of weakness during the summer when I had thought the thought. That I could be the man she wanted, give her what she desired. Because she was so fucking worth it. But I'm far too egotistical to make life-choices like that. I'm all too well aware of that. I can't change in the way that I'd have to in order to become hers for real. And maybe there's something healthy about that sort of self-awareness.

We are who we are.

TRANSCRIPT OF INTERVIEW WITH
MARTIN BENNER (MB).

INTERVIEWER: KAREN VIKING (KV),
freelance journalist, Stockholm.

KV: I don't know what to say. You broke up?
Just like that?

MB: Yes.

KV: So what now?

MB: Right now we're taking a break.
We've shut the office; we're leaving
it empty for a while. Helmer's on
leave, with full pay. I'm busy with my
rehabilitation and Lucy has taken a
temporary position elsewhere.

KV: But you still see each other?

MB: Absolutely. Belle would be distraught if
we didn't.

KV: Do you think you'll ever get back
together?

(Silence)

MB: Is that relevant, after everything I've told you?

KV: Not to the story itself. But on a purely human level, I'm very curious.

MB: Don't be. Your predecessor, Fredrik, never was.

KV: Sorry. What happened after you got home? I mean, with the murders you were suspected of committing?

MB: We managed to resolve that at least in part from the USA. After all, the Swedish and American police were forced to work together. But sure, there were still things to sort out when we got back.

KV: Was it hard to get them to believe Didrik's involvement?

MB: No, not at all. Well . . . the whole mess surrounding Mio was difficult to disentangle at first. But we managed to get hold of Didrik's son Sebastian's medical records from the hospital in Copenhagen. The doctors there said there was no way he could have survived more than a month after he was removed from hospital. After that, the police were forced to accept that the boy Didrik and Rebecca were raising as their own in their house in Denmark couldn't have been their son Sebbe. They found strands of hair in the

house, and using DNA analysis were able
to confirm that they belonged to the
missing Mio.

KV: But Mio isn't still missing, is he?

MB: No.

KV: So what happened?

MB: There was another adult in the car when
the accident happened. And that person
removed Mio from the scene and made
sure he was safe.

KV: Because they thought Lucifer was still
looking for him?

MB: Which he was, of course. Then.

KV: What about now? There's no threat
against Mio today, is there?

MB: No.

KV: So why is he still hidden?

MB: He isn't. He lives with an excellent
foster mother who'll love him as her own
son for the rest of his life.

KV: But . . . who else was sitting in the
car, then?

MB: Come on, Karen. Who do you think it
was?

KV: No idea.

MB: Rubbish.

(Silence)

KV: Not Rakel Minnhagen?

MB: Who else? Things started to heat up

in Stockholm and she fled to Denmark.
Didrik wasn't exactly pleased to see
her. When they were all in the car
together they were actually on their
way to Kastrup. He was planning to
send her to Spain. Apparently she had
friends there and would be able to go
into hiding.

KV: How do you know all this?

MB: I've spoken to her. Unlike the police.
They think Mio was snatched from
preschool by Didrik or Rebecca, and
I've no objection to that. Rakel was
Sara's only real friend in Sweden. She
did an awful lot of good things for
Sara and Mio. I refuse to hold her
responsible for the fact that she later
got dragged into Didrik and Rebecca's
deadly games.

KV: So the police know nothing about her
involvement?

MB: No, and that's how it's going to stay.
And I've said as much to Nadja, the
teacher who saw Rakel abduct Mio.
Rakel feels terrible about everything
that's happened. After all, she only
wanted to do what was best for Mio. It
was no coincidence that she applied
for a job at the Enchanted Garden. She
wanted to help Sara keep an eye on
Mio, and Didrik knew about that from

Sara, and exploited it when it came to snatching Mio. Then Didrik wouldn't let her go, and kept asking for help with all manner of things, from hiding Elias's body to moving him to my car. If she'd refused to help him, he would have got her put away for kidnapping Mio.

KV: Is she still in Spain?

MB: She's back in Stockholm. Studying. She left Spain once things had calmed down, and we saw to it that Mio was handed over to the authorities without her involvement. The police have asked a thousand times where Mio was between the accident and the moment he was suddenly standing alone on the steps outside Police Headquarters. I just shrug my shoulders and say I don't know.

KV: Sorry - he was standing alone on the steps outside Police Headquarters? I read about that in the papers, and they said—

MB: They said that the police had found the missing child as a result of diligent detective work. I know. But that's not what happened.

(Silence)

KV: I've got two more questions.

MB: Fire away.

KV: I don't understand how they managed to get Elias in the boot of your car. Don't you keep your car locked?

MB: Yes, but the lock's not good enough to beat a talented cop like Didrik. Don't ask me how he did it.

KV: And now the million-dollar question: who got Mio in the end?

MB: I don't know about 'got'. He ended up with Bobby's girlfriend. Bobby would never have been approved as a foster parent, but his girlfriend's a different matter. The sort of person who fulfils the criteria. Mio knew who she was, even though they hadn't seen each other in over a year. He needs someone like her. Someone who knows his history, his background.

KV: What about Boris?

MB: Ha! One question too far. Boris is fine. But I'm not saying where he is.

KV: And . . . the Porsche?

MB: Scrapped. I bought a Maserati instead. Much better.

KV: So, all's well that ends well?

MB: As well as it can be. We're alive and healthy. And that's really the most important thing.

KV: See. Maybe you can change after all?

(Silence)

MB: No, I don't believe that. Not in the slightest, actually.